House of Cards

The Curse of Alphonso

♣♦♥♠

R. J. (Rocky) Scarfone

M.A.G.I.C. Press
Atlanta, Georgia

First edition

Published by M.A.G.I.C. Press
Atlanta, Georgia
(770) 736-6890

Design and Production by Books International of Norcross, Georgia
Cover design by Paul K. Wilson
The paper used in this publication meets the minimum requirements of the American National Standard for Information Sciences Permanence of Paper for Printed Library Materials.

Manufactured in the United States of America

Library of Congress Cataloging-in-Publication Data
97–93064

ISBN 0-9657066-0-5 1995

Cover photo:
King - Joe-Pep, Queen - Nana Lou,
Joker - 8 year-old Joe

Dedication

MOTHER—for all her wrongs she never gave up; though she never owned more than a few housedresses, never took a vacation, never awoke to real joy or contentment, was tormented her entire life, she *always* stood by her children.

NANA LOU—she sacrificed in a way that only mothers and grandmothers can.

AUNT JOSIE—she took me in at a very troubled time in my life despite overwhelming problems of her own. She showered love and affection on my tired, lonely soul.

ANGELA—my sister and most dependable and cherished friend and adviser.

DANIELLE AND JEANETTE—forever to be my princesses and "punkins": lightning bolts that sparked change in my life. Though they would suffer through the beginnings of yet another generation of continuance, their beauty, caring hearts, perseverance, and loving Irish family would win reprieve . . . thus, for them, ending the Curse of Alphonso.

DENISE—who became my concrete support column bearing all. My vision to the real world . . . a world blinded by the words: respect, tradition, honor.

JULIANA ARIEL—born August 19, 1996 as a blessing to my world absent of Continuity and the Curse of Alphonso!

And to FATHER: I dedicate this book
and state to the world my regrets, love, and sorrow . . .
for my Knight in Shining Armor who wore
a trenchcoat and carried a .45

Introduction

I was born in 1953, but the trouble started 40 years earlier when my Great-Great-Grandfather Alphonso made a deal with the Devil: he asked Don Boccala (one of the most vicious criminals in New York City) for a better life for his family. How could Alphonso have known what sorrow and misery would come from this bargain!

Over the course of the following decades, one generation after another fell victim to the oath that Alphonso swore. By the time I was born, "the oath" had become "a curse" that afflicted me with a physical deformity that consumed the first five years of my childhood. By the time I was eight the Curse claimed my father who was brutally murdered. By age eleven, I ran away from home with my younger brother, and we began a quest for change: "Men of Respect"—I in my brim-feathered fedora, too small pin-striped suit and white sneakers; Carmine in clothes over PJs.

The happy, smiling faces on brochures of Pennsylvania led us from the New York World's Fair to the Pocono Mountains; but the Curse followed us . . . I was returned home where a group of my father's enemies lurked in the shadows—social workers appeared and took me in for three days of psychiatric evaluation. Once in Belvue, I was placed in an adult ward where three days became three months and, lost in a maze of suffering, the seeds of The Curse of Alphonso proscribed my soul.

My mind reeling in turmoil and question, I was released to the streets and was soon living in white and black checkered hallways that dotted my lonely landscape like the craters of a cold and dusty monscape. Soon I was running with a group of "wiseguys" in an effort to survive and belong. But even while I hung out with "the crew", I found time to teach myself how to read and write—then read every book I could lay my hands on! When my book and street knowledge congealed into a mass of opposing views, too large for my immature emotions, I dug an abyss deep in my mind and threw the file in. Soon I would find myself teetering on its brink, my questions drowning in a storm of hectic thought; inventing answers when I could find none. It wasn't long before I was returned to a reform school . . .

I soon discovered the awesome truth of my family's history: the facts behind my father's death and "The Curse of Alphonso!" The overpowering need to get even overruled any further thought—I'd leave New York and plan my course of action! But this time, my original desire for a "real" family, a father figure, and change in my life, competed with my plan of revenge and rescue!

This story demonstrates the fierce warfare between Good andEvil raging in our world; with its ever-evolving battles in which Evil places blame and demands revenge, while Good coaxes compassion and change. Throughout this quest, my battles are fought among many people on many fields across our great nation: Native Americans in New Mexico—discovering their faith in God; Baptists in Georgia—where my Catholic upbringing clashed with new views; Agnostic hippies in California—a culture believing in free love, drugs, and peace; African-Americans in Miami—falling in love with a young girl of interracial parents and discovering racial bigotry first hand.

I became a drug addict, a four-story burglar with Jack the Cat, a mascot with The South Florida Chapter of The Outlaw Motorcycle Gang, a junior member of a sixties version of the "Bonnie and Clyde Gang," and a disciple of Rah Lum Nah, a sixties California Cult leader.

I experienced a kidnapping, sexual abuse, confinement, religious experience, hunger, death, joy, happiness, love, compassion, friendship, God, Angels, Demons, hate, bigotry, loss, revenge.

All through this incredible journey, someone watched over me and guided me, rescuing me at every turn. Though sometimes I received more than a taste of my predicament, my appetite was usually satisfied in small bites. I was allowed to feel, see, and experience only so much at each stage until learned and ready, I would be guided through the next experience.

Eventually, I mastered the business world but I never seemed to be satisfied. I was always starting a business, pouring my energy into it until it became a powerhouse, then abandoning it to begin another venture! I was driven by a feeling that my life would cease if I became placid and content; that I had to run, run, run forward, never slowing down lest I fall flat on my face and cease to exist! Something was wrong . . .was it my background? When my last venture, featured in major newspapers, TV programs and magazines, with clients including Sylvestor Stallone, Bob Lee, Bob Beamon, Maynard Jackson and many others, blossomed four years in a row, threatening me with security and happiness, I began to truly believe I had discovered purpose and happiness . . .

But had I truly discovered my purpose in life? Was my purpose some how entangled within a web spun from the many roads I had traveled—including my most recent? Were my perceived disasters, just that . . . disasters . . . or were they an ending, a destruction, a release from a cocoon that had blinded me with its fragile, soft and comfortable, silken threads; threads pulled and refined from lies and false bravado—threads I had in fact woven myself in my attempt to hide the degradation, destruction, and perversion of my family?

And then, like the symbol of my new found home—Atlanta's very own Phoenix—rising from the burnt offerings of its troubled past—purpose—its wings of truth gracefully swept, reaching, striving, knowing its very depth, swept my thoughts and I discovered my destiny!

"Questions! Questions! Questions! Always questions . . . Am I to begin all over? . . . But the void is full! It overflows its banks with eternal sufferings! I HAVE NO ROOM FOR MORE QUESTIONS! Must I put my thumb out and travel the road in reverse? . . . A road I know is straight and direct? . . . One I can see ending in plain and simple truth? . . . Can you really ask me to substitute humility for the wall of pride I have built from all those fabricated memories? . . . Must I expose their truths and fears that have gathered into the vast and deep abyss? But, compressed are they; weighed down with the pain and suffering and torment and degradation of so many before me! Am I to resurrect their faults, their mistakes, their treachery, their vices, their very secrets . . . my secrets too? . . . Oh Lord, is this my only means for the reparation of the souls of my many and vast ancestors and the ending of the Curse? . . . What of Father? . . . What will they say? . . . And Mother? . . . Grandmother? . . . Even she? . . . The truth? . . . But she lives yet! And what of Great Great Grandfather Alphonso . . . What will become of the four generations of great and genteel ancestors I have invented and placed upon father-figured thrones of marbled thought and dream . . ."

* * *

Will Joe's His-Story open for the world to see and know after 40 years of waging battle after battle, finally end "The Curse of Alphonso?" . . .

Contents

♣♦♥♠

The Players

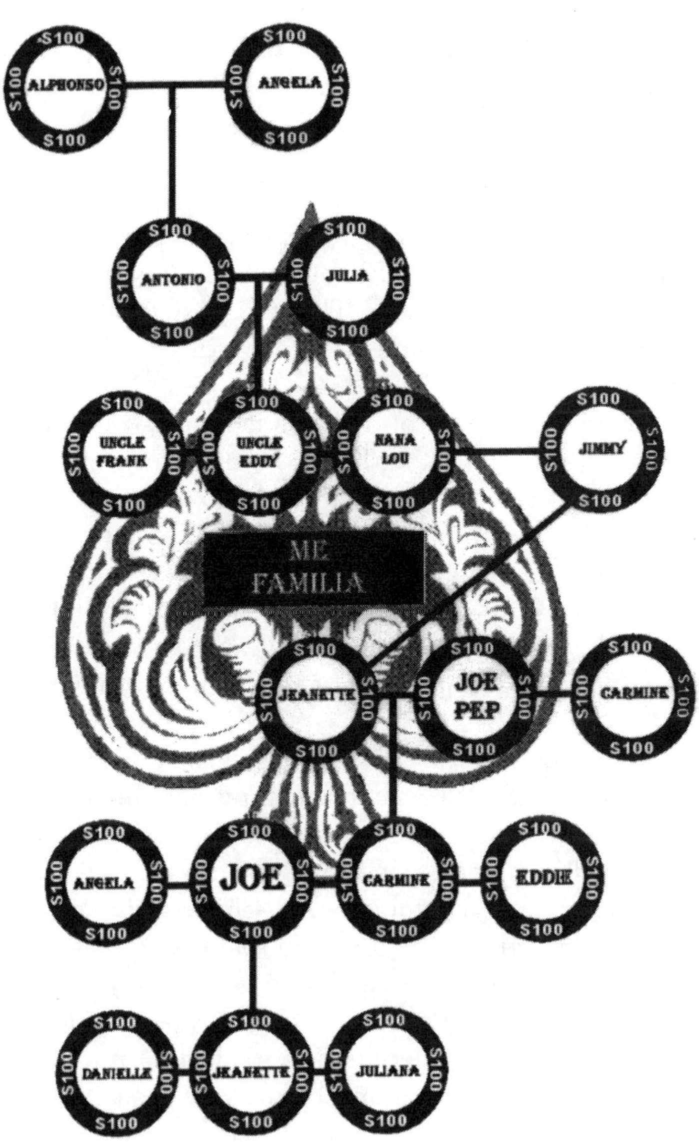

ALPHONSO
ANGELA
ANTONIO
JULIA
UNCLE FRANK
UNCLE EDDY
NANA LOU
JIMMY
ME FAMILIA
JEANETTE
JOE PEP
CARMINE
ANGELA
JOE
CARMINE
EDDIE
DANIELLE
JEANETTE
JULIANA

Preface

I have journeyed great distances encountering life's many pains, sorrows, joys, and happiness in my quest for knowledge. What began as a personal journey to find where I belonged in this maze of life became, in essence, my education—taught face-to-face by the many and varied people I met along the way. Yet, little did I know that purpose was laced throughout these times. For though my pilgrimage began long before I left home, it was the pursuit of the meaning of life and family that truly became my beginnings! Ernest Holsendolph of the *Atlanta Journal-Constitution,* in a front page article, described me fairly well, "Fatherless since he was [eight], he left home, first at age eleven. And like a Charles Dickens character, Mr. Scarfone scrambled about on his own, making a living from odd jobs and his wits . . ."

Those wits were wits of a continued endeavor to find a home in which to rest my aching heart. Throughout my journeys, God gifted me with a place of my own: I refused to sleep upon His bed of comfort, a bed that produces sleep so pure and refreshing that each awakening is new and alive with joy and revelation. I refused to welcome His roof of warmth and His walls of strength that protect us with mighty powers of dedication and perseverance—and yet He never quit in His just way to educate me for my purpose with Him.

Purpose remains the most confusing agenda that we must address each and every day. Without spiritual purpose life is mundane and has no true meaning. Faced with day to day, spiritless, mortal living we become leaves in the wind thrust hither and yon upon this vast earth in perpetual search for answers—answers that are often right in front of us! His truth—and the pain that is sometimes truth's companion—eventually delivered the answers to my questions about what I perceived as solely my own inequity, poverty, loneliness, and fears. His passionate understanding reached deep into my subconscious mind and wrenched out, by the very roots, the doubt, hate, and contempt planted there through seeds of despair and confusion. He permitted me to face my legacy.

Allow me to assure you, my history, as told in *House of Cards: The Curse of Alphonso,* is neither a "Mafia" story nor a religious narrative. It's a revealing and true history of a mother's love and compassion; of a mother's son who must come to terms with his past; a proof of the existence of a family's ability to beget more than its traditions—even a wretched curse of continuation. A legacy whereby their succeeding generations will pay a sometimes dear and expensive price!

House of Cards: The Curse of Alphonso is truly more than a simple story of rigid fact—it is one of gentle persuasion in the face of savage reality; a touching of minds, hearts, and souls upon a slice of time—minute and insignificant in this vast universe of reality, yet much to many!

I have legions of folks to thank for the many important lessons of life that made me who I am today. To those who nourished me, protected me, and forgave me when I sometimes "bit the hand that fed me," I deliver my story so that you may share in my joy and happiness—for you, my times of trepidation eventually became times of joy!

Isn't it incredible that we can rejoice in memory of horrid experiences and put to voice His truth and justice? Can you believe that? Isn't it fantastic that God gifts us all with the ability to shed the skins of so many snakes? Yes, faith and perseverance achieves all! Just maybe, a young man, a young woman, a mother or father, lonely in spirit, hungry of mind and thirsting to belong, will be swept along this journey of truth and history and discover their power through Him, Our Lord and Savior, our spiritual Father Figure—Jesus Christ! For only through faith is purpose revealed! So, with much joy and purpose in life, I praise Him. Thus my fears, hungers, and pains have become but a few yellowed pages of my life.

In His glorious name . . .

JB/RJS

Acknowledgments

House of Cards: The Curse of Alphonso is a true story. I have chosen to compress the timeline and to detail only the main events that dictated the course of my personal history and that of my family.

The statements about my ancestors and the murders of my father and uncle are true. Copies of newspaper stories about the gangland slayings are included in the book. Of course, occasionally when our family's verbal history has blanks I have filled them in using reasonable fictional license.

All of the experiences of young Joe are completely factual, though to protect certain persons' anonymity I have changed names, times, and dates.

Special thanks to "Tony" of Miami, "Tony-Pep" of Atlanta, "Fat Freddy" of Hallendale, Florida, "Tony-Thumbs" of Hollywood, Florida, "Sonny Black" of Miami, "Joey Tre" of Miami, "Johnny A" of Atlanta, "Angelo" of Atlanta, "Bob R" of Atlanta, "Anne" of New York City, and "Rock Crusher" for providing me the opportunity to discover the myths, truths, ways, and lifestyle that led to my father's death.

I'd also like to thank John of the Atlanta office of the Federal Bureau of Investigation, Don, Joe, Chuck, Bobby, Steve, Shawn, and others of the FBI, Secret Service, and Organized Crime Strike Force. Their assistance and cooperation made much of this possible. And finally, thanks to my new friend and editor, Marc Bailey. It was a struggle, but we got it done!

R.J. (Rocky) Scarfone

House of Cards

The Curse of Alphonso

Is There Life After Death?

Words of Wisdom

"Be careful, I love you!" Mother's cry.
Our cherished authors who plagiarize
those words of wisdom that rectify
our thoughts and feelings piper pied . . .

He entered the terminal care wing of the hospital in search of his wife. Passing a glass-enclosed, five-bed ward, he noticed her making her rounds and stumbled into the room. The sight of one particular patient stopped him dead in his tracks.

She lay directly in his line of vision, propped up on the bed, tubes running in and out of her body like a modern, crowded freeway under construction; they entered and exited her frail five-foot frame without warning, depositing their massive cargo of morphine, oxygen, and nutrients. He knew—and he was sure she did also—the numbers were absent from the dice . . . but he also knew he wouldn't peep a squeak.

As he strolled past the bed he was determined to force himself to display some sort of candor or irrelevance toward death's own determination; though, he was sure, death knew his end: for death towered over the dismal hospital room with its odors and bleak, pale-white entourage. He was immediately struck by a terrible thought . . . like man in his determination for power and wealth, did the devouring beast of cancer reckon its own quick death at birth and rush to its end in an effort at life? He could not answer himself nor could he comprehend her misery: 'Who was this' woman? Did she ever realize her wishes, her hopes, her dreams? What were her thoughts?' She seemed outwardly unconcerned in her pained and drugged state, but a slight trembling of her lips, quivering with untold efforts at persuasive thought, and hands tightly clasped in prayer, seemed to deliver a message of some awesome belief that God could defeat the enemy within. And then, an overpowering thought crossed his mind: "Is there life after death?"

Part One: The Beastly Soul Broker

IN THE YEAR OF THE BEAST, NINETEEN HUNDRED AND SIXTY-ONE

Beneath a terrified Battlefield Earth, in a dark, sinister, blood-red cavern, the bellowing Beast, the Evil Knight of Darkness, sat upon an imposing throne of contorted human skulls; stripped of their flesh, their chalk-white bony mouths screamed, prayed, and begged in a rhythm of perpetual motion—their chorus of infinite pleadings for another chance only adding to a din of eternal torment permeating the huge and fiery gathering of Demonic Warriors.

"Let it be known throughout the Realm of Darkness, on this One Thousand, Nine Hundred and Sixty-first Year of Earth, A.D., that Antonio "Squirm-in-Blood" Feranzi, Lieutenant of the Third Degree, is hereby promoted to Captain of the Red Forward Warriors of the Devil's Brigade! Come here and accept your dishonor."

Captain Feranzi hesitantly approached the platform. Aware of the Beast's ferocious appetite for warrior skulls, he was frightened the Beast would promote him and then order his soul to join those of the Court of Gesture: the ultimate fate for all condemned souls . . . including his. 'If he could continue to produce, then maybe, just maybe, he could remain an active Warrior,' he thought, as he stood meekly before the platform.

"You now have a problem, *Captain*!" the Beast began.

The cavern hushed, all lost souls and active Warriors viewing the newly promoted Captain's countenance. Anticipating him joining in their misery, a deep, low, hum of chanting began to evolve.

"Take. Take. Take. Take. Take . . ."

"I desire his soul! I *demand* his soul. He is *not* with the program. What will you do?" the Beast asked gently in his best sarcastic voice.

"Take. Take. Take. Take. Take . . ." the chanting continued.

"Sire, I am presently working on him. I have already delivered Alphonso, Antonio, and Jimmy's skulls. That is three generations! And soon, the skulls of both Joe-Pep and his brother, Carmine, the fourth generation, shall dress your throne! Yes, you shall receive the balance of Alphonso's lineage in due time! They are all living—

excuse the pun, your Majesty—down to their bargain of death. In fact, I am presently working on a plan that shall include Joe-Pep's son, Joe! You will have many skulls and souls before the year is up!"

"Well, confidence, ay?" The Beast cracked out loud. "YOU HAVE CONFIDENCE, DO YOU?" he screamed even louder. "I DO NOT WANT HIS OR ANYONE ELSE'S SKULL—YET! I WANT THEM ON EARTH CARRYING OUT MY ORDERS!"

The chanting grew louder: "Take. Take. Take his skull. TAKE HIS SKULL. TAKE HIS SKULL!"

"And if you make a wrong move, if he joins The Other One, I will take yours and every one of your descendant's souls and skulls on earth . . . DO YOU HEAR MY OATH . . . CAPTAIN?"

Captain Feranzi, his terror gleefully familiar to the multitude, stuttered his reply: "O Lord of Darkness, I shall deliver to your specifications. I shall deliver his and all of his descendants to your service. I shall also impose your will of sadness, suffering, and destruction to all involved and dedicated through Alphonso's contract! May I place my skull upon your throne if I fail!"

The cavern exploded in wails and chants and misery to the delight of The Evil Knight of Darkness. The Beast, wallowing in the self-pity and torment of his subjugated souls, let out a tremendous roar of pain and suffering: Agony ruled the walls, floors, ceilings—the very throne.

"Ah, Captain, your soul delivers warmth of fire and brimstone to my cold, cold, heart. Return to earth and do battle for me! *NOW!*"

Feranzi abruptly turned into the masses of Demon Warriors and grabbed several Lieutenants of the First through Third Rankings, then scurried through the Tunnel of Damnation for their journey back to Battlefield Earth.

"General Grogeninin, come here!" the Beast commanded.

"Yes, Sire," the General said as he bowed upon one knee.

"I command you to offer in sacrifice several million living souls on Battlefield Earth—this instant! Rain sorrow. Deliver pain. Beget misery. The battlefield must be joined!"

The screaming and moaning deep within the fiery cavern was soon joined by an earthly moan of misery . . . warming the cold black heart of the Beast!

Chapter 1: A Loan of Desperation

In the year of our Lord, 1908—as it was called in those days—a ship, under the commercial flag of U.S. Industrial Works, sailed packed to the deck with natives of Naples, Italy. The perishable, illiterate cargo crammed into its hold included Joe's Great-Great Grandfather Alphonso and his family. Believing prosperity could be found on the great shores of America, Alphonso had signed on to work for this trafficker of profits and was given free passage for himself and his family. In a secret pocket, along with other valuables constituting the wealth of his entire clan, he carried one of the flyers which had circulated in their small village in the old country. It told a tale of riches that could be gained by signing on to work for this industrial giant, U.S. Industrial Works. This great benefactor would supply all you desired: a home, a job, plenty to eat!

"Just sign here and we'll pay all your expenses."

For Alphonso, a smart but poor businessman, it was not a difficult decision. Bolstering the invitation was the old fable of the immigrant, who, upon arriving in New York City, observed a ten dollar bill lying on a cobblestone street. Exhausted from his long journey, he decided to leave it where it was and get some rest, returning the next day to pick it up. When he returned the ten was gone—replaced by a twenty dollar bill! By the time the tale reached Alphonso's village, the twenty had grown to one hundred!

Yes! America: rich, generous, compassionate; willing to share its wealth with all who came! Thousands of acres of land available to decent folks.

If only he had spoken to the Irish who had preceded him . . .

* * *

The lumbering ship docked at the Brooklyn pier in New York City, and Alphonso's family, worn out from the long journey, stood propped one against the other on the filthy, muck-encrusted deck, amazed at the sheer size of the smog shrouded city.

Gazing at the wharf, teeming with immigrants speaking in a multitude of tongues, Alphonso Dicanio hurried to produce documents that would speed up the perplexing immigration process; a process the agents of U.S. Industrial Works spoke of in their quest for souls. Without these documents he would have been unable to enter this great new country as a man of connection. Instead, he would have entered at Ellis Island and W.O.P. (with/out/papers) would be stamped on his immigration documents. Thus, he and his family would have begun the horrible and fearful process: health check, quarantine, separation, and a host of other terrible things including possible deportation.

As soon as Alphonso and his family were whisked through customs and taken to their new home, he realized the information he had been given was just a story: the "home" turned out to be a squalid tenement on the lower east side of Manhattan; the "job"—a 5 a.m. to 7 p.m. back-breaking laborer's position; the "plenty to eat"—scarce. He attempted to go his own way and was told to go back to work—or he would be deported. He went back to work.

In 1913, after five years of desperate times, in harsh, miserable conditions, Alphonso screamed a sacrilegious oath against God: "God, why have you put us in this place? I would give my soul to Lucifer in exchange for prosperity!"

The following day a man called Feranzi appeared and informed Alphonso that his services were desired by his "family." He stated that Alphonso could become quite wealthy, but that once he agreed to join this other "family," he was destined never to turn back! Alphonso agreed with this bargain and a "sit down" was arranged with the neighborhood representative of the Black Hand—the predecessor of the Mafia—Don Antonio Boccala.

Don Antonio Boccala was a "man of respect" aligned with gangster Salvatore Maranzano. Maranzano and his family operated from Sicily, but had strong ties to America. In 1925, Maranzano himself would come to America, where he would rise in power to become head of one of two Black Hand families battling for supreme control of the seedy and dangerous underworld. Until the dawn of mobster Salvatore "Charlie Lucky" Luciano—the true organizer of the modern day Mafia—Maranzano would rule with an iron fist . . . and a stiletto.

The Black Hand originated in Sicily as a small guerrilla force to combat the many oppressors who had ruled this island south of mainland Italy for thousands of years; Viking, Arab, Norman. The list of conquerors varied with the power and politics of the given time. Once these men had established themselves as a force to be reckoned with, they became known as "Men of Respect," for they respected their fellow brethren, country, and native traditions. Openly opposed to the ruling classes, they assisted the berated population in everything from housing and loans to settling disputes—to the people the Black Hand *was* the government. Eventually, as the oppressors were defeated through changing world events, these men of respect evolved and Evil entered the fray: power married greed, giving birth to an evil, sinister, repulsive creature named Sicilian Organized Crime.

Organized crime would continue to breed, producing bastard offspring along the way. Eventually, a collection of these cloned misfits arrived in every Italian community across the globe, dominating, thriving, and perpetuating their vile, greedy, self-indulging ways. Their rule was enforced with guns, baseball bats, Molotov-cocktails and explosives. This death-dealing monstrosity was a "men-only" fraternity. They enforced their own laws of fear and intimidation on one hand, and benevolence and compassion on the other. You had to agree with the first law to receive the second. By the time of Alphonso's arrival, the Black Hand had sown its treacherous seeds of destruction; seeds which were sprouting and blooming into massive, cannibalizing, soul-eating Venus fly-traps. Firmly rooted in the rich, fertile soil of Alphonso's immigrant neighborhood, this mutated abnormality fed off the hopes and dreams of its brethren . . . the very descendants of its once proud ancestors.

The Black Hand was the true mover and shaker of the Italian community, holding its own "court" from strategically placed "social clubs" in each neighborhood. From these dens of iniquity, justice would be dispensed and favors granted with a twitch of an eye or a puff of a cigar. Petitioners who had connections would use an associate of a particular family as their "advocate," thereby assuring a greater chance of success, while others would proceed alone. Whichever way they chose, a fact remained: for a favor granted, a small favor was requested in return—your soul.

Schooled since they were old enough to understand, most Italian men understood the traditions of respect, and Alphonso, believing his family's fortunes rested with the Don's assistance, realized his respect was paramount to that success. Yet he viewed this meeting with apprehension.

The sit down would take place in the family's "Social Club"

located in the same neighborhood Alphonso's predecessors had originally settled in. New York City had by now engraved the proud title of "Little Italy" upon its turf; its architecture the only remaining emblem of its American birth. Crossing the border into Little Italy, Alphonso entered the Old Country.

Mulberry Street, a stall-lined main thoroughfare in Little Italy, was alive with the hustle and bustle of commerce. Carts, piled high with a menagerie of color, texture and aroma, swarmed with shoppers engaged in the fine art of spirited bartering. Essential for the daily sustenance of this vast enclave, each wood and metal cube of rainbow and song embodied the economic spirit of the immigrant. Numerous Italian businessmen began their careers hawking wares from a cart on Mulberry Street—rain, snow or sunshine. Behind these symbols of territorial continuance, store fronts lined the sidewalks, each displaying their specialty in bold, proud, hand-painted lettering upon their windows. The entire neighborhood moved to a cadence of gentle and persuasive custom and culture, beckoning Alphonso's participation. Invigorated by the sights and smells, Alphonso temporarily shuttered his worry within his mind and briskly walked down the middle of the street. Soon, the vibrant rhythm caused him to dance in tune to the busy, ant-like shoppers, who left trails of bargains for others to follow. Passing a street sweeper with broom and catcher, engaged in an endless pursuit of refuse, he joined a mass of humanity congregated in front of the Alto Knights Social Club—this was his destination.

Mr. Eddy Bianco, an experienced vender, noticed Alphonso as he approached and began a serenade, "Fresha ripa tomata, fifteena cent a pound, zucchini only tena cent a pound, picka right offa vina thisa morning, aguaranteeda," and without a moment's hesitation continued, "Gooda morna, Alphonso, fora you, I throwa clova garlic eacha pounda you buy!"

Alphonso knew Bianco as a man of respect. In addition to the fruits and vegetables he hawked from his cart he also hawked a gambling concession for the "family." Alphonso stopped at the cart and expertly sampled and bargained until he was able to slip in his question, "How does the street news blow?"

Mr. Bianco waited until Alphonso made some selections, bagged the fresh basil, peppers, and tomatoes he chose, threw in a few cloves of garlic, and handed them back—along with his advice.

"Alphonso, youa musa member, staya calm, usa the words, 'I forever ina your deta, Dona Maranzano. Howa can ahumbla person sucha I, assista a man so esteema asa yourselfa.' An sita down . . . Befora you aska da fava!"

"The word was on the street already," Alphonso said quietly under his breath as he reached for the bag. "Thank you for your words of wisdom—and the garlic."

"Tella youa son Antonio I saya hello . . . ," Mr. Bianco called out as Alphonso stepped up onto the sidewalk.

Outside the unadorned, brown-brick storefront, with its large glass windows and white, neatly painted words, "The Alto Knights Social Club", a group of men dressed in boldly striped suits, fedoras, and spat-encased shoes were throwing dice. Each with a cigarette in his mouth, they spoke like a group of James Cagneys, "Mom, I'm on top of the world."

In the middle of a dice-roll, Francis "Franky Boy" Calabrese noticed Alphonso approaching and halted his throw. "Ha ya doowin, Alphonso babe?" he said frisking him. Not finding anything to worry about, he thumbed toward the door and said, "Tha Old Man's in da back, he's 'specting ya."

Alphonso had never been in the interior of the social club before, so it was with apprehension that he opened the door and entered the dank and moldy, smoke-filled room. Seated at three felt-covered card tables, on brown and weathered bent cane chairs, were a variety of men, from gangsters to local wannabes—wanting to be gangsters and pleased to be in their company—engaged in a variety of heated card games. Behind the tables, on stained and peeling papered walls, were pictures of the old country, each a demonstration of fealty, respect, heritage, family, and politics. The room buzzed with the racket of a gambler's den.

"Eh, Jimmy, I'll giv' ya 5 for 7."

"Go $%#@ yourself Monahan! That's why they call you 'Ball Buster' . . . Zippy already offered me 5 for 6!"

"Yeah, but where the $%#@ is Zippy now, huh! Tell me!"

"Come on . . . are you in or what?" Pauly Ham yelled.

Alphonso knew Pauly Ham. He ran the games for the Don. Hearing Pauly's voice, he strolled over.

Kissing Pauly on the cheek, Alphonso spoke greetings of respect. "The day finds you well. I pray your family is well."

"I can't complain. Junior was made last week!"

"May I extend my congratulations. May God bless you and your family. I have come to pay my respects to Don Boccala."

"The Old Man's in the back, he's waiting for ya."

Alphonso walked to the back of the room and gently knocked on the lone door. The door opened with a creaking sound and there stood the Ape—all six-foot-four of him.

A monster left over from the dark ages, thought Alphonso. Grasping the bag in his hand as if it were his protection from the giant, he greeted The Ape, "How are you, Angelo?"

"Cou'dent be better . . . how's ya son, Antonio?"

Knowing that this question was a mere formality, Alphonso replied, "Just fine."

"Come on in, I'll be right wid ya," the Ape said while motioning Alphonso into the Don's office.

Alphonso, bag in hand, his face wrapped up tight in a nervous smile, walked into the office as the Ape walked out.

Elaborately decorated, Boccala's office was a complete opposite to the other rooms—mahogany paneled walls—bookshelves holding leather bound manuscripts—statues of marble . . . and facing Alphonso was an imposing desk intricately carved with designs of snakes and lions locked in mortal combat. He read the Latin inscription elaborately engraved in the crest centered between those figures of life and death: "Veni, Vidi, Vici"—I came, I saw, I conquered.

How appropriate, he thought to himself as he inspected every aspect of this reflection of Don Boccala's mind. It was identical to that of Maranzano's Sicilian family's mind-set, *to be Caesar is to die Caesar*, he mused.

Alphonso knew of the rumors of this man's ties, and his facade could not hide the true facts of their purpose in life, not just to be a Caesar, but to ruthlessly conquer the souls of those around them—regardless of the consequences to those souls.

As if the President of the United States had stepped into the Oval Office—unannounced—the room became still with all attendees standing at attention, eyes focused on the Man himself.

The physical embodiment of a ghostly culture sauntered to his museum piece and sat down.

Alphonso stood as stiffly straight as he could, and in his native tongue, he recited what protocol demanded:

"I am forever in your debt Don Boccala. How can a humble person such as I, assist a man so este . . ."

"Slow downa, slow downa, hava seata, resta you tired feeta . . ." the Don interjected as he reached into an ancient, hand-carved cigar humidor.

Nervous energy emanating from his person, Alphonso sat down in the richly upholstered chair in front of the desk. No matter how hard he tried, he could not halt his fingers from fiddling with his hat.

"Senore Alphonso, I will come to the point. You come asking for a favor, and I have the power to grant much. But you must give your heart, your mind, your body, even your soul to the family. For we are a special family of power and wealth. Do you desire entrance to this special family?"

Alphonso sat back and thought for a moment of this question. He was about to join a highly respected family of men of honor whose families went to Church, spoke of God, and ran their businesses with iron fists—for the good of the people. Alphonso thought, If I could buy a house and have money then I could help my family.

Alphonso's thoughts overruled his heart.

"Don Boccala, I offer all that I am to your family. I give to you the allegiance of my own family as long as we breathe air."

"Senore Alphonso, I will help you . . . but remember, you ask something of me and I demand all of you. If I ask something of you what will your answer be?"

Alphonso, with the dignity his word of honor called for, rose to his full height and in a proud, sincere voice, replied, "Just ask and I will obey."

With business completed, the Don extended to Alphonso his hand with its bright, glowing, diamond-clad pinkie ring.

Antonio stood, kissed the ring, and departed.

* * *

Mr. Respect sent a message to the President of U.S. Industrial Works, a Protestant businessman from an established, wealthy family, and an associate of the elite, inner circle of social upper-crust leaders who ran the state of New York. His ties to the international business community extended to Palermo, Sicily, a city from which the man of respect imported olive oil—as well as Soldiers of the

Hand. His relationship to the underworld would eventually deliver political power and he would rise to become a leading member of Tammany Hall (the leading democratic organization which set the rules and elected most of the key party politicians of New York). The note, delivered that very same day by way of that loyal underling, Angelo "the Ape" Depicio, was simple and direct:

> *Remove A. from the roster and see that Mr. Berkowitz confidentially extends his assistance in securing our student a position in the Acme Land sales office. Let me know how that last recruitment fared. The ship should be docking in two weeks. —AB*

* * *

Thus Alphonso believed he had paid the gangster with his promise of equal favor—due upon request; his problems would be "fixed" . . . and the souls of his descendants would be assured a proper place in heaven after living a happy, bountiful life on earth. He never fully realized his oath had mortgaged his soul and the souls of five generations with a payment plan sure to go into receivership—the outcome being a life in Purgatory and an eternity in Hell. By the time Alphonso would realize the sacrilege he had committed, it would be too late!

Chapter 2: Payments of Interest

Father

Father, is it wistful the thought, to be born a tree . . .
My pennant a bark of strength, beauty, and serenity.
To plant my feet beneath Thy sacred earthen ground
And guard Thy torment without a sound.
With a message of brotherhood written on my leaves,
For all humanity broadcast to the breeze.
And seeds of peace cast to the sea
Sap wars of man; deliver true victory!
Then to depart this world from which I sprout

Begetting a dozen seedlings—hear them shout?
Their heritage of Father, their respect for me,
Through branches of wisdom as if to please;
My thoughts, My dreams, My future's hope
That now lie dormant, buried in the slope
From which they sprung with vigor and pride
One hundred years before I died.
How wonderful it would truly be,
If *You* had ordained me but an oaken tree?!

An efficient killing machine, consisting of three evil but mortal beings and a black, nondescript '61 Buick, had become immortal in the eyes of its master, who, upon the slightest whim, would set it into motion, bringing about a chain of events effecting not only the lives of those chosen for death, but the entire fabric of their lives. The Boss had made his decision: "Hit 'em!"

Right or wrong, the two up-and-coming racketeers who were targeted for death would have no appeal; their sentence was to be carried out with an emphasis on sending a message rather than revenge or payback.

On a wet, foggy, dreary night, Mario's Italian Restaurant & Pizzaria resembled a wake. The usual laughter and cheerful enthusiasm which greeted each patron in the form of one tall Robert Mitchum look-alike was missing. Always joking and carrying on, he would normally show each customer to the "best table in the house" where his inseparable brother, the ever-present "Professor"—slight of build, wearing simple, round spectacles—would complete the magic that kept the till brimming and made it hard to find an empty seat. But like the chill that tenaciously hugged the cold, wet city of New York, tension had permeated the establishment all night. As if death had been the main entree, a solemn, priestly individual, dressed in black, seemed to anoint rather than greet each patron.

"See youse gize lata . . ." Tony Black mumbled as he escorted the last patrons out through the old glass and mortised oak door. " . . . it's just the flu or somethin."

Turning on the heels of his pointy-toed Italian fence climbers, he grasped the handset of the desk phone with his right hand and dialed a number with a diamond-clad pinkie-ringed left hand.

As he waited for his party to pick up, Tony toyed with his ring of respect, his pride and joy, polishing it by breathing loudly on its surface and rubbing it against his black suit jacket until a brilliant, blue-white reflection danced a rhythm of sparkling star bursts against the dark and gloomy interior ceiling.

"Yeah, who's callin'?" a distinctive voice inquired.

"Tony Black . . . listen, tell da guy dat we're closin' da joint early, I'll see im at three . . . Oh, and yeah, Pauly Ham passed away."

"O.K."

Tony hung up the phone and sauntered to the pizza counter to count his meager tips. Standing under the wood trellis that draped the cluttered counter, he turned the tip glass over. The loose change that jingled to its surface was as devoid of substance as the dusty plastic vines that drooped and dripped from the Italian garden-looking contraption above his head. For Tony, the entire past week was a void. The only thing even resembling normalcy were the patrons who had sampled the pasta, and even they showed their dissatisfaction with the absence of ambience that usually overpowered all in its intoxicating, invigorating way. The pieces-of-eight that flooded the joint and lined Tony's pockets were slow in coming. As Tony would say . . . "Da tips waz as slim as fleas on a goldfish!"

Tony Black had two jobs: protecting the brothers and handling the pizza counter. The past two days he'd taken on the additional responsibility of "official greeter." He was supposed to stay until the brothers left, but tonight, he had asked for and received permission to leave early.

As he turned to leave he yelled toward the swinging doors of the kitchen, "Hey, Carm . . . Yo, I'm leaving . . . Do ya hear me?" Only silence. Turning on his heels he headed for the front door shouting: "I'll lock da joint on da way out. See youse gize tomorrow."

Stepping through the doorway and into a realm of pervasive darkness, he turned and closed the solitary door with a hefty thump. Turning once to scan the streets, he briskly walked to his parked Caddy.

As if Tony's departure provoked demons to suddenly play a loud and boisterous chess game upon the spoiled and sauce-stained red and white checkered table cloths, the blast of a sudden, heated argument in the kitchen ricocheted through the dining room, abruptly piercing the eerie cloak of silence.

"Let's just leave town, go to Ohio or somethin'!" The Professor was shouting forcefully as he nervously cleaned the sparkling, clear lenses of his gold, wire framed glasses.

"It's still on the table; we're safe until we get called on the carpet," his brother cut in as he turned the lights back on. "Let's just finish up and get home. It's nine-thirty. You're the one that has to drive all the way to Westbury, not me. I'll see you tomorrow at the house. We'll talk then . . . I'll call Joe Pag—get a sit-down, O.K.?"

"O.K., but I just got this feelin' we should just lie low until this thing blows ov . . ."

"Come on, I know what I'm talkin' about. There's nothing to worry about!" he shouted back with assurance—trying to hide the fear he felt. "The heck with those jerks, I could give a damn!"

Relentless in its stealthy pursuit of game, the predator rounded the bleak, dimly lit corner and eased to a stop at the curbside in front of the shuttered restaurant—allowing its contents to spill upon the sidewalk. There it remained, engine idling, a man-made carnivore of hopes and dreams, ready to pounce on all unsuspecting quarry. The brothers, unaware of death's grim reapers lurking just outside their door, continued to argue: "Why don' you ride with me to Long Island?" The Professor asked, not at all reassured by his brother's comments. "We can call Jean, let her know."

"Listen, I'm tired of this bull. We're not responsible for what . . ."

With sudden, shocking force and perfect precision, the hit crew, one tall and one short, crashed through the front door.

The brothers pivoted as one to face this sudden intrusion of fate.

A hail of deadly hot lead greeted them, each projectile finding more than just flesh and bone in which to burrow; deeply, mortally, these bearers of death silenced forever their dreams, hopes and feelings.

The diabolical chariot of death, sleek in its shroud of pitch-black midnight, with only a door-thud in the night, swallowed its two cold and sinister companions. Then, with fervent determination, it zoomed off for its next intended victim in a never-ending quest to satisfy an acquired taste for blood and power.

The repercussion was immediate—and once again, like waves of time and hurricane alike, smashing upon an unprotected shoreline, dividing, removing, changing, the waves of The Oath of Alphonso permanently altered and condemned the families of these two Soldiers of the Hand to uncertainty, sorrow, and a life of drifting sands.

Chapter 3: Characters of Principal

Life

When we are young and growing old,
Life, a story, often told:
"Life so simple, trusting and true,
never a worry.—How 'bout you?"
Then the midnight comes and goes.
The age of reason. Don't you know?
"Life not so simple, trusting and true.
Always a worry . . . How 'bout you?"

It's Thanksgiving Day, 1961; a day all good Catholic, Italian-American families esteem. There will be a grand celebration in honor of the first immigrants's arrival on the shores of America, a sharing of family goodwill and happiness, and a feast that will include an abundance of Italian delicacies reserved for this special occasion. Aunts, uncles, and cousins will attend this banquet adorned in their finest attire; strutting and squawking like a flock of resplendent peacocks —each one seeking the acknowledgment these displays entail. Elders will narrate tales born of heritage and legacy. But most of all, eight-year-old Joe, excited and anxious, will be there with his father: wearing a pin-striped suit, brim-feathered fedora, and diamond pinkie ring—just like him . . .

Convulsive sounds of thunder woke him, not the alarm clock so carefully set the night before. 'The forecast called for a bright and sunny day, not rain and lightning', he thought with dismay. Rolling toward his window's beckoning flash and vibration, he pulled on a frayed cord that held down its stained and discolored shade, releasing it to snap back to its place of refuge. Through the sooty, dirt-specked window, torrents of rain battled with filth and grime shrouding the city. Like the seldom cleaned grease trap in Uncle Tony's pizza parlor, the predictable outcome paralleled man's own battle between good and evil: the storm would rage with honest intensity and cause, only to exhaust itself against the overpowering and ever-present shadow of dusty gloom . . . testimony to its fierce battle, those remnants of vigor and pride with which it attacked its enemy, small pools of water and minute pockets of moisture, now befuddled and entwined in filth's death grasp; themselves infected with the stain of sin, doomed to evaporation, a legacy of grime in their wake.

Surveying the panorama below, a never-ending megalopolis of cars, people, confusion and noise, Joe felt that man had precipitated a horrible mutation of nature's once tranquil and orderly countryside. His family had recently moved from Ronconcomo, Long Island, a place of beauty and serenity. How he longed for its clean, damp, moss-covered woodlands, where the only sounds were the whispers of the breeze as it gently stirred the acorn-studded oaks, and the occasional call of his friends—squirrels, chipmunks, birds—as they scurried about their business, gathering nuts, building nests, all in harmony. A beloved place where he could shed his emotions in privacy with only his small companions, those magnificent silent trees, and God bearing witness.

His mother had a problem with living "out in the country": his father. His father was always in the city working. His arrival home was as unpredictable as the weather. To invest in an Italian restaurant on 81st Street in Manhattan, his father needed to sell their house to raise the down payment. At first his mother was dead set against selling, but the fact that they would move to the city and be with his father compelled her to concede. She was now the happiest woman he ever saw! Singing and dancing while she cooked, laughing and hugging them all the time. Joyous in every way! A flash of lightning transported him out of his daydream and back to reality.

On the street corner, Bianco's Deli was open for last-minute shoppers, who swarmed and buzzed like bees to honey as they gathered the fruits of harvest on display. Joe didn't have to look too hard to see the ever present figure of Old Man Bianco. The old man stood out on the sidewalk, protected from the deluge by a huge green awning that proclaimed in bold white letters: "Bianco's Deli and Meats." Wearing a bright yellow raincoat and hat—a perfect imitation of a ripe oversized banana—he blended perfectly with the brilliantly hued fruit and vegetables amassed on the stands.

Old Man Bianco, the neighborhood counselor, therapist and medicine man, would gather, store, and analyze massive amounts of intelligence each and every day. Then, with uncanny, precise, almost mystical powers, he would will his deductive reasoning to those it concerned. A leftover from the "Mustached Petes", he began providing his legacies in '23 from a vegetable cart located on Mulberry Street and knew Joe's father, Grandfather, Great Grandfather, and even his great great grandfather! Presently, Charlie Pinito, owner of the Three Chair Barber Shop, was the humble recipient of some of his words of encouragement or advice.

As Joe watched this familiar sight, the rain abated and the men in the neighborhood began calling on Mr. Bianco. They were purchasing carnations, pinning them to their lapels, receiving their advice, and swaggering away. Joe had recently earned thirty-five cents—enough to buy his own carnation—running errands after school for his father, a job his father had given him just a week ago. After he got dressed he would go to Mr. Bianco, buy a carnation, pin it on his lapel, receive his advice, and swagger away!

Jumping out of bed with an enthusiasm he seldom possessed, he dashed to the closet and carefully grasped the hanger holding his brand new, black pin-striped suit. Delicately laying it on the bed, he thought of all the trouble he had gotten into the past two weeks daydreaming about feasts and dressing up. Turning back to the closet to reach for the hat box holding his most prized possession—a miniature duplicate of his father's favorite fedora—he knew it was worth all the castigation he'd been through. After removing the hat from the glossy black container with all the dignity and reverence this ritual deserved, while still in his pajamas, Joe walked to the mirror and gazed at his reflection. He donned the hat and proceeded to tilt and adjust it this way and that: He'd look "as sharp as a ten dollar razor" just like his father. Grinning, he turned and walked back to the closet and from a recess above its top shelf, he picked up his least favorite possession: a brown, paper-wrapped Macy's shoe box containing a pair of black, Italian-made, pointy-toed fence climbers.

"How could something so beautiful cause so much pain?" Joe had asked his father after suffering through an entire day of wearing them.

"When you get older, you'll learn that many beautiful things can cause pain," he replied with a sadness in his eyes Joe was not used to.

Not understanding what his father meant, he drew his own conclusion: it had to be an Italian tradition—the pain, that is—for father and all the men that came to see him always wore them.

Next he searched his dresser drawers for that elusive shoehorn (he would never even dare attempt that most laborious and dreadful feat of putting these toe crunchers on without it). All that was left to complete his attire was the crowning jewel, one which all men of respect possessed: A diamond pinkie ring—and he had one!

His ring had what was called a diamond chip, but he imagined it to be a ten-carat diamond. It was kept in his father's jewelry box and only with his permission, on special occasions, could he wear it. His father always told him it was a symbol of respect and tradition. Respect and tradition were very important to his father. To him, they represented more then mere words: they were a way of life, and he made sure they were etched indelibly in his mind. Realizing he had spent so much time admiring his wardrobe, Joe decided to find his father to obtain his ring.

Joe lived in an apartment called a "box car flat," named for its series of rooms arranged end-to-end like railroad cars. Each room had doors that slid into the side walls when they were opened, thereby creating a corridor of space from the front of the flat to the back with no hallways. His mother and father's room (shared with his one-year-old brother, Eddy) was located on the opposite end of the flat, followed by the living room, then the kitchen—with the only offsetting room being the bathroom—followed by his sister Angela's room, and finally, the bedroom he shared with his brother Carmine.

Joe slid open his bedroom door and looked out into the flat to find his father. It was instantly obvious the usual noises and aromas associated with the Thanksgiving feast were missing. His mother was not skirmishing with his sister, Angela, an everyday occurrence. The kitchen symphony of clanking and banging pots, pans and utensils, conducted by his mother, grandmother, and assorted relations, was mute. Ancient, musty odors, which identified their worn flat as home, were not replaced by those tantalizing fragrances of the preparation of the feast—which certainly would have commenced by now. It was like the time their television malfunctioned: a fuzzy image with no sound. Though Joe's conscious mind was slow to grasp the unfolding events, his subconscious mind was already assimilating this vignette at a phenomenal rate.

In the far-off bedroom was his mother, laying in full repose, encircled by a group of women who were gesturing and whispering in a frenzied and chaotic manner. In his shocked state he could see their lips moving, but he heard no sound. A sudden movement caused his eyes to dart to the left. There stood Nana Lou, his grandmother, changing the diapers of his youngest brother, Eddy. She turned to him and their eyes met. He knew something was dreadfully wrong—the eyes that bore into his were not the beacons of warmth and radiance he knew so well, but blackened embers of a once proud fire; her smile, always present to convey love and understanding, was transformed to a grim, red slash—sending shock waves of sadness and confusion. Her movements were those of a robot programmed in slow motion.

Like the thunderstorm that appeared so suddenly on this bright and sunny morning, fear and anxiety replaced his cheerful enthusiasm. Without a word, he raced to his mother's room, desperately seeking the answer to the question he was too terrified to ask.

Angela's voice stopped him dead in his tracks, temporarily halting this ghastly nightmare . . . a nightmare that had voraciously annihilated every thought and feeling he possessed.

"Joe, there's been an accident," Angela said, her voice trembling with emotion.

His sister's words cleared the screen and brought the sound back on that broken television with a magnitude and intensity of an exploding bomb. Sounds and vision that weren't present seconds before, overwhelmed his senses. Nana was mumbling to herself rapidly in Italian as she wrestled with the arduous task of diapering Eddy. His aunts weren't whispering—they were weeping. Absent was any evidence of the presence of his father, brother Carmine, or any of his uncles.

'An accident?' he thought. 'Did she say accident? What did she mean . . . an accident?'

Turning toward his sister, he noticed she was sitting on her bed—a bed still rumpled from her own dreams of the coming day's excitement—excitement which now seemed to be nothing but a fabrication of those dreams. She was dressed in her nightgown and appeared as if she had inherited all the sorrow and loneliness in the world. Instinctively, his arms moved to comfort her as his mind raced like a roller-coaster attempting to sort the gravity of the scene.

Some of his father's words of wisdom came to him. "Father, I'm lonely and miss you. When are you coming home?" he once asked him on the phone.

"You don't worry about that. Just worry about taking care of your mother, sister, and brothers. I love you and until I get back, you're the man of the house!"

Needless to say, after that phone conversation he assumed the air of a dictator. His lofty position didn't last long as his mother put him back in his place with a swift kick in the butt.

Some of his mother's words of wisdom came to him. "Mommy, what does 'man of the house' mean?" he had asked her after the swift-kick-in-the-butt program.

"It means that you help take care of the family. Do you remember the time your sister hurt her leg and she cried?" she asked.

"Yeah."

"Well, do you remember what I did?"

"You bandaged her leg and held her till she stopped crying."

"That was taking care of the family. As the oldest son you are the little man of the house. When I need you to be the man of the house I'll let you know. This is not the time. Now go and throw the garbage out."

In his mind, this was an appropriate time to temporarily assume that position of responsibility and respect. This thought brought a semblance of sanity back to him. As soon as he could calm his sister down he'd find his father—'he'd know what really caused this horrendous change of events.'

"What happened. What's going on? Who had an accident?" he asked her. At that moment, the menacing dark clouds on Angela's horizon erupted, a flood of tears secretly held in check, burst forth.

"Angela, don't cry . . . calm down and listen to me! You have to calm down and tell me what happened. Who had an accident?!" he demanded, imbued with authority as the transient man of the house.

She interrupted her tears for a moment and softly said, "Father. Father had an accident . . ."

The only time his father had had an accident that he knew of was when he was "pinched" (later he would learn this meant he was arrested). They were living on Long Island, and one Sunday before dinner his father went to the store to pick up some Italian bread. When he didn't come home after several hours his mother began to worry. Late the next night, after they had gone to bed, Joe had heard the commotion of his father's return. He slipped out of his room and silently sneaked to the hallway door to see what had happened.

There stood his father, suit rumpled, a stubble worth two days of shaving, yelling in an agitated voice, "Those bastards pinched me!"

He had never seen his father in such an unkempt and distressed manner. Not understanding, the only thought he had was of his father standing in the doorway of an old house with a group of Uncle Tonys—he always called his Uncle Tony a "bastard"—pinching him over and over. For the next few nights the nightmare of this thought continued to plague him. Finally, he questioned mother.

"Why did Uncle Tony pinch father?"

His mother, not wanting to cause further distress, replied with a laugh, "Uncle Tony didn't pinch your father. Do you remember the time you caught your hand in the door and it pinched you?"

"Sure."

"Well, that was an accident. Your father just had an accident."

Joe had still wondered what his Uncle Tony, the bastard, had to do with father's "accident," but he decided to drop the subject to preserve his growing aura of being The Man of the House.

Shaking himself out of his reverie, he held his sister in his grasp, not so much to soothe her pain as to quell his own emotions—which were now boiling over. He wanted to scream out for someone to wake him; for someone to tell him it was all a dream—he wanted to cry!

Joe's father had forbidden him to ever cry. He would be ashamed of him if he let his feelings show. He would say, "Men of Respect Don't Cry."

The last time Joe remembered crying in the presence of others was when he was five. . . .

> Born with severe club feet and curved leg syndrome, Joe suffered with constant pain. This fact, combined with the cruel jokes of some neighborhood kids, slowed his normal childhood development. Joe was a late bloomer. If walking was a top priority, so was potty training—an issue that became a great source of consternation to his father. Once, while preparing for an extended business trip, Joe's father demanded that his mother have him "sitting on the stool" by the time he got back. When father arrived home—along with two of his brothers—the first thing he did was ask his wife, Jeanette, if Joe was "using the stool." Jeanette replied, "He is making progr . . ." But, before she could finish her answer, he grabbed hold of Joe's arm and, along with his brothers, dragged him to the bathroom. Once there, he pulled down his pants and shoved him on the commode. Frightened and embarrassed, Joe started to cry. His father's immediate reaction was a slap across Joe's face as he exclaimed, "Men don't cry or wet the bed!" He then snatched the electric hair trimmers and shaved little Joe's

head. Needless to say (with his mother's assistance) he never wet the bed again.

. . . Those reflections of his father along with his new position as "man of the house" appeased Joe's raging emotions. Everything would be all right. With relief, he now knew why the women were weeping and moaning. Women were sensitive and inclined to dramatize trivial incidents—such as pinching. A change of garments? A shave? Come on, a little aggravation? Is this what they're crying about? As his father would say, "Take it like a man of respect!"

The only thought that didn't fit was the image of Nana. It kept appearing in stark contrast to the assumption he'd imposed upon his mind. But he shoved it to a remote corner and replaced it with a vision of his father coming home and everyone telling father that little Joe did not cry!

"Angela, Angela, don't cry. Listen to me," he whispered, looking directly into Angela's beautiful brown eyes, eyes which were now a tempest of tears and subjects of her grief. "Stop crying. It's O.K.! I know what happened, Father got pinched!"

Angela's bellowing was reduced to a rapid series of sobs; she wanted to say something, but Joe, feeling much more the man of the house, continued in earnest. "Do you remember the time father went for the loaf of bread and didn't come back for two days? He had an accident. He just got pinched! Mother told me!"

A look of confusion and amazement replaced the tears of anguish which proclaimed Angela's disarray. It became evident that she had regained her composure when she spoke in a clear and compassionate voice, "Oh, Joe, Joe, Joe, you don't understand. It's the Curse! Like Grandpa Antonio! Father and Uncle Carmine will not be coming home! They can't! They're in heaven! They're with God!"

"No, that's not right! It's just another accident! He just got pinched!"

Something about the look in Angela's eyes quieted him. She repeated the words, "They're in heaven," and his life came crashing down. At that moment life was suspended. There were no visions, no thoughts, no feelings, no dreams. Gone were the thumpings of his heart sending its message of life—his ears ceased to hear, his eyes refused to see, he wasn't there. His world turned jet black. He ceased to exist.

Chapter 4: Portfolio of Sorrow

Memories

Twilight and soon,
a sliver of silver,
gliding, glistening,
will contrast the cimmerian.
I kneel, prayers said,
tears shed.
I hear a voice?
Distant . . .
Is it yours?
No . . . Just echoes.
Oh! Great Thespian shores!
Mute and mime.
Merged are you with antiquity.
Wave upon wave,
Prompting,
Suggesting,
Rendering the current
to the past
the past
to the future
I shall join thy waters
Misty blue,
With tears of tempest
Stormy hue,
And chance again
Another day . . .

It is Thanksgiving, 1961, a day of catastrophic misfortune for our Catholic, Italian-American family. Hushed, dismal talk of a somber mass replaces the expectation of joyous greetings. Aunts, uncles, and cousins, adorned in their finest attire, tiptoe with empathy as they seek to console grieving family members. Elders Eulogize and Exaggerize tales born of misery. But most of all, young Joe will be there, wearing a black, pin-striped suit, brim-feathered fedora, and diamond pinkie ring, just like the one father wore . . .

Stinging sensations stirred him from his faint. Joe fought to recall why he was lying on the floor while a multitude of arms, hands, and assorted extremities reached for him. Through this mass of determination his mother's face appeared. She was pleading with the benevolent apparatus to make way.

"Move over! Out of the way," he could hear her wail. "Is he breathing? Is he breathing?"

'Is he breathing?' he thought to himself. 'Am I dead?' The prospect that he was among the departed did not alarm him—an eternity of Medusa-like hordes did. 'This must be what Purgatory is like,' he thought to himself.

"Mom, I'm all right, I'm all right," he yelled toward her.

"Oh! My Joey! My poor little Joey! Are you O.K .?" she asked as she lifted him up and into her arms.

"I gotta headache," was all he could reply.

"Just lay down awhile. Mommy's gonna get something for your head," she said while placing him on Angela's bed.

"Angela! Where are you, Angela?" she called across the flat—which by now felt like a rush-hour train crammed with mourners.

"I'm right here, Mommy," Angela said, standing no more then two feet from her mother.

"Get your brother some aspirins and a glass of water. And, when you're done, put some coffee on and see if anyone is hungry," she commanded. Reality returned with his mother's request: ". . . and see if anyone is hungry." It seemed bizarre to him. 'How could anyone eat with Father and Uncle Carmine in heaven?' Joe thought.

He wanted to ask her, 'What are Father and Uncle Carmine gonna eat today? Do they have food in heaven? What happened to them? Did they feel any pain? Do you go to heaven with your earthly injuries? Is it cold in Heaven?' The mortifying consequences of these questions kept his silence. On the verge of tears, he firmly recalled his father's words, "Men of respect don't cry."

Angela placed a coaster on the tired, archaic nightstand, then set the glass of water and aspirins down. The nightstand, its spindly legs fatigued from ceaseless quests at permanent mooring, held an ornate silver frame containing a photo of Joe's father. It depicted a powerful man with hard, chiseled features, dressed in suit, overcoat, and fedora. A look of strong-willed determination was written on his face as he boldly posed for posterity.

"Here are your aspirins," she said, averting her eyes from the portrait. "I have to go and put the coffee on."

She turned and walked to the kitchen. The only sign of her crippled emotions was the lethargy with which she performed her assignment. . . .

As a child Angela had always been cheerful and optimistic, but her father's death fomented an obsessive devotion to her mother—a devotion that would cause torment and tribulation throughout the rest of her life. She was blessed with beautiful shoulder length brown hair which became her most cherished asset but also a constant source of irritation: she was forever in the bathroom—much to the dismay of the rest of the family—fixing her hair. A day would not go by without a skirmish between Angela and her Mother concerning such trivial items as hair spray, brushes, and time spent primping in front of the mirror. The family would start the battle, but Angela would eventually win the war.

Intellectually, she possessed a wisdom far exceeding her years. Being the only daughter of a household of a "man of respect," she inevitably received more than her share of the responsibilities, chores, and hardships. Yet she never complained because she had this remarkable perception of the adversities that her mother had to endure. The great and demanding burden of assisting her mother in the rearing of her brothers began immediately following Joe-Pep's death; the day he passed away became the day her childhood passed away.

From that day on, she never had the time to cultivate friends like the boys did. When they were playing, she would be cleaning house; when they were watching television, she would be washing clothes. Selfishness and hatred never became a part of her personality; on the contrary, the times you would expect her to be angry, she would convey goodwill and harmony—always mending the fences. Eventually, while the boys were out gallivanting around the countryside, she would quit school to help with the bills. It would be many years before the boys became aware of the fact that without her, their mother would have been lost. It would be with a combination of amazement, compassion, and sympathy that they acknowledged the loss of her childhood and the way she masked her feelings.

. . . As Joe watched Angela serve coffee to the grieving relatives seated around the dining room table, huge, dense plumes of smoke arose from the habitual chain smoking which had replaced conversation. It was as if someone brought the Con-Edison power plant into their flat, turned it on full steam, and allowed its huge chimney to belch all day. The eerie scene brought back the memory of Joe's first cigarette episode . . .

> Joe's father was seated at the dining room table savoring a demitasse of espresso. As he sipped this strong, sweet brew, he held his ever-present unfiltered Camel. Joe watched him smoke this contraption with fascination. Wanting desperately to emulate everything this illustrious man did, he waited impatiently until his father went to the bathroom. Then, he pounced from his hidden spot behind the sofa (with an eagerness he was to regret), grabbed that burning symbol of maturity and took a heavy drag. The response was immediate—he coughed, spat, turned colors, and nearly threw up. In a blink of an eye, his father was standing in front of him.
>
> "So you wanna smoke, do ya?" he demanded.
>
> Uh-oh . . . here it comes, Joe thought.
>
> He sat Joe down at the table and produced a cigar that looked like a dozen people could smoke it and still have some left over. He lit it with flair and stuck it in Joe's mouth. "Let's see you smoke that," he said seriously (while trying to conceal his own amusement).

* * *

Joe-Pep was over six feet tall with black hair and gray eyes. He liked to smoke Camel cigarettes and an occasional cigar. He dressed as sharp as a "ten dollar razor" in a suit, fedora, and diamond pinkie ring. Born of a long line of Sicilian racketeers, his education consisted of one class: "Street Smart 101." The most realistic representation of his father was "Sonny" in the original movie *The Godfather*—right down to his mannerisms and temper. "I'm Joe-Pep and my business is giving people what they want," Joe could hear him say—it was a term he borrowed from "Mr. Capone."

If giving the people what they wanted meant breaking some heads, he'd chalk that up to business. He always had a pocket full of cash—even if it meant no food on the table—and drove a late model Caddy. To the men he was a dominating presence and would back it up with a left or right hook . . . or a combination of both. To the women he was trouble—which was the cause of considerable misery to Joe's mother. It was his lack of attendance at the home front that made the kids use the term father rather than "dad," "pop," or "daddy." It was always, "When your father gets home . . . Your father is . . . Your father will . . ."

When it came to the children, Joe-Pep demonstrated his love with gifts of emotion; emotion dispersed in such tiny fragments, he kept them hungry and thirsting for more. Every word spoken would resonate to Joe's very soul. Joe worshipped Joe-Pep, he was his knight in shining armor who wore a trench coat and carried a .45. He could do no wrong.

It was that .45 which always held Joe's attention. It was the day before his seventh birthday that his father brought home the gift that he would cherish until his death.

Wrapped in bright, colorful paper, the box felt heavy. Holding it up to his ear, Joe shook it in his determination of its content.

"You can't open it until tomorrow," his father informed him with a delightful, yet serious look.

Wondering what was in the box caused Joe to roll and toss in his bed that entire night. The following morning Joe jumped out of bed and ran to the living room to check the box again. There sat his father, fully dressed, white-on-white silk shirt, old creased leather shoulder holster strapped and ready, talking with several other men who also wore holstered guns. He stared in fascination at these men of respect, 'Boy! they looked cool!'

Joe's father turned, saw him, grabbed the box, and tossed it to him, "Open it, go on, open it," he said, a smile beginning to break upon his face as Joe tore through the paper and ripped open the box.

A Colt .45 six gun . . . and holster! His first response was to attempt to wear the holster like his father wore his . . . but it wouldn't work—a western-style six-gun was made to wear on the hip. Joe's father came over, unbuckled the belt and strapped it on him. "When you get older, I'll buy you one like mine. Happy Birthday!"

Never in his limited time with his father was he more proud! From that day forward he believed that no one, not even God himself, could defeat his knight in shining armor . . . that is until his death.

Joe was told his father died in an automobile accident with his ever-present shadow, Uncle Carmine. Joe's father and Uncle Carmine were inseparable. Their bond was legendary. You didn't mess with one without having to contend with the other. His father was the brawn of the duo, his uncle the brain. However, both could rumble with a fierceness that kept most of the other wiseguys at arm's length. Family tradition played an important part in the naming and raising of their offspring. They both gave their children the same names: Joseph, Angela, and Carmine, with an Edward (in deference to Joe's Uncle Eddy on his mother's side) and a Cookie, Donny, and Richie breaking the pattern because his uncle had three more children. At family gatherings, whenever someone would call out "Carmine," six different Carmines would answer.

Though they both loved and protected their families with a passion, Uncle Carmine was much more constant in his home life. Joe-Pep always had a girl friend on the side and Uncle Carmine would cover for him—a perpetual dilemma between morality and loyalty. His uncle's imperturbable demeanor was frequently tested by Joe's father's explosive temper which could ignite without a moment's hesitation. Inevitably, when fate, in the form of The Curse of Alphonso, called their hand, it was as if a tornado had ripped through Joe's peaceful, sleepy town, altering forever his dreams and visions of his future with his father.

Part Two: Beastly Debt Collectors

IN THE YEAR OF THE BEAST, NINETEEN HUNDRED AND SIXTY-FOUR

Thousands of sunken, piercing, blood-red eyes, grimly reflecting off the chalk-white, contorted masks of howling skulls, created the perfect macabre atmosphere. The repugnant Knight of Darkness, The Beast of Death, stood above the masses of bowed infantry upon a platform built from an orgy of human skeletons; his voice, booming above a furor of lamenting souls, in conduction of ceremony.

"Bring to me his soul!" demanded the Beast. "I desire the fulfilling of the contract! It called for all generations, Do you hear me? ALL GENERATIONS! It is the Earth Year of One Thousand, Nine Hundred, and Sixty-Four! I am DEMANDING HIS SOUL!"

"Sire, we realize your concern," Captain Antonio "Squirm-in-Blood" Feranzi of the Red Forward Warriors of the Evil Knight's Devil's Brigade cried out. "We are presently working on him. But Sire, he is a Squire of The Knight of Good over Evil, he is with the Holy . . ."

At the near mention of the Holy Spirit, the enormous cavern went into exclaimed silence; mouths of skulls jittered in speechless dread.

A full ten seconds passed before the Beast recovered and, in a display of torrential anger, lightning flashed throughout the regimented soldiers of the devil's brigade as the Beast's right arm shot forward, its jeweled hand-claw, index probe extended, pointed directly at the Captain.

"You dare to deliver a message of failure? You dare to use an excuse of such minor consequence . . . TO ME? THE ALL-MIGHTY, MOST POWERFUL, AWESOME EVIL KNIGHT OF DARKNESS? THE ONE WHO CONVERTS, CONNIVES, SUBJUGATES, AND INSTIGATES ALL THAT IS EVIL IN THE UNIVERSE, IN THE HEAVENS, IN THE EARTH . . . IN MANKIND?" the Beast shouted in a firestorm.

Cowering in fear, Captain Feranzi stepped forward as the horrendous screaming and moaning resumed.

"Sire, understand, I do not come to bring you a message of failure on the part of your Warriors . . . just that a change of plans . . ."

A crash of ear splitting, thunderous rage erupted within the cavern, interrupting the Captain's sniveling reply.

"All I have heard in the last ten years is your excuses and innuendo. You have become a constant failure! You have had your plans backfire. The very oath that has delivered thousands of souls is in jeopardy because you screwed up! How did the information of your past planning reach those who have caused this disaster! You were given the responsibility of inducing the sin I required of this person eight years ago! Your plans have not succeeded! I never requested his father's early demise. It was you who caused his father's skull to be impaled upon my throne before he had the chance of converting and instigating his proper share of misery upon the earth! His children are now free to learn of the Other One! It was you who informed me of your plans to engineer a birth defect with the idea it would add to his son's misery and therefore plant the seeds of subversion upon his soul! All it has done is make him stronger."

"But, Sire, I have brought you many souls to dress your throne and fill your Tomb of Future Torment. It was I who engineered his family's demise and subjugation through the oath of allegiance taken by his forefathers! It was I . . ."

"How dare you interrupt me!" the Beast screamed. "IT WAS I WHO BARGAINED ALPHONSO'S SOUL, NOT YOU! JOE HAS INVOKED HIS NAME! HE IS IN THE POSITION OF ENDING MY RULE UPON HIS PEOPLE! TELL ME WHY I SHOULD NOT TAKE YOUR SKULL FOR MY THRONE THIS INSTANT!"

Pleading, begging voices joined in a chorus of, "Take His Skull, Take His Skull!"

The Captain, sensing his abrupt demise into eternal damnation of pain, grief and misery—a thousand-fold return of which he had given—dropped to his knees and began to beg.

"Oh, Mighty Master, Ruler of the Dark and Evil World of the Living Death, it is I, a loyal and faithful soldier of the Devil's Brigade, a servant of twenty centuries of service . . ."

Feranzi never had the chance to complete his points of dedication, for the Beast, moved on by a cacophony of misery, arose in full display of his hideous form and, with an electric, blue-white energy that momentarily danced a static maze of angles around the throne, shouted the Oath: "I, The Knight of Darkness, of Evil over Good, command you to join the Court of Mournful Gesture. There you will remain for eternity as pleasure for my ear tufts!"

Suddenly, the multitude of moaning, pleading voices rose in pitch and fervor into a crescendo of hate and misery. Echoing throughout the vast chamber of horror, they combined into a deep, appalling, electrifying burst of black energy, as pitch as the darkness of a moonless, starless, immortal night, streaming from the Beast toward the Captain, devouring all within its path.

Captain Feranzi, along with several thousand Warriors, was swept into the void: they appeared as moaning, fleshless, chalk-white skulls, implanted in the throne, walls, and very heart of the cavern.

"Now, step forward—my new Captain!" the Beast demanded of Lieutenant Gregory "Snatching Soul" Rumkof. "You are promoted to the rank of Captain. You will take the name of Feranzi from this day forward. Now—journey henceforth and deliver Joe's soul . . . NO MATTER WHAT! HEAP MISERY, CAUSE PAIN AND SUFFERING, ANYTHING AND EVERYTHING. DELIVER TO ME THE BALANCE OF THE CONTRACT EVEN IF YOU HAVE TO FOLLOW JOE TO THE ENDS OF THE EARTH!!"

Chapter 5: What Happened to Father . . .

PERPETUATION!

Ah so, said the monkey, as he scurried up the tree.
You'll give me two, if I return you three?
Yes said the snake, as he slithered right beside.
I promise and swear: By the legs that I hide.
The monkey was shrewd; he really thought he knew!
A snake has no legs, I'll take him for a few.
So he scooped up the bucks, and went upon his way.
Laughing, and joking, As he spent and spent all day.
Up popped the snake, a smirk upon his face.

Its time to repay, or I'll have a little taste,
I'll bake you and stew you, I like my monkey pie
So give me my money for I never, never lie!
The monkey just chuckled, swinging way up high.
Laughing, and heckling; You never tell no lies?
Where are those legs, the ones you say you hide?
I'll not repay you, I took you for a ride!
Not a cent will you get, and this I guarantee,
Said the monkey to the snake, as he swung from tree to tree.
The snake waited patiently, curled upon the ground.
As the gleeful monkey, jumped and flew around.
Then the cagey monkey, in his jesting haste,
grabbed a broken branch and to the ground he raced . . .
Ah, so! said the rabbit, as he hopped a round the tree,
You'll give me two, if I return you three?
Yes, said the snake, as he picked his gleaming teeth,
I promise and swear by my little, hidden feet!
The rabbit was shrewd, he thought he really knew.
A snake has no feet, I'll take him for a few . . .

Three years of arduous deprivation have passed. Times are changing. There's talk of a place called Vietnam. President Kennedy has been assassinated. The Peace Corp . . . Teamsters . . . Civil rights . . . Conspiracies . . . front page confusion. For our Catholic, Italian-American family, times have changed also. They have their own battles . . . their own executions: Destitution has replaced content; turmoil displaces serenity—their Peace Corp is welfare; Teamsters is spelled M O B . . . Civil rights are ever-present social workers, their justification for conspiracy, confusion their breakfast. . . .

The roaring, screeching clamor of a train rambling down the elevated track outside Joe's bedroom window woke him with a start. No matter how long they lived there, he would never get used to the incessant racket reverberating through the paper-thin walls of their new apartment on the outskirts of Astoria, Queens—even the rodents timed their morning calls to the seven o'clock express.

The welfare folks found this apartment for Joe's family a year and a half ago. It was your basic two-and-a-half bedroom slummer—the "half" means a broom closet with a curtain. Joe's sister had the half, his brothers and he shared one bedroom, his mother had the other. Whenever they complained, his mother would tell them about people in other countries who had to sleep on the ground, the bare earth. Somehow, he just could not identify with that image, for the scene that kept popping into his mind was one of pioneers in western movies—now that could not be all that wrong, could it?

Joe pulled the shabby, water-stained draperies from the window and peered out to see what the weather was like. A windy, cloudy, late spring-time day greeted him; the kind of day when the sun plays hide and seek—it hides and you seek. It had to do, he mused, for today was the big day: He had made up his mind to seek his fame and fortune—and thereby out-run the thugs. He was going to be a "man of respect"— even if it killed him. No more would he be a burden to his mother. No more would he take the ribbing from those Greek and Irish jerks. No more would they laugh at the way he dressed. I'll show 'em, he thought to himself. No more would those police who had known father laugh at him when he asked for their help! He would don his suit of respect and show them all!

As Joe continued to stare out the window, his thoughts went to the place they had moved from only two years ago. Boy had times changed . . . again! Instead of Old Man Bianco's cheerful Deli on the corner, there was a dismally monotonous, red brick building that housed Bernie and Yetta's Candy Store. Survivors of the Nazi Holocaust—with proof imprinted upon their person—Bernie and Yetta would tell their stories to all visitors who would listen through a thickly worn diary Bernie possessed. From this chronicle of sadness and carnage, this tattered ledger of horror and trepidation, Bernie's stories would leap from the pages as if each and every soul were buried within those written words. Joe, in desperate need of a father figure, soon became his youngest and most ardent admirer.

As Joe intently listened, Bernie would speak of terror, hope, and joy—all experienced simultaneously. Gesturing vigorously with flailing arms, as exuberantly as any Italian storyteller could, while weaving and bobbing as if to a Hungarian polka, he would talk to Joe for hours.

Though full of compassion and lingering pain, Bernie and Yetta inevitably bore the brunt of harassment from the neighborhood wannabees, who, mistaking their sincerity and desire to help for weakness, preyed upon them with the viciousness of a hungry school of sharks stranded in a depleted and antiquated goldfish pond—with the two aged survivors of that catastrophic holocaust.

Even at 7:00 in the morning, a group of toughs stood outside Bernie's demanding tribute just to enter. Joe would have to brave the requests of his mother when she asked him to get something from the store.

"What's the little punk want today? Probably wants to listen to the Jew talk that crap!" Jimmy Lendahan would say.

"I betcha he's got some bread," Joey Esposito would inject in a hostile tone of voice.

"Well, let's see what he's got in those pockets," Jimmy would reply.

He could not recall how many times he stole cigarettes or got them from Bernie to give to his mother after being mugged.

"Honey, do you have the change?" His mother would ask.

"I lost it." He would reply, guardedly.

"How many damn times can a kid lose change? You have no responsibility!" she would scream as she smacked him around.

Since the day his father passed away, Jeanette began resorting to physical abuse in ever-increasing tantrums. She placed her blame on tradition and the family, which caused her to repent those words and all they stood for—yet her repentance would become a source of even more sorrow. She did not want her oldest son to become like his father and felt that by avoiding the past she could rescue his future. But it only got worse.

Joe was caught up in the old world of the men of respect: a world he envisioned as "Knights in Shining Armor." He had not the slightest indication of the facts of his father's world, nor how his father really died. Continuation ruled his life; his fragmented memory of his father as a powerful, loving, and caring man of respect tore at his very soul: 'Father would know how to deal with this situation! He would not put up with this lack of respect! It is mother who is making life miserable! Why did she want to leave the old neighborhood and move to this horrible place? Was it that she wanted to keep him from receiving his legacy? Could he allow anyone to do this to him!'

Joe desperately desired to be loved, to be part of a normal family. To Joe, "normal" meant "men of respect," men with guns and sharp, clear, orderly lives; men who did not cry! Yes, this is what love meant! So, he created a family in his mind, one he could be proud of—which caused him to become increasingly embarrassed by his "real family"! He would think of what might have been, what could have been. He lived in a make-believe world where he was the only active participant. He used those old day-dreams of the past to rescue the future, thus creating a facsimile of reality—a "paper dream" to be lost, burned, thrown out, and trampled. He yearned to be back in his old neighborhood with Mr. Bianco . . .

> "Good morning, Mr. Bianco, sir," he would say. "It's a beautiful day." Then an apple would suddenly appear like a magic trick with the words, "Youa wanna apple?"
>
> "Oh no, Mr. Bianco . . . I can't accept that." All the time knowing that by the end of their chat the prize would be in his grasp.
>
> "Youa taka da apple. I nowa tela noa one . . . Youa hurta my afeeling if youa dona taka!" Old Man Bianco would state in his true-to-form sincerity.
>
> At which time Joe would anxiously reach out and take the bright red apple with a "thank you very much" repeated between huge bites of that delicious treat.
>
> As he thought about Mr. Bianco, he made a promise that he would return to his old neighborhood and thank him; Mr. Bianco was always there to assist him!

. . . Joe pulled the draperies closed—so no one could see him in his hour of action—and shook his younger brother Carmine with so much force he thought the world had ended.

"Carmine, Carmine . . . Get up! We have to go before mom wakes up."

"I don wanna go!" he cried.

"Be quiet, you'll wake her! You promised you'd go. Don't you want to see Pennsylvania? Don't you want to learn about tradition and respect?"

"You promised to take me to the World's Fair if I went." He said in a voice barely above a whisper.

"Well, if you get up and get dressed I will."

Joe wanted his brother Carmine, now seven years old, to become his pupil . . . someone he could hand down all the tradition Father had taught him.

Today was the start of Carmine's "education"!

It was 1964, the TV, newspapers, and everyone was talking about the New York World's Fair. Even though it was a short train ride to Flushing, Queens—where this grand fair was to be held—his mother couldn't afford to go, let alone take them. It was the monumental bribe to take Carmine to the fair that convinced him to join Joe in the adventure that was to be the inauguration of things to come!

Joe had solid plans. He'd seen brochures of Pennsylvania on his teacher's desk. They all had one common and recurring theme: beautiful streams, brooks, towns, forests, fishing (could be fun!) and happy people—all saying how they should visit! This is where he would go, the Pocono Mountains . . . or something like that.

After waking Carmine, he went to the closet and flung open the door. Hanging neatly in its shroud of plastic was his Suit of Armor: his three piece, black, pinstriped suit! This, his most cherished item of clothing, remained entombed since that terrible day almost three years ago. He had wanted to wear it to his father's funeral, but as fate would have it, he didn't go.

The funeral was held a few days after his father and uncle's accident; everyone was dressed in black—as if midnight could be worn "on the sleeve." Joe was depressed but he thought if he could see his father one more time he could say good-bye. Unbeknownst to anyone, he stole into his mother's room and carefully removed his diamond pinkie ring from the jewelry box. He did not intend to wear it, instead, as tribute to father, and in secret, he'd put it in the casket. He dressed in his suit, fedora, and tight shoes, then silently joined the solemn gathering.

His mother came over and complimented him on his attire, "You look very sharp and handsome, Joe."

"Thank you," he replied respectfully, standing erect to his full height.

"There is a favor I must ask of you," she said in a soft and gentle tone. "Do you remember the time you asked me about being the man of the house?" She looked him directly in the eyes.

"Yes," he answered in a voice that was as manly as he could muster.

"Well, you're the man of the house now. I know you want to attend your father's funeral. But I need you to take care of your brothers and sister while I'm gone. Would you do that for me?"

Her voice was on the verge of breaking up. He could see a mist of tears forming in those lovely eyes. Fighting back his tears, disappointments, and sadness for the umpteenth time, he agreed with a simple nod and a "Yes, mother."

For the first time he didn't care about respect, tradition, or being man of the house. What were these concepts? He couldn't taste or smell them . . . he thought he'd seen them once, but he sure couldn't feel them. Later that evening, when everyone returned, he snuck out and went to their church, The Immaculate Conception, only to discover that the funeral had not been held there. He didn't know where it had been.

"Oh, God, please tell me what to do," he prayed out loud. "I don't know what I should do." No answer came to him.

God had come to Joe a long, long, time ago. It was during a dismal time in his life when his birth affliction kept him confined. . . .

> Joe couldn't play with the kids in the neighborhood. Joe couldn't have fun. Joe just sat in a chair or push-walker and had daydreams of nightmares. He'd wake to the shouts and cries of his siblings and their friends playing with his father in the back yard. Jumping out of bed, he'd run toward the gleeful noise, but just as he burst out the front door, his feet would shrivel and he'd fall on his face . . . in front of his father!
>
> One day, his father, in his determination to motivate him to walk, surprised him with a brand new shiny bicycle. All of his siblings and their friends were riding bikes—he wanted desperately to join them.
>
> For an entire five months the bike stood silent, like himself, waiting to join in happy excitement with the others. The doctors warned his father that this experiment was detrimental to their treatment and his progress, "If he can't ride the bike the whole affair will cause damage to his will power." But, every day his mother would place him on the bike's soft black seat, wrap his

hands tightly around the multi-colored tasseled hand-grips and, placing his bandaged and twisted legs upon the boxy foot pedals, push him off. Holding back his tears, using all of his will power, he would push and push and push and never get anywhere—and every night, mounted upon his dreams, cool, sweet, spring time children, cheering in the breeze, would turn to laughing blizzards.

"I'm stopping. I don't wanna ride this stupid thing! Take it away!"

"But you have to try," his mother implored.

"I have. It ain't gonna work. Give the bike away!"

His mother looked at him with sad, moist eyes, and wheeled the bike away. Later that night she came to his room and sat on his bed. Held tightly in her hands was a blue and yellow book. She looked directly into his eyes and said, "Joe, I know, more than anything else in the world, you want that bike. Your father and I want more than anything else for you to be able to ride that bike. Sometimes it takes more than what we can give or show you for you to be successful. We pray to God every day and ask Him to help us in our lives. We must continue to pray to Him. He will help you. Of this I am sure. If you truly accept Him in your heart, ask Him to help, and you don't give up, He will help you! You must confess your hopes and wishes to Him."

"But Mother, I do pray, and I have asked God for help. I prayed to God last night and all of the other nights."

"But you must ask of Jesus . . . You must use His name. This book I have in my hands is a very important book." She said as she handed it to him. "It is The Lord's Prayer. I want you to memorize it. When you can recite it by yourself you will have his power behind you."

Joe sat on his bed, eyes and hands glued to the bright, blue and yellow book, waiting until she had left the room, then he swiftly opened the cover.

A colorful picture of Jesus greeted him: yellow halo, a touch of thorny brown, white flowing robe. His face seemed serene and divine. He was looking toward the stars which were perched, silvery-white and glittering, upon a deep blue background. His arms and hands were outstretched, as if imploring something of His Father. And then, Joe saw His sturdy feet encased in a pair of thong sandals, they rested upon the brown, rocky ground.

"Yes, sandaled feet . . . Oh, Jesus, how I want feet like yours," he thought.

He turned the next page. On a delicate, pastel blue background, within soft, white, billowing clouds, rich, black, Roman letters spelled out their urgency, "Pray with me."

He began to memorize the prayer. He would open the book, look at the words, close the book, and recite—over and over . . .

Children playing in the yard awoke him. He was dressed in the clothes he had worn the day before, the book lying open upon his chest. He closed it and looked out his window onto the patio. His bike, glimmering in the morning sunlight, like a knight's patient steed, fully dressed in battle armor, stood waiting for its master.

Boy, was he ready! "I will ride it . . . How fast will I go? The Lord will bless me!" he thought with happiness.

He reached for the book, picked it up, and started to read . . . suddenly, he had a change of mind and closed it. He shut his eyes and began to pray.

"Our Father, Who art in Heaven,
Hallowed be thy name.
Thy Kingdom come, Thy will be done,
On Earth as it is in Heaven.
Give us this day, our daily bread
And forgive us our trespasses
As we forgive those who trespass against us.

And lead us not into temptation
But deliver us from evil
. . . and help me ride my bike!
Amen"

"I want you to push very hard," his mother encouraged. "I'll start you off . . ."

The bike moved—just as it had so many times before—down the road. He struggled with the handle bars, with the pedals, "Oh, Jesus, please help me. Oh, please," he pleaded.

It seemed like his feet were moving the pedals with the ease of an adult! HE WAS RIDING HIS BIKE!

He zoomed down the road, secret tears wetting his cheeks, past all of the other children who had laughed at him so many times.

Zoom . . . zoom . . . zoom . . . he went, by the crowd of adults who were cheering him on . . . Joe had prayed to Jesus for His help and it was He who provided Joe with the courage and strength to ride that bike. Jesus would be his secret Father Figure. He would never tell anyone when they talked late at night. Mother would put him to bed and he would wait until everyone was asleep, then he would get out of the bed, falling softly upon bent knees, and they would talk in prayer.

You see, Joe's father never truly got over the fact that his oldest son had a deformity. Joe-Pep's secret of a slight deformity of his right foot was kept locked in a file in his mind. This birth defect that plagued his oldest son revealed his own faults. Thus, Joe-Pep would take Carmine with him whenever he could. He did not realize his favoritism of Carmine ever effected Joe . . . but it did.

When his father was taken from him all sorts of thoughts went through his head, Did God take him because of his treatment? Had Joe's prayers in some way caused his father's demise?

The questions and facts were overwhelming. A car accident! A car accident! How did he die! Joe felt in some way he had caused his father's death. Hadn't he asked God to convince his father that Joe was "normal?" Hadn't he asked Jesus to come down and be his father? Confusion had taken over his life. His father was taken from him just as he was beginning to be a son Joe-Pep could be proud of. And Joe-Pep was starting to act like a proud father! Hadn't he given Joe a job? Weren't they living together again? What was the truth? What were the facts? Who was responsible? Rumors crept the streets . . . rumors of a bloody death! What had really happened?

A battle developed within his mind. A powerful, purposeful, planned battle. His decision to run away from home would be the first step in a continual war of wills: a war begun with The Curse sixty years before. A war that had terrified and consumed so many of Joe's ancestors.

* * *

The morning after spending the night in the Church, Joe went to school as if everything were normal. Uniformed police and detectives were waiting for him along with Nana Lou, his mother, and Nana's brothers, Uncle Frank and Eddy. Rather then being happy to find him alive, they were quite angry. Even the two uniformed policemen, one tall and balding, nick-named Jolly-Green-Giant, and the short and dumpy one called Ball Buster, seemed quite upset. Although Joe's Uncle Frank was a connected wiseguy, and seemed to know the police very well, they were sinister to Joe. He felt a chilly breeze coming off their persons. His mother's demeanor changed when she noticed the frightful look; she came over and he melted in her arms.

On the way home he told her that he had slept in church and prayed to God—she grabbed him in her arms and cried softly. Though he felt good, confusion ruled his mind. What had happened? Had father's death affected her so severely she didn't care anymore? What had happened to cause her to jump in and out of what seemed like dual personalities? One moment she would be demonstrating her love, and the next screaming her head off as she chased Joe around, beating him with a kitchen spatula. Pushing that unruly memory aside, he thought once more of her caring arms wrapped around his small, frail shoulders that morning three years before.

Joe felt good and began removing his suit from the closet. He would discover the truth, search the world if he had to. He would find out if those rumors were true.

Temporarily satisfied, Joe ripped the covering off with such a fervor his brother Carmine jumped out of his bed.

"Get dressed," he demanded, "and hurry it up!"

Carmine immediately began to dress, putting his clothes on over his pajamas.

While Carmine was dressing, Joe thought of his father and God and how he had prayed to Him . . . like he had done so many times before—he had prayed for an answer, "Dear God, what should I do? Can you send me a message? Like what you did in that bible story that Sister Claire told me last week. You know, a miracle?"

He had even stepped over every other crack in the sidewalk as he said, "He'll let me know"—step—"He'll let me not"—step. But he wasn't very truthful. He kept landing on "He'll let me know"—on purpose. The only message he seemed to receive was an urge to leave home and discover for himself the facts about his family. He was in desperate need for answers. He wanted a Father Figure in his life; someone he could learn from; someone he could share the good and the bad with; someone that he could be proud of; someone that he could brag about and tell stories to and someone who would listen to a man of respect . . . for a man of respect could not talk with the women.

He had thought of Bernie . . . but he would not do, he was not very strong with those guys who bullied him!

He thought of Mr. Bianco, well, he wouldn't do because he was always so busy helping everyone else.

Joe decided to go out and find someone or return so wealthy and famous he'd be the man of respect . . . and rescue his mother and family from the evil thing that had taken over their lives.

He started to put on his suit, but found he had grown too big to wear it. After all his planning how could he leave town as a man of respect. How was he going to stop in front of Bernie's and show those idiots what a man of respect looked like? What about all of his dreams of arriving in Pennsylvania with all the people bowing from admiration at such a man of respect?

After studying this minor setback, he decided to shoe-horn his "Suit of Armor" on and proceed with his plan. Reaching for his jousting helmet—his brim-feathered fedora—he put it on. In a split-second he realized he had outgrown it too. As he muttered to himself he grabbed the now-stained and soiled brown paper-wrapped Macy's shoe box. His feet rebelled! If he was going to complete his mission he'd need to pick up some shoes somewhere. Until then, his sneakers would have to do.

His mother was sound asleep, her purse on the dining room table. He opened it up and discovered there was sixty-five dollars in bills and some change. He picked up a pencil kept by the phone and wrote her a note:

Dear Mom,

I'm leaving home with Carmine. I love you, don't you worry none. When I make my fortune, I'll come back and we'll move back to the old place . . . and I'll repay you the $40.00 I borrowed.

Love,
Joe

And so, like a modern day "Don Quixote" La Astoria, Queens, with "Sancho" in tow—wearing his clothes over his PJs—Joe set out on an adventure searching for respect and tradition; fame, fortune, and a Father Figure . . . in his ill-fitting suit, fedora, and sneakers!

Chapter 6: And Mother's Father!

Under a meadow minty green,
roosts a family—hardly seen.
Rich in character, poor in name,
not a worry, they look the same.
They're always busy, always on time,
building their burrows all in a line.
They huddle as one in the winter's cold,
caring for their young and very old.
No money to spend, their pockets dry,

sometimes they laugh, sometimes cry.
Friendly little fellows in sympathy,
caring for their fortune of dignity!

Jeanette awoke with a deep pain in her back. With a slow and difficult turn in her bed, she twisted her swollen feet until they were over the bed, then, with a push that sent waves of pain coursing through her body, she heaved herself upright. "Joe! Hey, Joe! Angela, Angela. Come here, Angela!"

"I'm here, Mom," Angela said as she stepped into the room with caution.

"Where's Joe?"

"I . . . I don't know . . ." Angela stated as she cringed with the thought of what was going to happen when she discovered the boys gone. She hated the fact that they had left her to face the music.

"Help me up," Jeanette asked Angela as she lifted her arms up and out for Angela to grab hold of. Jeanette arose with a series of grunts and moans. After stretching the pain and cramps away as best she could, she reached over to the old nightstand her mother had given her. An array of pill bottles competed with the silver framed photos massed together upon its dulled surface as if to remind her that she once had a father, husband, grandfather, and a mother who bore her!

"What's happened?" she thought as she studied the faces of her family and their surroundings. Halting on a photo which showed her and her father at the beach, Jeanette suddenly felt a familiar feeling raging from deep within her chest. Tears washed her swollen face and dripped as rain upon the gilded frame. As they washed across the scratched and scarred glass, a thought crossed her mind, the one thing she was sure she would never run out of were her tears of grief.

The picture of Jeanette at the beach—wearing a bathing suit, splashing gleefully in the water with an adoring father—held a different story for Nana Lou than the one Jeanette saw and remembered, for in the background, barely noticeable, a woman stood talking to Jimmy.

The picture was an actual representation of Nana Lou's life with her husband, Jeanette's father, Joe's grandfather—Jimmy. And, in fact, the last time Lou had looked upon that picture was the last day Jimmy had been around to beat her . . .

Jimmy was a handsome and debonair man who wooed and romanced young Louise. His racketeer lifestyle and slick way with words created a fable in her mind . . . a fable as savage and deceitful as if he had used force and intimidation to vanquish her maidenhood.

A few years after his conquest of Louise, Jimmy saw another piece of territory to conquer, but his first territorial success had to be secured . . . phase two of that time-tested plan of subjugation: divide! He made sure her defeat was complete, her dependency a fact; he created friction between Louise and her father, Antonio, after she was pregnant, then he flew the coop, only returning occasionally to eat, sleep, and accuse her of everything he was doing—then he would beat her and leave to bed with his whores again.

Louise finally left Jimmy and moved to White Plains. She got a job working in a gambling joint where the pay and tips were great and, with her brothers—Eddy and Frank—loaning it 5 for 6, she figured she'd have enough in a few years to buy a house on the Island. Then she could be with her daughter, Jeanette, full time. But Jeanette had been left with Louise's sisters and had become confused as to who mommy was and why she had to move around so much. It was that fact that caused Lou to catch a bus to New York City for Jeanette's fifth birthday celebration. Lou wanted her appearance to be a surprise, and she hoped that her father, Antonio, would be at the party too. She hadn't spoken to him in years. He had first objected to her early marriage to Jimmy—even though he in fact had married his sweetheart when he was fifteen and she thirteen. He was further enraged when she left Jimmy—though he knew of the beatings! He was a too-proud Mafioso to talk to her about the situation, but she was thinking of apologizing on her own.

Deep in thought, Nana Lou sat by the only piece of furniture she cherished, an old night stand. Its legs turned, curved, and delicate—the rich, hand-rubbed finish superb. It was built by her grandfather from the limb of an old walnut tree that had grown and prospered on the grounds of a sacred church in the village of his birth. He brought it to his new country, her birthplace, in the hope it would cast its forebearer's blessings on all who touched it, that they would grow and prosper. What it was casting then wasn't luck, but an image of her face, contorted, twisted, and lonely. Louise had shuddered and turned her focus to the elaborate, silver-gilded frame that held the beach photo of Jeanette and her husband Jimmy; she shut out Jimmy and focused on Jeanette . . . yes, she would tell her she loved her and take her with her.

The deep thought of how they would share their love was arrested by a knock at the door. She got up and answered it . . . Crash! Bang! Boom! Jimmy tore through the opening as soon as she turned the handle.

"You $#%@^%$ whore! You piece of garbage!" he screamed out as he smacked and beat her.

"Oh! Please stop! Please stop!" she pleaded.

You want me to stop? You %$#&^%$!" The tirade continued. Bang! A slap - boom! A punch! "Stop this . . ..you $%^#^&% whore!" Wap! "So you want to leave me?!"

"Jimmy please . . . I didn't do anyth . . ." Louise screamed, trying to protect herself from the blows raining upon her without letup.

Like a bulldozer knocking down an old, weathered, clapboard house, Jimmy and all his six foot might, beat five-foot, delicate Louise black and blue.

Jimmy wasn't done. He pulled out a garden hose and proceeded to beat more! Screaming at the top of his lungs, "You want to leave me? Huh!" . . . $%#@#$% dame. You ^&#$#$% . Boom! Bang! Boom!*

By the time the neighbors got up the courage to check on Louise, Jimmy was long gone and Louise was unconscious on the floor.

After this terrible beating and the subsequent situation it created with The Family, Louise lost her job in White Plains. But soon, with the Don's blessings, she would begin a new career as a gaming hostess and piano player at an upstate New York mob-joint called the Mt. Kisco Cabaret. Little time would be left to cultivate her gift from God. Jeanette would become a vagabond domestic in all of her relation's households.

. . . The only flower to bloom among the weeds sown that fateful time was that beautiful child Jeanette; a divine, sweet, innocent little girl who was born with a common and dreaded disease . . . continuation, or, The Curse of Alphonso.

Jeanette's childhood was a constant search for a father, a mother, a home, and someone to play with. Not too much for one so young.

Chapter 7: The Quest Begins . . .

The store had a handwritten sign in the window, "Beatle boots only $12.95." Joe reached into the tight pocket of his undergrown suit and pulled out his wallet containing the forty dollars.

Carmine was complaining about being hungry. "I wanna eat," he sobbed. "Com'on let's get somthin' ta eat . . . I'm hungry! I'm stavin . . . matter fact!"

Using his best man-of-the-house voice, Joe told Carmine, "Look, I need to get some shoes. After that we'll eat. Why are you complainin'? There's starving people all over the world—didn't mommy tell you?"

"I don care 'bout stavin other people! I'm stavin!" Carmine whined.

"Just give me a minute, O.K.?"

"O.K." Carmine replied. "One Mississippi, two Mississippi . . ."

'I gotta hurry and get those shoes,' Joe thought to himself, but he didn't want to spend any of their traveling funds. This called for quick action.

Entering the front of the store, he noticed the cashier was busy at the register. She couldn't see the back of the shop. He went up the aisle and looked with ambition at those boots. As he contemplated what to do, a vision of the Beatles and Aunt Connie appeared. . . .

> After Joe-Pep passed away, Jeanette had to make some choices. The estate of her deceased husband consisted of one silver ring and a mountain of debt. She was penniless. No one offered her assistance. Some of their relatives would occasionally drop by

with some cast-off clothing—second, third, and even fourth-generation hand-me-downs, and an occasional few dollars on Christmas, but the money she initially received in the envelopes at her husband's funeral lasted only a few months. Their predicament led to emotional turmoil and depression that she never recovered from. She blamed the family and all it stood for. She wilted under the pressure of her circumstances and tried exiling herself—along with her children—as far as possible from the influence of the old guard. She discovered that men of respect had no respect. They talked of taking care of their own . . . but never seemed to remember to do it. Jeanette soon began to live in two worlds, one where she cursed the family and all it stood for, the other where she maintained occasional contact in order to survive.

By their fourth month alone she had to find work. With no education or experience her options were limited. The only logical step was welfare, but welfare didn't supply enough money to take care of five hungry mouths, clothe five naked bodies, and put a roof over five tired, lonely souls. The one hundred and fifty dollars she received along with a once-a-month ration from the government food surplus program, consisting of powdered eggs, milk, cheese and dry, tasteless peanut butter, was not enough to support them. She made a decision to find work and collect government assistance—but there was one complication: Federal law stated that she couldn't work and collect assistance too. She had to work at night because social workers always made surprise visits during the day.

The only job that met these stringent qualifications was tending bar; her only offer, a joint owned and operated by the mob—the hours 9 p.m. to 4 a.m. She took the job. Her title was barmaid.

The bar business in '61 was a physically demanding occupation; especially for a woman. Jeanette's problems with weight control complicated matters. Long hours standing on her feet, combined with her obesity, proved to be a factor in the deterioration of her health. Over the years she was beset with a multitude of diseases caused from all her grief, hard work, and failure to properly take care of herself. When Jeanette returned from work, she'd grab a few hours of sleep and then get up to see her children off to school. This continuing pace wore down her ability to deal with even the slightest problems. She would become abusive and resort to sudden violent outbursts when even the simplest situation arose. In the mornings she would wake up tired, in pain, and with what seemed to be the weight of the world upon her shoulders. Both she and her children grew to hate the mornings. Everyone would tip-toe through the house to avoid waking the beast of anger that brewed deep within each of the occupants of this tragic play of life.

So, with Jeanette working at night, she needed a baby-sitter in the evenings. Good luck! First there was Marsha. Lovely, teased, brunette Marsha. Whenever Jeanette went to work, Marsha "went to work" inviting men over—sometimes three in one night. It became so bad Joe developed a crush on her. She was fired. The second, third, forth quit. Then came the woman who would stay with the family for seven years: Aunt Connie.

Connie was not their true aunt . . . she demanded that title, and received it without reservation! She stood six-foot-four and walked with so much force, they knew what an earthquake felt like. Her favorite attention getter: "Get the #$@*! over here," spoken as if her deep baritone voice were complemented with six fog horns all blaring at the same time. Their entertainment was giving her heck—and she reciprocated! She would arrive at 5:30 p.m. sharp with brown paper bag in hand, say "Hello, Jean," then smile as if she were a combination angel and Saint Bernard. After Jeanette left for work and the door was shut, "Get the #$@* over here!!"

Connie's favorite pastime was sitting in front of the TV watching Jackie Gleason in The Honeymooners. Joe concluded that during the day she was probably Ralph Cramden! She would sit in front of the TV, open her bag in a flurry of sound and movement, then reach inside to pull out a loaf of Italian bread and a jar of red, hot, Italian cherry peppers. She'd place them on the coffee table, turn the TV on, and start feasting.

One night the Beatles were guests on The Ed Sullivan Show. Joe and his sister were excited like everyone else they knew. His mother told them they could stay up and watch the show and Connie agreed. But when Jeanette left, Aunt Connie sat in front of the TV and turned on The Honeymooners. When Joe and Angela complained that they had been given permission to stay up to watch their special show Aunt Connie screamed, "Get your butts in the #$@damn bed!"

Angela and Joe decided to get even and have some fun, too. During a commercial, when the behemoth stomped to the bathroom to make room for her gluttony, they scooted to the table and grabbed her jar of coveted peppers. Screwing the lid off in a rage of giggles and muffled laughter, they replaced the vinaigrette with nail polish remover! Out came the monster . . . she farted as she sat down, reached for the jar—while they hid behind the couch as official observers—and unscrewed it with determination. Dipping her meaty paw into the jar, she plucked one bright red cherry pepper, juices dripping all over, opened that big cavern of a mouth, and placed the object of her craving into it: WHAM! THE ELEPHANT RAMPAGED!

"Who the ##%# did this? I want to $@@%$ know! Right #$%%@ now! Angela, Carmine, Joe get your $%#@# a##$# over here."

She absolutely, positively lost it . . . they got their butts beat bad and were punished for a week, but they never regretted it!

. . . With a snicker, Joe reached up and took down a pair of those sparkling new black Beatle boots.

As he untied the sneakers he wore, Carmine's inquisitive voice stopped him.

"Whacha doin?"

"Trying on some shoes," he said nonchalantly.

"Can I try dem on?"

"Listen, Carmine . . . I'm not buying 'em. We don' have enough money," he whispered.

"Then why you tryin 'em on?"

"Do you wanna eat?" Joe demanded, wanting to thrash his hide.

"Yeah, but you're gonna steal 'em, ain't ya?"

"I'm gonna borrow 'em—now shut up before the lady hears you!"

"Oooh, I'm tellin . . ." Carmine replied in a smug voice.

"Be quiet! Do ya hear me?" Joe snapped, totally losing his patience.

"I'm tellin' mom!"

The sales clerk showed some interest in their conversation; conversation that by now had become heated—Joe had to shut him up!

"Listen to me . . . You wanna eat, right?" he whispered seriously. "You wanna go to the fair, right?"

Carmine started to nod his head affirmatively while tucking his small hands into his pockets.

"You don't wanna get into trouble—do you? Well, if you keep talking you'll get a spanking when that lady calls Mom and she comes down here!"

With that, he was as quiet as a cat on the hunt.

Joe removed his sneakers and placed them in the empty spot on the shelf, then slipped the shoes on his feet. They were two sizes too big, so he left the fill-paper in them.

Turning to see the clerk busy, he nonchalantly shuffled out of the store.

It was his first theft besides the Kool cigarettes he had pocketed for his mother after he was mugged, and he didn't even think about it! It was easy.

Though it was difficult walking in those shoes he mastered the pain by the time they were two blocks away. They continued down the street noticing everyone staring at them. He felt proud—he was finally getting some respect.

As he stepped with pride—Carmine was shuffling—they passed a packed, silver and black diner. In blazing red neon were the words, "All You Can Eat—$2.95." The sign caught their attention and the aroma of food cooked on a grill greeted their senses. His mouth salivated and his stomach groaned. Carmine stopped dead still and wouldn't move. It was time to eat their first meal on their own.

They entered the establishment and strolled to one of the empty booths and plopped down. The waitress came over and inquired if his mother was in the restroom.

'Did she know mother?' he wondered, his heart skipping a beat.

But then he realized that she was not expecting to see a young man of respect with such a little kid. He informed her that they—that is he and his pupil—were going to the fair. She just looked at him with a puzzled look and handed him the menu. Carmine proceeded to ask for everything he could think of—that's how hungry he was.

When the waitress came back, Joe mustered the courage to ask about the "all you can eat" and she showed them the buffet in the back of the restaurant. It was a feast with pancakes, French toast, eggs, bacon, sausage, hash browns, every kind of jelly, real butter, pastries . . . the list went on and on. They had not seen food like this in three years. Carmine and Joe grabbed plates and began heaping everything they could fit without spilling!

The other diners sat watching in amazement as this comical duo—The Don and Sancho—stuffed their faces like there was no tomorrow. After several plates, Carmine stopped, looked up at Joe, and vomited!

After the waitress cleaned up the mess Joe apologized for such bad taste and asked for an espresso! She brought him milk instead.

Drinking his milk, Joe felt a little strange, "Men of respect drink espresso, not milk!" But he let it go. It was obvious that this young lady did not know the ways of tradition!

With this grand feast consumed, he asked for the bill. It was seven dollars and some change. He reached for his wallet and those two precious twenty dollar bills . . . they were not in his wallet or pocket! With the waitress keeping an eye on them from behind the counter, he held his breath and thought about what he should do. His life was rushing before him . . . as if he died . . . again!

He was in trouble and he had to do something!

Calling the waitress over, he asked her if she had any pie. She was flabbergasted. "Are you sure you can eat anymore?" she asked.

He replied that it was for his brother—seeing that he now had an empty stomach. Then, with her standing there, he told Carmine to go to the bathroom and wash off, he'd be there in a minute to help. He then reached for his empty wallet, placed it on the table, and asked her to bring a slice of apple pie. Before she left, he excused himself—leaving the empty "Trojan Horse" in full view.

This was his second time in less than two hours that he had used dishonest means to accomplish goals. Using his present circumstances as justification for his theft, he simply said a prayer to God asking Him for forgiveness—and then it became easy to forget! He assumed that if he told Him he was going to commit a sin because he had too, it would be all right.

Entering the bathroom, he looked for Carmine and the window that he knew had to be there.

Carmine was standing in a stall. Joe grabbed him and ran to the little opening five feet off the ground. It was pretty high, but he had no choice. He had to get out of there and find the money he dropped. Snatching the wastebasket, he turned it upside down and jumped on top. His brother, recognizing the distress, was not only moving to his commands, but improving on them. They smashed the glass and squeezed out into an alley way. 'That was close,' he thought, as they ran back to the shoe store.

They approached the building from the opposite side of the street. Joe saw two familiar police officers standing in the doorway, one tall and one short. He remembered them from his experiences on the street and the day after his father's funeral. Pulling Carmine close to him, he whispered to him to go to the "el" (that was short for "elevated train"), climb the stairway, and wait for him. Carmine did as he was told.

Looking across the street on the ground, he spotted the two bills. They were next to the trash can where he was standing at the time he took out his wallet. There was no way to get them without those two cops spotting him. Then he saw the trash can on his side of the street.

Joe had taken a few things with him figuring they might come in handy on their adventure. Reaching in his pocket, he removed a lighter that once belonged to his father. Stepping to the trash can, he lit the refuse overflowing its rim. Swift in their pursuit of life, spiraling flames soon began leaping, crying, bellowing in their misery of dark, putrid, black smoke. Ball and Jolly saw this conflagration and ran across the street. Joe crossed too, and for a moment their paths met. Eye to eye but for a moment's breath, Joe felt that chill once more—as if death had laid its hand upon his brow. He hit afterburner and reached the front of the store without losing stride. Reaching down in one swift motion, he snatched those two twenties. Turning with the grace of a ballerina, he scooted past the cops once more. They recognized him, shouted his name, and blew their whistles, but Joe just kept on hitting the pavement. Another battle was won; a battle in a war that these men in blue would wage against Joe until he found the cause of their anger.

Carmine was waiting for him when he arrived at the station. Pulling his arm, they flew over the turnstile, ran down the station landing, and hopped the train.

What a start, he said to himself as doors closed on the packed Flushing-bound express.

There were no seats available—and no one offered to make room—so they pried enough space open to reach the corner and safety. In fifteen minutes they would arrive at the World's Fair. In the meantime, Joe evaluated the commuters on this train of dreams.

Standing next to him was an extremely obese woman, sloppy in dress and speech, chastising what seemed to be her clone.

"You listen to me, you little brat!" while holding this compilation of habit by one hand—literally lifting her off the ground.

The clone was screaming in duplication, "I don' wanna go, I don' wanna go!"

Over by the door, crammed between its portal and the mass of bodies, which were the essential ingredients of this hot, smelly recipe, stood a man with gray hair, mustache, and a funny looking cap-sort-of-thing on the back of his head (like the one worn by Bernie; called a yamica or something?). He wore thick, black-framed coke bottles with a prayer shawl around his shoulders. He was attempting to calm the scientific experiment and its clone. "You should treat that child better," he complained, rather than advised. "Otherwise, she will grow up just like you!"

Next to this gentleman was a priest, who, viewing the situation in a different light, put his two cents to work. "Jesus will prevail . . . do not worry about how she will grow up—the Lord will look after her."

This display caused a man in work clothes and a cap with the words "Tonto Tobacco Chew—The Working Man's Choice" written on its front, to address the situation, "Why don't everybody just shut the #@%! up?"

On and on, throughout the car, this continued; with passenger after passenger adding their own two cents until the piggy bank was full and nothing further could be added—yet the woman and her clone kept singing.

As the court jesters practiced their wisdom, Joe returned his attention to Carmine. Joe could see he wasn't feeling well, so he raised his spirits with conversations of marvelous anticipation.

"Carmine, did you know they have cars that go in the water?"

"Rrrreeeally? Will we ride one?" he asked, eyes suddenly wide with excitement.

"Not only will we ride in one, but we will also see color televisions, eat food from all over the world and . . ."

"I don' care fa food—my tummy hurts," he exclaimed, rubbing his stomach as he gave Joe this "don't you feel sorry for me?" look.

Knowing he had to keep Carmine's mind off this subject Joe continued, "Well, we should be pulling into the station any minute and then we'll go on rides and have lots of fun, O.K.?"

Seemingly satisfied, Carmine answered. "Yeah, that soun's 'ike fun. But why'd we hav ta run?"

This last question he ignored. The experiences so far this morning were perplexing to his young mind, but soon, he would forget all that had happened.

The train screeched to a halt, doors opened with a swish, and the crowd of rude, sweating offenders stampeded through the opening—as if chased by a fire-breathing demon.

The first thing they saw were the large signs placed at strategic spots along the way. "The New York World's Fair—Gateway to the Future!" they exclaimed, each colorful picture creating just the right amount of excitement. They *were* excited! Approaching the entrance to the fair, they passed a huge steel globe, fountains with tall sprays of water, loud triumphant music, and a multitude of gaily dressed citizens. It was a sight that mesmerized Carmine . . .

"Ooh! Look at that!" he cried out in a voice that turned everyone's head at one time.

A policeman swinging his nightstick walked over to them.

"What are you young fella's doin' here?" he asked in an authoritative tone. "Why're ya dressed that way? Where's your parents?"

Joe started to stammer, "They . . . uh, . . . they . . ." when Carmine's voice stopped any thought of explanation.

"I did'n do notin'—he stole the shoes! Joe wanna run away . . . Not me! I just wanna see the . . ."

Chapter 8: With Tears of Déjà vu

"Oh! My God! Where are they? What did they do? Call Joe-Pag! Call Uncle Frank! Angela, call someone now!"

Jeanette had discovered the note and her mind was in turmoil. She feared for her boys as she had feared for her husband, her grandfather, her father . . . To this Italian-American family, the word "men" had become synonymous with death, loss, or "moved away"!

Jeanette had shed so many tears in her life. Every time she thought of her father, Jimmy, the tears would flow. Oh how she missed him and cried her way to sleep so many, many times. And then came her 'Knight of Rescue,' the one she transferred her emotions of her father toward . . .

An unfamiliar, uncomfortable sensation would sweep over Jeanette whenever she sat close beside Joe-Pep, paying ardent attention to each and every word that recklessly erupted from his mouth.

"Let me tell ya, I'm gonna be da top guy in town one day! Hell, I'm already collecting, and I got a five-hundred dollar book!" Joe-Pep would exclaim, transforming his voice to fit the image he envisioned.

"Wow, really? That's a lot of money!" she would exclaim. "Do you have a girlfriend?"

"I got twenty or more," he would brag, head thrown back, unfiltered Camel dangling from his lips.

Sliding closer to her Knight in Shining Armor, Jean would gaze into his gray-blue Sicilian eyes, mesmerized with awe as she continued her questions.

. . . But now he was gone and her hopes and dreams returned to her original knight in shining armor: her princely father, Jimmy, whom she wished would appear and rescue her from a nightmare that seemed to begin after he moved away.

She was forever telling Joe and Angela of her recollections of his love and handsome countenance. A picture she carried for twenty years, one which showed grandfather Jimmy in creased baggies and spats, center-parted hair with thick mustache and handsome, gentle features, had become wrinkled and worn from her perpetual demonstration of it.

She once heard rumors he was living in Chicago and swore she would find him one day—a fantasy she would never part from because in reality . . .

Jimmy reposed on a soft, silk-covered bed, thinking of his situ-ation. The Don had warned him, "You keep your hands off Louise, capisch?" And then . . . well . . .

When the word had hit the streets, Jimmy soon discovered he was a dictionary of four letter words!

"Can you imagine? After all, she deserved it, she left me!"

He had tried to get a sitdown. He'd called and called and called and called . . . but he couldn't get anyone on the phone. He kept getting, "He's not here"—"Went out of town"—"In Miami"—"Over in Brooklyn"—"Queens"—"The Bronx."

"Awe, %$#^ him," he said to himself, he was in Chicago now . . . and no one was aware he'd left town, let alone where he was—he could care less what the Don thought. The only thing on his mind that he cared about was the blonde sitting across the room. 'Look at her', he thought, 'A picture of the goddess Venus.'

Arriving in town, Jimmy had immediately called Louis , "Little New York" Campagna—his best friend, someone he could trust. They had hung out on the streets of Brooklyn and Manhattan, attended street school together and dated the same "broads." They were closer than most brothers by birth. Jimmy, the younger of the two, was the pupil, Louis the older brother and teacher. Little New York had come to Chicago to work for Al Capone, and Jimmy knew him as someone he could count on.

"Lou, baby, it's me . . . Jimmy!"

"Hey, Jimmy, how's it hangin?" Little New York asked.

"I heard about the ruckus in the city . . . wha happened?"

"Just a bunch of bull, Louis. Nothing to worry about. Seems everyone wants to play marriage counselor. Listen, it happened before, it'll happen again. So, what the hey. Listen, don't tell anyone I'm here—you know what I mean?"

"Yeah, I know what you mean. Who's your man? Huh? Who?"

"You are, Lou!"

"Where you at? Gimme your phone number and I'll call you back."

Jimmy gave him the number.

Later that night, Little New York called Jimmy back and told him he had a "Welcome to Town" gift for him.

"Jimmy, I gotta gift for ya—one hot chick! The kind you like! I'm gonna send her over. It's on the house . . . have some fun, I'll see what I can line up for you. Where ya staying?"

"At The Drake."

"What's your room number?"

That's how the dame showed up . . .

The commuter train pulled into Chicago's busiest station, moaning and groaning as if death were a passenger. Two fearsome-looking men, one tall, one short, in long overcoats, exited. They sauntered to the stand, hailed a cab, and instructed the driver in two words, "The Drake." They made one stop to use a phone. "Hey, Feranzi, tell the Ape we're here." They jumped back in the car and didn't say another word until they arrived at their destination. Handing the driver a fifty dollar bill, the tall one said, "Keep da change . . . and your mouth shut!"

Entering the lobby, they went to the desk and handed the clerk a card. The desk clerk read the card and immediately called for the bell hop, "You take the gentleman's bags, and . . ."

"That's all right, sonny. We'll carry our own bags," the taller of the two said.

"Oh, yes, sir. Yes, sir. I have the Royal Bamboo Suite ready for you. Mr. C. reserved it this morning. If you need anything, just call room service."

"$%#@ the room service. Some broads, steaks, and a case of Dom, you got that?" the little one asked.

"Yes, sir . . . now if you just sign here," the clerk replied, handing the register to the tall one.

The short one grabbed the register and threw it in the clerk's face.

As Jimmy undressed and laid back on the bed watching, the buxom blonde performed a series of perverse acts. Jimmy enjoyed wild, kinky sex—like his life, which evolved in a world of perverse thought and action, his preferences would ultimately dictate his conclusions—and Little New York, "his best friend"—had provided what he deserved.

The tall goon finished his steak, drank his Dom, and patted the broad on her bare behind as she cleaned up the bed. To the other he said, "Now this is the life! You made the arrangements . . . didn't you?"

"Yeah, the train leaves in half an hour. Tony A's got a car waiting and Joey B. set up the alibi. The Ape gave the O.K. We got no problem. Let's get rid of dese dames and get it over wit."

"Gussey boy said the Old Man will be very happy with this finished," the tall one replied.

"Closes the book. Let's go and clip that rat. My wife's expecting—gotta get back ta da city."

Fluffy and Jimmy, locked within each other's arms, were mute to anything other than their pleasure. Rolling upon the silk-covered, king-sized bed, they were completely surprised when the door burst open—two men wearing trench coats with fedoras pulled low over their brows, stood menacing . . . deadly black revolvers drawn.

One said calmly, "The Don sends his best wishes," as he leveled his instrument of destruction.

"Hold on, hold on!" Jimmy pleaded with these soldiers of death. "Please . . . I got money . . . I got money!"

The shots, muffled by silencers attached to the short barrels of the pistols, struck Jimmy and Fluffy with deliberate force; a force which one could not walk, run, nor hide from. Both soldiers emptied their guns, reloaded, and walked up to the corpses to fire a coup-de-grace into the back of the heads of both.

A couple more lives ended in this world of respect, legacy, tradition, honor, and the Curse of Alphonso.

. . . Jeanette wanted so much to just sit there, lost in thought, until the facts of reality matched those of her self-imposed memories, but, for now, her children needed her. And in several hours, the house, packed full of relatives, police, and mobsters alike, would be a world of whisper; word that the boys might have been kidnapped rushing in rumors of pale pain and foreboding innuendo; the streets crawling with cops and mobsters—all in pursuit of two boys . . . one seven and one eleven.

And Angela? She would bear the brunt of the mishap through her obedient servitude. She made and served sandwiches and coffee.

Chapter 9: The Poconos or Bust . . . ed

Joe pushed the officer, who tripped over a small retainer wall and into the water of one of the fountains, pulled Carmine's arm, and ran as fast as their small legs could carry them into the large crowd and the camouflage of the masses.

Joe had to get control of this situation. "Listen to me! I'm the man of the house and you must respect that . . . so let me do the talking from now on, fair enough?"

"If I can git som' cotton candy!"

Thus began Joe's second lesson to his pupil: "Respect for the man of the house."

Joe was at a loss on a procedure to gain entrance to the fair. The main gate was too risky, so he decided to investigate the possibility of climbing the fence.

Approaching the Fair from the east side, Joe spotted a service entrance. Walking over, he noticed it was manned by three police officers—one on foot, two on horseback.

Grabbing Carmine by the shoulder, he stopped, hid in the bushes, and thought things over. There was a gate, a small booth with one employee in it . . . not busy, just a few delivery trucks and those uniformed officers of the adventure-ending squad. Spying a garbage can loaded with trash, he went over, pulled out his lighter, lit the garbage inside, and hid once more in the bushes to await the show.

The flaw was obvious. The mounted police saw the flames and went to investigate while the footman stayed on duty. Just when Joe thought his plan was doomed, a delivery truck stopped in front of the bushes and its driver jumped out, fire extinguisher in hand, dousing the fire.

While the policeman and driver were busy playing fireman, Joe was busy playing hide and seek; running from his place of concealment while dragging Carmine in the process. Joe raised the back door, lifted Carmine up, and climbed in to wait as the "firemen" congratulated themselves.

"Thanks for your help."

"No problem," the driver replied, and with that, climbed into the truck and entered the fairgrounds.

When the truck stopped in front of a building, and the driver went inside, Joe raised the door and the boys hopped out onto the ground and into the crowd.

Joe stood in front of one of the many pavilions dotting the giant landscape, a futuristic building sitting upon an expansive, concrete, "mushroom" shaped tower, with curves and whirls and widely spaced open areas dotting its circular roof.

Carmine was ecstatic and wanted to eat, so Joe decided to find a food vendor. He soon discovered that food was abundant—and abundantly expensive! It was then he noticed the pavilion of The Bell Telephone Company with its army of eager, uniformed matrons enticing the public with free hors d'oeuvres. Yanking his brother's arm, they joined the crowd and proceeded to stuff their faces. Two women in Bell uniforms gave them this pitiful look . . . he wondered why, but continued to gorge himself.

Throughout their seven hours of exploration they saw sights that amazed them: telephones that enabled a person to see the person they were talking to; little gadgets that would add and multiply for you with a press of a button—'sure would be handy in school,' Joe thought—also large things with colored lights whizzing and whirring called computers. The pretty lady said one day they would be used to run the world . . . but he wasn't that stupid! And then the finale . . . a ride in the amphibious car! By the end of the day, they must have walked ten miles! They had visited every free exhibit within the complex and they were tired and facing reality, "What do we do next?"

Leaving the fair, they headed toward the train station and the next leg of their mission.

Arriving at the Ticket Master's booth, Joe inquired of the uniformed gentleman when the next scheduled train to Pennsylvania departed. He looked down at him and said, "Sonny, you mean Penn Station?"

"Yes, that's it! Pennsylvania Station!" Joe replied as the clerk stamped two tickets and he paid the dollar fee.

As they boarded the train Joe informed Carmine with great bravado that they were on their way and to take a seat and get some rest. Carmine was seated and snoring before he could think of a smart reply.

At last they were on their way to Pennsylvania! It was not long after the train rumbled off and began bumping along the track that Joe joined him in sleep.

"Penn Station, last stop! Penn Station, last stop!" Joe and Carmine were being shaken by the conductor.

Though Joe awoke with enthusiasm, Carmine proved to be in a cranky mood. "I'm tired . . . I wanna go home!"

"Listen to me, we're here! We're in Pennsylvania! Come on, let's go, then we'll find a place to sleep."

Carmine hesitantly followed Joe to the exit and they left the train.

As they ambled toward the exit Joe realized there was something wrong. They were still in New York City! The Ticket Master had written up two tickets for Penn Station, NYC!

Crowded by commuters coming and going, oblivious to anything but their aching feet which methodically carried them on preprogrammed paths, Joe was overwhelmed. He made attempts to interrupt several of these robots in discovery of a train heading to Pennsylvania, but each answered without missing a step, "Ask the cop over there." He was ready to call it quits when his brother began wailing about going home. Afraid of attracting too much attention, with Carmine's moans and tears echoing off the high stone ceilings, he searched around until he spied a gift shop.

Dressing the window was a miniature power boat with two props which would spin with sound when wound up! He pulled Carmine toward the brightly painted object. "Carmine, look at that! Wow, ain't that neat? A real power boat—almost like the car we rode in!"

Carmine's eyes lit up and he forgot about going home; all he wanted was the boat in the window . . . they were both learning new things on this adventure.

Entering the store, Joe asked the clerk the price of the displayed boat. She opened a new box and pulled a yellow and red duplicate of the one in the window while deftly winding it up. To the tune of the motor whirring away she said, "This is only $6.50 . . . would you like me to wrap it?"

"No, don't bother to wrap it. Mother told me to find something for my brother to play with on the train to Pennsylvania," he said with authority.

The sales woman looked at him quizzically and said, "You mean the bus . . . right? There aren't any trains going to Pennsylvania."

This statement was the answer to the question of his next move, "Yeah . . . that's what I meant . . . the bus."

With Carmine once more happily in tow—winding and whirring away—he proceeded to investigate the layout of the Greyhound bus depot which abutted the train station; it was a center of swarming activity: Rushing red-capped men in uniform loaded heaps of baggage into the deep bellies of a regiment of buses lined up as if on military parade—their "color of order," destinations announced on lighted signs above their front windows: Buffalo, White Plains, Hackensack . . . while people scurried to catch last minute departures.

Joe knew he could not buy tickets and was worried by now there would be a warning to look for two runaways. He had Carmine sit down and play with his boat while he searched for the opportunity he needed.

As he walked around the depot a young punk of sixteen approached him. "Hey you, you lost or sumthin?"

"No, just getting some tickets for Pocono, Pennsylvania," he replied cautiously.

"Well, ya gonna have a hard time. Cops are gonna get you!" he said with assurance.

"What do you mean . . . I'm just taking my brother home." Joe replied, worried this guy might know something he didn't.

"Yeah, right! I've been watching you—you're a runaway!" Then, in a chummy tone, he continued, "Listen. If ya want, I'll buy your tickets . . . How much money ya got?"

Joe reached into his pocket and brought out the bills and change he had from one of the twenty dollar bills, while keeping the other in his pocket. He handed this to the punk.

After counting it, the young stranger looked at him pointedly and inquired, "This ain't enough. You got anymore?"

He had to get those tickets . . . he reached into his pocket and handed him the last twenty.

"If there's any change I'll give it back, O.K?" he said as if he was his best friend.

"Sure, that's great!" Joe answered with relief.

Joe had been waiting twenty minutes when the kid appeared as suddenly as before . . . with a new jacket, transistor radio, and two tickets to the Pennsylvania mountains. Joe asked him for the change; his flippant reply . . . "There weren't any!"

Joe looked at the tickets and noticed $3.00 was stamped on each one. He looked at the radio and jacket.

The punk was ready, "Listen, I had to grease the Ticket Master! You know—-pay him off." And with that, spun on his heels and danced away to the blare of the small radio held to his ear.

Joe knew that he'd been taken—a new lesson for the rapidly developing man of respect.

Broke, exhausted, and alone, Joe went to get Carmine and boarded the bus to Pennsylvania.

They were seated in the very back of the bus when the driver came up and inquired of their destination. Producing the tickets, Joe told him they were going to visit their grandmother. He advised Joe he would keep an eye on them and would wake them when they arrived at their destination—around one in the morning. After about an hour, the bus was full and they left the station on their way to a new life. His brother was soon fast asleep. Without looking at the other passengers, Joe also fell into a deep sleep.

Chapter 10: As Continuity Rules

Nana Lou hovered over her Jeanette. Though she had been fretful and awake for twenty hours, it had taken a heavy dose of sedatives to knock her out. Asleep, quiet, and peaceful, Jeanette resonated long-lost thoughts and memories of her own childhood, her own family, her own father, her love, her future . . . dashed and crumpled had her dreams been vanquished, pain and suffering their offspring. What had happened . . . and why? And her daughter . . . she had planned so much for her. And now, her grandchildren.

Tears dripped off the cheeks of her memories of what she once had been—an innocent child! She had culled that portion of her own childhood from the larger memories of her life. For so long she would think, 'Was I ever a child?' For so long she could not answer that . . . she could only recall working and slaving, and her mother, her siblings; the desperation for a dollar that ruled her thoughts . . . the demand that the children work. Yes, she could recall the memories of her hard work . . .

The strong stench of sour bath-tub gin, stale cigarette smoke, and dried sweat, which reeked throughout the enormous bedroom, stirred Louise from a deep sleep. Sluggishly sitting up, she adjusted her vision to the bright rays of the sun as it cast its shafts of light through the parted, red velvet draperies. Focusing on the particles of dust that danced a trapeze in and out of this disharmonious mixture of life and death, she pulled the satin coverlet over her head. With each morning's sunrise came the reminder of the dreaded day's wait for evening to return.

It was in the darkness of the night, consorting with high rollers congesting the gambling tables of the Mount Kisco Cabaret—a joint "Charlie Lucky" controlled—that Lou lived her life. Decked out in her finest, a jeweled cigarette holder laced between her fingers (though she never smoked), she could whip up a smile, flash her golden brown eyes, and stare down even the most hardened fellows in a heartbeat. Here she was, entirely at home among the overpowering fragrances of the ladies of the night as they mixed and mingled with the onion and garlic of the obnoxious wiseguys.

Last night she was very much alive, making a C note entertaining Dominic. "Big Dom" was a player in a world of games. He had recently come into some heavy cash, and when he had it, he spent it. Last night he had it . . . and she got it—along with her normal hangover. A knock at the door had announced her maid's arrival with her breakfast: an elixir consisting of tomato juice with garlic, salt, tabasco sauce, and a hard roll.

"Good mornin', Lou. Las' night you got a phone call from yo brother, Franky," she said as she placed the morning tray upon the bed. "I didn' wanna botha you wid it, bein' that you was wid that man, Big Dom. He's one sharp, heavy looted man . . . an he's sure enough got sumthin' for you!"

"You just mind your own business and get this room cleaned up and ready for tonight," Lou directed in a civil yet commanding tone. "I'll be wearing my black dress . . . the one with the sequins and my white mink stole. Make sure they're clean!"

. . . Yet, Louise often wondered, was her soul clean?

All her life she'd lived for money and self-sufficiency on the pretext she was doing the right thing, even if it meant leaving Jeanette with friends and relations . . .

Her father, Antonio, had begun early in Louise's life to imprint much in her mind: that men of respect make money and women help men of respect make money . . . and make children!

In the late nineteenth and early twentieth-century, the career of choice for women was reproduction, and her mother Julia's fruits of labor were six healthy children: Francis (Franky), Anthony (Tony), Theresa (Tesi), Angela (Anna), Edward (Eddy), and Louise (Lou).

While Julia struggled to raise the children, Antonio, along with his father and the mob's assistance, worked his way into owning four apartment buildings in Long Island City. Each four story building had twenty families paying rent. Antonio would make Frank, Eddy, and Louise—at ten years of age—take a trolley, rain or shine, from Hicksville to collect the rents! It seemed Louise's entire childhood was spent working in the absence of fatherly love. Desperately attempting to discover that love, she tried to please him by demonstrating her devotion to earning money for him; yet another perversion of thought and life accomplished through The Curse of Alphonso and its subsequent acts of selfishness, greed, and perpetuation.

. . . As the years went by, and Antonio's ties to organized crime developed and grew stronger, the cash flowing to the bank began producing into reality those dreams that once ran rampant in all of their minds: dreams of plenty; dreams of splendor; dreams of opulence—those wishful dreams of desperation, once vanquished from a sleep of absolute poverty, had returned, not to their sleep, but to their awakening—for in payment for this temporary reversal of fortune, their dreams soon became nightmares; breeding, reveling, tormenting, until they in turn became the substance of their awakening . . .

Antonio had just finished his lunch and was enjoying an espresso as he looked out the silk draped windows of his ante-bellum style home. His gaze absorbed the huge, fluted colonnades, a large veranda that swept the breadth of the facade, a spouting statue-circled fountain;South Carolina-style mixed with

Greek revival (a duplicate of a picture Antonio had seen in a magazine) at the two soldiers, who, guns in hand, patrolled the expansive grounds while a third, The Ape, sat reading the paper. The war of the past three years had claimed many lives of close relatives; such as Che Che and Zippy. In fact, it was at one of his buildings in Long Island City that Antonio's jovial cousin, Che Che, had joined his ancestors . . .

With five men manning the busy phones, Che Che had been running book in one of Antonio's apartments. It was a calm, sunny Spring day with just a chill of the lingering winter—a day that brought the promise of a beautiful, evolving season. Antonio had just stepped outside and was breathing in the cool, fresh air when a black automobile pulled up. Six men jumped out and, as one grabbed and thrust him against the car, five others proceeded to the door and up the stairs. No words were spoken—only a silent, deadly attitude warned the danger of uttering a sound.

Reaching the third floor, the lead gunman motioned for the others to proceed to apartment #301. There were no guards in front of the reinforced door. The troops took up position. With tommy guns drawn, the lead man tapped on the door.

Inside Che Che was ecstatic. Business was proceeding better than planned. "In two more weeks," he thought to himself, "I'll expand the operation." He had been given permission to bring in four more associates. Being a "made" soldier, he only lacked proof of an ability to command respect and teach others to become "earners" to advance up the ladder. He could now provide his "Capo" with sufficient proof (and loot) that would filter up the chain and catch the attention of the underboss. He was sure the Boss himself would then promote him to Capo. With his own crew he could maybe attain even higher status: "Don Cheech!"

There was a familiar knock at the door: rap, rap, stop . . . rap, stop . . . rap, rap, stop . . . rap. Che Che went to answer it thinking it was the Ape. He was doing so well, the Ape assisting him . . . said he wanted to make sure Che Che looked good in the eyes of the Don . . . said he'd stop by that day.

These thoughts led him to disregard security measures he had so rigorously implemented. Zippy, on the phone taking a bet on the horses, looked up and noticed Che Che removing the elaborate locking mechanism. He was in the process of reminding him to first identify the caller by using the simple peep hole when the door burst in.

The callers didn't utter a word—just ripped a hundred rounds into the main room. Che Che was nearly cut in two, Zippy's mouth gaped in silent warning. The phones rang with continual determination of clients who now would have to place their bets somewhere else. Only the smoke lingered beyond the fading echos of those bursts of lead and fire. And the phones . . . the phones kept ringing . . .

The gunmen left calmly down the stairs and out the door. Before entering the car, they warned Antonio about further business with his mentor. Leaving him with the words, "Your new partner will be in touch."

Antonio had spoken to no one about what had transpired nor of the warning. He told the Don he was not at the bookmaking operation at the time of the hit. The family's disposal crew arrived at the apartment thirty minutes after the incident and incinerated the evidence—including the bodies. None of the neighbors uttered a word, no one helped, looked, or said anything. The accomplices and substance of organized crime went about their business as usual. Only the suspicion of a traitor in the midst of this "loyal and trusting family" served as a reminder of what transpired.

'Yes,' thought Antonio, 'this was the reason the Ape had been given the responsibility of Antonio's protection.' After the last episode of "war," finger-pointing began immediately and a cannibalizing purge of rivals and a clearing of debts was being accomplished—under the guise of loyalty! The Ape had been with the Don for twenty-five years and the Don respected and trusted him.

"It's time to go," the Ape reminded Antonio—returning him to the present and away from his reverie of horror.

"Did Feranzi call this morning?" Antonio inquired in a respectful tone of voice.

"Yeah", replied the Ape. "He has some good news."

'Good news,' thought Antonio, 'means bad news for someone.' He picked up the phone and dialed the number.

"Hello?"

"Feranzi?"

". . . wait a minute, I'll get im."

It was Joe-Pep.

Antonio thought the kid acted a whole lot older than seventeen. He'd become liaison to Louise who was working in some mob joint up in Mt. Kisko. He would pick up Jeanette and bring her to see her mother once a month. Big plans were being made for Joe-Pep and his brother Carmine. Joe was already running numbers and making pick-ups for Pauly Ham. But Antonio would keep his sons as far away as possible from the Family. He heard rumors of Feranzi backing Franky with a loan-sharking book on a small basis. He understood Joe-Pep was the courier of funds between Louise and him but he would not complain. He didn't want to rock the boat and have them sink deeper into the sea of depravity.

The phone clicked with Feranzi's voice in a frenzy of excitement. "Listen, Jimmy and some broad got it this morning in Chicago . . . something about a jealous husband or something. He sleeps with the fish!"

Antonio held the phone in his hand staring at it like it would come alive or something. Though he wanted revenge, he now wished he'd never agreed. "Well, he should have kept his thing in his pants, I'll see you soon . . ."

A rusted out truck with East Side Plumbing painted on its side pulled up at Antonio's mansion. Three men dressed in white uniforms got out of the back while two stepped out of the front cab. Their cautious attitudes revealed a motive other than plumbing for the sudden, unannounced appearance of such a large work force. They had no interest in fixing any pipes—they were there to "fix" something else.

The two alert bodyguards canvassing the grounds noticed the "plumbing crew" as they walked up to the door with "tools" in hand. With hand signals and body language, the loyal, experienced duo silently positioned themselves to the rear of the hit squad. One of the heavy set, walking brick walls, a large, meaty hand wrapped around a black revolver, twitching with anticipation, asked in a low, chilling, rumbling voice, "Can I help youse guys?"

An icy blast of Arctic wind, the voice froze the group. Nobody could speak cause their minds were too busy racing with computations: How many?—Should I make a move?—Shoot first . . . then ask questions?—Who the hell was in charge of scouting the situation?

Antonio was seated at the dining room table when the racket of a firefight in his front yard startled him.

The stalemate between the hit crew and Antonio's bodyguards had lasted only moments. Without further warning, the quiet, still air, tense with apprehension, exploded with blasts of gunpowder, careening hot, swift lead, and shouts of determined orders.

The sinister group had moved as one—as if telepathically commanded by the "foreman" of the plumbing crew. Someone appeared behind Antonio's loyal men—blasting away. When the smoke had cleared, the two bodyguards were dead . . . so were two of the plumbers—a third was wounded but there were still two capable assassins.

When Antonio stood up to investigate, the door opened and three men entered—The Ape, had taken care of the bodyguards from the rear as was part of the plot. One of the men—"Micky Two-Shoes"—without any explanation or communication other than, "Just keep your mouth shut and we won't hurt you," tied Antonio up, dragged him to the truck, and threw him in . . .

. . . In a dark, cold room, on a bare mattress, Antonio lay in deep thought. After a shoot-out at his place, he was hog-tied, blind-folded, and taken to this seedy location—which he presumed was a safehouse used by the new Boss who demanded new tribute to be paid. He realized decisions were being made about his future and he knew that future didn't look so bright. Overpowering memories, long since buried, leaped from the deep dark past into the deep dark present of his thoughts. Friends killed, lives ruined, rumors of his daughter, Louise, living in a world of prostitution, Eddy and Franky loan sharking, father Alphonso dead . . . yes, and all due to Antonio. He had balked at the demands. Alphonso had intervened only to keel over by a heart attack at the revelations of his granddaughter and the threats and demands of those who now gave the orders. Yes, he had been a willing participant in This Thing of Ours. He had wallowed in its muck and slime in piggish delight, standing tall on the porch of his mansion, proudly dressed in his finest attire, all paid for by souls of the deceased—past, present, and

future—squealing in delight as his property and cash grew in leaps and bounds. He was sure he would now pay the price for his transgressions and those of his ancestors.

Flashing in and out of these thoughts were the questions of denial that hammered home the reality of his situation. 'What day is it? How long have I been here? Why me? Haven't I done everything correctly? I didn't ask for this heritage. I knew what I wanted in life. I worked hard for it. Why should I take the blame?'

A scraping sound of the outer door as it was pushed open checked his thoughts. Tensing his bound hands, he strained to listen for sounds that would identify his caller. A thought streaked across his mind, It's Mickey Two Shoes, that Irish %$%^%#@ returning, not to check up on him, but to end his life!

The commotion and noise coming from the outside alerted him to the fact that no matter who was on the opposite side of his locked cell, he was not alone. Rattling of keys in a lock, and the metallic clicking of its removal, notified Antonio of the next event . . . the door to his cell slowly creaked open and a flash of blinding light rushed in, illuminating the silent chamber of horrors that had become Antonio's prison of the mind—as well as the body.

While Antonio, blinking away the pitch-black that coated his eyes, desperately sought to determine the identities of captors, a silent silhouette of a large figure blocked the sudden, brilliant invasion. With his cell cast once more into darkness, he pushed aside his mounting panic and questioned the specter in his most demanding tone, "Who the hell are you?"

The figure entered the room and untied the ropes that bound Antonio. He was lifted and shoved toward the light that poured once more through the opening. Antonio, with slow, deliberate steps, moved toward the irradiated portal of life, abandoning Lucifer to wait, laughing in the dark, for his return.

Passing through the doorway, his eyes darted about, searching the dingy room in semi-blindness as he was pushed toward a lonely chair placed in front of a threadbare sofa. As his vision returned, he swept the room again to identify the players. He was shocked to recognize the Ape, Pauly Ham, and Feranzi; three close friends and associates who'd removed him from his cell. Three other men, who sat on the sofa, remained unfamiliar . . . though he thought he recognized the one in the center, he just couldn't place the scarred and cratered face. The only aspect of these wiseguys he was sure he could recognize were the heavy caliber weapons of death and enforcement perched in nests of leather, worn by each. Intimidated, he gently sat in the wobbly wooden seat, shaking his head trying to escape this nightmare.

Barely above a whisper, the pocked-marked face spoke. "Eh, Antonio, how ya feelin'. They treatin' ya right?"

"Just fine, I'm O.K."

"Ya know, we don' wanna do ya, we wanna help ya."

"Help me with what?" Antonio demanded, concealing the fear and anxiety bubbling deep within the pit of his stomach.

"Weez got diz problem. I'm da new guy on da block an I'm callin in da notes ta all dem places in Queens dat waz set up wid our bananas, capisch? Ev'ry body is doin somthin'. It's time for you to divvy up. You can do da right ting or you can sleep wid da fishes. It's up ta you."

Without a moment's hesitation, Antonio, shocked at the implications of such a request, blurted the words, "You can @#%# yourself!"

For what seemed an eternity, silently, the expressionless soldiers of The Hand gazed upon Antonio's defiant facade with indifference. Then, abruptly, the peaceful volcano erupted. Spouting out a time tested reason for immediate death . . . "You ain't got no respect" . . . in a blur, he pulled the shiny revolver from its birth, cocked the hammer, and fired a shot that creased Antonio's skull.

Dazed, ears ringing, Antonio fought to retain his position in the chair as the howling shape spit out a pledge. "Who da hell do ya dink you are? I'll kill you ya @#%$^%$#@ idiot! That's what I dink I'm gonna do, I dink I'm gonna blow your $%^&%#@$ brains out myself! From now on, you don't pee widout askin' us! You got dat? Da guy on my left is Lou Parrilli. He's gonna set up da books an collect fa us. You just sign dem papers he brings! Maybe you can keep ya place on da Island, but if ya mess wid us, we'll kill you an dat son of yours! Ya got dat?"

With that, he turned, motioned to the others it was time to leave, and walked to the door. The two wiseguys got up and followed. Before exiting the door, they whispered something to Feranzi and the Ape, then left. Feranzi shut the door, went to his overcoat and, as Antonio watched in horror, removed a large pair of metal shears from an outer pocket.

Petrified, Antonio attempted to rise from his chair but seemed to be frozen in this living nightmare. "Hey whaddaya . . . you . . . need those for . . . ?" a distant shrill voice cried out with dread. He could clearly see Pauly Ham grabbing someone's left arm, could hear screams of pain as fingers plopped to the floor, convulsing with apprehension, fear, and hope, alive, wriggling, one with a wedding band still attached—its design vaguely familiar. He could feel pain as if the appendages that dropped onto the bloody floor were his. Then, the screaming stopped and he floated along a river of wet blackness. . . .

. . . The flood that became that river of blackness had begun its descent upon Louise's family in 1913, washing away the colors of happiness, joy, and the very essence of family.

Just like her childhood . . .

And Momma Julia's

And Jeanette's . . .

And her love . . .

And Jeanette's Joe-Pep . . .

And now these poor "little ones" . . .

Too soon.

Leaving bits and pieces of faults and mistakes to surface, rumbling from their very cores in quakes of memory; for they would also live in that world where memories haunt forever.

And so Nana Lou would come to love little children with all of her heart . . . but, when they reached the age of five and above, she would shun them. The memories were just too strong, they mixed and mingled with the pain of her husband, Jimmy; her father, Antonio; and grandfather, Alphonso. She had long ago bleached this ragged bit of destiny from her mind . . . yet all it took was a visit to her daughter to prove the stain was permanent!

Nana Lou sighed and said, "Angela, you go and get some sleep, don't you worry about your brothers . . . they're men and will be just fine."

Chapter 11: And Adventure Calls

The low, soft voice of the driver, combined with his gentle nudging, awoke him: "Young man . . . you're here. Last stop—c'mon, wake up."

Joe woke up and shook his brother and they got off the bus.

The driver asked if someone was picking them up and Joe replied, "Yes."

With that, he closed the door and drove off.

They stood next to a bench on a cold, dark, nearly silent road. Not a single sound of a car, truck or human pierced the cloak of silence. The only sound was the occasional cry of an animal as it delivered its message of existence. There were no tall buildings, only the dark images of giant mountains bordered by a multitude of stars which sprinkled a pitch-black sky. No street signs pointed the way. No friendly face greeted them in cheer. They were alone!

Carmine, frightened to the bone, began crying that a bear was going to eat them. He was crying for his mommy. Joe told his little brother not to worry—they just needed to find a place to sleep. In the morning they'd find people. Not giving him any more time to think, he started walking down the road with Carmine following in a hurry!

As they walked for what seemed like an hour, Joe questioned God. Why are people lost in the world? Why is there not enough food? Why did father leave? Is he with you now? How long is the ride to heaven? Did you use a train or did angels take him to you?

The questions bothered him. He couldn't comprehend the situation. 'How did father die?' became his greatest question. 'A car accident?' He pictured two Chevy Impalas colliding at an intersection; both father and Uncle Carmine dead . . . a recurring nightmare!

Walking in deep thought he almost passed a sign indicating the entrance to a golf course—a pleasure resort that opened in the summer and closed in the winter. When he saw it, he turned into the entrance and came upon a barred and locked chain link fence. Climbing over, they discovered a pro shop with several doors and windows. Cold and needing shelter, Joe broke a window and entered. The place was bare of all but boxes of golf balls, cigarettes, books, and candy bars. They went for the candy, loading their pockets as well as their mouths. After satisfying their hunger, Joe decided they should sleep somewhere else because of the possibility of getting caught in the building. Taking an armful of books, they walked down the driving range and plopped on the ground. Joe started a small fire and they tried to sleep.

During several hours of tossing and turning on the hard, frost-covered ground, a dream of his mother—"there are people who sleep on dirt floors"—came to him, and Joe began to think once more of those secret, whispered conversations he occasionally overheard. They usually popped up among the women during times of sadness or sorrow. After shooing the kids outside, when they thought they were alone, their sobbing became their music, tracking their scales of sorrow to the lyrics of prayer mixed with the emotional bursts of oaths of revenge, forgiveness, and utter pain. It was after they would exhaust themselves against their misery that the questions and answers would flail his ears with talk of a Curse!

Joe became vaguely aware Jeanette had spent her entire childhood with relatives, sleeping in borrowed beds, beds just as lonely and desolate as the cold, hard ground he now rested upon. He had heard bits and pieces of his mother's sorrowful tale of being surrounded by people who had their own children and were too busy with their own problems to care about hers.

Was it true that mother grabbed onto what she perceived as a lifeline to love, family, and a bed of her own when she met father? Had her love truly doomed her to misery like those women said? Was her choice of family truly an ingredient of lasting servitude—her bed never to be made?

To Joe, the forests surrounding him represented those that surrounded her, and now him: beautiful, full of life, providing shelter and sustenance . . . but totally silent.

Joe's cramped back had delivered its hard lesson: he could now understand what his mother meant when she told them stories of children sleeping on dirt floors—and sorrow pierced his soul!

"Oh, God help us, I promise I won't run away again . . . I'll go home! Just find us a place to sleep and something real to eat," he pleaded in his sleep. Suddenly, a sharp pop startled him, caused him to jump to his feet in one bound.

Carmine was seated, shivering with cold, tossing golf balls into the fire. As Joe yelled for him to stop, another loud pop pierced the stillness of the crisp, clean air. Then, all hell broke loose! The pops turned to explosions sounding like the Fourth of July! Golf balls exploding in the fire. Sparks lighting up the night.

The boys ran as fast as they could through the dark virgin forest; branches and brambles tearing at them with a vengeance—punishing them for their transgression upon its reposing soil. By the time they spotted the huge, white house, they were scratched and bleeding.

"Look at that!" Carmine yelled. "It looks 'ike a castle. Do you dink they gotta phone?"

"It looks like the place is empty . . . lemme check," Joe said in a low tone.

Approaching the stone and wood mansion, it became apparent the place was empty. Large windows overlooking a wide, terraced lawn were boarded up; a set of huge double doors with massive steel chains binding its handles and a large padlock securing it, barred any thought of entry.

Calling for his brother, he went around the side of the house and discovered a cellar with two doors—like the one in the Wizard of Oz, where Dorothy hid from the tornado. Reaching down, he lifted one of the doors, it opened with a loud and piercing screech. Looking down into the dark bowels of this grand house, he was tempted to close the door, but they had no choice. He could hear a fire engine somewhere in the darkness. Flicking his lighter as he climbed down to the bottom of the stairs he cried, "We can't let em find us tonight!"

Moving through cobwebs, tripping over many obstacles cluttering the way, he stumbled into a stairwell leading to a door with a hasp and lock. Turning back, he searched the dirt floor until he saw a rusty old ax. Swinging so hard that sparks flew, Joe finally broke the lock and entered the upstairs of what he expected to be a palace.

Though it was dark inside, the huge white sheets covering the furniture acted as reflectors, and he could make out enough to get his bearings. An embossed, green-tinted metal ceiling was twenty feet above him. The front door was a good forty paces straight ahead, and, like a scene out of a Boris Karloff movie, tapestries draped the walls surrounding huge fireplaces, their large mantles towering above him. Chandeliers were covered with cobwebs, but their crystal still twinkled in rhythm to his lighter's flickering, each star-burst reflecting into numerous elaborate candelabras holding tall candlesticks—spooky but beautiful!

He knew he'd better light some of the candles before Carmine came in. Descending the stairwell, he left as he came and soon was surveying the house from the outside. He had lit candles throughout the house and no light penetrated the boards covering the windows! They now had a castle to live in! Calling his brother, they went back inside to investigate the layout: twenty-five rooms, including a library, a kitchen stocked with canned goods, five bathrooms, a pool parlor with all sorts of card and billiard tables, bedrooms with huge canopied beds, and a music room, competed for opulence and comfort! Carmine went crazy. Running into a large bedroom, he began jumping up and down on a bed screaming, "This is my room!" over and over. Joe told Carmine to get some sleep and soon after starting a fire in the fireplace, Joe joined him in deep sleep.

The next morning they woke refreshed and hungry. Racing down the stairs, they entered the kitchen and opened a pantry which revealed shelves filled with canned food.

"Peaches!" Carmine yelled in excitement, "I want peaches!"

Grabbing a huge can of peaches, he searched for a can opener. The only one available was an ancient electric contraption, so with knife and hammer, he mutilated the can open.

After feasting on a wide array of delicacies they decided to explore the grounds.

"Are we going home now?" Carmine asked.

Forgetting the promise he had made, Joe lied. "Yeah, later on."

They left the house and proceeded to the woods he loved. Entering its canopied tranquillity, he was once again in tune with its powers. He was immediately calmed and at peace; he had no cares, he was in charge. Joe was showing his little brother the wonders of the forest when Carmine noticed a wide stream with fast-moving rapids. Carmine had never seen such a river and he ran toward it.

"Hey, Carm, be careful."

But Carmine had reached its edge and was trying to make his two pound metal boat float, when it sank. In his desperation to recover it, Carmine jumped in. The currents that were playing with his boat were fun! It felt like some invisible friend playing games in the water. But this friend wouldn't let go when you got scared. Carmine wanted to call for Joe but he knew the ridicule he'd be in for. He decided to work it out by himself. If he could just find a good foothold on a rock that wasn't so darn slippery . . .

Joe was getting aggravated. 'Little brothers are a pain in the butt,' he thought. "Yo, Carmine, where are ya?"

He wandered in the general direction Carmine had been running. When he got close enough to hear the rapids, he saw a shock of color in the freezing water . . . it was Carmine . . . in the water! "Hold on, Carm, I'm comin!" Joe screamed, as he ran through the brush, leaping into a calm, deep pool just past the swift current . . . the water was so cold he got an instant headache . . . it hurt his eyes to open them in the water . . . his clothes were soaked through and feeling so heavy . . . Joe's foot hit something under the water—his only hint that he was not drowning alone in this freezing stream . . . Joe dove down into the pooled water grabbing for anything he could feel . . . he brushed against a moss-covered tree limb—no, it was Carmine's arm . . . but the water was so cold . . . the weight of Carmine and his sodden clothes were pulling him down deeper into the blackness.

Chapter 12: More Facts Arise

Franky searched the entire neighborhood once more in search of Joe and Carmine with no luck. His grand-nephews were causing quite a stir; causing old wounds to surface. The rumors had attracted law enforcement officers who were putting the heat on . . . and no one enjoyed being in the limelight, especially not Ball and Jolly!

They were upset and vowing revenge for the reprimand they had suffered for not "finding two little kids lost on their beat." Franky was at odds at what to say or do; after all, his own "business" had been effected. The sooner they were found, the sooner this situation would be resolved. Franky was well aware of what could happen after a minor "situation," like the one those two cops had participated in . . .

Slinky Gina, red silk dress glued to her sensuous frame, purring rather than communicating, was the epitome of the gangster groupie—beautiful, dumb, and ready. Gina knew her stuff; she began her education at thirteen years of age, Pauly Ham her teacher! She was hand-picked and trained personally by Pauly—who liked them young, and would use his converts to get the facts on other wiseguys. Even though Gina had grown up since that first date with Pauly, she maintained her "cute and dumb" personality . . . and for a very good reason: Mobsters didn't pick women for girlfriends who were smart. Mobsters wanted stupid, ignorant girl—friends to hang with. Anyone who was smart was going to tell them something they didn't want to hear. They wanted someone who looked like a whore and acted dumb! Plainly speaking, a trinket to wear on their arm to show off to their wiseguy friends. But the fact remained: most of the women who associated with mobsters were smart—they just learned how to act dumb . . . Fast!

Throughout the history of the mob, many a tough guy had been brought down by the phrase, "Dat dumb broad don' know nothin', so don' worry boudit!" The stupid dame on the mobster's arm was always around—always secreting information to use when the time was right. From wiseguy to wiseguy they traveled; planting seeds of greed, selfishness, loyalty, respect, or devotion. Occasionally, sprouting seeds never reached maturity and full bloom before a storm would arise to flood and destroy them—yet, whatever the season called for, they would plant it and work the garden. Gina was a pro at this form of revolutionary gardening. A seasonal change was in the air, for Gina wanted to get even—she would work her garden.

The driver pulled to the curb and shut down the motor, exited the rich, yellow, Cadillac, and made a show of unbuttoning his overcoat. Walking around to curbside, he opened the rear passenger door to allow Salvatore and Anthony Donitelli's brother, Jimmy "Big-Jim" Donitelli, and his dame to step out. The automobile noticeably raised several inches as Big-Jim's corpulent body, encased in a light blue, silk ensemble—more like a sack than the three-hundred and fifty dollar, custom tailored, suit that it was—removed itself. Flagrantly disregarding the mass of anxious patrons mobbing the threshold of Boccala's Bistro, he swaggered into the joint with Gina wrapped around his arm.

"Oh, sweetheart, isn't that Pauly Ham over there?" Gina purred as she made a display of pointing toward Big-Jim's nemesis. "I heard he was on the Don's personal list."

"What the hey you say? What #$^#$@$ list ya talking about?"

"Oh, sweety, you're jealous!"

"I'm not #%$#%#@^% jealo . . . Wait a minute, waddya talking about, huh? I'll wack that ^%$$#^&&*$# W.O.P . . . ," Big-Jim yelled, his temper running far ahead of his judgment.

Several people in the crowd overheard the last portion of Big-Jim's remark. Soon the news reached Pauly Ham—who kept an eye on Jimmy all night . . . as Gina smiled inside.

No one thought of this minor situation as what it was . . . a mistake on the part of the gardener.

"What's the word about Sally and Big Jim?" Pauly Ham asked nonchalantly of Tony Black.

"I ain't heard nothin', why'd you ask?" Tony replied.

"Hey, I don't know either. It's just that they split seven large last week and . . ."

"What are you talking about, they only made one . . . at least that's what they sent up!"

"I don't wanna cause any problems, let's forget about it, O.K.?" Pauly said, further advancing the situation.

"Where did ya . . ."

"Listen, forget about it. I don't know what the story is . . . .must be a rumor . . ."

The message traveled the street and by the time it reached the Don, it became truth!

"But Boss, we gotta do sumthin'. We can't allow dis to jus go away! Setting up their own expansion widout your permission! An, pocketing da lion's share of the green! Youse want me ta uze da crew down on da docks?!"

The Don did not reply. His face remained blank as he thought of the answer to this situation of respect. Big Jim had assisted in many sensitive aspects of his takeover. The territory he was awarded was hotly contested by Pauly Ham; he had officially entered his objections. His "beef" was that Harlem was opened up by his own uncle. A rumble was in the making and it might throw a glitch into the wider picture. A question of the Donitelli's loyalty and respect might just be the reason for their elimination—clearing the way for the return of the territory to Pauly Ham—while he remained in actual control of the real estate. The other item that weighed heavy on the scales was the fact of Big-Jim's knowledge—this fact could lead to an even worsening situation with the other Dons. He made up his mind, "Make da call . . ." he commanded, " . . . but just for Big Jim and Anthony, I want you to get word to Pauly."

The Don had spoken. Pauly had the contract and he relished the thought. He would have rather let Big Jim know so he could squirm in fear, but he knew he could not toy with him—he was too powerful. Even with all of the precautions taken, word soon leaked out on the streets that Big-Jim and Anthony were in disfavor with the Don. Their brother Sally was told to "sit it out or else." Everywhere Big Jim and Anthony went, shoulders turned. Soon they were living in a cold, unfamiliar world. They knew something was amiss but could not put their finger on the cause. It took several months for Pauly to set them up, but the contract on Big-Jim was not carried out until Anthony had conveniently disappeared. Rumor was, he had been an added ingredient to a mix of cement and was now an integral portion of a newly refurbished Brooklyn pier. It was said his own guys had carried out the hit because of interpersonal reasons and a juggling of power. But Big-Jim knew the reason, if not the cause.

Like countless other mobsters who felt change in the atmosphere forewarning of the coming storm, Big-Jim believed that he would be safe, that he could regain his stature; that the storm would blow over and he would still be firmly rooted in the mob structure. After all, he was in-

vincible. His answer was to take precautions and wait it out. He did not assume, he presumed. He dropped all routines and appeared as suddenly as he left. His meetings to conduct business were as sudden as his temper. Except with Gina . . .

While Big-Jim had nightmares of being a leaf blowing in a wind of seasonal change, Pauly deduced, reasoned and planned. "How can I get close enough to him?" he said to, rather than asked of Joe-Pep, who was proud to be part of this great occurrence. He was participating in a hit! He was becoming a man! Joe-Pep was with his Father Figure, his mentor, Pauly Ham. He was teaching, sharing, showing, and including him in a hit! When he had real sons, he would show them the way also . . .

Thus, a vengeful turn of events had become the final, essential ingredient of total pervasive change in the life of another descendant of The Curse of Alphonso. That night, alone in the company of his Father Figure, Joe-Pep became him. From then on he would view life, death, and procreation with a unique perspective: life evolved around the continuance of the family, not personal family, but Mafia Family. He decided he needed a wife to beget sons—he would then be complete in the ways of "This Thing of Ours!" But first, he desperately wanted to answer Pauly's question—he knew he had the answer.

"Gina! That's how! Gina!" he blurted out with glee. "Pauly, he's close to her. I know we can use her to set him up! She won't even know!"

"What the $%$ . . ." Pauly began and caught himself. His look converted from serious, thoughtful consternation, to relieved, concluded answer. His demeanor changed and a proud, beaming smile resonated from his face, lighting up the quiet room.

"I think all my years of grooming you has paid off . . ."

Gina patted her face with make-up as she thought of the situation. Joe-Pep had visited her last night. He came over and they had spent the night in abandon. She enjoyed his pure and ravaging love making. "He is sexy and thorough," she thought as her body purred with visions of his youthful manhood. "What a change from that fat #$%#@#$%." She had had a great time, but certain questions nagged at her subconscious all night. Joe-Pep asked questions and made innuendoes about Big-Jim all during the night. She was sure they were more than important, and soon she combined them with the word on the street—and her own future! It was evident Big-Jim was marked, not Pauly! But how could she benefit from this situation? Bing! A light went on. Quickly she completed her face, then left to find Pauly.

Fat Freddy picked up Gina at 8:30 sharp. Guided by his bodyguard, she entered the car and planted a large wet kiss on Freddy's lips.

"You love me, don' ya?" Big-Jim asked, wiping a smear of lipstick off his lips with a silk handkerchief

"Oh, Baby, I can't get enough of you," she answered, lightly running her hand along his thigh.

"You want some of this, don' ya?" Big-Jim said as he grabbed himself. "Listen, we'll stop at the club for a minute and then go to my place."

"Oh honey, do I have to wait?" she said coyly, as she cuddled real close to Big-Jim's sweaty, silk-draped flesh and zipped down his pants. Content, Big-Jim relaxed as Gina began performing. She made him wait, toying with him until the car pulled up at the curb outside of the club—then bang! . . . she finished.

Big-Jim was trying to compose himself as Gina got out of the car. The bodyguard, flushed and embarrassed, was sorting his own composure when the sound of a terrific explosion cut his thoughts to blackness.

Gina was violently thrown to the ground as five hooded gunmen blasted Big-Jim into the cushions of his seat. His body wilted in the progress of his endeavor as he lay upon the fabric of death with his zipper still open, his mouth set in grim disbelief.

A crowd assembled around the bright-yellow emblem of power to gaze in awe and concealed delight at this spectacle of crushed might. Talk of the "hit" would enable these witnesses of mob justice to bask in the spotlight of temporary fame. Muted answers to police interrogators would convey a lapse of memory while loud thoughts of stories to be told, grand in testimony, were tossed and turned in mind. Many a thoroughly boring and uneventful life would succumb to these thoughts and, for a short time at least, an oration of fable and witness would combine producing a fiction of events which converted weakness to power. Enthusiastic responses from a multitude of thrill-seekers to the statement, "I was there when . . ." would promote inspired awe of the mob and its ways. But a fact remained no one was aware of: a young man named Joe-Pep was one of the men who participated in the hit that obliterated Big-Jim from the planet.

Chapter 13: To Be Like Father

When I awoke the other day
Life was painted a dismal gray
Just before the evening had
Locked me in a cage so sad
People of all nations races
Trapped behind these steel braces
Fight for justice win or lose
False accusations simple clues
Turn Key Turn Key where are you
One simple hour seems like two . . .

Joe fought the current and the cold as he pulled Carmine to the surface.

"Let go of the boat!" Joe screamed.

Incredibly, Carmine had recovered his prize boat and hung onto it throughout the ordeal. Now he wouldn't (or couldn't) let go.

Yelling and praying at the same time, Joe pried the boat out of Carmine's hands and got him to cling to his jacket instead. With more effort than he ever imagined would be required, Joe wrestled Carmine out of the pool of water and the threatening current.

He decided it was time to go home.

Joe practically dragged Carmine through the woods on their way toward the road. They were soaked and shivering. When they reached the edge of the road, a group of rowdy early-teenagers approached. A tall, blond-headed boy, trying to be the leader, shouted to Joe and Carmine, "Hey, what are you doing in my forest?"

Joe was startled and surprised by the sudden appearance and size of the youth, but with his brother by his side, he had to demonstrate he was a man of respect. "Whaddya mean, 'your forest!' We have a castle here and it's *my* forest!"

The kid lunged, but Joe side-stepped and grabbed the kid's jacket collar, flinging him to the ground.

Sensing he was in trouble and alarmed by his bad judgment, the kid never had the chance to recover his pride. Joe turned to the group and told them, "Listen, we're mobsters from "The City." We're hiding out at our castle. If you want to see it, come with me!" The group, dumbstruck by the swiftness of their dominance, followed. Arriving at the boarded-up building, they were amazed!

"This place is yours?" the tall kid asked. "We always wondered who owned this place."

"Well, it belongs to my father . . ." Joe lied.

Carmine was looking strangely at Joe's blatant lie. But, before he could ruin the situation, Joe began giving them a tour and story about hit men and such.

Within a week they had every kid within ten miles around hangin out in their "castle."

Soon, they became known as "The Motley Crew!"

Sitting high above the throng, on a throne atop a pool table, Joe gave orders to his guys, "Put the TV over in the main study, I'll take the jewelry." He ordered two kids who delivered their recently acquired loot, "Go and get yourselves a drink. You deserve it."

His Motley Crew was the terror of the empty, boarded vacation homes that dotted the mountain sides. They were enjoying the fact they belonged to a Mafia family; their proof: the booty they brought to their castle—jewelry, TVs, furs . . . the list grew and grew.

'Boy, would father be proud of me!' Joe thought.

Joe had become the eleven-year-old Godfather of the mountains with a fortune of goods—though he had no clue what to do with the stuff.

A crime wave had hit the Pocono Mountains resorts and soon the authorities became aware of the "mobsters" from New York City. They reacted swiftly.

Wailing sirens atop jeeps reached the castle without warning. Police encircled the castle's keep, then announced their presence via bullhorn. It was chaos! Thirty kids hit the basement at one time. A candle was knocked over and a blaze erupted. All of the kids got out, and in the ensuing madness, twelve got away, including Carmine and Joe. The manhunt to find the "criminal element" encircled the mountainside. For the next day and night the brothers hid out in a cold cave. When it seemed the hunt had died down, they walked out cold, hungry, and wet, looking for signs of life.

They were crossing some railroad tracks when they heard the order to halt. Turning around, they saw a state police officer with his gun drawn. Looking at two bedraggled kids in weird clothes; cut, dirty, tired, and hungry, he replaced the gun in its holster and shook his head. He pointed to the open car door.

Joe grabbed Carmine's arm and sat down in the patrol car. They were cuffed together and off they went; quiet, tired, and wanting to be back in their own beds . . . asleep . . . with full bellies!

The boys' fame had spread; the old stone jailhouse was crowded with angry townsfolk who had heard of the capture of two mysterious mobsters responsible for the out-break of crime and subversion of their children. Joe immediately thought they were going to be real life subjects of a movie: a lynch mob, waiting, ready, rope in hand, taunting the sheriff . . . who holds off his former friends with words . . . and a double barrel shot gun!

Joe halted, pulling Carmine back several steps as his nightmarish thoughts continued, 'The mob rushes . . . shouting . . . screaming for vengeance . . . storms the sheriff . . . knocks the gun from his hands—grabs, pulls, tears . . . and hangs them from the nearest tree!'

Frightened, holding Carmine's hand, he was led through the crowd to a cell, and shoved in.

With the rattle of keys, the jailer locked them in their newest castle, where they remained for several days.

The dismal gray iron bars; cold, stone gray walls, and gray steel bunk eclipsed the dirt floors of his mother's visions.

The sights and sounds of this experience ingrained another cold, hard, gray picture into the core of Joe's mind, drastically altering his perceptions of adventure. "Dear Jesus, I just want to go home," he prayed; not sure He would listen again.

The New York "kid hunt" never reached the mountains of eastern Pennsylvania—no one even knew they'd left New York. After final consultations with the NYPD—and some guy named Salvatore Donitelli—the sheriff decided not to press charges. He just wanted them gone.

Jeanette arrived at nine o'clock that night, very exhausted and *(very)* angry. All the way home she smacked and beat Joe—while Carmine slept peacefully—yelling that it was costing her money to come and get him; screaming about how he should be ashamed of himself for causing the family grief, and danger to his brother . . .

Joe had known he'd be in a lot of trouble at home for this escapade, but he also felt that his mother demanded that he emulate his father. What confused him was that she despised the fact that he tried to be like Joe-Pep. As oldest son, his family traditions were a part of his present circumstances. Joe was trying to handle things like a man of respect would—take the blame and don't complain. He took the blame like a man . . . but he didn't like it!

Chapter 14: Sowing the Seeds

The ride back from the Poconos was terrible to say the least. Joe heard over and over how everything that went wrong in the entire universe was caused by his vacation. He understood his journey had been a disaster, and that being home with some security—a warm bed, a caring, loving family—was better than fending for himself. He made a commitment to himself that in the future he would take care of his problems in other, less drastic ways. But life plays its strange and sometimes cruel games. For a reason he couldn't fathom, the police (Ball Buster and Jolly Green Giant) were determined to press a vengeance on him. They called the Department of Social Services and pushed to have him taken from his mother for "psychiatric evaluation." Social workers appeared on their doorstep with orders to take him to Belvue Hospital for examination.

The three women and two men who came for him were like an army of determined storm troopers. He fought them tooth and nail, but they overpowered him, placed him in a straight-jacket, and injected him with a substance that turned his world into a woozy, placid, serene dream. Without further struggle he was on his way. Jeanette was screaming and crying on the doorstep with his siblings—who added to the chorus of tears.

Everything was neat and white: the shiny clean ambulance with sirens blaring; the starched and pressed uniforms worn by the attendants; the straight jacket they had put him in; the sheets on the stretcher they used to transport him. When they pulled up to a massive, white tomb of a building with small black windows, he thought he was entering a world of the colorless afterlife . . .tranquil but imposing—and permanent.

Doors opened and they led him into a brightly lit, immense room with waxed and polished floors reflecting spotless white walls with white lights hanging from a spotless white ceiling. Another injection and he drifted off to sleep. His last thoughts . . . 'Where am I? Who am I? This must be a dream.'

Then . . .

"Ah! No! Please!"

"Get the #$%@#%$!" Bang! . . . Boom! . . . Crash!

"What the #$@% . . . "

"Leave me alone! No—NO—HELP!"

Crash! Scuffle . . . "Hit im with the sticker!" Crash! Bang! Boom!

Joe awoke with a start. The white, gleaming thoughts he had must have been a dream. He was lying in a bed covered by a dirty gray blanket in an institutional green painted dormitory, its walls covered with the stains of brutality; its floors dulled by the constant traversing of wild-eyed, mumbling figures; some semi-clothed, some entirely naked. Windows, covered with bright red metal gratings—as if they were on fire—completed his immediate thought pattern . . . 'Am I in Hell?'

As his vision and hearing returned to normal, he found the cause of the violent commotion that woke him up. In the corner of the dorm, three demonic creatures—two black, one white—with needle in hand, were molesting a man. In Joe's drug-induced nightmare they became three appalling apparitions.

"Oh, God! Where am I? Father can you hear me? Why . . . why am I here? I must have deserved this—I must have! What did I do? Where are you . . . why did you leave?" He wanted his mother . . . he wanted to be home!

"Home! Home! Home!"

The next thing he knew, he was fighting with two orderlies.

"Get his arm, get his $#%@^%$ arm . . ."

"Get your hands off me . . . leave me alone!" he screamed, as an orderly attempted to inject something into his arm.

Joe was screaming out loud about home as two orderlies tried to calm him down. Having witnessed the molestation just minutes before, he was petrified that he too would soon be in the same "position." Totally berserk, he fought an obstinate and savage battle!

Out of the bed, kicking, biting, clawing, cursing, Joe was an enraged, beastly, Tasmanian Devil. It finally took four, full-grown men to hold him long enough to inject him.

He awoke for the second time in twenty-four hours, totally naked in a frigid, bare cell. He had nothing but a cold, hard, puke-stained floor on which to rest. His immediate thought: he'd been molested and would soon be again. Like a terrified rat in a box-like trap, sensing he is in danger, he scurried to and fro trying desperately to find a place to hide both his fear and his nakedness. But, like that rat, trapped and confused, there were none. This reaction only confirmed to an ever-watchful orderly that he was truly emotionally disturbed—which translated into insanity.

Was it a dream . . . the white on white on white, or did he pass into an after-life where gentle, white-robed angels, seated in billowy, soft, white clouds of heaven, judged, admonished, and then vanquished him to a place called Purgatory? The madness, confusion, and horror seemed identical to what was taught by black-robed, straightforward nuns in catechism. Here he would remain, he was convinced, lamenting, despairing, while enduring horrors that even man could not invent to torment man. Purgatory was not death, Death was Hell . . . and Hell was a permanent place of suffering. Once you arrived in Hell you were doomed for eternity with no hope of rescue. In Purgatory, on the other hand, one could be forgiven and reinstated to that white, warm, beautiful place called Heaven. Like the tranquil, protecting forest that he had come to cherish and desire, Heaven was a place of serenity; where you could live forever among ancestors as white-clothed angels in harmony and peace. There he would see his father . . . Oh, no! he thought to himself, 'Was father here? Was he roaming this vile, rabid, vermin-infested house of horrors? Was he one of the semi-damned! Begging, moaning, perpetrating? Oh! God! Let it not be so!' he prayed; not for *his* forgiveness, but for Father's.

He prayed, not to God, the Virgin Mary, St. James, Paul, or Peter, but to those still among the living; still residing in heaven's waiting room—Earth.

"Please light candles for father's soul . . ." he prayed out loud, "and if you have an extra dime, light one for me. Say prayers, for we are here among the damned . . . waiting, suffering, missing! Can you hear me? Please, pray for us!"

As he prayed he realized he was not floundering in a repulsive nightmare; the repugnant, sickening feelings that were boiling in his stomach, the visions bursting forth with sound and color, the rancid odors that permeated to his very soul, convinced him that he had truly arrived at Hell's waiting room! He began to plead for his own soul. He begged God to give him a second chance!

He recanted all his sins, praying: "I will never run away again—I will stop throwing the pastabazool out the window—I will eat the oatmeal . . . even three days a week and not flush it down the toilet bowl! Please, I promise, I promise . . ." he cried out loud. He beseeched God to deliver him, safely, soundly, and untouched to his home and family. "I will not think wrong thoughts of mother, even when she yells and slaps me! I will not give Aunt Connie a hard time!I will not steal any more . . . nor skip school!" Profusely, thunderously, he recited Hail Marys, Oh Gods, and Our Fathers until his voice, raw, hoarse, and on fire, gave out.

No angels, swords of justice and truth in hand; crushing, smiting, defeating, routing these mercenaries of the devils harvest ever appeared. No sudden light, delivering warmth and benevolence upon his forsaken, terrified soul burst within his cell. He was dropped into this world of madness . . . entombed forever?—naked, cold, filthy, hungry: a Dante's Inferno . . . winterized and real! Never again would he see Angela's beautiful smile, never again would he hear his mother's voice in compassion—or even in reprimand. The only "angels" that appeared were those dressed in dirty, white smocks, with needles in hand, to further "crush, smite, defeat, and route his soul!"

He awoke again without an idea of the time, what day it was, or what had happened. Until, for the third time, he saw the green, slime-covered walls and steel door with its barred glass window framing an ever-present callous, smirking, perverse attendant. Feeling the cold, dirt encrusted floor on which he lay, he knew there was something worse than dirt floors or gray jail bunks on which to sleep. When a paper plate appeared through a small trap door with a sloppy, mucous-looking substance, purported to be food—he made a commitment: if God gave him a second chance, he would never again complain about, nor refuse a meal.

Then screaming shouting souls, lost and afflicted with pain, agony, and misery, echoed through the odious, obscene corridors of this forsaken place. They seemed to end in his lonely, cold cell, festering, terrorizing, and tormenting his aching soul. He ceased praying and shuddered at the thought that crossed his mind, '*Am* I in Hell. Oh, man, I am in #$@%$#@ Hell . . . not Purgatory!'

Hell was not a place where demons, dressed in long-tailed red nakedness, roasted lamenting sorrowful souls over huge open pits of intense, molten fires for all eternity. Hell, in fact, was icy cold, where demons dressed in dirty white cloaks of hate roasted the imprisoned bodies and minds of the damned in a fire of torment: not external, not visual, but internal, constant, burning—overpowering the mind—eventually changing, twisting, converting each and every soul into replicas of themselves. 'Now it makes sense,' he thought to himself, 'where the devil's apprentices come from.'

Eventually, after enough torture, the damned would in fact become willing subordinates of Lucifer: evil, black-hearted, delighting in their contemptuous, villainous occupation; further recruiting souls through actual defilement and depravation—not fear, intimidation and hope! By the time you reached Hell, fear, intimidation, and hope were dropped from the vocabulary of the damned. Even though you spoke, thought, and dreamed these words in the hope that by doing so you could improve your predicament, it had no basis whatsoever. There is no intimidation, fear, or hope in Hell. There is no reason nor need for these mortal, living words, only physical and mental punishment; continual, without interruption, until having had the personal entertainment of your pain, Lucifer's ever-present army presses on until you are converted without your knowledge, into a facsimile of the horrid living dead. You are an appendage of the devil's sinful, wicked, heinous, corrupt, and immoral soul; perpetuating debauchery, depravity, and inequity. Furthering the outrageous and malevolent atrocities that are synonymous with the word Hell. All semblance of who you were, or might have been, are forever erased, including all memory of decency, loyalty , virtue, morality, goodness, love, compassion, and kindness.

'Do I deserve such punishment? Could anyone really deserve this? It is not human! It's Hell! Yes! That's what it is! Hell!' He wanted to cry but knew he could not show his emotions in such a manner, so he flew into a furious and uncontrollable rage.

From that moment on, whenever he felt an emotion that would bare his inner-self and show weakness, he would throw a tantrum; he'd hit someone; cause a fight or change the situation by starting an argument. Using fear and intimidation he would hide behind that paper wall he had erected . . . thin . . . ready to tear at the slightest breeze—boasting of accomplishments, endeavors, real or imagined, before anyone could decipher his own fears and intimidation. Loudly, boldly, he would create in a split of a split-second a personality, complete with mannerisms, ways, and ideals to meet the prescribed circumstance. He became a living, breathing, human-reptilian creature; a chameleon of change, jumping in and out of identities, as one changes into various outfits before picking the right one to wear to an important occasion.

The consequences of this behavior would become both an asset and a detriment to his character development—to his very existence. Success and failure would be his constant companion; with success, like a rocket, taking off in fantastic, phenomenal, leaping bounds; then failure as the rocket sputters; the enormous amount of energy it took to lift off exhausted—its landing pad an ocean of trouble!

Sitting in his cell, sorry, lonely, with fear tearing at his soul, Joe heard the abrupt creaking of the door as it swung on its hinges. Three orderlies gathered around the doorway taunting him as a fourth stepped through the doorway and placed a can on the floor. In this, he was supposed to perform his bodily functions? It was Joe's mistake all the way, as he exploded into the orderly, delivering in one blow his pent-up and displaced emotions. Attacking with all his strength—yelling, spitting, clawing—he hit the orderly with the can of refuse, urine and all. Then he slung the plate of slime they called food right in his face. Standing over the prostate man, he declared his rights as a man of respect and stormed toward the door.

The respect he received was a wrestling match with the other three orderlies—enraged, screaming soldiers of the devil's brigade; their weapon of choice, the stainless steel stilletto of sleep found its mark—sending him drifting . . . floating . . . into a cold, semiconscious state.

After several days of this "treatment" by the welcoming committee, Joe was weak and mentally defeated. It wasn't until someone finally realized he was sick with pneumonia that a doctor was summoned to treat him. The M.D. gave him another dose of tranquilizer, sent him to the infirmary and prescribed shock treatment.

No ink blots, no questions, no nothing.

Joe awoke on a stretcher; arms, legs, and torso restrained by large leather straps with huge silver buckles locking them down. A strap was placed across his brow and around the bed, thoroughly immobilizing him. Then, while one attendant shaved little round circles into his scalp another smeared a vaseline-like substance on each spot. It felt weird and Joe begged them to tell him what they were doing.

"Don't worry, kid, it's just a test. It'll be over in a few minutes."

Thin wires, with disc-like objects on the ends, were placed at both of Joe's temples and each bald spot. They forced a piece of leather-covered wood between his teeth and told him to relax. . . . Right!

Zap! . . . the current of electricity shot through his body.

Dazed . . . trying to gather his thoughts . . . fuzzy images . . . blurry vision.

"Wait . . . . . . uh . . . listen . . . ah . . . stop . . . please . . ."

Zap! . . .

"Fath . . . Moth . . . ah . . . phew . . . just wait a min . . ." Zap!

Steady buzzing, buzzing, buz . . . buz . . . buz . . . Zap! . . .

Zap! . . .

Simian creatures . . . Scrambling . . . Climbing about . . . Screaming . . . Ranting and raving . . . Urinating . . . Curled, clutching hands . . . Devouring their food off crud-infested floors . . .

The appalling nightmare returned in full intensity—tearing, wrenching, cannibalizing his very mind. He was sliding into a seizure when the face of an angel appeared to him: beautiful, kind, with flowing golden hair and crystal blue eyes. She blocked out the vile, evil specter that was consuming his life and soul. The Angel spoke in a harmonious, melodic, trusting voice as she gently squeezed his arm, "Someone made a terrible mistake . . . you're not supposed to be here. You just lie there, sweetie, and everything will be all right."

The words seemed to float along a music bar, making him want to sing along! Golden Angel turned and barked orders to the attendants who quickly moved Joe, bed and all, to B-wing where the other child-patients were staying. "Angel" was soon alongside him wiping the sweat from Joe's forehead and whispering soothing phrases to him. Whenever she touched him, Joe felt waves of gratitude and compassion coursing through his body.

Had his prayers been answered? Did the Angel appear to deliver him to Heaven? Had Hope, Happiness, and Relief arrived in the form of a real Angel in a clean white smock? An Angel that could give orders to bad guys and have them followed without a moment's hesitation? The orderlies had moved his new rolling bed, with him in it, to the West wing of the hospital and into an infirmary full of bright joyous colors, clean, white-sheeted beds, and happy kids his own age! It was a miracle rescue!

By evening, Joe was asking everyone who came into his room for the name of the lady with the blonde hair—the Angel.

"Excuse me," he said to the candy-striper who brought his meals, "Where is the nurse with the blonde hair that sent me here?"

"I don't know any nurse on this floor with blonde hair. You just eat, O.K.?"

"Doctor, who's the tall nurse with the blonde hair and blue eyes?"

"Just a second, let me finish these notes. . . . there . . . now, a tall blonde nurse you say? Wish we had one; preferably single too. No, there's no blonde, blue-eyed nurse, or doctor for that matter, on this staff that I know of."

"Sure you do, she's the one that made those jerks stop zapping me. When she talked, they listened . . . and moved quick-like."

"You got me, kid. This is where you're supposed to be. That's all I know."

Time had just evaporated. The hours Joe had computed were, in fact, days; the days, weeks; the weeks, months. The bald spots on his scalp, the marks and bruises on his body, his total weakness, were proof of his experience. Throughout those days of treatment Joe's mother had been making futile, desperate attempts to free him. She was not allowed to visit him—the explanation: "It would be better for him if you didn't." She called everyone, including their priest, but for some reason. his "several days" of examination had been prolonged into *three months* of electric shock torment!

Chapter 15: Nourishing the Pain

Old Man Bianco, his vocal voice
stripped of all its octave choice
creaked and crowed in age and vice
"Liquor, tobacco, you pay the price!"

After Joe was released from the hospital, he discovered he had a "Father Figure"—courtesy of "Tough Joe Pag", the owner of a bar called The Cheetah Lounge in Queens, New York. Jeanette was working there now. She had started dating Joe-Pag while little Joe was being evaluated. Jeanette had not married Joe-Pag—but *he* sure acted like she had! Joe Pag had little Joe released into his custody with several stipulations: Joe had to obey Joe-Pag without question. Eventually he had to make amends to his friends for damages, and he had to receive counseling from the Catholic Church . . . every day.

Joe Pag picked him up from the hospital in a new blue Cadillac. While he drove he used a cigar as a pointer to drill his message home. "Youse can't treat your mudder that way—youse cost me a lot of dough. You cause any mo' $%#$ an I'll kick your butt! Your fa'der wud be ashamed of your $%#$. I knew im well. You gonna straighten out and gid wid da program!"

Since Joe-Pag was responsible for engineering little Joe's counseling at St. Joseph's Catholic Church in Queens, he was determined to turn Joe into his spitting image—complete with vocabulary—while punishing him for Salvatori "Sally" Donatelli's loss.

It turned out Sally owned the resort that burned down, and Joe-Pag was his best friend. Joe-Pag informed the priest that little Joe needed counseling to save his soul—then promptly donated $500 to the Rectory Renovation Fund. After two months of this assistance—"That's not how you handle this situation, give me your hand!" WHACK! WHACK! WHACK!"— Joe was determined to wake up from the nightmare that began that rainy day so long ago!

By the age of eleven, Joe had journeyed a lifetime, his small brain packed to capacity with hardship and its loyal companions, hopes and dreams. His solution? The first opportunity he got, he ran away.

The going was difficult. Joe slept in hallways (the top-floor landing next to the roof door was the best) especially if the building's boiler chimney ran alongside the outside wall where heat would radiate through the wall! The only problem with this scenario was the fact that you'd have to turn constantly all night long, like some rotisserie, warming one side of your body at a time. Joe ate his meals by roaming the A&P super market; eating as he went—until he got caught and turned over to Ball and Jolly:

Clothing ragged and worn, eyes darting about in terror, an uneaten portion of bread squeezed into a dough ball in his hand, dripping melted snow and mud onto a trail of torn and pilfered packages . . .

"Sonny, is your mother in the store?"

Silent, head downcast, mind clicking like a two dollar slot machine. Pictures, images revolving with no end in sight. . . no prize.

His wrist is clenched without protest as he is dragged to the office. Once there, nose running, face red with shame, the questions continue.

"Where do you live? Who do I call to pay for all of this? Let's see, chocolate chip cookies, one missing—potato chips, a handfull-gone—one loaf of Italian bread . . ."

"I'm sorry, Sonny, but I'm gonna havta call the police."

Swaggering through the door, Ball and Jolly again, their stoic faces unmask. "Well, looky here! Yummy Yummy!"—child-eating giants who prefer children named Joe—offspring of deceased gangsters!

The car pulls into an alley way. Doors open and slam shut . . . crunch, crunch . . . goes the snow under heavy-booted feet of long-legged dragons, to be compressed into sheets of thin, dark ice. Clung! The back door opens and blue-sleeved arms reach into the interior to snatch him out. Whap! The blow catches his face and knocks him to the frozen ground. Voices . . . hazy . . . a mist of confusion . . . jig-sawed words. "You think you're . . . your fath . . . I'll . . ."

Whap! Stars explode, deep red flashes of light move in tune to the choppy language confusing his mind. Dizzy. 'Speak!' he commands his paralyzed mind.

Bang! Wop! Boom!

Sounds and grunts piercing the air . . . strange ringing . . . pounding . . . a surf . . . SMACK!

The numbness is knocked from his ears . . . a radio's blaring . . . its voice in emergency.

The giant . . . blue monsters . . . turning!

A voice inside his head commands . . . demands . . . RUN!

He rolls and scoots the alley . . .

Behind him, crunching sounds in rapid sequence; louder!

'Don't look back! You might turn to stone or something.'

Willing his feet to move . . .

You have to reach the alley through-way under the building.

"STOP! STOP!" shouts pierce his concentration.

'You gotta reach the steps . . . take you under the building . . . to the other side . . . alley divides into ten more! You've got to make it.'

A slip on the stairs . . . tumbling through garbage cans, full . . . stacked . . . blocking the entrance . . .

'Daylight ahead! Forget the bleeding leg!'

"STOP! HALT! WHEN I GET . . ."

'Climb the cans! Climb the cans!'

Ankle bruised . . . I feel the pain . . . I feel pain . . .

'The pain will keep you going! . . . feel the pain . . . Scurry right. Turn left . . . Go straight . . . Turn right . . . Lungs on fire . . . KEEP RUNNING, THEY'RE RIGHT BEHIND YOU!'

'An empty apartment? There on the second floor of the Marine Terrace Apartments? Wonder why they call it Marine Terrace . . . it's a dump! Along the wall . . . go along the wall! Hide your footprints along the wall! Up the stairs! On the roof! Over the roof! Down the side . . . Jump! Jump!' the voice commands.

'IT'S TOO HIGH.'

'You gotta jump! . . . JUMP!'

Jumping onto the fire escape landing, scurrying down two flights.

Break the window! Fall into the apartment . . . FALL!

Holding his breath . . . peaking through the corner of the window.

Voices . . . "Where the heck did he go? See any footprints in the snow?"

"@#$# NO!"

* * *

Compared to hiding in white and black checkered hallways that dotted Joe's lonely landscape like craters of a cold and dusty moonscape, living in abandoned apartments was a major step up in life—Joe even felt a sense of safety.

Marine Terrace was a series of interconnected three-story buildings, each with underground alleys and interconnecting fire-escapes; perfect for eluding anyone or anything in a moment's notice. The area he chose began at the corner of the East River and the Con-Ed Power Plant, and ended at the intersection of 21st Avenue and 21st Street. Joe soon discovered he could simply turn on the power and gas in the basement of each building.

Using the gas stoves, Joe set up "mobile" homes throughout his new neighborhood; alternating between apartments at his whim, or danger. During the day, he seldom left his secure hide-outs, and when he did, it was in the safety of a maze of alleys and hallways. By the time anyone figured out an apartment was being used he'd switch to another. In an emergency he could always pick a hallway. Experience taught him when an apartment he had commandeered was about to be rented, or when an occupied one would soon be available. His main—and constant—problem remained nourishment; he spent most of his time scavenging for food or thinking about what he'd eaten last, and when.

"Let's see, two spoonfuls of ketchup, one stale piece of bread."

"Didn't the teacher say we needed two glasses of milk a day?"

"Well, I'll drink half a glass of the stuff I got from the milk box of the Sweeny family."

"Left two bottles, should have taken another."

"Naw, I shouldn't!"

"Nice of them to share . . . I know they wouldn't mind."

"I'll make up for drinking only half a glass by getting another bottle tomorrow!"

Though an occasional quest to an outlying food store, or a raid on the early morning deliveries left outside major neighborhood grocery stores, delivered extra goodies, the bulk of his rations came from his explorations of newly emptied apartments—Joe got there before the clean-up crews arrived. It was on one such raid that Joe had his first personal exposure to hard liquor and cigarettes.

The apartment had been abandoned after a raid by the police. Joe had been keeping an eye on it since a group of men came in the middle of the night and emptied it of all furniture and valuables. After three weeks had passed and only trash remained, Joe climbed the fire-escape, placed a towel on the windowpane next to the lock, and with a quick and solid blow, silently knocked a hole in the glass. After turning the catch, he climbed through, and began rummaging through the garbage scattered throughout the four rooms. It was not long before he discovered a half-full bottle of Smirnoff vodka and a carton of Marlboro cigarettes. He wound up smoking the cigarettes and drinking the vodka to relieve the boredom, and prove to himself that he had become a man . . . he got so sick he couldn't move for two days!

While Joe waited out the rest of the cold winter, his main staples were condiments he recovered from his apartment "explorations":

mustard; ketchup; left-over sugar; and other junk that had little substance . . . but they did keep him alive two-and-a-half months until spring's sunshine and warmth delivered melting snows, neighborhood kids . . . and the police.

Chapter 16: Harvesting the Hate

Long the Hate, tumbling 'round, absent of boundary, naive as it sounds . . .

Besides all the fact and innuendo, for a long time there had been bad blood between the two cops, Joe-Pep, and Uncle Carmine. Though these cops had been "mobbed up" for twenty years, the brothers refused to pay them and had actually scammed them on several occasions. Joe-Pep thought the two were acting too big for their pants. When threatened with a loss of protection, Joe-Pep had Pauly Ham, their mentor—a wiseguy running the rackets in Harlem—"speak up" about the cops' broad latitude in the way they were "shaking down" these everyday soldiers. When the Mafia Commission heard of this accusation, they called the cops on the carpet and reminded them that over the previous years they'd committed as many crimes as anyone else. Told to lay off the brothers, they obeyed . . . but they were steamed, and watched for opportunities to stick it to Joe-Pep and Carmine . . .

Joe-Pep rounded the turnpike's banked curve at ninety miles an hour, as Gina, giggling and carrying on with the delight of a teenage school girl, hung on to his arm for dear life. In the back of the '61 Caddy, Carmine was yelling at Joe, "Your wife and kids are waiting for ya and you're drivin like a maniac, with a whore in the front seat, shooting her mouth off! Whaddaya think Lou will say if she finds out about you and Gina—and you know she will! When is this garbage gonna end? We gotta work tonight! And you know the facts. Pauly Ham is on his way out. If Pauly's gone we gotta watch our backs! He's the one what got the contract pulled! That guy from Florida is gonna wanna get even! Ya hear me, Joe! Pauly was the one got those jerks off our backs . . . short of whacking them!" Carmine was shaking with rage.

The brothers were still arguing when they came up on the gleaming structure of the Triborough Bridge. They didn't see the car darting onto FDR Drive . . . it nearly side-swiped Joe's sedan.

As the intruder grappled with his steering wheel in an attempt to keep his tires on the road, Joe lost his temper. "You #$%%^%$#-%%$#, who the $#%$%$# do you think you are?" he screamed through the open window at the driver of the careening car. "I'll blow your ^%$^%^&^$ brains out!" he continued, pulling his revolver out and pointing it straight at the guy.

The driver, realizing a madman was pointing a black revolver at him through the window of the Caddy, slammed his brakes to avoid the shots but several hit the car anyway. Carmine had had enough. He yelled at his brother to slow down and pull over.

"Let me out of this #$%$@# car!" he demanded as he tried to open the door of the moving vehicle.

As Joe-Pep slowed down to get off the highway a police cruiser pulled alongside.

"Hey, Pep, pull that piece of $#!@# over."

The two police officers, riding in the cherry-top, pulled up to the curb in back of Joe-Pep's car. Hustling out of their patrol car, Ball and Jolly Green approached the brothers—who had also hit the pavement. Though dressed in custom-tailored uniforms and strutting with an arrogance hard to miss, they were a comical duo. One was extremely tall, probably six-four but thin; the other was short and dumpy. But the laughter abruptly stopped whenever they spoke—having the dubious distinction of law enforcement officers with mob connections—they could shut you down in a heartbeat.

"Listen, you guys think you're it! I been around longer then both of ya. You keep doing this #$#@ and I'll bust you both!" Ball hammered, standing directly in Joe-Pep's face.

"Who do you think your talking to, huh? You're garbage, that's what you are! Pieces of $%#$ on the take! You guys never had the guts to do it no other way," Joe spat back, his eyes flashing.

"Put your $%#$%#$ hands on the car . . ."

Joe-Pep tore into Ball. By the time Carmine and Jolly Green got them apart, Ball's face was a mess.

"Someone's gonna hear about this! You hear me? Your @#$#$#@ not gonna get away with this!" Ball Buster screamed, as Jolly tried to calm him down. Jolly finally convinced Ball to get into the car. Joe-Pep could hear him shouting revenge through the window as they roared off.

Chapter 17: A Bounty of Desperation

Gaby the Gator lived in a swamp
in the muddy water he liked to romp
catching daddy crawfish for dinner he would
rather eat a pizza if only he could.

Gaby the Gator slept in the dark
wished he had a light so he could mark
all the things he wanted from a magazine
A basketball! A dolly! A Nintendo machine!

Gaby the Gator dressed in gator hide
must be something better, he'd confide
I'd rather have Nikes or Reeboks instead
to place underneath my own waterbed.

Gaby the Gator had a boring day
sitting around with no one to play
should I watch the sun set into the trees?
boy, I wish I had my own color TV!

Gaby the Gator moved into a home
away from the swamp he felt all alone
even with his sneakers and his waterbed
Gaby the Gator missed the life he had led!!!

. . . "Hey, Man! Whachoo doin' in here!"
"Nothing."
"Watch you mean nothin'? He asked you a question!"
"Go fly a $#%$%^$# kite or something!"
"Wham." Stars exploded . . .

Spotford Detention Center was a cold, hard, wake-up call: a place that would forever influence Joe's life as a youth. Later, whenever he was stopped by the police during his journeys, he wouldn't tell who he was, or his real age, for fear he'd be returned there . . . He learned it was better to lie and go to a jail for things like vagrancy, than risk return to a place like Spotford.

A bleak, drab, overcrowded building with huge walls surrounded by chain link and barbed wire, Spotford was divided into sections; dormitories and rooms secured with steel doors and wire-reinforced windows. Run by "supervisors"—who seemed in reality ex-Spotford inmates—Spotford relied on the trustee system to keep order.

The power and command of the trustee system was everywhere. Nothing was accomplished without the trustees's approval and assistance. In order to protect themselves and control the super-violent inmates, supervisors chose most of the trustees from the most hardcore inmates. They were given the day to day chore of keeping everyone else in line. A typical morning would begin with a homosexual rape of some child who could not take care of himself. Muffled moans would signal the dawn. Then, "On your feet! On your feet! Make your beds! Make your beds! YOU GOT TWO MINUTES! ON YOUR FEET! TWO MINUTES TO CHOW! "

The inmates, who averaged thirteen to sixteen years of age, would scramble to make their beds in the tight marine corp style. The trustee would flip his quarter, yell, smack, kick, and tear the bed apart. Then, as he ate your breakfast, you scrubbed the floors with a piece of cloth, five-inches-square.

The military chores were not the problem; the trustee system was. No matter how well you did your job, unless you paid them off with sex, violence, cigarettes, or food, your stay would be violent.

"LINE UP, TOE TO HEEL! EYES FORWARD, HANDS AT YOUR SIDE AND OFF THE ASS! DON'T LET ME FIND YOU PLAYING WITH SOMEONE'S ASS! DON'T MOVE YOUR FEET OR YOU LOSE YOUR SEAT!"

"WHAT ARE YOU LOOKING AT! HUH! MR. FANCY ASS! WHAT ARE YOU LOOKING AT! TRUSTEE!"

"YES, SIR."

"TAKE FANCY ASS TO THE SHOWER ROOM!"

The shower room was the worst. The shower room meant being strip-searched and "paddled"—beaten would be the best word. Next time Mr. Supervisor said, "EYES FORWARD," you better believe your eyes would be forward.

Grabbing, shoving, and sexual horseplay would accompany the inmates on their way to the chow hall. And it was here, at the tables, that trustees chose and traded their prey. It was here that trustees made their moves.

"Gimme yo breakfast, pretty boy!"

Now, if you were intimidated and allowed him to take your "munch", he would take your lunch . . . and then . . .

After chow, they would return and begin clean up: Wash, Scrub, Wash, Rinse, Hand Hard Wax, Hand and Foot buff.

Then they would be given a smoke break—the State of New York felt a child could smoke if his parents signed a consent! Cigarettes therefore became the main currency and cause of retribution and intrigue. Trustees traded human beings for smokes; both were a commodity. After the smoke break, they would go to a school room.

Literacy was not on the agenda. Formal education consisted of a street education: breaking into homes and businesses, stealing cars, which booze was best, sex perversion, mugging, how to cause the most damage to the body when getting even, gambling, etc. Usually the teacher, who was a supervisor with a new hat, would play cards with trustees while others were molesting the weak in the bathrooms.

Lunch time, the scene repeated.

Dinner time, the scene repeated.

Two things were assured in Spotford, the first was clean, shiny floors; the other, fear and misery.

At night, after dinner and clean up, inmates were given one hour to watch TV, play pool, or play a few hands of cards. Bets, using the cigarettes and the weak as collateral, were placed without care nor interruption.

Then, to the dorms—or rooms, if you were a trustee!

The worst fear was the dormitory at night. The supervisor made his rounds three times a night and everyone knew. More often than not, supervisors slept the nights (agony) away!

It was during the night that the homosexual attacks occurred with the frequency of the clock's ticks. The grunts of the strong and moans of the weak were horrifying. No one dared "inform" on a trustee or his "friends" who were part of the team. Many a cracked head, swollen eye—even attempted suicide—were testament of the perversion and trepidation that ruled the night.

Once, every two days, the yard would be opened and basketball, cards, and more degradation would be practiced.

Joe's eighth day brought more of the same: "Yo, gimme your dessert!" Through a bruised and blackened eye, he saw the demented, scowling face with terror, hope, and joy . . . all at the same time! He really understood Bernie now. For the past week, while facing the terrible thought of what these angry people could do to him, Joe had hope that if he gave up his food he could avoid the reality of that thought—and with joy he gave up his meals! But today, while standing in line, he saw the trustee who'd hit him and taken the majority of his meals, huddled in a group, pointing at him. When they whistled at him—laughing and slapping each other on the back while they grabbed themselves—he knew they wanted—and intended to get—more.

"HEY, BOY, GIVE ME YOUR ^&*&^%$# DESSERT! YO, SWEET BUNS! COME ON TO THE SHOWER!" Energy, hateful and determined, flashed in angry vibes from the trustee's pores.

"YOU HEAR HIM, PUNK? HE SAID GIVE HIM YOUR %$%^&^% SWEET BUNS! GET UP AND GO TO THE SHOWER!"

How many times would he have to fear? How many times would he be tempted to cry? When would this awful nightmare end? Hands trembling, emotions tearing so loudly you could smell the fear oozing from his pores, Joe vowed he would be dead before he'd go along! Summoning an extraordinary strength, a spiritual strength whose origins would remain a mystery to him for many years, Joe's swollen lips parted and the sound of four years of rage tore through the two hundred inmates who were seated in the chow hall—sweeping silent the unending echoes that pervaded the institution: "ARRAUGHHHHHHHH!"

In that instant of astonished silence, Joe had jumped up on the table, clearing the heads of inmates seated next to and across from him. His hand shot down, snatching a steel tray, and, coming down on the opposite side of the table, slammed it down on the head of a six-foot trustee/demon, dropping him where he stood. Then, twisting as in one practiced movement, Joe threw himself at the trustee table in revenge for all of the young men who had been abused, violated, and tormented. By the time anyone could react, he had struck three more . . .

"Yo! Chow, bro," a familiar voice rumbled through the small sliding door.

Reaching down, Joe pulled the tray into the interior of the five-by-four "ice cell".

"Thanks, man," he said with sincerity.

"Hey, I heard they were gonna let you out next week. Your mother's picking you up. Listen, the guys are proud of what you did. I'm getting out today. When you're released, come by Astoria Park, under the Hell Gate Bridge . . . where the trees are. You know, next to the doors. Remember my name—Paul Wheate."

After the rumble in the chow hall—a rumble that was joined by several "good" trustees and a multitude of inmates—Joe was hustled to the "ice cell."

The ice cell was a five-by-four-foot cell of concrete. No bed. No nothing! They took your clothing and you were put naked in the cell. Total, cold darkness greeted you twenty-four hours a day. He had been on "ice" for two weeks. The trustee—Paul Wheate—who delivered his once daily meal was from his neighborhood. He invited Joe to meet with him and his friends when he got out.

"A friend! At last, my first friend!" Joe was elated.

Part Three: A Beastly Inflation

IN THE YEAR OF THE BEAST NINETEEN HUNDRED AND SIXTY-FIVE . . .

Chaos reigned in the cavern of death. The Beast roared in abstract painful pleasure; tormenting multitudes of newly implanted souls, among them . . .

"So, Captain, you are well on your way. I am pleased with the situation you have connived and subverted. Your training in the black arts is invigorating. Destruction, murder, helpless fear! AND JOE'S PREDICAMENT is pleasing to my heart! I commend your expert handling of the others! Look! See them over there," he said, pointing towards the highest reaches of the cavern.

The Captain searched the living, grotesque masks two-hundred feet above him until he had located all of the minute, familiar visages of his recent acquisitions; each face of bone, their features—minus flesh—intact, their chalk-white, bony lips twisted in spastic grimace. Everywhere he looked, legions of mouths invoked forlorn entreaties to God, desperately anxious to end their personal, living-in-death nightmares. Though reality, maintained through a flowing and ebbing of tides of memory and pain, produced a consistent series of sane recollection and demented torture, it was thoughts of hope—a fact never lost on the Beast—that constantly created new buttons. The Beast would violently push in return for his personal, sadistic pleasure. You never sleep in HELL; never dream in HELL; you are forced to return to memories of good, for good memories were The Beast's tools of anguish—for all eternity. Recalling good memories would only add to the misery of the captives' everlasting predicament.

"So now, Captain, what do you have up your sleeve? How will you continue your intrigue? I have noticed that only one of the participants of this skirmish has invoked He that is Good! But I expect this to change. Why don't you intensify your temptations?"

"Sir, I have implemented a two year program that I am sure will deliver vast amounts of suffering and conversion. He is putty in my hands. I am well on my way to provoking another series of disasters!"

"Be wise, Captain, for the mere invocation from the heart of another of these subjects of yours could well bring down the wrath of The Knight of Good over Evil; He, the Salvation of Man—The Son of God! . . . Then, another personal battle will ensue. Remember, they are well in my hands; their poverty and suffering a fact . . . but do be perfect in your plans. For if you slip, you will join the others!"

"Your Majesty, I am aware of the pitfalls of over-confidence . . . But, I shall succeed!"

"Return to Battlefield Earth and get on with it. I want your full complement of souls. In fact, because you are so sure of yourself, I want an increase of forty thousand subjects to dress my throne over the next fifteen years!"

"But, Sire, forty thousand more souls? How can I . . ."

"HOW CAN YOU WHAT!" bellowed the beast called Satan; the Knight of Evil over Good. "YOU WILL DELIVER SIXTY THOUSAND SOULS! IN *TEN* YEARS! Now, be gone! Remove your lowly, worm-filled vessel from my four eyes or I'LL BLEACH YOUR SKULL!"

Yellow, red, and orange flames of emotion, launched in mighty blasts of sound and motion, splashed the chalk-white, timorous, vanquished souls. A terrified, clamoring repentance, pitched in reverberated horror, flowed over the cavern as Captain Feranzi the second made his exit.

Confused and desperate, Captain Feranzi vowed loudly to meet his quota, now, no matter the situation—"Jeanette, Angela, Carmine, Joe . . . and, Oh Yes! Young, 'innocent, Eddy!'" How many souls could they count for? he thought . . . an avalanche of souls, building in volume, until the very core of humanity is perverted;wrenching the once innocent, into depths of the vile Beast's demented cavern! "How wonderfully evil!" he shouted.

He was no longer confused or desperate! He had the answers! HE HAD THE CHOICE!

Chapter 18: "Street Smart 101"

Hanging out with a "crew," composed of younger brothers of established street hoods, developing into his father's spitting image . . .

The crew consisted of Joe and six other guys: Donny and Danny Lendahan, Paul Wheate, Nicky the Greek, Pete, and Crazy Eddy.

Paul "Pauly" Wheate—the guy who befriended Joe in Spotford—introduced Joe to the crew. Joe's reputation had preceded him, but it was Pauly's interpretation and broadcasting of that reputation that afforded him instant acknowledgment. Of German and Italian descent, Pauly was blonde, powerful in build, and daring. He was the crew's "locator" and driver. He would find cars to steal, plan jobs, and assist in settling disputes. He became Joe's closest and most loyal comrade.

Donny and Danny, younger twin brothers of Jimmy—whose reputation as a street brawler inspired all of these "young punks"—were as opposite as day and night. Donny, a macho Beatle wannabe, complete with hair cut and boots, had a habit of singing the Beatle's most popular tunes: "I Wanna Hold Your Hand," "Michelle," "I Love You," "Yeah! Yeah! Yeah!" In an out-of-tune, deep, monotone voice, crooning with determined and serious facial expressions, he sought the praise he felt he deserved . . . only to receive the lambasting they felt he deserved—which never dampened his enthusiasm for singing. Donny was loyal and always ready for action. You could count on him, even when it was just you and he facing down twenty thugs! On the other hand, his brother Danny, a gentle, quiet, serious person with a tendency to act in an effeminate manner, was prone to disagree with the collective thoughts of the crew. Always arguing the reasons why they should not do something, but never offering an alternative, he was not so popular.

Nicholous Aphrodopolus, a.k.a. "Nicky the Greek", was a giant of a youth. He could pick up a guy who weighed 150 pounds with one hand! Bright and trustworthy, he and his family had recently immigrated to the States from Greece. As loyal as a person could be, he had the personality of a Saint Bernard: very protective and a true follower. The only English-speaking member of his extensive immigrant family, he was overly protected by them. It became a vocation just to come up with excuses for him to join them everyday—but they would manage it.

Crazy Eddy was something else. Born with a growth handicap, his body had remained four-foot-four while his arms had grown extra-normal, almost touching the ground! He had huge amounts of body and facial hair. His voice box was misshapen, causing his speech to be barely comprehensible to anyone but his close friends, family, and the crew. His greatest asset was his ability to rumble and get away from the police by pretending to be crazy! That's how he got his moniker "Crazy"—the law had classified him as deranged.

The final player on this dream team of independence was Big Pete. Big Pete was a mentally handicapped and gullible Puerto Rican—easily manipulated . . .

The crew, standing across the street from Ditmars Boulevard's most famous jeweler; watching the scores of shoppers packing the sidewalks four and five deep, wondering where their next "score" will come from . . ."

"Ah, man, you're #$%$#$% wrong. He'll do it! I know. Pete's got heart!" Joe says out loud—defending a mute question.

Pauly picks up on it immediately. "Let me tell you . . . he ain't cool man. He ain't got no heart!"

"Listen, he'll do it! He's a cool cat, man. Pete is the guy with the largest @#$# of anyone of you!" Joe cuts in.

Pete listens intently.

"Hey, Pete. You know what Pauly said?" Donny whispers.

"No. What?"

"That you couldn't run over to that jewelry shop, break the window, and grab those jewels and watches in the window."

"Oh, yeah?" He tears across the street—in broad daylight—smashes the window, grabs two handfuls of jewelry, and scoots through the crowded streets towards the East River and safety.

Later, the crew meets behind Bernie and Yetta's Candy Store.

"Hey, Pete, that was bad man . . . real bad. You got it, man. You're a man of respect even if you're a Puerto Rican!"

"I did it, didn't I . . . I did it. I'm cool. I'm bad! I could be Italian, couldn't I?"

"Yeah, but listen, we gotta hide the stuff! We got to stash it until the heat dies down. What about them rocks over there?" Joe questions, pointing to a group of rocks by the wall.

They bury the jewelry and everyone goes home to "hit the mattresses" and hide out until the following day . . . while Joe and Pauly sneak behind Bernies and remove the jewels. They immediately go to Fat Joe's pizza place.

"Hey, Joe! We got some swag that'll knock your socks off. A heist from Ditmars Jewelers! Class stuff. Real merchandise! The ladies will flock to tick your clock for a piece of this here stuff!" Pauly shouts as they strut into the small, oily, hot, grease-specked joint.

Fat Joe—a 'he's-with-us guy'—big and fat in guinea tee and chef's hat, sweat pouring from every pore of his body; cigar stub, the same one he has been chewing on for the last week, jutting from the corner of his mouth—snatches a few pieces of the merchandise, gives it a glance and declares, "Dis stuff's paste. Not worth the air youse gize jus polooted my joint wid."

"You're full of #@%^! This stuff's the genuine article! We know cause we snatched the frigging loot!" Joe snaps back.

"Youse gize oughtta watch ya mouds! Dis iz a respectable joint. Wad wood da customer's sayz . . . Huh? I'll giv ya four large, an' a pissa a day fa two weeks."

"Ah, you can do betta dan dat offer," Pauly says, imitating Fat Joe.

"O.K , youse gize got me. I'll give ya seven big ones and five pissa, an dat's my final offa."

The next day the entire crew meet at Bernie's.

"Hey, the stuffs not where we put it!" an excited Pete yells.

"Yo, Pauly, was that James Kirt that you seen when we were leaving?" Joe yells. James was a guy who the crew believed was informing on them. He was their enemy. But, due to his imposing connections with the law, neither Joe nor Pauly could deal their retribution. They decided to leave him alone until they could figure a way to deal with him; and Joe had found a way.

"Yeah! That's who took our stuff—and after all Pete's bravery!"

"Yo, Pete! You gonna let James get away with our stuff?" Danny called over.

"Hell, no! I'm gonna go find him." Pete found the thief and whipped his butt, causing James to hide out for a few months.

"Hey, Pete. Great job! You're the enforcer now! Yeah. You deserve to be paid by the crew . . . we took up a collection. It happens to be part of our war chest, but you deserve it!" Joe says as he handed Pete a brand new, crisp one-hundred dollar bill.

Pete, tears in his eyes, refuses the money but, after the guys convinced him it had been worth the sacrifice to see James put in his place, Pete accepts.

"Hey, Pete. Let's go to Fatso's joint and I'll buy us a pizza!

The crew yelled their war chant and proceeded to go pig-out on pizza Joe "bought."

It was events such as this that demonstrated Joe's intrigue and connivance. His past lessons were paying off through control and command. He had not only rid the crew of its enemy; but he'd given Pete his fair share disguised as a gift—a gift that gave the crew their own enforcer who'd be used on many occasions.

The crew's daily routine was simple. On week days after school, they would meet behind Bernie's and roam the surrounding neighborhoods, planning and scheming, until they made a score—then they would plan the evening's entertainment.

On weekends they would spend the days shoplifting. Basically, two of the crew would enter a store on Steinway Street (made famous by Steinway Pianos) and act like they were fighting. When the manager tried to break it up, the rest of the crew would storm the door and heist whatever they could. In the confusion, everyone would get away and meet at Fatso's Pizza Parlor on 21st St. at 21st Ave. in Astoria, Queens. Fat Joe would buy whatever they had. They'd take the money, divide it up, and sneak into the movie theater with their girls.

Movies became more than entertainment for Joe—they were a great part of his education! Each picture show brought him views of the world—past and present. Where mobster movies reinforced his father's traditional views, shows like *Ben Hur, Sparticus, Gone With the Wind, The Ten Commandments, The King and I, Guess Who's Coming to Dinner?, Robinhood, Boys Town, It's a Wonderful Life,* and *King Arthur,* planted seeds that would eventually change his basic view of life. After each movie, his guys would find him in the library reading about the characters, times, and countries of the show's contents: Swashbucklers, Cowboys, Indians, Romans, Russians, Greeks, Napoleon, Alexander the Great, The French Revolution. They were his fascination, his heroes, his dreams.

Joe soon became torn between what he saw and read and what the crew saw and did! What initially began as a simple plea for friendship, a cry for attention, a need for a father figure, developed into a desire to be accepted. The crew was already established before he arrived, but by the end of three months and several fist fights, he had assumed leadership of this group of wannabes. He named them the Motley Crew—from his first adventure in the Poconos. Soon he was hanging more and more. They would show up at school, leave after roll call, and meet at the church. It was in this majestic atrium of the Lord that they met, not to worship, but to plan their day's events.

Organized religion represented poverty, sorrow and loneliness to Joe. He could not comprehend its message. To him, the individuals associated with the church were the same people who were part of the system. Though he maintained a direct line with Jesus, confusion alternating with lucid reality kept him either on the ropes or in the thick of battle. The family priest had recently told Jeanette that "victory was waiting on the wings of an Angel, an Angel that was slow in coming, waiting for the opportune moment to release the angers, pains, and realities of his existence".

"In other words," Jeanette had commented in agreement, "when he is truly ready."

At five in the evening, he would go home for dinner, wait for the Beast's arrival, then sneak out the bedroom window and climb down the fire escape—joining the guys again. Carmine would pack his bed with a dummy and let him back in before his mother returned from work. When the school called, his sister answered—pretending she was his mother offering excuses. Notices began to arrive as frequently as the mailman. It was easy at first to intercept them before his mother could see them. Eventually, the truant officer arrived at his front door. That's when he went before "The Judge."

Chapter 19: Social Intervention

Smurphy the Smirker stood upon the hill
Jumping and smashing all the daffodils.
Why are you standing on my flower way?
Asked the Lord's nature, dressed in sunny day.
Must be a color, or the way they smell,
Could be the beauty, really couldn't tell!

Smurphy the Smirker stood upon the beach
Jumping and smashing everything in reach.
Why are you standing on my coral way?
Asked the Lord's nature, dressed in tempest day.
Must be the crabsters, or a flocking bird,
Could be the salties, really sounds absurd!

Smurphy the Smirker stood upon the woods
Jumping and smashing everything he could.
Why are you standing on my tree full way?
Asked the Lord's nature, dressed in forest day.
Must be the squirrels, or a tree top snake,
Could be the pine cones, really, give or take!

Smurphy the Smirker lay upon the ground
As the Lord's nature jumped and smashed around.
Why are you standing on my tummy round?
Asked Mr. Smirky, in a pleading sound.
Could it be an omen, or a fit of glee,
Must be the answers that you gave to me!

"The court has found your son to be delinquent. You seem to have no control over his actions. He demonstrates a tendency toward criminal actions. We have decided to send him to a special school in Queens. It is like any normal school—the only difference is it's all boys, and the teachers are trained in dealing with emotionally troubled children. You will take him there this morning and register him." The Judge glanced at the Rolex watch on his arm and then continued, "Before we recess, I'd like you to step forward young man."

Joe stepped up to the sturdy oak table separating him from the bench and stood at attention.

Looking directly at him, the Judge started the ball rolling, determined in its direction, setting a course that would continue for the rest of Joe's adolescent life, "Young man, you are the problem with this country today: a juvenile delinquent who has no regard for your school system, your mother, nor any authority. You, young man, are not owed a single thing! It is your responsibility to overcome your hardships! You have no excuse. When I was a youth my father beat my butt for doing a fraction of what you have done! Our country has done much for your family. Your family came to this country on the goodwill of this nation! Do you truly want to grow up like your father? Do you want your life to end like his? Left on a cold, muddy street for people to step over? Do you?"

"What are you talking about? What do you mean my fa . . . ? Joe interrupted.

"YOUNG MAN. DON'T YOU DARE INTERRUPT ME! I'M NOT YOUR MOTHER! YOU MIGHT FOOL HER, BUT NOT ME!"

Joe was confused, lost, dumbfounded. He had no idea what the Judge was talking about. Pictures of his father, lying on a cold and muddy street, with people walking their dogs over him flashed across his mind in living technicolor. 'Did he mean at the accident site?' he thought to himself.

" . . . and if you appear in my court again, I'll throw the book at you!" Bang! The gavel came down. "Court recessed!"

Joe never had the chance to say anything in his defense; to ask the questions that were rattling around in his head, or to pay attention to anything that occurred after the Judge mentioned Joe-Pep. And Jeanette, feeling the appropriate answer was silence, kept quiet—though this would have been the best place and time for proper intervention. No one knew or attempted to discover the complications of this family . . . continuation ruled the day . . .

A picture of a medieval apparition greeted them upon arriving at the "special school." Stark, lonely, and sinister, the large filth-shrouded building had steel-bar-encased windows and a high, wrought iron fence running completely around its perimeter. There were no children playing in its large playground and athletic yard, and this left Joe with a feeling of foreboding.

Climbing the graffiti blanketed steps to a set of massive steel doors, which creaked and groaned a message of ageless torment, as they swung out and open on tired, rusted hinges, gave Joe second thoughts of entering its darkened, hollow-sounding entrance. No happy sounds reverberated from within; not a single echo of busy, striving students bounced from its stained and dingy, institutional walls. No colors of the rainbow gleamed and shouted with cheer from its bulletin board—only internal memos and warnings of the punishment to be conferred on those the system determined needed it.

The gloom-filled building Joe had entered would become a dungeon to many lonely, desperate, emotionally hurt castaways of an unforgiving society, who, upon abandoning these misfits, continued on its glorious way—while these pupils of the storm relied upon their wits, strength, and fists. Left to fend for themselves, these students of an archaic juvenile system would develop into devious, cold-hearted criminals, who, until they left this mortal earth, would haunt their tormentors.

At the main office they were introduced to the principal. George "Lefty" Simmons seemed to be a tall, easy-going, Afro-American. He asked them to have a seat, while an assistant prepared the paperwork and left the office. In order to wash away the thoughts of his father, which continued to crop up in his subconscious mind, Joe began to concentrate on the pictures on the walls. He noticed there were plenty of pictures of Lefty in boxing rings, but no degrees or testaments of his educational experience. But, he thought, 'If the pictures were correct, maybe he would teach him how to box . . . like a good father figure!'

He tapped his mother on the arm and pointed to the walls. Jeanette, also lost in another world of thought, looked and shrugged her shoulders.

Lefty soon returned, sat down behind his desk, and began speaking of the changes Jeanette would see in Joe after a few weeks of attending his school of "higher" education. Then he stood, gently took Jeanette's arm and, while laughing and joking, escorted her out of the school—leaving Joe to continue contemplating this change in his life.

About twenty minutes later Lefty returned and sat down behind his desk. "So you're the young punk that Judge Milton Gordon sent down? You're a "W.O.P." that's gonna learn that I have the last say! I tell you to jump, and you don't jump, I will kick your @#$!ing Italian butt from here to Italy . . . You %$@#ing understand? Do you?"

Joe was stunned and devastated by the change in this gentle, considerate man. He demonstrated how sorry he felt for himself by acting nonchalant.

"Yeah, man, I understand," he said in his usual casual way.

"You little smart $#@! You address me as 'sir'!" the principal shouted as he jumped up, smacking Joe so hard he saw stars.

Instead of crying, Joe transferred his erupting energy into an anger that splashed red neon across his now grim, rock-hard face. The message to Lefty was ugly and direct, "Kiss my ass!"

"I'll show you who's boss," Mr. Principal said. "Hey, Larry," he asked of his assistant, "what class are the Jones Brothers in?"

"371, with Bartholomy Samuals," Larry replied—as if this was a normal request.

"You! Personally escort "Mr. Wiseguy," and get him signed up in 371."

Joe entered the class and immediately realized the pupils, a racial mix of White, Puerto Rican, and Black, were all five inches taller than him. Hostility greeted him the moment he entered the door. 'This is gonna be a bummer,' he thought to himself.

As the day went by, the principal called the Jones Brothers in for a consultation—Joe was frightened the rest of the day. When the bell rang, he grabbed his coat and rushed for the exit . . . he didn't make it in time. The Jones Brothers, with several of their cohorts, caught him in the stairwell.

"So, you're the %$#%t %$#@ eating W.O.P. that thinks he's too good to be here!

The entire group began taunting him.

"Let's just $#%@ him up!" another cut in. "Yeah! He can take his butt to the hospital after we're through with him!"

Joe had no choice but to go on the offensive and hit the first guy who began the situation—it was his last punch! They grabbed him and started to beat the heck out of him. Bam! Whack! His mouth was bleeding, his nose broken, his eye swollen and red. Before long, the principal "happened" to arrive and rescue him.

After a brief appearance at the infirmary, he was allowed to leave and go home. All the way home he held his tears and grief; thoughts of his father. Oh! How he wished he could be here to help him! He was devastated! He had to go to school the next day and face that same group. Arriving in his neighborhood, he snuck to his apartment—lest the crew see him in the shape he was in.

Entering his apartment, his mother took one look at him and started yelling, "What the heck happened? Who did you get upset in order to deserve such a beating? What am I gonna do with you!"

Hurt, sad, and expecting sympathy, Joe strutted "without a care" to his room to clean up and get ready for dinner. But once behind the security of the wood door, he fell upon his bed, begging God to end his life.

A loud rapping upon his bedroom door aroused Joe from the sleep of exhaustion he had drifted into. He tried to ask who it was, but a sharp pain shot through his jaw before he could utter a syllable. Angela's voice, asking if he was all right, broke through his pain and he stood up, opening the door for her to come in. She entered and without saying a word, put her arms around him, and started crying.

Through Angela's tears, Joe knew she could feel the pain of his soul; his inner-spirit that longed for the old ways. She knew of his suffering, both physical and mental. She could feel his embarrassment, his feeling of failure, his shame. A wave of compassion rushed through his body, touching his heart, relieving his mental and physical pain. Her understanding and sympathy were demonstrations of emotions long absent from the world of those infected with The Curse!

With his strength and pride once more renewed, Joe stood straight as an arrow and wrapped his arms around his sister. Reversing the roles, he once more became the man of the house that had emerged that rainy day in '61, "I'll be fine. Don't you cry any more! It'll be OK." Then he started kidding her about her concern. "What? You my mother, or what?"

Soon they were both laughing and joking around, with him making comical, distorted faces, complete with swollen, red marks and bruises—she imitating.

It was in this way they buried the questions; questions she knew from her own traditional training, were not to be asked. As a man, he was expected to deal with his own troubles . . . No matter what!

They both were sharply brought back to reality by Jeanette calling them to dinner; a ritual as inviting as kneeling in a church for an hour while reciting one hundred Hail Marys as twenty nuns and priests recanted all of your sins to the public . . .

Chapter 20: Ancestral Retribution

— *Lisa Chapo* —

Become a wreath, my flower of youth
and live a rainbow garland
kaleidoscopic in nature
brilliant in stature
boasting tomorrow's song

Become that song
my budding minstrel
always bold and strong
be a melody of harmony
in a chorus of lasting love

Become that love, my cherished friend
and bless your endless run
of faith in God
and tests of will
and bestow a rainbow garden

Gathered around the old, metal-legged, formica-covered table, Carmine took one look at Joe and asked in a loud voice, "What happened to you?!"

"I got hit with a truck," Joe mumbled sarcastically through his swollen mouth.

"Really, you did? When?" he asked, leaning forward intently.

"Carm, come on, I'm kidding . . . it was just an accident . . ." He trailed off. 'Just an accident' had become the answer to all questions which could not be answered, and to all situations that were reserved for their own memories—to be dealt with and recalled only by those who had reserved them under: "Accident/Personal."

Joe's desire to brush away any mention of his mishap was of paramount concern to him. He knew how a simple situation could snowball into a major confrontation at the dinner table. All Italian men learned from a young age not to discuss business with children and women.

"Let us say our prayer of thanks," Joe said. Everyone folded their hands as he led the blessing. They passed a bowl of pastabazool, a concoction of pasta, peas, beans, onions and garlic, in a light red sauce—a favorite staple of his mother, because it was cheap, nutritious, and filling—around the table. His brothers—Carmine and Eddy—began to eat with relish.

Angela and Joe, on the other hand, talked of her day at school as they picked and played with their food—to them, the memory of great Italian cooking brought back vivid memories of Joe-Pep. Jeanette, running around in a frenzy as she dressed for work, approached the table and reminded Angela and Joe there were starving children all over the world. She ended with, "Look at your brothers. See, they eat everything because they understand!"

The evening's meal was progressing like any other. At first, Angela and Joe never blamed their brothers for the stress that dinner, with their help, heaped on their lonely hearts. But he knew they'd eventually have to put them in their place; it was affecting everything they did. Lately, at the dinner table, all he could do was think about getting even. Joe finally frowned at Carmine when he started to take his "I'm a good guy" too far. He started to say that Joe probably caused the accident that resulted in his Halloween mask. Mimicking his mother, he harassed Joe for running away and causing him anguish—a word he had no idea how to pronounce correctly, let alone understand.

The developing argument caught the attention of Connie, who had just entered, sack in hand, stomping and swaying as she asked matter-of-factly, "Jean, is this young man giving you a hard time?"

His mother, caught up in the situation, told her to punish him by limiting him to his room. Connie did this immediately, causing his sister to stick up for him, which caused his mother to tell Angela to clean the dishes, throw the garbage out, iron the clothes, shut her mouth, and then go to her room. It was time! He really had enough! His sister and he looked at each other as they parted from the table. He winked and left for his room.

As he sat in his room, sounds of his crew yelling their war cry, "Ave' Ho!," reverberated through the streets and up to his room. He opened the fogged-up window, yelling for them to come back later and climb the fire escape to Angela's room.

Later that night, after his mom had gone to work and the Beast had retired to *The Honeymooners,* he crept to Angela's room. He lightly knocked on the door that one of Joe Pag's men had built for them and she opened it. He motioned for her to keep quiet, going to the window to inform the crew to come on up.

After everyone climbed into the closet, he told them of the situation at school. He was fed up with his situation and had no one to turn to, but his friends. After informing them of the dilemma, Donny's eyes lit up as he told them the Jones brothers were part of a black crew that worked for the Gallo brothers—"made guys" of the mob who used black guys as hitters, drug runners, and collection strong-arm troops for some of their territories. They came up with an idea. But first, his immediate problem . . .

Pauly, Donny, and Joe crept into the kitchen and grabbed Carmine, who was eating graham crackers. He placed his hand on his cracker-filled mouth, while Danny opened the clothes dryer and shoved him in—along with the balance of the large pot of pastabazool! Nicky turned the machine on—around and around went Carmine—with his favorite meal.

They retired to Angela's room to celebrate. Each time they heard the Clump . . . Clump . . . Clump . . . of Carmine taking his tasty ride, they cracked up! By the time Connie realized the dryer—which had its heater disconnected and was not supposed to be turned on—was running, they were screaming with laughter. She lifted herself from the couch and stomped to the kitchen to rescue a crying and garlicky Carmine . . . then she went on a rampage!

Hearing the steamroller approaching with all her fog horns blaring, they rushed to escape through the lone window, but they didn't make it. With a, "Who the @#$! is in there? Who in the heck put Carmine in the dryer?" the door, closed and triple locked, was ripped off its hinges. A sight both comical and frightening greeted them.

Aunt Connie, door in one hand, metal Electrolux vacuum cleaner extension in the other . . . glaring . . . wild eyes stuck in her red, bloated face . . . gaping, wide-open mouth . . .. screaming obscenities without pause. The crew went into emergency escape mode! What a racket they caused! Everyone was running, pushing, squeezing through any opening they could find.

Nicky the Greek's huge frame stuck in the window.

The Beast senses opportunity . . . Attack! Attack!

Beating Nicky on the butt with her "magical wand."

Nicky yelling for rescue, (they weren't frightened; on the contrary, they couldn't stop laughing!)

The rest, running in circles, laughing so hard their stomachs hurt.

Pete tries to escape through the giant's legs . . .

The Beast stands in a wide stance, swinging, grabbing.

Pete gets stuck!

The giant, steam-rolling Beast displays an amazing dexterity for dance and action, holding the door and pummeling Nicky while performing a Polish, foot-stomping Polka on top of Pete.

That's when Pauly, Donny and Joe rushed her as if playing tackle for the New York Giants.

. . . a tremendous crash . . .

. . . driving her through the doorway . . .

. . . Uh Oh!

. . . No! . . .

. . . not into mother's only remaining piece of fine furniture!

. . . the heirloom of their ancestors! . . .

THE NIGHTSTAND!

The nightstand, handed down from her mother, handed down from her father, handed down from his father . . . who made it by hand. It had traveled the world of the family legacy, until its present, intertwined relationship with The Curse of Alphonso. "If only it could talk," Jeanette would often say.

It was supposed to bring good luck to all who protected it. It held several ornate, silver-framed photographs of various family members who once owned and ruled its predicament. A picture history of the great father figures who had produced the heritage that ruled his life. Did they own it . . . or it them?

NO! NO!

Crash . . . Boom . . . !

There sat Connie . . . dazed . . . dress pulled-up . . . exposing large, meaty thighs . . . red cherry peppers dangling in her hair. She looked like a large, distorted Christmas tree, with a loaf of Italian bread stuck between its limbs. Dazed, confused, angry; she was up in a flash and ready to begin again. The crew, sensing they had lucked out thus far; beat it to the door and freedom.

Figuring it was a done deal—the trouble he was in so far—he went for broke. Starting with the church and ending with the Jones Brothers.

Joe gathered the crew and walked to the church and its sanctuary. Entering the open doors, they began looting the poor boxes. As the guys filled a paper sack with change, Joe felt a draft of cool air cross his brow. He stopped dead still and looked down the aisle toward the alter. He wanted to shout to the guys that they should forget about the money, but his mouth wouldn't respond. His voice was as frozen as the plastered images which stood upon their pedestals gazing mutely at this sacrilege with pity.

As they were leaving, a Priest approached them: "My poor boys, what have you done?"

"Taking what belongs to us!" Pauly stated emphatically. "We are the poor, thank you!" he continued as they trooped down the stairs—laughing all the way.

Joe's guilt, pushed aside by the emotional turbulence of the past years, raised its head, but using excuses of hard times and the reactions of society—no one really cared—he managed to will it back in its shell.

Stopping by a liquor store, Nicky used his fake ID to buy a bottle of Muscatel. They walked to Astoria Park, sat under the Hellgate Bridge, and drank the cheap wine.

Throughout the night they toasted and incited their bravery and their plan for tomorrow's vengeance on the Jones Crew. Then the crew went home to warm, happy beds; and he, to a dimly lit hallway, where people walking their dogs stepped over him as he slept on the cold, hard, checkered tile floor.

At 4 a.m. he awoke and went through the neighborhood rousing the guys. After stealing some bagels, rolls, and milk from the front of the A&P Supermarket (deliveries were made at 4 a.m. and left in front of the store) they ate their breakfast and headed for the dungeon.

There were nine guys in that hallway at school when Joe got beat up; *they* were just six. The guys they were going to show a lesson to, were bigger than Joe, but not his guys. They arrived at the school at 5 a.m., pried the bars off a window, shattered the glass, and climbed through. Positioning themselves at the top and bottom of the exit stairwell landing, Joe entered the hallway and waited for the arrival of the Jones Brothers.

By 7 a.m. the school began filling up. Because the entrance and exit stairwells were separate, the crew remained hidden, patiently waiting for Joe's plan to begin.

Joe had never thought of racial issues before. He never used slang terms that were given to the various racial groups that made New York so rich in culture. In fact, his crew was composed of various ethnic backgrounds. But this situation required him to learn and say new things. The bigots had arrived in his life and were demanding loyalties he would surrender to. The devil was in a bragging mood; triumphantly on his way to another victory.

"Hey, you ^%^&$%# $%%#$! Yeah! You #$%^%$! Come and get a piece of this if you think you can!" Joe yelled through the crowded hallway at the gangsters who had assembled.

The Jones Brothers took up the challenge and charged toward him. "Get the #$@$ing W.O.P. boy!" they yelled, as they turned the steam up.

He dashed for the exit stairwell, opening the door with determination. Giving the Motley Crew war-chant, "Ave' Ho!"—taken from the Ave' Maria sung in church!—he jumped down an entire landing, turned, and watched with glee as the Jones Crew entered the stair well unprepared for what was to be their greatest surprise!

The group rushed into the stairwell and down a flight of stairs before they had any clue they'd been set up! As they scrambled to gain position, they were greeted by a flurry of fists and pipes—the Motley Crew destroyed the leadership of the Jones' Brothers Crew.

Strutting, heads held high, chests inflated, gloriously cruising the hallway, they commanded the respect of students who parted way to allow plenty of room for the Motley Crew and its half-pint leader to swagger away.

The police were called in. Though no one received severe enough injury to require more than the attention Joe had received for his own injuries, the cry went out, these criminals have to be punished!

Their great educator, ego permanently damaged, waged a war to get Joe punished for his "transgression" against his sacred right to abuse, humiliate, and embarrass anyone he chose.

Word of the revenge of the Motley Crew spread far and wide. As all stories go, by the time it hit the social workers and court system, they had killed, mutilated, and buried the entire school. They, the defenders of the just, had become perpetrators of the unjust.

Joe began once more to live on the streets and in empty apartments throughout the neighborhood. Smoking Marlboro reds and drinking rum and coke, he commanded respect wherever he went; backing it up with a fist or pipe. He began to discover bits and pieces of information on the various operations of the wiseguys who occupied the neighborhood. He soon discovered many of the older associates treated him with a sort of special deference. Talk of his father and other relatives trickled down to him.

He began to pump information in his quest to discover what happened to his father. One guy in particular, an old man named Feranzi, took a special interest in him, and Joe was proud of it. By his fourth month he had established a reputation for taking care of business. Feranzi began sending wiseguys to him when they needed a car for a "job," or some windows broken.

"Hey, Joe, Feranzi sent me. We need a red, '62 Volkswagen . . . you get a hundred bucks. Deliver it to Junior's place—here's an advance of fifty."

Pauly would heist the cars; Donny deliver them. After a while it became easy. They dressed in fine clothes and always had money. Joe was even dating several girls, but one in particular caught his attention: Aggie McDonald.

She had red hair, freckles, and a smile that lit up his world. Her family was originally Catholic, but converted to fundamental Christianity. She would preach the GOSPEL all the time. The crew would get upset every time she was around. But Aggie provided a semblance of understanding and love—two items of his vocabulary which were constantly missing. How he met her was a story unto itself . . .

* * *

Early that spring, after performing his morning functions in the bathroom of the Shell gas station—a place used to keep a toothbrush and comb—on 21st St. at 21st Avenue, he stepped out and into the bright, sunny day. He immediately noticed a beautiful young lady in a desperate situation. A group of thugs surrounded her, grabbing and harassing her. He approached this collection of free-booters and, as his education happened to be taught in the movie theaters of Steinway Street and the libraries where he hung out while the crew was in school or at home, challenged these "Black Knights" to a duel in the proper way.

"Remove your hands from the lady!"

They took up the challenge . . .

Chapter 21: Love, Sex, and Change

I miss you, I miss you!
I shall always miss you!

Gone are the simple ways,
that we, as lovers, shared our days.
A chance, perhaps, to love upon the shore,
Kissing, embracing, craving so much more,
Love was like a new life beginning,
Born into this world innocent and thrilling.
I miss you, I miss you,
I shall always miss you!

Our fervent thirst, our impatient hunger;
satiated by a love as strong as thunder.
A thunder that would herald a raging storm,
and wash away our naive and exalted dawn.
Oh! Do you remember,
what we shared that late November?

I miss you, I miss you!
I shall always miss you!

Lying . . . in the lap of a princess; she, wiping the evidence of misfortune off his face with a damp cloth. Green eyes, warm freckled face, stirring his emotions. Emotions he fights helplessly to dispel.

He was in love! He continued to act like he was hurt; he didn't want the feeling to lapse as they always seemed to. His first serious relationship was in bloom, and this experience would lead to the most unusual situation of the streets. Joe's image of Aggie as a princess, combined with his view of respect led him to cherish the relationship to the point he honored her by refusing to engage in sex (all of the guys were engaging in sexual intercourse by now) with her. He made a commitment that he would live up to. This extraordinary event was not lost on the crew. She became a liability to the guys. From this moment on, they would fear the ending of the relationship of the brotherhood and begin to plot her removal from the scene! In the meantime, Joe made an attempt to lose his virginity to a street-walker, ten years older than he was.

Her name was Carmen, and she was a Puerto Rican prostitute who was the neighborhood squeeze. One night after Joe dropped Aggie off at her home, he ran into Carmen on the street. After a half-bottle of rum, in the back seat of a '49, flat-head Plymouth, the opportunity presented itself. Carmen sat on the back seat teasing Joe.

Joe—slightly intoxicated, absent of his blue-jeans; aroused—suddenly figured he was finally at the gate of pleasure. He was actually with a naked chick! Yes! He was gonna do it!

Carmen settled back on the wide seat. Her feet up on the seat cushion, knees bent out, wide open, pulling him towards her. Her hand guiding him, taunting him, pulling him . . .

Joe, in the darkness, kneeling on the floor, coming closer to her, desperate to view this wonderful object of man's pounding desires.

A car roars down the road, headlights piercing the darkness. It zooms past the Plymouth; its glaring lights illuminating, for a fleeting moment, the sacred object of his desire! Joe thinks, 'Unreal! Is that what men fight, lie, connive, and dream for! I bet, if I asked father how could something so ugly cause so much pleasure, he would have replied, 'When you get older, you will learn that many things ugly can cause you pleasure!' But, before he can lose his excitement to this stunning revelation, Carmen grabs and pulls him to her.

He is at the door, poised and ready, her hand guiding him.

This is it! This is what all the guys talk about! He's ready! He begins to push . . . and wham—he ejaculates all over the seat!

Later he would brag to everyone that he had "done it," and then find out everyone who had "done it" with her, had to go to the doctor to get shots for a venereal disease she was transmitting like a one-woman plague! But Joe was smart, he just made believe he'd gotten the injection!

As Joe fought a battle between the message of His Word, as taught by Aggie, and the word of the street, orders were coming in for four and five hundred dollar jobs. One night, he was approached by a guy who was from a crew captained by some guy named Tony Black. Tony wanted cigarettes: two hundred cartons. Paul and Nicky picked out the place and planned the job.

Aggie heard of the job from one of the guys, who thought if he told her, she'd get upset and leave Joe alone to the crew!

She did tell Joe that what he was about to do was wrong. She said it was getting worse—the crimes—and he would have to pay one day. She quoted Biblical verses in an effort to back up her statement. He flatly stated that he had to meet the guys and quickly left. As he trotted to their prescribed meeting place, he heard her tears of grief over and over in his head. He kept thinking that it would be all right—it was a simple job!

Good Food was a supermarket on 21st Avenue in Astoria, Queens. They agreed Joe would keep "chicky"—a look-out that kept an eye for cops. Paul and Nicky would disable the alarm system, climb the roof, cut a hole in it, and wait in the back. Donny, Danny, and Crazy Eddy would climb inside, load the cigarettes in carts, and deliver them to the rear door, where Paul and Nicky would load them up. This left Pete to be the intermediary between Joe and Paul. If something went wrong, Joe would signal Pete, Pete would yell to Paul, and everyone would make a dash to a prearranged safe house—which was a nearby empty apartment.

On the night of the job everyone was ready. A '58 Buick Special—stolen by Pauly in Flushing, Queens—was parked during the day at the rear exit. The crew left it there so any cops who saw it would assume the owner worked there and store employees would get used to seeing there. That night, as they walked toward their rendezvous, they passed Bernie's. The thugs, growing increasingly jealous of the Motley Crew's success, started their symphony of cat calls and harassment.

"Hey, look who's across the street," Joey Esposito yelled. "It's the Mickey Mouse crew, M-I-C-, see you real soon, K-E-Y—why? . . . because we're gonna kick your butt! You are $#@#ing m-i-c-e."

Joe returned the talk, "$#%@ you!" They took off with ten of the older guys chasing them down the street. As they turned the corner, a police cruiser was waiting.

Although Joe had mostly overcome the problems of his congenital club feet, he still suffered occasionally from the after effects of this affliction. He could walk as well as any healthy person, but couldn't run a lick! He would see nothing but the rear-ends of his buddies as they steadily increased the distance between themselves and the hunter . . . leaving Joe to become the prey. It was a standing joke within the Motley Crew, "You don't have to outrun the cops, you just have to outrun Joe!" Since he was always left behind when his guys hit their after-burners, Joe developed his gift of communication; learned how to talk his way out of tight spots—sometimes it didn't work . . .

Hands shot out and grabbed him, throwing him against the car. "You $#@%ing little piece of #$@%!" Ball Buster screamed at him as he beat him with his open hands, slapping and pulling.

"He's like his father—a %$#%ing punk!" Jolly Green Giant added, joining in the evening's entertainment.

"Who the $#@$ do you think you are, huh? We know what you're up to." Ball said. "We want information . . . And you're gonna give it to us, you %$@%!"

Joe's mind was trying to fight off the pain as he tried to organize an answer that might sell.

"O.K., O.K. I'll tell ya! Just leave me alone." he shouted, eyes misting, voice cracking. "We're gonna break into a bar on 38th and Ditmars Boulevard tonight at 1 a.m., I swear, I swear!" he screamed, feigning fear.

"You get your butt outta here—we'll be seeing you soon."

As he walked away, he could hear them patting each other on the back as they laughed and jibed each other.

Joe arrived at the Church playground later that evening; the crew was assembled, waiting for him.

"Hey, Joe . . . what happened?" Pauly asked.

"Nothin'—those #@$#%^$ cops . . . I talked my way out."

Even though he told the cops a lie, he didn't want to let his guys know that he had given them wrong information: wiseguys did not even talk to cops!

They prepared for their job by dressing in all-black clothing and checking their tools and equipment. Soon they were on their way. It was midnight; a full moon was bathing the city in light as they scurried like rats into the night. Reaching the supermarket in thirty minutes, Joe climbed the tree across the street and from his vantage point, Joe could see all of the routes connecting their location. Pete positioned himself on the opposite corner facing Joe. The others went about their business defeating the alarm and cutting a hole in the roof.

Over the course of the next hour, the cigarettes were loaded into the car; but the guys inside (after helping themselves to beer and wine) were drunk. They were running up and down the aisles playing bumper cars with shopping carts, turning lights on and off, making all kinds of noise. Someone must have called the cops because Joe saw the red flashing lights of multiple cop cars approaching, sirens mute. He frantically yelled and waved to Pete, who stared dumbly at Joe, frozen in fear and confusion!

The police surrounded the store, arresting those outside, but Donny, Danny, and Crazy Eddy continued their gallivanting inside unaware of the commotion right outside the window. Then, with a neighborhood crowd gathering in front of the supermarket, the police used their bull horns,

"THIS IS THE POLICE! WE HAVE YOU SURROUNDED, COME OUT WITH YOUR HANDS UP! LET ME REPEAT . . . THIS IS . . ."

When Donny and Danny saw the crowd in front of the store, they wet their pants! Ball and Jolly had been the first to arrive and he could hear them saying, that they, the Motley Crew, had a rat in their midst! Joe remained motionless in the tree, until after much prodding, Danny, drunk and believing that it was Joe who gave them up, pointed to his secret spot. The cops started across the street as Joe leapt out of the tree, running faster than he ever had, to the safety of Aggie's house.

He called his mother and told her he was in serious trouble. She pleaded with him to turn himself in. "I've worked so hard to keep you off the streets . . . is this what I receive in payment? I've been praying for you . . . please come home!"

Joe replied that praying made no difference; that she should not worry. He hung the phone up, thinking he was now an out-cast; black-listed, with no friends, no protectors, and a family that was worried sick. Fearing to return home—knowing the police would be patiently waiting—he racked his brain for answers. 'Who told the cops?' Men of respect would not inform, even if they were of several different nationalities.

While Aggie kept repeating, "I told you, I told you!", he kept answering, "It's Fate! It's Fate! It was meant to be!"

With word of the bungled burglary on the street, and Ball and Jolly gleefully tracking him, Joe left Aggie's for Ravenswood and his cousin Billy's house. After arriving and informing Billy of his dire need for cash "to get away", Billy called his buddy Sergio . . .

Sergio was an aspiring boxer; a piece of work! When he wasn't in the ring, he was scamming how to "make a score." When he wasn't scamming, he'd be in Manhattan with an old wash tub, placing it upside down, he'd stand on top, daring anyone to knock him off his "mountain," by hitting him in the stomach with a baseball bat (one he carried religiously everywhere he went)—for ten bucks a pop!

Joe was impressed by what he thought was the young man's bravery. "Wow," he said to himself, "I'd like to be like him! Maybe he could be my father figure!"

Like Joe's ancestors before him, Sergio had dreamed dreams of plenty; dreams of splendor; dreams of opulence . . .

The first thing Sergio did was take Joe under his wing. He taught him how to box during the day; how to break into houses at night. They were in the dough, and living large. After several months, Joe decided to return to the old neighborhood.

Bernie's Candy Store . . . the ever-present group of toughs standing outside the entrance. Joe sauntered to the door with Sergio. Arrayed in front of him were the same punks who used to steal his money. Pauly had left the crew—which was temporarily fractured due to the fact that three of its members were doing time in Spotford for the grocery job—and moved up the ranks. Pauly stood with his back against the wall as Joe approached the group.

The ring leader, Joey Esposito—the one who mugged him so many times—started in immediately, "Look who showed up—the rat!"

Pauly, due to his friendship—and knowledge that Joe would never rat on the crew—decided to come to the rescue. He stepped in to put a damper on the situation before it exploded.

"Hey, Joe's all right!"

Sergio then stepped in, and with the confidence of two supporters, Joe began to feel he could whip the world. Joe pushed Sergio out of the way and challenged Joey.

With false bravado Joe yelled, "Look who's talking! I think you're the rat!"

Spoiling for the entertainment of a fight, one of the guys began to taunt Joey with provoking words, "You gonna let 'im say doze dings to you!"

"Kick 'iz butt," another chided.

And then, the corner came alive with reverberating chants from the entire group.

Joey Esposito was several years older, five inches taller, and fifty pounds heavier than Joe. As the reality of the moment dawned upon him, Joe began to get butterflies in his stomach. He'd truly thought that in boast and banter the majority of guys would see him in a different light, step in, and squash the whole situation—but even Sergio got embroiled in the situation.

"THE ALLEY! THE ALLEY! DO IT IN THE ALLEY!" chanting reverberated throughout the entire block.

Among the various adjoining shops that made up the strip shopping area on 21st St. between 21st and 22nd Avenue, in Astoria, Queens, Bernie's place was at the corner. Behind Bernie's ran an alleyway the breadth of the one story, dingy, red brick buildings housing the other business establishments, serving the area. This alley was the site of innumerable fights, involving everything from fists to guns and knives. The alley became synonymous with "jousts." Whomever had a beef would challenge; the champion who emerged, would claim truth on his side . . . no matter the hard evidence!—just like the days of knights and kings!

Joe started toward the alley, thinking any moment he'd be called back with a, "Yo, forget 'bout it," or something—but he knew he was about to get "his head handed to him!" As he turned the corner, a thought of fleeing zipped through his mind . . . 'NO! YOU CANNOT!!' . . . A thought of prayer . . . YES! PRAYER . . . "God . . . ugh, I . . . Oh! God, help me: I'm sorry, . . . truly! I am!" Entering the alley . . . Joey and entourage rapidly approaching behind . . . 'GOD!!' he thinks again, as he spies a large chunk of chipped red-clay brick lying upon the ground . . . Pictures of David and Goliath in desperate battle cross his mind . . . he bends down . . . stretching his arm . . . Joey Esposito turns into the alley . . . Joey's right hand grips his jacket . . . Joe's mind screams, 'HIT HIM WITH THE BRICK! THE BRICK!' . . . Joe's hand grasps the brick and begins to rise . . . Joey pulls and begins to turn Joe around . . . Joe's right hand, securely attached to the brick, comes 'round and into Joey's view . . . he speeds up his motion . . . his left fist . . . tight . . . huge knuckles . . . straining to greet Joe's face . . . swinging 'round with tremendous force . . . Joe's face cringes into a mass of compressed fear . . . as the fist approaches . . . speed of light and . . . PLOP! Joey slips! His feet fly out from under him! . . . WOP! . . . He hits his head so hard on the paved alley, it sounds like a pumpkin has busted! . . . 'He's out cold! Praise the Lord!' Joe pounces on top of him just as the "wannabe wiseguys" come around the corner. A vision of a victorious , intoxicated, animated Joe greets them—sitting on top of Joey beating him about the head—"So whaddaya think now, punk?"

TOTAL AMAZEMENT RULES THE CORNER!!!

Joey was a mess. His mother had to be called to take him home. Joe was the hero—at least that's the way he saw it that day! The group gave him a leather jacket (three sizes too big) and he became one of them.

Sergio left to go back to Brooklyn, urging Joe to go with him; but

Joe was swept up by the victory. He was a hood! He was with the "Big Guys." *He was in!*

Pauly and Joe started hanging together on the corner with their new crew. When his old pals came to speak to him, he emulated his new friends in their taunting and despising of these "pieces of garbage." Over the next several weeks, Joe broke all of Bernie's car windows—because his new "friends" said he had to show Bernie who was boss!

Joe had arrived. He was now a member of the thugs he once despised. And they, deciding that he should go all the way, gave him an invitation, "Hey, Joe, let's go to Spanish Harlem!"

Chapter 22: A Mainline Trip to God

I see an apparition
Vile of all tradition
An appalling, dreadful, horrid man
The phantom of our sacred land
The ghetto his dominion
The crackhouse his pavilion
His melody
A symphony
Of poignant, servile, misery . . .

The guys had invited Joe to go along for a ride to a dope house in Spanish Harlem. They journeyed over the Triborough Bridge in a beat up '57 Chevy, belching huge, blue-white clouds of smoke, as it ticked and burped over the bridge. Entering Manhattan with a bang, they made a turn and proceeded along the East River.

The dope house was located in an area close to the neighborhood his ancestors had originally settled in 1908. New York City had engraved proud titles upon its turf: Little Italy; China Town; Spanish Harlem . . . the only remaining emblem of their American birth was their architecture. When you came upon the invisible borders of each territory, you entered into another country simply by taking that one additional step. They proceeded through Little Italy and soon passed through the neighborhood that Joe remembered with great pain—the dark days of change in his family's life. As they passed Bianco's Deli and Meats, he shouted for the driver to stop. There it was! And Old Man Bianco was open!

Proudly exiting the car, he proceeded up to the door and announced his presence with a loud and happy shout, "Yo, Mr. Bianco!"

An old, worn-out man turned and a grin of delightful recognition appeared upon his face.

"Joe! Howa you! Boy, youa grow! Youa look lika youa father."

"Oh, Mr. Bianco, I've missed you and I'm sorry I haven't come before."

"Youa wanna apple?"

"No thanks . . . well, yeah! I'll take an apple!"

"Howa youa moma?" he questioned, wiping a large, juicy apple with a rag.

"Oh, she's OK . . ."

"Eva since youa father wasa murder . . . I meana ina acciden . . ."

"What did you say? What . . . ? Did you say 'murdered'? Father, murdered? Are you crazy . . . ? Or just senile? He was killed in an automobile accident!" Joe exclaimed.

But Mr. Bianco's stunned face said more than any words ever could. That face said, "I'ma sorry, mya boy. Buta itsa true." The pain and disappointment . . . and truth . . . was plainly there. Joe's own face lost all its color; he turned ashen white as a picture of all the innuendo of the past rushed together in a self-assembling jig-saw puzzle.

"I noa mean he wasa murder . . . I mean . . . I'ma so sorry, Joey."

With a sense of pain and betrayal coursing through his consciousness, he turned in rage and vaulted out the door and into the waiting car. "Let's go . . . Now!!"

Mr. Bianco appeared in the doorway, limping, but moving quickly toward the car, a look of sadness written upon the deep lines creasing his leathered face. Joe suddenly knew the old man had made a terrible slip, possibly the first of his lifetime! This fact only further added to Joe's misery. He was devastated to discover his haunting thoughts and dreams were minor compared to the reality of this revelation! He had placed his father's memory into that secret compartment labeled "Accident:Personal," even though rumor and innuendo caused him to second-guess, he had been sure there was nothing to it! He'd assured himself he would be at peace with his memory as soon as he made his fortune and married Aggie. Now the doors had been flung wide open, revealing more torment and sorrow. As they drove off, Mr. Bianco's small, bent shape changed rapidly into a smaller and smaller figure that continued to beckon his return. He desperately wanted to drown the pain. Soon he would . . . drown . . .

* * *

They reached 117th Street and rounded the corner. The neighborhood changed as suddenly as the turn in the road. Filthy, red and brown three-story buildings lined a debris-cluttered street. Hulking remnants of abandoned and stolen cars littered the street side—cannibalized skeletons of rusted steel separating the worn and used family heaps. Grubby, half-naked children played in the street. An open fire hydrant spewed water as they gleefully jumped in and out of the cool, wet gusher.

Stoops of buildings, built of plain, stone steps and rusted iron railings, jutted out onto cracked concrete sidewalks, like tombstones lying stacked one on top of the other. A slice of concrete desert, its face creased by age and sorrow, with towering wind-scathed monuments of suffering looming in a surreal landscape of crime and death. Residents of this sweltering enclave crowded upon their cool, weathered-smooth surfaces, like the deceased of the apocalypse; dead, yet alive—longing for hope; but receiving pain.

All along the block, dealers and users mixed and mingled in a never-ending cycle of master and slave. Addiction crawled along the thoroughfare in the deep-set, black-ringed eyes of the damned. It seemed that all of the occupants of this slum were evil, mean-spirited, dangerous hoodlums; but, behind the filthy brick and rusting iron, above the mass of death and deception, through the hallways of inequity; Joe knew that families huddled in fear; alone; not daring to leave the semi-protection the flimsy, old, tired wooden doors of their musty, rat-and roach-infested apartments, afforded them.

In New York, it was said that all Puerto Ricans lived with roaches, it was said that if you had one, you had the other. The fact was, these great people lived in an infested slum because it was the only place they could afford. Joe, in fact, could identify with this truth!

They stopped in front of one of the buildings, exited the car, and approached the stoop. Dealers and users who sat across it, moved to the side with scowling faces at these Anglos from Queens who dared interrupt their peaceful ambiance. Tromping past a peeling door jamb, they climbed creaking steps through piles of trash and people, draping them like multi-colored shag carpets in drug induced stupor. After the fourth landing, they turned into a narrow corridor and knocked on one of the doors. Several locks clicked loudly and the door slowly opened . . .

"What's happening, how you doin'?" a squat, bald-headed man—who would turn out to be a member of the Jones Brother's crew who peddled dope for a mobster named Joey Gallo—asked as they swaggered through the door.

"All right, man . . . just looking for the white horse," Pauly answered.

As the negotiation went on, Joe looked around the place. It was a three room apartment with peeling, century old, wall-papered walls. The main room was furnished with three worn sofas. The kitchen was filthy—rust stained porcelain sink, mounds of garbage heaped in every corner. People of all ages, dressed in decrepit clothing, in various states of consciousness, were crowded into the three rooms. A foul stench invaded his nostrils and he fought the urge to vomit.

Through a doorless bathroom, above the chipped, black and white tile floor, one guy sat on the toilet, rubber hose wrapped around his arm, needle piercing a main vain in his arm, while a second guy "booted" the plunger. As he pulled and pushed the plunger in order to boost the drugs over and over, a morbid pallor flushed the face of the first, as he teetered back and forth in rhythm with this exercise. In the bedroom (a hot, filthy cubicle that contained a single sweat-stained bed) a young girl, about thirteen years old, lay nude; stoned. She seemed unaware of the perverse acts that were being committed to her by several, semi-clothed, drugged men of various ages.

As they sat on a raunchy sofa; Pauly negotiating for the dope, Joe viewed this place of horror with eyes that misted with pain from his recent revelations. Frightened and alone with his thoughts and these sights, he wanted to bolt through the door. A powerful force was ordering him to leave. He realized this was an impossible situation, but he didn't leave . . . he just vowed that he would never do drugs.

When the deal was consummated, one of the guys came over and began to wrap a belt around his arm. He protested. He said he didn't want to shoot dope but peer pressure combined with feelings of wanting to belong overshadowed his thoughts and commitments.

"Come on, it's great! You'll love it. Be a man. It won't hurt you! Just try it. Come on, whattaya think . . . you'll become an addict? That's bull! Give me your arm!"

Joe noticed Pauly had slouched into the couch. He was surprised Pauly would do the dope. But Pauly had been shooting the stuff for a month and had told Joe he wasn't hooked. "Listen, if you don't like it, then, you don't do it no more. But, man, these guys do it all the time . . . you gotta at least try it!" The thought of Pauly as a novice never crossed his mind—someone once said that misery loves company!

Joe gave in, put his arm out, and sat in a semi-conscious state as the needle entered his arm with a slight pinch. The plunger was pulled and he could see his deep red blood enter the vial. Staring, lost in a trance, his blood slowly mixed and then gathered speed. The drug seemed to boil with impatience as it realized it had another slave. Alive, a parasitic embolism, it swirled with excitement, screaming in silent motion to be released into the healthy body of this young man. It wanted to tear through the rich, life-giving blood and attach itself forever, sending its physical and mental pain for succor.

The belt was loosened, the plunger sank half-way, and a warm feeling traversed rapidly up his arm. It coursed through his vessels until it entered his heart and brain. In an instant he was lost in a world of slow-moving peace. All thoughts and worries were cast aside. The plunger was withdrawn and plunged again and again. Soon he was throwing up his insides—and feeling good about it!

In a split second he was transferred into a world that seemed to answer all his questions by eliminating them. 'What was that thought I had about father? What was I worried about?' All his questions and doubts were swallowed by the alien substance which was gleefully transforming him into a creature of habit. The thing allowed only moments of pleasure when compared to the long and desperate cravings for the next shot. Sending just the right amount of pleasurable feelings pounding within his brain, it wrenched all other feelings. He soon fell into a dreamy sleep.

He awoke, filthy, vomit dried upon his clothing, and with the urge to shoot again. Soon he was lost again.

They spent four days "shooting up." He didn't eat at all. He didn't wash himself or brush his teeth. He just plunged that filthy, bloody needle into his arm over and over, until finally, he missed the sore and worn out veins and shot the drug into the muscle of his arm. His arm began to swell and an abscess formed; so he just switched arms under the pretext of killing the pain.

The demon was within him. It controlled and demanded sacrifice. Friends, acquaintances, and even family, were suddenly prey to its sinister and evil intent to subjugate. The only demon to rear its head was him! Lost within the hazy warmth of the drug, he would have no cares—except how to regain the feeling. His life began to move up and down in tune to the plunger. The urge to shoot heroin became the only reason to live.

They hung out on the corner scheming and devising ways to steal and con, in order to race over to Spanish-Harlem and journey to the land of the living dead! He'd sneak in the window of his mother's apartment and steal money to support his habit. And, on many occasions, he'd swipe the keys to the beat-up-hunk-of-steel she called her car to get his fix—until one night, after shooting up with his friends, he wrecked the car and left his mother without her meager transportation!

This went on an entire summer. He became one of those filthy, skinny, drug users who traversed the streets in packs, ready to pounce on any weak prey that happened by. His eyes were black-ringed, his hair filthy and knotted—yet he continued to hang out with the new crew. He was using more drugs than any two of the others.

One hot and humid night, he was hanging out behind Bernie's. He had just shot up a "nickel" bag of dope, taken two "reds"—sleeping pills—and was sipping on a bottle of wine, when he realized someone was pulling at his arm.

Looking up, he recognized Aggie. She was pleading with him, "Joe, Joe! Come on wake up!"

"Leave me the #$%@ alone!" he screamed at her, as he fought her like the demon he was.

She grabbed his arm as her tears dropped in a storm upon his face. He swung his arm out and hit her so violently, she staggered and fell to the ground. As she got up, he realized what he'd done! He tried to stand in an effort to apologize, but fell back to the ground as she disappeared into the darkness. It was like a nightmare—yet he knew he had not been asleep. He yelled at God. Blamed Him. He screamed so loud, that all of his friends rounded the corner expecting to see some new disgrace.

As he was yelling at Him, an old woman, dressed in black and pulling a hand cart filled with packages, passed the alleyway. She was a wrinkled woman of approximately seventy. When the guys saw her, they spied her bag. In a second they were upon her and had wrenched her pocketbook as she tumbled to the ground.

They scattered like roaches before she realized what had happened. Joe was jolted back to reality by the sight of that vicious crime. Though still drugged, he was somehow rational. He could distinctly hear the old woman thanking God that she was not hurt as she got up off the ground. When she saw him on the ground she rushed over to him.

"Sonny, are you all right? Did those hoodlums harm you?"

Here was a seventy-year-old, frail woman who'd just been violently assaulted and her bag stolen, yet she was assisting him—the devil incarnate—with care and concern! He was both embarrassed and ashamed. He got up and helped her put her packages back into the handcart. Telling her he was alright, he thanked her for her kindness. She replied that Jesus would watch over him!

That very night he went to the church and slept once more upon a pew, like he had done the night of his father's funeral. When he awoke, he felt as if he had slept for several weeks. He was truly refreshed and at peace. The cravings of the monster within him were cast adrift in a sea of acidic reality and he soon realized how disgusting he felt. He was wearing blue jeans that hadn't been washed in months; his fingernails were black with filth; the taste in his mouth was revolting. He swirled his tongue around in contact with the slime coating the enamel of his teeth like a fungus, shuddering at the thought of what he looked like.

He stood up and slowly walked to a metal bowl hanging on the wall by the entrance. It was brimming with Holy Water. He wasn't thinking at the time, he just had the urge to see what he looked like in the reflection of the stainless steel mounting. He was shocked! The face that stared back at him was one he could not recognize! He desperately scooped up the water in his determination to wipe off the mask someone had glued to his face. With both hands cupped together, he reached deep into the curved interior and washed his face.

It was the most refreshing water he had ever splashed upon his being. He was renewed with the thoughts and angers that had essentially driven him to dive so deep into the living world of nightmares; but this time he was in control! Yes! He was once more in control of his feelings and emotions. He was suddenly facing the consequences of his actions. He knew he would have to leave this place in order to remove himself from the demon's grasp.

Joe was not in tune to the facts of this sudden miracle! Though cravings still tugged at the core of his being, he felt he had to find the answers to the truth he was seeking and face the facts. This sudden feeling was the armor God had blessed him with that terrible night long ago. He returned that night to the corner and his buddies. Soon, Joe was arguing with the guys. "I don't want to be doin' drugs, I want to take a break."

"Hey, who's your buddies? Huh? Who watches your back? Just come for the ride in case we need you, O.K.?"

"Listen, I'm going to stay at Aggies house for a few days. Clean up, get some rest."

"Just come for the ride! Come on. Then we'll drop you off!" Pauly said.

"Hey, Pauly. You looked in a mirror lately? You got tracks runnin' up and down your arms! Black and blue bruises and puss-filled abscesses all over you! You look like you got leprosy! Man, it ain't cool no more."

Pauly looked down at himself. Joe could tell Pauly already knew how he looked. His family knew. His old friends knew. Sure, he knew. But, to quit . . . "Cold-Turkey?" It was a word he feared more than death!

"Yo, Joe. Let's jus go one more time. We can get enough to quit slow. Come on. I'm your best friend. We'll quit together!"

Even though Joe felt he could quit right then and there, Lucifer wouldn't abandon the struggle . . . Though Joe was dead set against staying with the guys, the craving for dope began to overtake his body and mind. Being around the only friends he'd ever known; the only people he felt cared about him; made Joe's battle that much harder. But the picture of the old woman and her final blessing appeared in his head and, just as suddenly, the warm feeling of that first shot of dope momentarily invaded his picture—wiping the old woman from his mind, as if his mind were an etch-a-sketch! Then he saw pictures of Aggie in tears.

Joe's mind was at war—his feelings raged against his thoughts. As visions of Aggie and the Old Woman tore at his heart, the memory of the warm, peaceful feeling that the needle brought him whispered hypnotically. 'What should I do, sweet Jesus', he plead in silence as he pressed against the brick wall behind him. He was surrounded by the power of evil. He was being consumed by its total authority! He was about to relinquish the last vestige of his newly discovered independent reason and thought; about to be consumed: If he took that trip he'd never come back!

In the speed of light and revelation itself, a white "Rotor Rooter" van appeared on the corner as if zapped by an alien entity, and a huge man dressed in green over-alls and cap, got out. He strolled over to the wolf pack, a cigar stub clenched between his teeth . . . "Which one a youse is Joe?"

Joe stood still in the middle of the crew with his back to the wall, waiting for his pals to tell this joker to fly a kite.

When he bellowed the question again—adding colorful details of what he was gonna do to the two guys he had snatched by the throat—the entire gang parted, leaving Joe alone to face the music.

The big guy looked him over; spat on the ground; and left.

Turned out he was Mr. Esposito. He'd come to take care of the guy that beat up his kid Joey several months before. When he saw this shrimp standing there, he went home and—the story goes—beat his son again!

Joe finally figured it out: the guys he thought were his friends had thrown him to the wolf! They didn't give a damn about him, when push came to shove. Joe walked away and never looked back . . .

During the next several weeks Joe enjoyed one of the most fantastic times of his life. He revisited his family; discovering how much his mother had been praying to see him safe and sound. Angela, Carmine, and Eddy became his siblings once more. He talked to Pauly's family and they placed him in a treatment program. As Aggie took care of him, showering him with love and understanding—with God—Joe returned to being the person he was, before his addiction—maybe even the happy-go-lucky guy he was before his father died.

Aggie and he spoke of living their lives together, forever. They went to the Museum of Natural History and to Central Park in exploration of nature's nooks and crannies. Hand in hand, they climbed the park's large black boulders that jutted from the landscape, their once-jagged edges worn smooth by the harshness of time to become warm and gentle shapes which were pleasing to the eye and touch. Soft and friendly, yet tough and unmovable, they were like the old Italian men Joe knew in the old neighborhood. Aggie said they were solid examples of God's nature, a fact of His M.A.G.I.C.[1] She said man could, with God's grace, become like those aged pieces of a once, large, uncontrollable mountain—reshaped, settled, inviting, providing strength, peace and serenity to many lost and hungry souls.

Rarely in his young life, had Joe had the pleasure of being part of a true family. Like a wildflower that blooms among the weeds and then gets choked out, his family would sprout for a few precious days, then disappear for long periods of time. This was a special moment. He ate dinner at his mother's, and the entire family celebrated just being together. A rare feeling of blessed love descended on them. It was a M.A.G.I.C. moment that Joe held very dear to his heart. And then, the greatest moment occurred: Aggie brought Carmine and he together in a rare moment of brotherhood. She said to Joe, "Why don't you invite him to come with us to the park tomorrow?"

"He won't wanna go," Joe replied.

"Don't you think he wants to be with you as much as you with him?"

That next day Joe, Carmine, and Aggie went to Central Park and spent hours exploring and climbing its boulders; the same boulders that were smoothly shaped by the harshness of time. And like those transformed boulders, Joe felt more the older, caring brother and less the man of the house. He wanted so much to demonstrate his love to Carmine. It was just when he was about to directly tell him of this fact that Joe noticed a few strange shapes sliding down the face of one of the boulders thirty yards off. They could have been other individuals doing the same thing they were doing. But in the rapidly fading light of the coming night, they looked bizarre. Seizing the moment, Joe grabbed Aggie's hand and yelled to Carmine, "Hey, Carm! They're coming. They're coming! I'll protect you!"

---

1 M.A.G.I.C.—Most Amazing Gift In Christ

Carmine, not knowing what Joe meant, came tearing through the woods dragging some girl who had joined them, and they all began to run. As they reached the blacktop bike path that encircled the park, several strangers heard them shouting and began running with them. Soon, twenty people were running—causing even more people to join in—when finally the entire park seemed to be running!

The combined sounds of over one-hundred people running and screaming, "They're coming! They're coming!" reverberated throughout the park! Joe, Aggie, Carmine, and the girl were at the head of the group, which pounded the pavement to elude whatever was "coming"! As they broke through the bushes onto the street in front of the Plaza Hotel and turned in hysterical glee, the people broke through in total confusion. They streamed onto the road yelling, "They're Coming, They're Coming!!!"

All the way to Queens, with the train moaning and bumping along; in front of a car full of silent, depressed faces of strangers who could not comprehend their emotions of the moment; they; Carmine and Joe, hugged and rolled on the floor of the car laughing so hard their stomachs hurt and their faces were red and wet.

Aggie was right, as usual. The brothers had a great time. It was like they had never been apart. During the next several days even Jeanette had the pleasure of watching her two boys laughing and playing. Her prayers were answered. Her boys were home, safe and sound. The boys enjoyed many M.A.G.I.C. moments, and became the happiest kids in Queens.

Chapter 23: Until Continuity Calls . . .

How soon we forget: Like the pain that warns of injury, once removed by cure, we soon forget the cause as well as the injury. Joe didn't remain in His grace for more than a few weeks. Though his heroin habit was gone, his environment—full of evil intent—

drove him again into the clenches of sin.

For the next month "home" returned to normal—that is, if you can call living with Aunt Connie normal. Connie was overjoyed to have him once more under her wing, and demonstrated it by encouraging him to rebel.

As for Angela, she had begun her odyssey into the world of hair spray and curlers.

Carmine was rapidly gaining weight as he tried to eat his way out of the miserable conditions that surrounded them—he took "eat all of your pastabazool" literally.

Eddy was walking and talking.

Jeanette was her old self, trying hard to show she loved them by sacrificing everything for them; while that sacrifice in turn produced in her a hatred of her circumstances.

To Joe, Jeanette acted as if she detested the mob and what it stood for, yet, she continued to play both sides of the fence. So, though Joe displayed emotions which 'went with the program'—he received Holy Confirmation at St. Joseph's and was registered at PS.141—he had this tugging sensation telling him to leave. Joe had become a cog in a wheel of misfortune—and the road was about to get bumpy . . .

The catalyst for change revealed itself sooner than expected. Joseph "Joe-Pag" Pagerello, insisted that Jeanette allow a bookmaking operation in her flat. Jeanette agreed because of her situation—she needed her job, and the extra fifty bucks a week promised a small but very real elevation in their lives.

"Mom, why is that guy always here using the phone?" Joe asked.

"He's just working."

"What kind of work?" . . .

For eight weeks, the bookmaking continued, until one night, "Open the damn door, it's the police!"

Ten police officers—including one federal agent whose presence caused a temporary lapse of the protection Joe-Pag enjoyed—busted the door down. Jeanette was home watching TV—it was her night off—and she barely got up before they grabbed and handcuffed her in front of her children.

The police ransacked the house and took everyone—well, almost everyone—to the 114th precinct. What a scene: Angela, Eddy and Carmine crying; Jeanette screaming epithets; police threatening and speaking roughly to all of them. And Joe? . . . he got away!

After he escaped in the confusion, Joe went down to the corner, where his old buddies had moved up the ladder and replaced the addicts—who were now like lepers to the mob associates. They were now hanging in front of Bernie's demanding tribute! As Joe approached the corner the group greeted him with pretend punches and macho hugs.

"Yo, we heard about the raid!" Donny exclaimed.

"Who got busted?" Pete cried.

"Ow 'uch bred 'id 'hey git?" Crazy Eddy squeaked.

"We heard you guys had a shoot out!" Danny questioned.

"How many guys went down?" Jimmy Lendahan inquired, as if to join in the questioning was an apology for his actions of several years before. To all, Joe was once again a celebrity.

Nicky had gotten a job at Bernie's—the owner figured the windows would stay in their frames longer—and the crew was hanging inside, using it as their headquarters.

A long lunch counter ran along the right side of the store. On the left were the tables, juke box, and a new glass display refrigerator that Yetta had recently installed.

Their favorite beverage, Chocolate Yoo Hoo, was kept there. They'd buy one, sit near the cooler and drink it down; reach into the cooler for a new one, replacing it with the empty can.

At first it became a great thing to hang on the corner all day, but soon it got boring. They say the grass always looks greener on the other side—but to Joe, it didn't feel any better!

Joe longed for the family that had sprouted several weeks before. Though he couldn't let it show, he hated coming back to the streets. The streets brought memories of his father back . . . and his murder. Despite Aggie's love and support, a furious rage boiled beneath the facade he had erected in defiance of the inequity he perceived. 'What was happiness? Was it the love of a girlfriend? Lots of money? Was it freedom from the confines of his predicament? Was it his family?'

Now that was a question! Could a new and normal family, change his life and views? And if it could, what of his real family? Could he forget the love that simmered beneath the trepidation his mother faced each and every day?

And the question of God and Devil, as living entities, loomed on his horizon. Were they real? Can you imagine if fate was the cause, and not God!

"Blasphemy!", the priest would shout aloud!

Yet, if God was real, his life could easily be viewed as a petty masquerade. A theatrical drama where the enlightened could turn the lights off and change the script. "Oh! God! Why must I return again and again into this foreboding place, a place of question after question? Happiness is all I want."

Joe's envy made him despise the kids who came by Bernie's everyday from school or their homes to buy candy or "Egg Creams" from the soda fountain, while laughing and horsing around.

It was this jealousy that caused many of "the punks"—as Joe once called them—to react in anger to anyone who demonstrated happiness. Yet, some of those same kids wanted to hang with the crew. A few tried and were sorely disillusioned—they had seen a group of kids, though tougher-looking and street-smart, hanging all day and acting as if they had not a care in the world; when in reality they were a group of hungry, lonely, emotionally troubled children who had grown up too fast.

It didn't take long to grow tired of sitting in a candy store thinking of ways to get money for your next meal. But this was the preeminent breeding ground for future wiseguys; guys who lasted through the drugs, violence, arrests, purges, and other hazards of the streets; who might one day make it to the next level.

Like a football program, each level was kin to the next, related in the basic study, only more intense as you moved up. Though only thirteen years old, Joe had reached the Senior High level in street crime. Like most of his "buddies", who were now sixteen and seventeen, he was set to be recruited for college—the pros would be calling soon . . .

* * *

On a corner in Brooklyn, a group of loud racketeers, wearing suits, fedoras, and pinkie rings, performed their morning ritual. As each soldier approached the intersection, they would seek out the next upper-ranking member, lightly grasp him with their arms, and place a kiss upon his cheek. This ceremony was repeated in a pecking order until all ranking members received their morning's respect.

It was a sight that made all young street hoods envious of 'This

Thing of Ours.' Just to see a two-hundred-and-fifty-pound enforcer, bedecked in his finest, offer his respect to a five-foot-three, one-hundred-and-fifty pounder, dressed in simple attire, sent waves of awe coursing through the veins of aspiring young criminals.

Though this view of loyalty, friendship, and tradition provoked an imagery of fealty in its purest sense, what lurked beneath the surface of this seemingly orderly society was ambition, greed, selfishness, and terror.

The La Costa Nostra enforced its ways with brutal efficiency. The soldier who placed a kiss in deference in the morning, could plant the kiss of death in the evening—with just as much ease.

The figure of a young boy, clothed in jeans and cotton pullover, with a cigarette stabbing out of the corner of his mouth, advanced down the street toward the busy congregation. He stepped from the pavement to the curb with purpose and turned into the crowd. The assembly of soldiers, capos, and associates parted way, allowing him access to the hub of activity. He immediately walked up to an old man, kissed him on both cheeks, and grasped the envelope that appeared in his hands as if it were an apple. . . .

Chapter 24: And the Demons Arrive

The driver of the Dannon Yogurt truck made his first stop of the day. Pushing his hand-cart; stacked to its top bar with fresh yogurt; he casually entered the store like he had a zillion times before, leaving the keys in the running truck. Pete was in the truck and zooming down the street before the driver could even turn around.

They hijacked twenty trucks in two weeks and still could not keep up with the demand. No matter the product, a buyer could be found—in fact, even two-hundred cases of pigs feet, discovered in a truck purported to carry cigarettes, sold for twenty-five cents on the dollar! Money flowed and Joe was living in a motel by the airport. He even had a phone! Though Joe was not the leader of the pack, he operated as the captain of his own crew.

Good old Feranzi, a "retired" mobster who knew his father, had opened many doors. The older guys knew it was due to this unique friendship that Joe moved so easily among those many years his senior. Though some flack had been generated by those who desired a piece of the action, his new group of "punks" were holding their own, that is, until the appearance of Ball and Jolly.

"Where'd you get the bananas to pay for this room? Listen, you little punk, you don't even $%^% without paying twenty percent! And I don't care about Feranzi or anyone else! This is our territory and everyone pays! *You'll pay just like your father did.* And you can take that whichever way you want!"

"And you can take that whichever way you want!" " . . . take that whichever way you want!" " . . . whichever way you want!" " . . . you want!"

Joe awoke in a sweat. Over and over the dream kept coming, and he could hear the words, "*You'll pay just like your father did.* And you can take that whichever way you want!" He called Feranzi to ask him a few questions and only got more of the same.

"Listen, just like the big guys do . . . you do. Those guys will deliver protection, capisch? You picked up a lot of bread so far, an there's plenty to go around. How many of them punks make two-three hundred a week? And remember, the big guys always gotta get their due. As far as your father goes, I ain't gotta clue. Do ya think I'd be pushing you up the ladder if I didn't give a damn? None of your father's guys would have hurt him! Anyway, that's a league you're not in yet. You gotta be groomed while you grow up! This is the way it is, but I'll see what's on the streets."

To mobsters street news is the most rapid network going for dispatching and gathering information . . . and for the dispatching of retribution! Faster and more complete than the daily newspaper, the word supplied all the details and intelligence a mobster needed. Rather than spending the time to read a paper, the only news that was important was the "the word on the streets;" you received the latest word by milling around the corner, frequenting bars, mob headquarters, social clubs, mob hang outs.

In fact, the only reason most racketeers purchased a newspaper was for the daily sports page and racing forms. The Mafia's main source of solid revenue and opportunity was the business of gambling and loan sharking. They went hand in hand. A business owner, housewife, truck driver, or even a bank president, would borrow money to finance a deal, purchase something, or more than likely pay off a debt—usually from losses due to gambling! When they were unable to repay the weekly vig (interest), the mob didn't take them to court; they beat the heck out of them; took over their companies; or intimidated them into turning over information that would enable them to commit crimes which satisfied the debt ten times over.

A week had gone by with no news from Feranzi, when Joe's Uncle Frank stopped by the corner, a cigar clenched between his teeth.

"Listen, forget this stuff about your father. Yes, he passed away, but it was an accident. An accident, Joe! And what's this stuff about you hanging around these punks? Do you realize your mother's worried sick? And why are you giving those cops a hard time? They're my friends, been friends for many years" . . .

"Franky," the next in line for the family throne, sat at an immaculate rolltop desk reconciling his records in his office in Ravenswood, Queens. Other than his ink well and leather-bound ledgers, the only other visible items on his desk were ten orderly stacks of worn, well-circulated bank notes. Nearly four thousand dollars in various denominations were the fruits of last night's collections. With twenty-large on the streets, the vig was coming in steady. His book was growing and it seemed it would approach thirty-large by next month. After concluding his chore, he picked up a bundle of twenties and counted out eight-hundred dollars into two piles. He then placed each pile into separate envelopes and sealed them. Arising from the desk, he slipped on his suit jacket and put the secured packages in his inside pocket. This was the mob's share of his business and the pay-off he made regularly to the police at the 114th Precinct in Queens. He was quite aware of the fact that no one operated without the sanction of the underworld and the protection of local law enforcement.

Heading toward the front door, he reached down, opened a carved walnut humidor he kept on a coffee table, and grabbed a handful of Havana cigars. Placing them in the breast pocket of his jacket, he opened the door and stepped into the hallway. Franky then strolled to the stair landing; his tall, clean-cut figure draped in a simple business suit, inexpensive overcoat, and plain fedora. Plucking one of the cigars from his pocket, he took his engraved silver cutter out, nipped the end off, stuck it in the corner of his mouth, and chomped down on it. He then descended the stairs to the cleaning establishment he used as a front. One of the few luxuries Franky indulged in were his cigars; you hardly ever saw him without one poking out of the corner of his mouth. It would be clamped between his brilliant white teeth, hardly moving, even when he spoke. His passion for these emblems of success, combined with his crew-cut, provoked an image of a young drill sergeant with a wiseguy attitude. As he descended the stairs, two police officers riding in a marked car pulled up to the curb in front of his three story building. Exiting the vehicle, they approached the doorway under the sign that read, "Frank's Cleaners." They shoved open the door and tapped a bell on the counter to announce their arrival.

Franky stepped through the draped doorway that led from the stairs to the front room. Seeing the two cops standing at the counter, he reached into his coat pocket and retrieved one of the envelopes. He handed it to the taller of the two. "How's it going, Fitz?" he entreated as he chewed and rotated the hand-rolled cigar in his mouth.

"Better with this," Fitz replied tapping on the package. "Seems like your business is doing fine."

"It'd be better with that territory."

"Well, you know as much as we do, what the situation is. Word on the street has it you're in line for Flushing! The Old Man's got plans for you. He just got back from Chicago. Went to meet with Batters."

" . . . and if I catch you on this corner again," Franky continued, "I'll break your butt! You get home!"

"But . . ."

"There's no "but" about it. Never mind, I'm takin you home!"

Jeanette was so happy to see her little Joe come home. "Oh, Joe! Are you hungry? Come here and give your Momma a kiss." But Joe wasn't home twenty-four hours when Joe-Pag walked in . . . and after Jeanette left for work that night . . .

"Who da hell do youse dink you are?" BANG! "Snatchin trucks on my turf!" BOOM! "Ya oughta gotten da %$%^ beatin outa youse a long time ago!" WHAM! "DON'T YOUSE EVER RAISE YA HANS TA ME! YOUSE HEAR ME!" SMACK! BOOM! BANG! "An rememba . . . dose guz are my friends! Been my friends for years!" CRASH! "An stop bringing dat stuff up about ya old man! He's dead, got dat? He ain't eva done nuttin' for your motha or youse guz!"

BANG! "He deserved what he got!" CRASH! SMACK! BOOM! "Ya just like 'im an I ain't gonna put up wid it! I call da shots! You $%$#$% little punk!" BOOM BOOM BOOM! "Da word iz on da streets, youse guz don move nuttin'! NUTTIN'!" BOOM! "An jus like youse father, a 'zample haz gotta be made!" CRASH!

Other than the TV and an occasional sound of a beer can being opened, the house was quiet as Joe lay bleeding upon the nicked, terrazzo-looking linoleum kitchen floor. Joe's siblings had stayed tucked deep within their beds, with pillows over their heads, while the horrendous shouting and dreadful blows, reverberated throughout the apartment. Wheezing through the mucus and red, foamy liquid, covering his face, he remained where he was for two long hours; frightened to budge an inch, less Joe-Pag return with his fists or belt. His attempt to defend himself had only made Joe-Pag madder and he knew there was absolutely no way to even contemplate a plan of action, let alone succeed at one. He was about to begin crawling to his brother's room when he heard the knock on the door. He froze in place and awaited the outcome.

"How's ya guz doin! Come in . . . Wanna beer?"

"No thanks. Just wanted to stop by 'cause someone called the cops . . . Ha! Ha! I was just telling Fitz how you was gonna kick his butt, when it come over the radio!"

"Well, he won't smart hiz moud off ta no one for a while! Listen, I wan youse guz ta pick up dat Pauly guy. Do a good numba. Let 'im know whose don it!"

"Sure, Mr. Pagerello."

"Oh, an danks for tellin me about hiz action. *An if ya seez Franky, tell 'im danks.*"

"Good night, Mr.Pagerello . . ."

Chapter 25: Revealing the Enemy

Joe put two and two together, and began attacking mob-related business; stealing mob cars and burning them up; burglarizing any place he heard was taking book or operating a swag (stolen merchandise) joint; ripping off numbers runners. He even threatened a Mafia Capo in Astoria, Queens, when he heard they had threatened reprisals against Carmine.

"Hey", he said, "I might be a punk, but I'll get a couple of my Puerto Rican and black friends, and take care of business. Remember, if so much as a lightning bolt flashes near my brother, I'll come for you. You, your wife, or your kids'll come out of your house and a brick'll drop on their heads. Listen, I'm not like your guys; you know where to find them. Me, I'm like the night . . . blending with the shadows. I can get you anytime I want."

Capo Bianco sent three apes in a black Caddy to teach Joe a lesson. They cornered him on a pitch-black midnight, several blocks from the Capo's home on 38th Street in Astoria with steel pipes in hand. Joe escaped with only a slight cut on his head by waking up the entire block . . . and then returned to rob the Capo's own home!

Nothing was sacred in Joe's determination for revenge. He was now more than that juvenile delinquent the judge had warned his mother of: he'd become a pupil of The Curse.

After convincing Pauly's father to send his son to Arizona for safety, Joe relocated near Aggie in Woodside, Queens; the center of a housing project where he aged several years in the five weeks it took to heal. Moving like a shadow in the night, he was seldom found in the daylight hours, and when he was, it was usually at Bernie's. He would appear unannounced in the early morning to conduct business and disappear . . . like a shadow.

One morning, after showing up at Bernie's, Yetta announced they had a doctor's appointment and would return later that night. Joe seized the opportunity to vanquish his pangs of hunger. Kidding around with Nicky, who was behind the counter, about giving the crew "somethin to sink their teeth into", he looked over to the huge, steaming, warming tray, and asked what was cooking for Yetta's "daily."

Nicky raised the tray top and the fragrant aroma of roast beef and gravy wafted over the counter.

Joe's stomach—on empty—caused his mouth to water.

"Hey, Nicky. Gimme the beef. Yo, Nicky we want the beef," he chided. Soon the place reverberated with the crew's chants, "Give us the beef, we want the damn roast beef, give us the beef, we wanna sink our teeth into the roast beef, so give us the beef; we wanna . . ."

"PLOP!" The roast beef flew down the counter on a river of gravy into Joe's lap. With gleeful laughter, he carried the roast beef out the door and soon, he and the entire crew were feasting like kings at Aggie's house.

Joe was with Aggie later that night when Bernie's regular customers came for Yetta's roast beef. The crew was gathered outside when they heard a horrendous noise. It was Yetta, throwing the large, commercial basting pan out the door! The next thing the crew realized, Yetta, meat cleaver in hand, was running after them!

Not to be intimidated, they dressed Joe's little brother Eddy in fake mustache and German SS cap, and had him enter the store with a 'Heil Hitler' (complete with salute) as they threw in a stink bomb.

Joe happened to show up just as Eddy came running out the door and the sight caused him to break into hysterical laughter. It was then that Bernie turned towards Joe and looked him straight in the eye as Joe loudly laughed in Yetta's face.

Joe turned and hid his embarrassment with more fake laughter as they ran hysterically down the block . . . but, throughout their night of drunken abandon, he kept seeing Bernie's face full of disappointment.

What happened? Had he become a thug who'd take money from a frightened, little boy? Was he one of those beasts, who terrorized lonely, lost children? Who was he?

Later that week, he stopped by Bernie's . . . alone.

"Whaddaya want?" Bernie asked, his hands shaking with a combination of rage, sorrow, and grief. "Haven't you done enough? Why don't you just leave my store; leave Yetta and me alone! You have a short memory! Don't you remember all those times we talked and I helped you? Ahh, hoodlums. What good is it to try?"

"Well I was just gonna apolo . . ."

"I don't need your stinking apology! Just get away from here or I'll call the cops! I don't care anymore what you hoodlums do!"

"But . . ."

"Get the heck out of here . . . din't you hear me? Get lost!"

That night, an embarrassed, humiliated, self-conscious, sad, and sorry Joe, desperate for sanity to enter his life, dropped by his mother's place and looked up into the lit windows.

"They're probably sitting down to dinner," he said to himself. He didn't want to bother them; he knew he'd have to make excuses for his appearance and he was not in the mood to lie—he had no reason to stop by.

"If I could wish one wish, what would it be?" he wondered.

A small voice seemed to answer him, "That's a tough question. It requires responsible reason."

"Reason? You mean like a reason for me to knock on my door?"

"There is no 'reason' to knock on your door . . . no, only love will allow you to have the sort of reason to simply knock and be accepted in. The 'reason' I'm talking about is the reasoning or thinking ability to understand your life and the life of people around you."

"How can I get that kind of reason?"

"You don't 'get' reason; it's a gift from others who already have it."

"But, if they already have it, where'd *they* get it from?"

"God gave reason as a gift to Adam and Eve. He gave them choice and reason. Everyone knows history repeats itself, but so do situations. Reason and choice give you the power to change! The things that rule your life have all happened before; yet it continues today! Why? Because the gift of reason has been absent from your life! It's the responsibility of others to award those gifts to you. It's your mother's fault!"

"No, it's not! And besides . . . there is no God! If there was, then why all of this . . . ?" he exclaimed as he pointed to the debris cluttered street. "How could my mother cause all this?"

The voice didn't reply . . .

As Joe turned to leave, Carmine came out the front door with little Eddy in tow; laughing and playing with each other as they took out the trash.

Though Joe was happy for them, a tinge of jealousy crept into his thoughts, "It's not fair!"

"What's not fair?" The voice was back.

"That they're there and I'm here!"

"Whose choice is that?"

"God's choice!"

"But, I thought God didn't exist."

"Well, maybe he does . . ."

"It's your choice to be or not!"

"Yeah, right," Joe thought with sarcasm. "You live in this world; you put up with the beatings, the hatred, the poverty and the loneliness . . ."

"I do . . ."

It was true, there was no 'reason' in his house . . . only the 'Oath of Alphonso' and its devastating continuance . . . and he rode this wildness as if it were a rollercoaster ride at Coney Island.

Joe watched as Carmine and Eddy tromped back into the house. How he ached to drop his shield, throw away his cloak, and rip down the walls he'd erected that day in Belvue so long ago. He wanted to laugh again; not in the false joy of torment, but with true happiness. He wanted to turn back the hands of time to that shattering morning, so long ago, and put his suit on to join his happy, frolicking, cousins in their quest for attention. *He wanted father again!* He wanted to play with his brothers and Angela; have them look to him with respect. Have them come to him when they were in need. He wanted his mother to be proud of him, to announce to relatives that her son was something special.

He recalled the look of sadness in her eyes when his aunts had stopped over after his first return from the streets; proudly showing off their children and boasting of talents, grades, and activities. Jeanette searched her mind, turning it inside out, desperate for just one proud moment of her own; but she had none. And Joe knew his boasts were empty. It's not that he couldn't achieve good things and it's not that he didn't want to; but something was holding him back. The lies, the dreams, the pretense and boast!

'Did he want too much? Were some people doomed to live a life of unhappiness? Was that the real world? Should he just accept it?'

The battle for the domination of his soul had only begun. He was still living in the world of dreams; not facts. He couldn't translate his thoughts into genuine feelings of love. He couldn't use his gifts because he was unsure of their power. Confusion reigned supreme. Was his only hope—to seek fame and fortune, then return home to rescue everyone—a corrupt and reluctant fable?

In a wave of understanding Joe realized his brothers weren't returning to some palace of tranquillity. That home was a haven of instability and pain! How could he, who had witnessed the suffering personally, blame them for this small sliver of happiness?

Joe was thoroughly confused. A battle raged on all sides with no peace emissary in sight. There would be no cessation of continuity; no offer of substance; of cure and rehabilitation . . . only the Demon . . . snatching souls, with his ever-present Curse!

Joe was journeying into the blame stage. Where once his thoughts were of rescue as a 'Knight in Shining Armor;' galloping through fields of poverty, leaping barriers of contempt and hate in his mad dash of rescue as the man of respect of the house; now they wavered in a deep fissure of self-pity—cracking along the remaining seams of his honor and strength . . . of God and family!

In response to this overwhelming temptation to place blame on his family—since God might only be an effigy of hope—Joe established a new defense, a Maginot Line he was sure would hold . . .

He watched Carmine and Eddy hit the front door to the apartment building and disappear into its warmth and comfort.

After dropping by Aggie's house and telling her he was taking a business trip; that he would write to her; he walked to the "el" where he selected a train at random and boarded. He had one hundred dollars in his pocket and no idea where he was going.

Joe planned to take the "el" and then the subway to Penn Station, where he'd select a bus to take him to his destiny. But outside the "el" exit, he noticed a large group of transit officers milling around the sidewalk, their radios chattering up a storm. As he descended the stairs, a police cruiser slowed to a stop right in front of him. Then several more cruisers surrounded him with lights flashing . . .

Officer Jolly appeared and, even though Joe was just a juvenile, he was packed off to Rikers Island.

* * *

Rikers is a detention center/prison on an island in the center of the East River—used to detain those awaiting trial and to house convicted felons. Determined to cause Joe the maximum possible duress, his jailers placed him in a cold, filthy cell-block with an assortment of criminals who had been arrested that night. Joe feared for his life.

Unending noise echoed off the steel and concrete of the overcrowded cell-blocks as his jailer moved him through a concrete and steel corridor. Arrayed on either side of the narrow passageway were steel doors with traps for serving meals and small, wire reinforced windows. Angry, twisted faces peered out at him as he passed, mouthing vile taunts and predictions; a lust for vengeance against any weaker species that chanced to enter their domain was written upon each contorted face. A shiver raced from his mind to his bones: which door would bang open with a loud metallic sound as the huge brass key turned the well oiled lock? When it snapped open and revealed its caged and hungry prisoners, what would they say . . . or do?

The guard stopped at a quiet cell-block door, behind which held sixteen to twenty-one year old offenders. He placed a key in the lock, turning it with force necessary for the huge tumbler to revolve, and brought forth a sound that would become familiar for the following several weeks: "CLICK! BANG! MOAN!"

It's message was promptly answered—immediate shouts; movement; jostling—the hungry, feeding sharks were dropped a chunk of bloody meat . . .

He was immediately swarmed with questions, pokes, and taunts as the caged animals tried, tested, and studied this morsel dropped into their midst: IS IT EDIBLE?

Joe was aware his answers, actions, and reactions would set the stage for his stay. This was the time when all new prisoners were assigned a rung on an invisible ladder of hierarchy; where you placed your foot, was were you'd begin your stay. The weak became subjects of amusement and enjoyment for the strong. The hesitant became the subjects of the determined. The loud, false pretenders became subjects of immediate fist-full bashing. Only the quiet, strong, and determined would be left alone to their thoughts and anger—and even they had to remain alert and ready for the slightest challenge of position.

"Yo, how ya doin? My name's Joe. If you want a piece of this . . . then just @#$# with me," he said slowly and methodically with a serious, poker-faced attitude as his heart raced with fear and apprehension.

His muscular build, two homemade tattoos (inked with India ink on a New York rooftop with needle and twine) and a determined soft persuasion, resolved the issue.

"There's a bunk over there," a sixteen year old (sixteen years was the age a teenager became an adult in New York) black guy said, as he pointed to an empty top bunk in one of the sleeping cells.

He walked into the cell and climbed up onto the steel bed with its thin, stained, white and blue striped mattress and dark brown, filthy blanket. There he remained for seven days and nights before being moved into a cell-block; wondering all the while why he was in Rikers. 'Was it the school incident? Why here? In a jail?'

The cell-block was long and narrow. On the left side were seventy-five cells arranged in three tiers of twenty-five, two men to a cell; one-hundred-fifty inmates when it was full. To the right, on the first tier, was a long day-corridor, with steel tables and benches anchored to a reinforced concrete floor. The second and third tiers looked down on the "Day Area." Grated windows; placed high above the tables and benches; delivered the light of day and the darkness of night. Sounds of the freedom from the city wafted across the waters of the East River, but were drowned in a bay of commotion and sound from the cell-blocks that lined the walkways; like so many cages of a city zoo. Each cell had a sliding steel-barred door controlled by automatic electric switches from the outside corridor. At night, guards made their rounds, while prisoners became subjects for viewing, and assumed that role with relish.

But during the day, the cell doors were opened and the prisoners released to congregate in the day area. Questions, answers, and ideas were communicated with grunts, heckles, and the angry motions of prisoners as they sat on top of and around tables. Those steel tables were the center of the universe to each inmate. They remained full with excited, loud inmates; consumed by games of hearts and spades for the prize of sweet smelling, tailored—store bought—cigarettes.

These man-made objects of addiction were the supreme being within this immense mountain of concrete and steel. Worshipped and prayed to, machine-rolled tobacco determined many things. It wrought death, brought happiness, and delivered suspense to the lives of its believers. Constant fighting over supremacy, places at the tables, games of chance, and use of the weak were the essence of daily existence. Joe was committed to maintaining a low profile. It didn't take long for him to realize that this place was more intense than Spotford. Unlike the first cell-block, meals were not dispensed in the blocks. Instead, the inmates went to a chow hall three times a day— and he could recall the word "chow hall" with no problem. The first morning he walked that route, he got all kinds of looks. The cooks and servers gathered around him, "What they got *you* in here for?"

Joe knew that sooner or later he'd be challenged by an inmate—or two. It happened during dinner chow. He was standing in line and someone kept bumping into him from behind. Turning around, he saw it was a large, eighteen-year-old Latino, who was trying to gain "points" by starting an incident.

"Yo! Watch yourself," Joe said, turning forward again.

Bump . . . Push! He did it again.

"Yo, what did I tell you ?" his stomach doing somersaults.

"Hey! On the back, when we get back!" was the guy's reply.

The challenge was clear; when they returned from chow, they'd face off. The winner would receive prominent status, the loser . . .

All the way to the chow hall Joe was in internal emotional turmoil. He realized that this definitely was not a Knight's Duel where the victorious would face the defeated and celebrate together—it was a Southern Dog Fight where death and dishonor ruled. He looked once more at the guy and saw he was twice Joe's size; all of the inmates could see this; the ribbing didn't stop until they returned to the cell block.

The line entered the block through the steel gate. Before he realized it, the Latino and he were pushed to the rear of the narrow corridor. Once at the back of the block, a solid band of inmates formed a deep half-circle between them and the main gate into the block. There was no way a guard could enter and reach them before someone was torn apart.

The chants began; goading them, pushing them, demanding them to lock horns. He threw up his hands like Sergio had taught him and began to dance. The guy came at him like a bull, head down, arms spaced wide. Joe feinted toward the center and then, at the last moment, came around "Latino's" left side and hit him solidly with a blow that contained every ounce of his body weight. BANG! The bull staggered. He hit him with a left to the body and he stumbled back. When the inmates pushed "Latino" forward, Joe hit him with an uppercut and he fell—cold stone out! Cheers went up from the inmates, competing with the sounds of a ruckus of ten guards with batons forcing themselves through the crowd. Someone grabbed Joe's arm and hustled him out of the way. He wound up in a cell on the first landing.

After they got "Latino: out of the cell-block, the inmates treated their five-foot-two, miniature "Marciano" with great respect. You could see him every day, sitting upon one of the tables, cigarette burning, cards in his hand, playing spades with the big guys. Taking advantage of his popularity, he bargained a few meals with a trustee for a needle; and with strings of thread from his blanket, fashioned a tattoo needle. With ink he made from the soot of melted plastic that he ground up with water, he traded his service for the necessities of life: soap, cigarettes, extra food and other toiletries.

A month went by without a word as—unknown to Joe—jailers and mobsters decided what to do with him. Though no one told him exactly what he was charged with, when he would go to court, or when someone would speak with him; he knew sooner or later they'd have to. He began sending notes out with inmates who were released; notes directed toward his guys in Queens. He'd been made incommunicado, just like at the hospital, and, he reasoned, by the same enemies! He started having dreams of punishments he'd receive for past transgressions. He prayed to God every day; informing Him he was sorry and asking His forgiveness. He told Him he was sorry for causing the pain and sorrow to those who cared for him . . .

"Oh, God . . . are you there? Can you hear me? Please, release me. I know that I ask you all the time to help me and then I go out and get in trouble again, but please!"

He started to think he'd never leave Rikers, when one Sunday, he met another person who would tend and nourish the seed his mother had planted so long ago.

The steel door opened and an old man entered the cell-block. The shouting, foul language, and card-playing stopped. Some of the guys went into their cells while the rest turned to face their visitor.

"Good day, Pastor Jacob."

"How are you young men doing?"

"Fine," voices answered in unison.

"I've come to hold our morning mass."

"Did you bring cigarettes?" a voice blurted.

"After mass, young man," the minister answered.

After a brief mass was held, cigarettes, books, and candy bars were distributed. Everyone then went into their cells to read, munch, and smoke away. Pastor Jacob then commandeered a table and began to converse privately with each inmate who requested assistance. Having accepted several books, a few candy bars, and a handfull of tailor-made smokes, Joe was reviewing his gifts when he heard his name called.

"Joe . . . Joe, come here please," the Pastor called.

"Yeah, what do you want? How do you know me?" Joe said, as he came out of his cell.

"I always find out who the new guys are." Pointing toward a nearby seat the pastor inquired, "Can I please speak with you?"

"Why not?" Joe said, seating himself on the steel bench.

"How long have you been here?"

"A few weeks."

"Why are you here?"

"I don't know."

"Are you sure you don't know? You seem awfully young to be here. You should be in the Spotford Juvenile Detention Center; not here! Shall I do something, call someone?"

"Pastor, I don't want anyone to interfere with my situation. I appreciate your concern, but it'll work out."

"Are you a Catholic?" he asked in gentle tone.

"Yes, sir."

"Would you like me to . . ."

"Listen, I don't want anyone rocking the boat. Please. I appreciate your concern, but don't do anything!"

"OK, . . . but I will pray for you."

Over the course of the next few weeks, Joe began to talk with the Pastor on Wednesday nights and Sundays. They spoke of Joe-Pep. They spoke of all of the acts of God that had rescued him so many times. Pastor Jacob explained that God would always take care of him. Joe wanted to believe . . . he really did. But the main questions kept nagging at him—why? how? who? Pastor Jacob explained how Joe should seek the truth; that he should concentrate on correcting the cause of his pain by coming to that truth and facing his situation. He explained that he should seek answers to the questions and then, only then, would he have the ability to defeat the demons which were tearing him apart. He explained that discovery of the truth and answers to the questions that tossed and turned would not mean a total absolution of worries and pain, nor bring automatic relief. He said "the cause would be known . . . and with the knowledge of cause, its defeat could be planned, initiated, and implemented. Through—and with—the power of God . . . though sometimes it takes a horrendous occurrence to discover the truth."

Joe thanked him and prayed that a solution to his immediate situation would enable him to find his answers, but, deep in his heart, he felt that God truly didn't care!

"Joe, get your butt front and center!" the guard's shout pierced the noisy cell-block.

"Where'm I goin'?"

"Don't you worry . . . just keep your trap shut until we get down to the visiting area."

At the visiting area, Joe was placed in a cell with a steel table and several chairs. The guard disappeared. Joe sat in a chair and lowered his head upon the table awaiting his fate. The opening of the cell door awakened him. Tony Black, a short, muscular guy, cigarette dangling from his mouth, strode into the visiting cell. Unconsciously polishing a large diamond pinkie-ring against his suit jacket, he nodded the guard off and snatched a chair. He screeched the chair against the floor with its back facing the table, straddled it, and while flicking smoking ashes off his cigarette, began to speak.

"How ya doin, Joe? What's da problem? You know if you don't stop hitting our joints your gonna be in a real jam!"

"Listen, what worse jam can I get in! I'm sittin' in a jail, don't know what charges have been offered, and you're sitting here telling me this junk!"

"You really dink dat I'm gonna put up wid dat mouth of yours? You're lucky you didn' get your head broke! I knew your father, very well . . .. You gotta have respect or you will spoil his memory."

"If you knew my father, then what happened to him? Huh? If you know so much, what happened? All of you guys act so mighty. All I ever see is trouble from people like you!"

"Dat's not my problem. You just udderstan' dat you're gonna get out tonight. You gotta guy who's payin' to keep you safe . . . you need ta do tha right ding . . . you udderstan'? Da guy dat is gonna pick you up will take you to da guy you bin stealing dough from! You can tell 'im what you told me."

With all said, he got up and swaggered out the cell—leaving Joe to contemplate the events.

Joe had no idea that some wise guy was paying the jailers to keep him incommunicado. As far as the police were concerned, he had not committed a crime! He was ecstatic. He was overjoyed! But, he had to meet with the guy he had been "hitting." He was still not out of the woods . . .

"Oh, God, thank you for letting me out."

Chapter 26: And Thoughts of Revenge

At eleven that night, three guys—two resembling oversized apes, the other, a Wall Street lawyer-type—showed up and escorted him out of the jail building and into the back seat of a brand new, black Cadillac. The driver started the engine and they proceeded toward Little Italy. As the car bounced in and out of pot-holes, he began to think of the mess he was in. 'Would they talk with him and understand?' He didn't think so! 'If they thought he was not going to stop, he would be in trouble . . . At least he could keep his mouth shut concerning the others involved . . .'

"Hey, Mr. Tommy "TEE" Dipicio," the driver spat towards the large beast who sat beside him, interrupting Joe's desperate thought process. "We heard you're in line to be made!"

"Yeah, I'm da chip off da ol' block."

"That's why they call you "Ape." I unnerstan your fadder was a big shot with Maranzano in the twenties and thirties," the lawyer-looking guy shot back . . .

Yes, the thirties, with Alphonso dead and Antonio no longer independent; but part of the Maranzano family that was at war with Joe, "The Boss," Masseria. Though "The Young Turks" were making moves to eliminate the "Mustache Petes" and assume power, Don Maranzano decided to defeat Joe The Boss with the assistance of these Young Turks. They fell upon the "Don Caesar" and, as Brutus, brutally assassinated him with knives! A war between the faithful of the old against the new consumed many lives . . . and the dreams of those lives. Alliances and allegiances were swapped as fast as bullets leaving a tommy gun. (Salvatore) Charlie "Lucky" Luciano finally assumed the role of top boss . . .

. . . Joe The Boss sat enjoying lunch at his favorite restaurant, the Nuova Villa Tammaro in Coney Island. Through the window, the sights were lively and colorful. Over on the boardwalk, teeming with happy visitors, the ferris wheel was packed as normal. Parents watched in glee as their children, screaming with joy, rode the winding rollercoaster. Joe's guest was informing him of a plan to "take out" Don Maranzano.

Salvatore "Charlie Lucky" Luciano; right hand to Joe The Boss; with soldiers loyal only to him, had made a pact with Maranzano to take out

The Boss—but Luciano also planned to hit Maranzano at the same time. As the fat man stuffed his piggish snout, Lucky excused himself to attend to matters concerning the restroom. Genovese, Adonis, Anastasia, and Siegal appeared as suddenly as Luciano had left and, with purpose, fed Joe The Boss his metallic dessert. When the explosive racket subsided and the smoke cleared the air, Joe The Boss was a note for the history books on mob tradition, loyalty and respect.

News spread like the winds of Cape Horn, with speed, might, and grim death; ships of dreams, cruising the tides of the underworld—sank—capsized by a storm of revelation.

To the soldiers of Don Maranzano the news was not of a better future; the fact that the "Turks" had finished a job they could not, meant that the hierarchy would change—leaving them stranded on an island with no hope of rescue. Over the next four months, goaded by these capos, soldiers and advisers—"You can't trust him . . . look, he wacked his own boss!"—"Capo Di Tutti Capi", the Boss of Bosses, Supreme Godfather; Maranzano "secretly" made plans to contract outside of his family for the removal of Luciano. History books claim that Lucky Luciano was informed of this development and "retired" Maranzano for it, when in fact, it was a pre-planned course of action for a man of Luciano's ambitions—only hastened by Maranzano. The plan backfired. On the day the hit was to be carried out, Luciano moved ahead with his own plans.

In his new, luxurious offices at the Grand Central Building in Manhattan, high above bustling Park Avenue, Maranzano, cornered in a back room, was assassinated unlike a "Caesar" with knives by his Romans; but by knives and guns at the hands of "Barbarians." The first order of the day was the removal of the high office holders loyal to Maranzano. The Ape was the first to suffer a fate he could not even contemplate . . .

The Ape strolled to his car thinking of his heavy schedule. He had to stop at the butcher shop to take care of an order his wife placed, drop by Joe Adonis's joint and pick up some receipts, ride to the Don's office and take care of several items, swing around town back to Brooklyn and then join his family for the Communion of his son, Tommy, on Long Island.

It was around eleven in the morning when he turned onto busy Canarsy Street in Brooklyn. Vendors, well into their morning ritual, forced him to leave his car double-parked. Perturbed at this lack of respect, he entered Joe's Butcher Shop with a pronounced, forced, dominant swagger. The crowd of shoppers, recognizing The Ape's massive bulk, meekly parted way. Swift, shuffling feet, and loud, boisterous voices became hushed whispered murmuring. The sudden absence of activity alerted Joe the Butcher to The Ape's arrival. He immediately entered the main shop from the cutting room with a wide, beaming smile. "Heya Apa Mana, taka look ata veal—justa prepared," he said, as he turned and walked back into the cutting room. The Ape followed Joe the Butcher with a knowing grin; he expected this special treatment; he was the enforcer for "The Man"—and was to be accorded his due. All he could think about was how he'd surprise his wife—and his stomach—with a gift of fresh veal!

The Ape passed through the swinging double doors. The sight of the freshly cut veal on the cutting table made his stomach groan. He pictured it lightly breaded, fried in olive oil, and served with a side order of tomatoes seasoned with oregano. As he turned toward Joe, deep in thought, a butcher knife cleaved his skull in two . . .he never saw it coming.

Joe immediately emptied the store saying, "I'm a sorry . . .I gotta closa tha shopa . . .Pleasa coma back alatta."

The team—well rehearsed and prepared—lifted the body onto the cutting table. In twenty minutes they had chopped up the six-foot-four frame and deposited the remnants into cardboard boxes. As a member of the team drove the Cadillac to a Brooklyn salvage yard (and its own dismemberment) a truck pulled up back. The boxes were loaded for delivery to a private Crematorium in New Jersey. Within two hours, all evidence of the Ape's existence had disappeared. The once proud and feared enforcer was now nothing but ashes . . . so were the dreams of his son Tommy . . . who would wait patiently for his father's return . . .

. . . "Eh! Don' you call me Ape, dat's not my name. It's Tommy an don' you guys forget it! Who da hell iz dis kid? Why da boss wanna sit down wid a kid?"

"Dats Joe-Pep's kid, you know, your dad's friend . . ."

"Whoa! Now ya gonna really tee me off. Joe-Pep? Alphonso—Antonio-Joe-Pep-Joe-Pep?"

"Right. THAT Joe-Pep," Mr. Attorney said.

"Well, like-father-like-son. Da Don oughtta whack him like his father . . ."

"I gotta go!" Joe suddenly shouted, holding himself.

"Da only wear you gotta go is fifty more blocks, dat's where you gotta go."

"No," Joe shouted, "I GOTTA $%#@$%$# go! Or I'll pee in your car!"

The driver slammed on his brakes. "You gotta be kiddin? Ya dink I'm gonna let 'im pee on my floor? I jus' got dese here wheels . . . let 'im out! Now! Tommy, you keep an eye on 'im!"

"So, you knew my father?" Joe asked Tommy as his mind rushed with thoughts of escape.

"Dat was many moons ago . . . hurry up! An don' ya go in dat alley . . . ya dink I'm stupid or sumptin?"

"Hey, listen Tommy. I know where a lot of bread is stashed. I can give it to you! You can keep it, I don't care! Listen. I'm just a kid. Where am I gonna go? Just let me go and I'll . . ."

"Whaddya dink I am? Stupid! Git yo . . ."

"Hey, Tommy! LOOK!" Joe shouted like the guys in the movies, pointing behind Tommy. "It's the cops . . . Look! Hey . . ."

At first Tommy was not fooled by his antics, but a cat ran behind him—scurrying into a group of garbage cans. Tommy turned his head around for one tiny moment. At that precise moment, Joe tore through the alley way and hit the first fire escape he saw. Grabbing a garbage can in one motion, he turned it over, jumped on top, pulled the ladder down, and kicked the can away as he swung his feet up and onto its rungs. He was on the roof before the trio knew what happened.

After hiding out for two hours, several blocks and a couple of dozen roof tops away; he made it to Manhattan's Little Italy at around four a.m. and proceeded to Mr. Bianco's Deli. "Mr. Bianco would know." This Joe was sure of. Mr. Bianco would know . . . but would he will his facts and deductions on a lost and lonely boy? That remained to be seen!

The streets were dark and silent as he slowly made his way to Biano's place of business. Mr. Bianco lived above the store, so he slipped between parked cars lining the street and found his way to the doorway. He buzzed the bell until a light switched on in a window above. The rasping of a window sliding against its old wood runners delivered a high-piercing screech, which broadcast through the still and silent night like someone's scream of pain. Ducking down, eyes squinting, he glanced at all of the windows of the buildings in the neighborhood to see if anyone was awakened by the abrupt noise; there he remained, a still figure, melting into a landscape of jumbled garbage cans, cold, black, iron railings, and empty shadows until a head poked out the window and he heard the familiar voice call out, "Whoa ringa mya bell thisa time ina mornin?"

"Mr. Bianco. It's me. Joe!"

"Joe, it'sa you?" he inquired. "Oh, you betta geta insida right now!" he exclaimed in haste, as his head ducked inside and a buzzer announced the opening of the door with a loud click.

Climbing stairs three at a time, Joe reached the landing and door before Mr. Bianco could open it. When the door did open, Bianco pulled him through—locking and double bolting it in a hurry. He then began talking as he rushed to the window and surreptitiously viewed the street below.

"You'a ina trouble? You should'a wenta the meet!"

Joe proceeded to inform him of the entire story, not leaving anything out. He told him of the hospital; the family; the agony of his life. His mind just opened up. "Mr. Bianco, what happened to my father? How did he die? What happened to my family, my grandfather . . . my mother? Please, I'm old enough to know . . . will you put my mind to rest?"

After preparing coffee, they sat down and Mr. Bianco began his tale. Soon, stories of life, of people, places and events, of several lifetimes, flowed as clear as a mountain stream from Mr. Bianco's wise and knowledgeable mind. At eighty-five years of age, Mr. Bianco had not lost a speck of information. Like an old, village wise man, informing a pupil and future leader of his ancestors's heredity, he spoke as if he had not spoken in twenty years. What a sight it was: two human beings, separated by immense time and journey, joined together in thought and story—the first; a vast reservoir of knowledge; begins to leak, then to flow, finally it pours forth in overwhelming facts and details; the other, a compressed sponge, absorbing all—even the overflow . . . until it is saturated . . .

"Ana besida the copa ana Tony da Blacka, thera was anota guy coulda dona da joba . . ."

"Clear skys and eighty degrees . . ." satisfied, Shorty turned the radio off. "Hey, Thumbs, get the car . . . we're goin' to the track for the meet!"

Sun, palm trees, humidity, dog tracks and "Shorty" were synonymous to Miami. One did not take a bet, loan money, nor approve a heist in South Florida without Shorty's approval. Though a ranking member of the Gen-

ovese Crime Family in Miami and Hallendale, Florida, Shorty was actually a diplomat to the many national crime families who did business in the open territory of South Florida. You could usually find him at one of the dog or horse tracks during the season, hobnobbing with some of the most prominent members of the ruling mob families. He was happy the weather called for clear skys—though no October showers were going to call off the meet between Meyer and the Big Guys from The City! With Castro in full power in Cuba, most of the top ranking members of the mob had lost tremendous amounts of cash and property. Plans were being made to topple Castro and to increase the lucrative smuggling of Cuban businessmen and their liquid assets to the shores of Miami. Shorty was buckling his gold watch to his wrist when the phone rang.

"Hey Boss, it's your brother," a voice called from the kitchen.

"I'll take it in the study . . . ," Shorty replied as he swaggered into an opulent room.

Picking up a gold gilded phone, Shorty sat on a leather couch, his feet smoothing the snowy white carpet he was famous for, "Yeah, what's goin' on?" he asked into the handset as he viewed the blue sky and blue-green ocean through the wall to wall glass doors.

"Shorty, Pauly passed away! That #$%$#& dropped $%&^%$ dead. The Ham is roast pig!!"

"Yeah . . . and?"

"Well, you know dat Joe-Pep don' hav a leg ta stan' on!"

"You know, if ya kept that mouth of yours shut, we would not be in this $%#^%^& predicament. I'm tired of your big mouth . . . you got that? Just because you're my brother dose not mean I'm going to keep bailing you out! You unnerstand me?"

"Well, I was just thinking about your reputation!"

"My %^&$%^* reputation! You listen to me! You may be my brother, but you're a punk! You keep putting your foot in your mouth. Those guys were right in smacking you around! The only thing was that you're my brother! You just keep that trap shut and I'll take care of the situation!!!" Shorty slammed the phone down and strutted through the apartment with a retinue of gophers scurrying to catch up.

Until he reached the kicker . . .

The diabolical chariot of death, sleek in its shroud of pitch-black midnight, with only a door-thud in the night, swallowed up its cold and sinister companions. Then, with calculated determination, it zoomed off for its next intended victim in a never-ending quest to satisfy an acquired taste for blood and power.

"Ana thatsa story of a youa Pop" . . .

* * *

It was nine a.m. by the time the one sided conversation ended.

Outside, the streets were teeming with traffic and people when Joe rose and kissed Mr. Bianco on his cheek and, with a hearty bear hug, thanked him from the bottom of his heart.

As he turned towards the door, Mr. Bianco provided the same time-tested words that he had embraced his Great, Great Grandfather Alphonso with: "Rememba, usa the words, I'ma foreva ina your debta, Don Gambino, Howa cana humbla person sucha I, assista man so esteema asa your selfa . . ."

Joe was now the only one who truly understood the truth, but just how would he react?

After his conversation with Mr. Bianco, Joe telephoned his grandmother and point-blank asked her for the truth of fathers 'accident'. Nana Lou broke down in tears when he confronted her. For the following hour, he was once more privy to a story of truth. Her recollection only differed with Bianco by the details as she knew them—and this only fortified the truth as told by Mr. Bianco . . .

" . . . and then, there was this guy, he borrowed money from your father . . . was supposed to pay him weekly. After several no-shows, your father and uncle caught up to him. He began telling Joe-Pep he was not going to pay them; that his brother was a big shot who had the "juice" to take care of things. When he mentioned Shorty's name, your uncle tried to tell your father they had better wait until they checked his story and then bring it before the commission. The guy kept running his mouth and your father jumped the gun and beat him up. When the word hit the streets, your father and uncle were "called on the carpet" and told to leave this guy alone. But, right after the sit-down, this guy went to your father's joint and began running his mouth . . . your father and uncle beat him again. But, their murderers remain a mystery, cause it could have been any one of them, including that guy from Florida."

"Was he dead when they found him?" he had asked as sorrowful pictures of his father's last moments flashed in slow motion in his mind.

"Your father was dead when they found him."

The need to overcome thoughts of his father; his 'Knight in Shining Armor,' who wore a trench coat and carried a .45; lying in a pool of blood . . . his dying thoughts of his family, his hopes, his dreams . . . filled his soul with a mixture of sorrow, revenge, and questions.

'Who was responsible? Sally? Tony Black? Uncle Frank? Genovese? Gambino? The Police? Shorty? All of them? And, how could these people go home and play with their children? How did they join their families in celebration, that day so long ago? How could they enjoy each succeeding holiday of family solace and warmth when they had destroyed the very essence of an entire family?' Death could not be simplified and dignified, especially when there were others who were mourning that death. So many thoughts converged within his novice mind. Revenge was the traffic cop . . . He would get revenge. They had stolen his mother's happiness and thrust Joe-Pep's surviving family into a world of sorrow and depravity; ending their lives before they began! He'd become a vagabond left in a wake of cold, hard silence; lost in nomadic journey upon an endless desert, burdened by a never-ending avalanche, with each step of hope foundering in a lucid, liquid sand-trap; finding relief and succor concealed in a host of additional questions as soon as truth had been discovered.

"The Family", "This Thing of Ours," had become a ravaging beast bent upon total destruction, leaving orphans of society in its quest for life. For a mere child of the storm, it was he who was left to pick up the pieces. Would he ever? Would he become the man who avenged the dishonor and sorrow placed upon his family with total disregard to the repercussions of this disastrous act of continuing greed?

'You will prevail! . . . 'But, what of Spartacus? What of all those heroes who battled injustice only to die a glorious death in the end! Was he ready for that? Like Charlton Heston in *Ben Hur,* would he return for the ending the hero who rescued his family with the assistance of God?'

"Oh, Jesus, where art thou now? Come to me and deliver your power to defeat mine enemies—they abound like a plague of locust. Send to them a shower of fire and ice! The death of the first born has occurred! Please, let my people go! This trial and tribulation has desecrated my soul, my 'Knight in Shining Armor' is gone. Will you to take up my cause?"

'Was God going to perform miracles of Faith? Those same miracles which had burst his soul with His power to overcome his handicap?' He could not answer those questions; later maybe, but for now, the overpowering need to get even overruled any further thought. He'd have to leave New York and plan his action!

After the meet, he'd leave once more, only this time, the desire for a real family, a real father figure and real change in his life would clash with his new plan—his plan of revenge and rescue!

"I am forever in your debt, Don Gambino, how can a humble man as myself, assist a man so esteemed as you?" Another soldier of the hand, the fifth generation to do so, had spoken those words of respect. This one, the youngest by far, did so with a mixture of fear and revenge welling from the depths of his being.

"You have committed an act of supreme disrespect yet you now show me respect? This is most encouraging. But listen to me, a thief does not steal from a thief. And a thief doesn't crap in his own back yard."

"But I . . ." Joe began to tell him that it was not his fault and then stopped, realizing that a man of respect only understood two things: Respect . . . or a .45! " . . . I apologize and will return your money. It may take some time, but I will return it."

"If it weren't for your age I'd have your head . . . but, for now, due to your mother, grandmother, and your Uncle Franky here, I'll allow you to repay your debt to me. I am not sure how, but you will find out shortly. I want you to go home and stay there. You'll help your Uncle for the rest of the year at his shop . . . and you'll hear from me shortly."

With that said, Mr. Gambino dismissed him to the care of Uncle Franky, who told him to wait in the car . . .

No sooner had Joe left "to wait in the car" . . .

did he zoom off . . .

. . . once again!

Part Four: Demon Skip Tracers

"It was I who allowed you to enjoy your infamy!

As the Beast, his whole being immersed in defilement, roared in dripping rage, a hush descended the desecrated crimson cavern. Impaled upon his massive, slimy, spear-tipped tail, Snatching Souls; he who was called the second Feranzi; fought a losing battle in his attempt to patronize his master.

"Sire! Sire!" he shrieked between disgusting bursts of putrid slime belching from his innards . . . "Yes! Yes! You are always right! I will listen. I will obey your every command . . ."

"At last, do we see??"

""Oh, yes, my bleak and black-hearted master. I see!"

"So, now that you have seen . . ."

As if a sweet and delectable object, swirling with pleasure in one's mouth, had instantly turned repulsive and revolting, Feranzi was spat off of the Beast's tail. As he sailed through the cavern howling with pain and the knowledge he was being processed alive; the flesh on his body began to sizzle, in bits and terrible pieces, strips of his melting flesh, rent in sheets of blinding pain, were gobbled by scores of chalk-white skulls. The more he screamed the more the skulls clamored to plant their mouths upon his being. Soon, hundreds of mouthing skulls, nimble sharks in a feeding frenzy of torture, gorged upon his soul!

"Step forward, Captain Nicolus Jobuly!" the Beast commanded.

Captain Jobuly, terrified by the demonstration of the Beast's power and pleasure—a demonstration none of the condemned members of The Devil's Brigade were immune to—stepped up and bowed upon the living, skull-full throne.

Immediately, writhing, fleshless mouths, caught up in the pain and suffering, contorted in their determination to feast upon his dead-yet-living flesh; razor sharp teeth and white-bony gums flashed in a crescendo of hunger as he lowered himself and planted a kiss upon the Beast's foul toe claws.

"Arise! For you are to lead the battle! Go and bring to me what is wrongfully mine!"

As Jobuly exited the grim cavern of death, he felt a sweltering rush of anguish and misery sweep as a desert wind, howling in the depths of scarlet affliction, across the writhing, blood-red, white-specked walls, floors, and ceilings. There was no end! There was no relief! Like all before him, he could only prolong the inevitable: he had to get Joe's soul!

Chapter 27: The Quest Continues . . .

He stood on the side of the road, thumb out, facing south. He had no idea where he was going, only that his continual quest to find a place to sleep, eat, and then move on, was becoming a never-ending cycle. You gotta keep movin and meetin new people—before the old ones figure you out. He knew his father and Uncle Carmine's deaths, which had overpowered his mind again once the threat of Gambino retaliation had wavered, would soon fade into the same dull, milky-white memory that had enveloped his mind after their "accident." He was sure they'd joined his ancestors among the lost souls that were now suffering a fate in Purgatory—or even Hell—which was something he could not dwell on. The best he could do was light candles at a Catholic church in its "lost souls" section—complete with deep, red candleholders and fragrant incense. He thought about what he'd do:

Kneel beside old grandmothers dressed in symbolic black; chanting prayers of forgiveness in tune with their ever-present rosaries. Then he'd place his dime, clinging into an elaborate change box, and ring an announcement in Heaven that another prayer had been entered for THEM. He wondered how many dimes it would take until they would be allowed to join God in Heaven. His reflections only reinforced a fact he knew; once he ignited his wooden match against the striker, an explosion of tired, old, wrinkled faces of despair would appear—revealing their pain of worry and hope.

Would Joe be that old and gray, before He heard Joe's prayers? What if He didn't hear them at all? Ever? Who'd pray for Joe-Pep and

Uncle Carmine when Joe was gone? Thoughts of vengeance entered his mind, even in this House of God . . . he'd get even!

The thought brought on a calming effect. Yes, he'd learn how to get even.

Peacefully alone with his thoughts; standing on the side of the road; Joe recalled his last ride: a slow-talking, southern trucker who never questioned his motives, just asked if he'd help him unload his semi when they arrived at his destination. For this, he gave Joe his first chew of "tabaky"and a free ride—with meals—and ten dollars.

They stopped for meals and rest at various truck stops along the way; each place teeming with magical people who roamed the towns, cities, and country-side of this great land.

Sitting in a corner booth in the company of gregarious people, munching on plates of home cooked food, was invigorating. With mouth full and ears wide open, he listened with fascination as they spun tales and drew him into their web of banter. He couldn't mask his curiosity and ambition to visit the strange, far-away places they talked about: A city so high the air was hard to breath!—A bridge spanning a wide, deep bay with no supporting columns!—The French Quarter, with buildings Andrew Jackson visited, and night spots where women danced naked on a stage! Really? Live alligators! Grizzly bears! Indians! . . . Wow! Movies come to life!

But now he was on the move again . . . in day-dreams, not thinking about his family, his problems, nor his fate. Just waiting for the next ride—and wondering where it would take him.

It was in the middle of the day and Joe had made it just north of Biloxi, Mississippi. He was famished. Checking his resources, he saw he had nine bucks and change—so he looked for a place to eat. It was then he saw the weirdest thing of all his life: a sign on the window of a restaurant announcing "BREAKFAST SERVED ALL DAY - NO COLORED ALLOWED."

Flabbergasted, he looked at it and tried to figure it out . . . but he couldn't. Curious and hungry, he walked in and sat down at the counter. The waitress came over and he asked her what the sign meant.

"It means that nigger's don' eat here. We don't care what them Yankees say," she said in a normal, everyday way.

He looked at her but didn't reply.

"You gonna eat, or jus sit there?"

"Eat," he said, snapping out of his reverie. 'What was this Yankee stuff? Was she talking about him?'

The waitress brought a menu and he thanked her profusely. 'Why am I nervous around her?' Joe wondered, 'She's the #@$@!&*.'

The greasy menu could have been written in Greek—he was lost as soon as he read it. "Hominy Grits"—did this mean singing food or what? "Pigs in a Blanket"—are they cold? "Flap Jacks"—he didn't even want to guess! "Molasses . . . maple syrup "—Ah, this he recognized."Sorghum"—what was that? Are they for real?

"Chipped beef and gravy?"

"Corn Bread?"

"Peach Cobbler?"

"Sour Dough Biscuits?"

The list of strange sounding dishes continued, so he just pointed to the special: grits, eggs, and sour dough biscuits.

It turned out to be fantastic food—he ate till he thought he was going to—bust and the bill was only $1.89!

He got up and went outside to investigate the town. Soon he was lost, all the streets seemed to end in the middle of town; where everything was divided into colors . . . not of the rainbow . . .but of people—black and white. Even the drinking fountains in the small park he walked through were labeled black and white.

When his fascination with this strange place waned, he asked directions to Miami from an elderly black man sitting on a dilapidated rocking chair on the front porch of a barbershop, "Scuse me, man, but which one of these roads goes east toward Florida?"

After a momentary hesitation, and recognizing no enmity in Joe, the old fella pointed meekly toward a dusty side road just as a worn-out beige Impala turned the corner and pulled over to the curb. Joe noticed the immediate change in the black man: eyes cast downward, rocking motion slowed to a stop.

Leaning across the seat and winding down the window the driver demanded, "Where you from, boy?"

Thinking "I've seen this routine before" Joe replied in his friendliest voice, "Up north."

"Get in the car."

When Joe hesitated, the man, face red with indignation, fished around in his shirt pocket and produced a tarnished sheriff's badge.

The old black man went into a wailing lamentation, "I'za don' do nuthin, Mr. Henry, sir. I swear, I'ze don' . . ."

With a sigh and a bland backward wave of his hand, the sheriff motioned Joe to the passenger door as he opened it from inside. Wearily, Joe swept the crushed Dixie cups and empty Red Man pouches onto the floorboard and dropped into the seat. After hearing a lecture about roaming "his" streets and "mixin with coloreds," the sheriff dropped him off at the right intersection and advised Joe to take the first ride he could get. After what seemed like an eternity, a trucker stopped and offered Joe a ride toward Birmingham. Joe's visit to Mississippi, that had started with so much promise in that corner booth in Martha's Country Kitchen, had ended on a sad and disappointing note. He'd remember the bigotry a lot more than the home fries and grits.

They arrived in Geneva County, Alabama, late in the afternoon and, after unloading the semi, he pocketed five bucks and was on his way again. As he walked a quiet stretch of two-lane highway with his thumb out, he noticed the traffic picking up—everything from mule and horse drawn wagons to open cars and pick-ups. In the distance he could see a huge red, white, and blue tent with streamers fluttering in the wind and crowds of folks milling around. He thought he'd discovered a carnival or what he'd heard called in this area "a county fair!" After washing up in a small pond behind the main tent, Joe hurried back to see the sights. By now the crowd was overflowing into the open field! He approached the crowd with caution . . .

" . . . AND THE LORD WILL CASTIGATE, HUMILIATE, AND FORMULATE YOUR SOULS INTO THE FIERY PIT OF HELL! SEEK YE HIS BLESSINGS! HEAR YE HIS WORD! EXCEPT YE CHRIST . . . OR YOU WILL BURN FOR ETERNITY! YES, I HAVE COME; NOT AS A MESSENGER OF DOOM AND GLOOM—BUT AS A MESSENGER OF ETERNAL LIGHT AND LOVE!

"SAY IT REVEREND, SAY IT! HALLELUJAH "

"COME TO JESUS AND BE SAVED . . . OR BE DAMNED INTO THE BOTTOMLESS PIT OF ETERNAL DAMNATION."

"AAAYYMEN! YES! YES! SAY IT, REVEREND!"

"AND I QUOTE, ROMANS 7-16 . . . 'YOU CAN CHOOSE YOUR OWN MASTER . . . YOU CAN CHOOSE SIN, OR ELSE, OBEDIENCE TO THE LORD. WHICH DO YOU CHOOSE . . .

WHOM DO YOU STAND BY?'"

"AAAYYMEN . . . OH, LORDY! AMEN!"

"THROW AWAY THOSE BOTTLES AND JUGS OF CORN LIQUOR . . . STOP THAT WICKED FORNICATION . . . TURN OFF THAT SINFUL MUSIC . . . REPENT! REPENT! REPENT! REPENT I SAY TO YOU."

"YESSIR . . . ALL RIGHT! . . . SAY IT REV . . . SAY IT. IN JESUS' NAME, SAY IIIIIT!"

BLOOOOOW YOOOOUR TRUUUUUUMPETS AND THE WAAAAAALLS OF JERICO WILL COME TUMBLING DOWN . . . SIN AND WORRY CAST INTO A HEAP OF WRETCHED RUBBLE . . . ONLY GLORY AND PEACE LEFT IN IT'S WAKE!"

"AAYYMEN! Amazing Grace, How sweet the sound . . ."

Joe did a double take . . . this was a Christian tent revival just like the one he'd seen Burt Lancaster perform at Steinway's corner movie house in Queens—Elmer Gantry! A tall guy with an awesome power of speech stood up on the stage, draped in sweat and righteousness, delivering a sermon that had these people writhing on the ground!

Joe was amazed! In his Church people just didn't act this way. In fact, it was a sin to even enter any church but a Catholic Church! He began to wonder if a tent could be a "house" of worship. Though he knew better, his curiosity demanded he determine if, in fact, it was Burt Lancaster who was delivering this fiery speech that had so many people singing, chanting, and generally going bonkers!

"SONNY, COME RIGHT UP HERE! THAT'S RIGHT! FOLKS, MAKE ROOM FOR THIS CHILD OF GOD TO RECEIVE CHRIST!"

"Is he talking to me?" Joe asked himself as he tried to get close to the stage—the man's eyes were on him and he was pointing directly at him!

"HELP HIM . . . I SAY HELP HIM . . . I SAY HELP HIM UUUUP TO THE LOOOORD!"

Joe felt faint the way he had on that fateful day four years ago in their box-car flat in Queens; a multitude of hands and extremities, all mish-mashed into a blur of motion, grabbed hold of Joe and lifted him high above their heads, passing him along the top of the swarming crowd to land at the feet of the preacher.

Angela, Jeanette and Joe. Check out the club feet.

Nana Lou 1950

Young Joe at Holy Communion

Find .38 Pistol Believed Used In Cafe Rubout

A .38 revolver, believed to be the weapon used in the rubout of brothers Carmine and Joseph Baffa, was found by a detective yesterday in a vacant lot around the corner from the Yorkville pizzeria where the brothers were gunned down Monday night.

DAILY NEWS NOV 29 1961

The weapon, its chamber empty, was turned over to ballistics detectives for testing. It was the

Joseph Baffa

Carmine Baffa

best clue the cops had in a case that Capt. Michael Clifford, of Manhattan North detectives, admitted "has us facing a blank wall."

Each Shot 3 Times

Carmine, 41, and Joseph, 39, each were shot three times at close range. Joseph was dead when police arrived at the pizzeria at 1528 York Ave., at 81st St. Carmine was staggering about the restaurant, but died before he could be taken to a hospital.

Detective Walter Curtayne, one of 30 detectives on the case, picked up the revolver from a lot at what formerly was 520 E. 81st St. shortly after noon.

Both the slain men, police said, were ex-convicts.

From *NEW YORK DAILY NEWS,* November 29, 1961

Two Brothers Slain Gang Style

By ARTHUR NOBLE and FRANK MAZZA

In a double murder with every appearance of an underworld rubout, two brothers vith long police records were shot to death at 9:30 last night in the kitchen of their 'orkville pizzeria.

Hit twice in the head and once n the chest, Joseph (Mario) [illegible], 39, apparently died in- [illegible]tly. But the elder brother, 'armine L. Baffa, 41, though ortally wounded in the neck and hest, was still on his feet, stag- ering around the blood-spattered oom, when the first cops arrived.

Patrolmen Thomas Mannion and oseph Seiter of the E. 67th St. tation asked him what had hap- ened, but he was incoherent. efore the cops could reach him, fell dead on his brother's body.

There was no sign of a struggle nd no indication of any attempt rob[illegible]ery. Both men wore wrist atches, Carmine had $6.55 in his ockets and there was $11 and ange in the cash register. Joseph had no money and there were no papers in his pockets, so that police were unable to establish where he lived. Carmine lived at 1069 Washington Ave., Westbury, L. I.

Tenants of the building told detectives they heard five shots and saw two men running.

Check Jersey Car

The brothers' records included arrests for assault and robbery and policy operations, and Capt. Michael J. Clifford, commander of Manhattan North detectives, said, "It looks like a racket knockoff."

Police were checking the ownership of a 1957 Chevrolet with New Jersey license plates which was parked in front of the restaurant. Leo Perry, superintendent of the building, said he had seen the brothers driving the car, but Capt. Clifford said neither apparently was the owner—that they evidently had borrowed it.

Perry said the restaurant had changed hands several times over the years and nobody ever seemed to make a go of it. The Baffa brothers bought it last summer.

The room is nine feet wide, with space for only nine tables. The whole shop is about 40 feet deep including the kitchen. If it was no great shakes as a restaurant, it was a good place to commit a murder. There is no rear exit, and the brothers were trapped when the gunmen walked in.

Article from the *New York Times,* November 28, 1961

From left: Jeanette, Angela, and Nana Lou. At Coney Island.

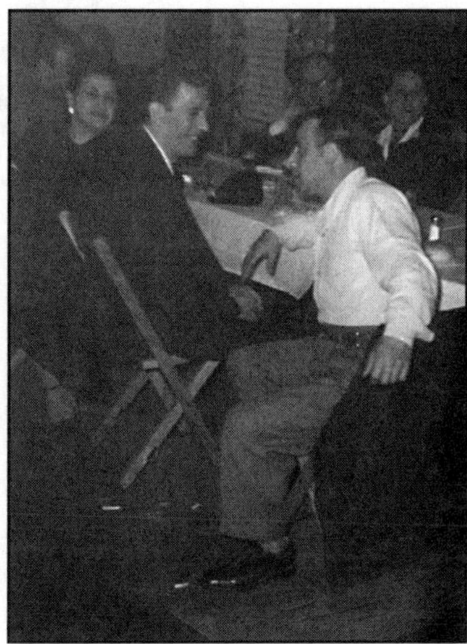

Joe-Pep and "Family" at the social club.

"IT'S TIME FOR HIS REBIRTH! LET ALL WHO DESIRE REBIRTH FOLLOW ME TO THE WATERS OF LIFE AND BE WASHED WITH THE POWER OF THE HOLY SPIRIT!"

The next thing he knew, the force of the crowd had carried him along as it swelled out the rear of the tent toward the pond.

"IN THE NAME OF THE LORD . . ."

Joe never heard another word or sound other than his gulps for air and the air bubbles that rushed out of his mouth as his head, bobbing like an apple in a wash tub, was pushed up and down into the icy cold water of the pond!

What Joe learned on his southern swing was that the people were friendly once they saw that you represented no threat. The challenge was getting them to see you weren't a threat! They saw enemies everywhere!

He was standing soaking wet with his thumb out when the police cruiser stopped and an officer stepped out.

"Boy, what are you doin here in my county? Let's see your ID."

"I have almost ten dollars . . . but I lost my ID . . . back there at the revival. I got baptized!"

This surprising news made the patrolman hesitate, then say, "You sound like you're one of them New Yorkers. What're you doin' down here?"

"I'm heading east, on my way to Miami."

"Baptized, huh? I bet you went for a swim. That Preacher Smithfield, he's somethin' else, ain't he? . . . What's your name?"

"I'm eighteen. My name's Mike Clark . . . Jr."

"Git in th' car—I'm taking ya in", he said, grabbing his arm roughly.

The patrol car stopped in front of an old concrete building with a sign, thick with countless layers of paint, reading, "Geneva County Jail - Home of Law and Order."

Sheriff D.T. Williams and his jailer-wife were the law and order. They ruled the county—along with the Judge. Their attitude was "This is our house—we're the law—order what you want."

The operation was simple. Officer Williams would keep the streets clean by arresting all hitch-hikers under the pretense of vagrancy. If you didn't have an ID or enough cash, then you were thrown into their bleak jail along with an assorted combination of riff-raff, drunks, town bums, and an occasional thief to await trial. The Judge would pass a sentence of 30 to 90 days or, if you had cash, a hefty fine. Fines were split by the trio. Those who couldn't afford to pay the fine would spend the next several months working on the Judge's farm. All food served in the jail was supplied by his farm and the county and state money allocated for each prisoner's sustenance was also pocketed by the trio.

The interrogation began, "Who are ya?—How old are ya?—Why'd ya run away?—Where ya from? Ya need a hair cut an we're gonna cut it!"

After all the experiences he'd been through, in a quiet but menacing voice, Joe informed Sheriff Williams he was in for the fight of his life if he so much as touched his head. After a momentary staring battle, Sheriff Williams thought better of it and welcomed Joe to a six-week stay in the "Alabama Cross Bar Hilton"—the hair cut was not mentioned again.

Joe was placed in a cell with several locals, including an old man who made periodic visits for town drunkenness, two deserters from the Navy, and some guy who committed an offense against the Judge himself. Joe settled down to evaluate his situation and examine his surroundings. The cells were painted black as if that could cover the filth. The beds, black-painted steel bunks sprouting from the walls, contained bug-infested mattresses and a single stained and grime covered blanket. After a single day he caught a bad case of the crabs, chiggers, or was it bed bugs? He went to sleep fine and woke up itching like a hound dog.

The "good ole navy boys" had the answer. "Take some of this kerosene and paint remover, mix it and pour it on your entire body. An don't forget your $#%&*!"

On the top bunk, naked from the waist down . . . jumping and hollering like a banshee, "Holy $#%* It burns like fire!"

Red and swollen, he jumped on that "good ole boy" and tried to beat him senseless! The navy boys laughed so hard they nearly busted a gut. Not only were his private parts red, swollen and sore—so was his pride. Sheriff Williams brought him some ointment, had the cells cleaned and disinfected, then re-evaluated his thoughts of Joe. "Boy, I'm watchin' you. You stay in the cell. No work detail tomorrow."

Time Joe spent in the library reading books—combined with another tradition handed down through the ages from father to son—the art of wine-making. This gave him an idea.

Joe-Pep had brewed home-made wine; Great-Grandfather Antonio had brewed home-made wine . . . and Joe was going to brew home-made wine—in a jail—using raisins, yeast and glass milk bottles!

There they were . . . all five of them . . . drunk . . . laughing . . . making money selling their home-made Raisin Jack to other inmates . . . Officer Williams walking through the cell-block complaining of the odor of sour fruit in the air . . .

"Fred, you worthless piece of $#*#@! Get off your butt and git these cells cleaned out! It stinks in here!" Fred, the trustee, only had two months left to serve on a dognapping "charge." Seems he had stolen the Judge's prize hounddogs and sold them to a black family in Wetumpka.

In Fred's thorough determination to obey Sheriff Williams (combined with Joe's natural ability to convince folks to do things they never even contemplated—along with the help of "Raisin Jack,") he not only cleaned out the cells . . . he cleaned out the Williams's car, his wallet, and the jail of several southern desperadoes, including Josh Webb!

Josh Webb and Joe got along great. Joe listened to his stories and vice-versa. Webb's father had been killed in World War II and he grew up in an orphanage. He had been abused as a boy, and been all alone for years. He'd been sentenced to three years in "The Big House," in Slapout, Alabama. Seems he had the longest criminal record in the county; full of petty crimes magnified by his ineptness—and the fact that there was very little true crime in this well maintained community. Joe hung with Josh for three weeks and, feeling sorry for him, eventually hatched the plan to free him.

Joe had convinced Fred that Joe's family was powerful, with mob connections. He told Fred he couldn't tell the authorities who he was because his family's name would be published.

On the night the escape took place, Williams was asleep and Fred—who had a key because he cleaned the cells and served meals—opened the cells and drove Josh and several others to the Georgia border in the Williams's car that Fred "borrowed." Fred immediately turned around, high-tailed it back to Geneva County, and claimed he'd been forced to assist in the escape. Only his knowledge of the Williams's and the Judge's operation allowed him to escape prosecution. But D. T. Williams discovered who was responsible: the conniving moonshiner from New York!

"What're we gonna do with you?" D.T. asked in all seriousness. "Why don't you tell me who you are . . . and I'll jes send ya home?"

"If I do that you'll be in a terrible situation. I'm a juvie . . . and you've held me illegally."

The look on Williams's face was most revealing. Joe informed D.T. Williams that his operation was also illegal and that the FBI would probably be highly interested. His conversation with Josh had produced the desired results. Officer Williams frowned, shrugged his shoulders, and sent him back to his cell. Three days later he was informed he would be leaving in two weeks; the county would pay his bus fare or give him the money to go wherever he wanted to go!

Back in his cell, though he partied with his cell-mates, he dreaded the thought of being alone again.

On a bright, cheerful, late summer day, keys clanged and doors flew open—he was free. D.T. Williams gave him a lift to the highway at the county line and one-hundred dollars!

Chapter 28: Discovery or Tragedy

They picked up a depressed and homesick Joe on Alabama highway 20. Their names were Robert and Gail Blount, a God-loving family who lived above Bainbridge, Georgia. They were down to earth, third generation farming people who lived with the land; alongside nature.

Joe acted like he was a grown man; for hours telling them of his travels and such. But they saw the truth with their hearts—a young boy who thought he was a man. They decided to offer their love. They didn't ask questions, just provided something which could not be bought nor traded for.

"Listen, you look like you could use some home cooking and some sleep. We're on our way to Tallahassee, Florida. We'll be gone for two days. But we'll drive you to town and you can stay with a friend till we get back. You're welcome to stay with us until you get on your feet."

It was an offer Joe could not refuse.

. . . The Blount "house" stood crooked within a pocket of green pines. A weathered shack, built upon four red squares of crumbling brick with rusty metal sheeting for a roof and an awkward brick chimney protruding through it at an angle—it brought to mind a picture combining The Cat in the Hat, Daniel Boone, and a mountain cabin in West Tennessee. 'Could this be the right place?' Joe thought, as he cautiously mounted two moaning stairs onto a crooked porch and grasped an empty screen door. Ripped and torn metal screen, remnants of the one that had once been placed to bar the horde of flies which buzzed around, like so many miniature sawmills, rasped against his hand as he opened it to knock on the front door. Through cracks in the door's hand-hewn boards, he could see Gail Blount as she hurried about straightening the front room. He was looking down at himself, tucking in his shirt, when the door opened.

"You found the place!" she said with a smile that made the shack seem a mansion.

"Yes, ma'am, it wasn't any problem," he answered her as he shuffled his way inside.

She closed the door and asked him to take a seat. He sat down and looked around as she talked about the visit to Tallahassee.

Just four rooms, divided by simple, flimsy walls of weathered boards nailed to rough two by fours. You could jump and grab onto any wall, pull yourself up, and see the next room. There was no interior ceiling; only the bright metal of the underside of the tin roof. The "living room," with its quilt-covered bed, rocking chair, old dresser drawers, shot guns, deer antlers, various animal pelts—squirrel, rabbit and possum—lining the walls, and a large cross, brought to mind a wilderness cabin rather than a family room. Through the entrance to the kitchen you could see a wood stove, shelves lined with preserves, and a hand-made table. There were two primitive bedrooms for four young children. There was no indoor plumbing, so water was drawn from a "dry well" that collected rain water! Joe was amazed.

"Are you hungry?" Gail interrupted.

Before he could reply, she arose from the squeaking wood rocker and walked into the kitchen to prepare a sandwich of homemade bread and venison.

After several days, Joe realized it was a tremendous love and belief in God that motivated these simple folk—it was awesome! They blessed God every day for their lives and were joyous, even though their lives required so much sacrifice. They were not caught up in a world of greed or denial; on the contrary, they found joy in the family, and lived for it! He knew he had been rescued through God. He knew he would enjoy this brief interlude from the harsh life he had been born to. He also realized this was to be a learning experience.

Robert worked at the local dairy where the pay was low and the work hard. With six mouths to feed, he also grew vegetables in a small plot of rich, black earth that bordered the house. Robert hunted whenever he could and, on his days off, began taking Joe with him to hunt the small game that dressed their dining table. As they stalked rabbits and squirrels among the pine forests and hay fields of the surrounding land, he would tell Joe stories of the Big Hunt "that was right around the corner."

"It's a time for all woodsmen of the county to assemble deep in the timberlands and celebrate manhood. It don't make no difference nohow whether you're rich, poor, a gas station attendant, or a business owner. Everyone shares in the chores and joys of the hunt; pretense and boast are lost among facts of courage and tests of will."

As Robert told the tale of the hunt, visions of a blazing campfire, crackling with sound and light; reflecting men seated 'round, bedecked in fringed buckskin with coon-skin caps; gleaming long-barreled rifles and long, sharp bowie knives tucked deep in belts of woven rawhide shot through Joe's mind, eclipsing all other thoughts and matters—if only he could . . .

Several weeks later, Robert secured Joe a part time job cleaning the milking stalls at the dairy. Joe bought a .410 shotgun—Robert said a 12 gauge was too big for his five-two frame—with his first two paychecks and Robert taught him how use, take care of, and respect it. The first squirrel he shot, skinned (preparing his own brew to rid its gaminess) and cooked, made him feel manly and proud. As the big weekend approached, he began to boast of his hunting prowess—hoping to be invited. A fatherless boy in the company of down-home fathers, he desperately wanted to be part of the experience. He also wanted to be a man . . . but Robert acted aloof and unaware.

The night before Robert was to set out, he called him on the porch. Expecting an apology and a promise of "maybe next time," Joe was thrilled when in stoic candor, Robert told him he was invited along!

Several three-sided, open front, log structures faced a cleared, clay earth patch. Hunters and their dogs milled about; some attending to various chores, others cleaning and preparing a large buck strung from a tree. Everywhere he looked there was movement and preparation. Robert parked the car and Joe jumped out to begin unloading their stock of supplies—canned goods, dry clothing, bed rolls, fire arms, ammunition, and dog food. A bearded, red capped, old sage of the woodlands suddenly appeared and began assisting him with a "Welcome Little Man! I'll show you where you'll bunk!" After they stored the supplies, Red Cap assigned to Joe the camp chore of gathering firewood.

He was in awe as he tramped through the dense and sweet foliage of a brushed and muted forest, splashed with reds, browns, and the deep, golden colors of falling Autumn leaves, gathering old, cast-off branches. On his way back to camp, with pieces of dried, moss specked timber crowding his arms, he stopped to gaze at the pink and purple setting sky—a part of the canvass of life.

By the time he reached the camp, a fire was snapping and crackling to life and a sliver of moon was poking a gentle path through a sea of jet-black. Owl hoots, rustling branches, and departing whip-poorwill soon joined in chorus with the soft, soothing, sound of a harmonica's persuasive language. Red Cap sat on a sun-bleached stump of oak, a brown jug at his feet, his whole being immersed, as he brought to life the small, metallic object he held with reverence. His eyes caught Joe's; he stopped, winked, took a shot of the jug, then set his lips dancing with glee, scurrying back and forth across his instrument with foot-stomping, hand-clapping, robust energy. His wailing, rustic tempo was soon accompanied by loud and boisterous whooping and clapping which drowned all other sounds in a sea of electrified men.

After expending enough energy to light up New York City for several days, everyone snatched a dented, silvery plate and shoveled upon them huge amounts of lip-smacking butter beans, crunchy hard drop biscuits, and delicious venison stew. Grabbing a cup of steaming, strong black coffee, each person found a place to enjoy his

When everyone had as many servings as a body could hold, the clean-up was shared by all. Robert and Joe took care of the dogs and the camp buzzed with activity. When everything was clean, fresh coffee was set on a grate over the fire, and they retired in a circle around the camp fire.

A mingling of dressed game, coon dogs, and hickory smoke swept through the night's crisp air, blanketing the men around the roaring campfire. With laced, leathered boots, tan, khaki pants, red and black plaid shirts, and an armory of trusty, long-barreled rifles and shotguns by their sides, the seasoned hunters began exchanging stories of the kill.

From enraged moose to rancid, snorting, wild boar, the stories of the hunt were as varied as the cracks and creases which swept across fire-reddened faces like dry, washed-out stream beds of ageless lands. Enthralled, he sat on the rich, red Georgia clay, within the circle of male bonding, sharing in each man's turn of historical oration as the hounddogs bayed for attention to fact and detail, for the dogs had vowed to the hunters, their eyes, ears and heart; and as such, vied for a spot as each master's voice was heard.

Red Cap nudged Robert, pointed to a man—who had been described as the camp jester—and winked at Joe before he spoke. "Hey Jack! You remember that there twelve pointer ya got last year?", taking a long swig from a brown, ceramic jug.

"Ya'll mighty sure hogging that stuff. Gimme 'at jug an I'll tell ya the story," Jack replied, tobacco juice streaming from his mouth with the quickness of a rattler's bite to explode in the campfire.

Splashing loudly, the jug was handed to Jack. He grabbed it with one finger, deftly flipped the container into the crook of his bent arm, and, in one motion, took a long drink. With a loud belch, he began his tale . . .

"There I was, that 30/06 six cradled in my . . ."

"Which gun was that?" Red Cap asked.

Jack took another swig, roughly wiped his mouth with a rag, then continued.

"This here 30/06 cradled in this here arm," he said pointing to the polished, gleaming, blue-black barreled rifle resting on his knees. "Hiddn in a stan' of oak . . ."

"Where were you hiding?" another voice chirped.

Jack gulped another large, hearty swig, and transferred the jug to his other callused hand before resuming his story.

"There I was, hiddn' in a stand of oak with Ol' Blue resting in the grass . . ." "Waoo. Woof, Woof, Woof. Waoo," a dog barked like he treed a whole forest-full of game."

"Gim'me another sip 'a that stuff," he demanded, squinting through bloodshot eyes for the jug he held tightly in his own hand! "Gimme . . ." Pop! He hit his mouth against the jug. Taking another swallow he continued, "so . . . ike I was sayin . . . the . . . uh, we was standin' in . . . the lake . . . with Ol' Blue . . ."

"Waoo. Woof, woof, woof. Waoo," the dog joined in; again interrupting Jack.

"Heh, gim . . . anothe . . . of . . . dat . . ." and Jack teetered over on his side as his dog bayed and howled into the night.

Everyone was rolling on the ground, sewing stitches of laughter as Jack snored in musical tune to Ol' Blue's deafening cadence.

As Jack ripped his logs—drowned in two-hundred-proof moonshine—the circle of fables came around to Joe.

"What do you hunt in New York?" a voice asked him.

Not wanting to be the party pooper, he wracked his brain for an animal that lived in New York and hadn't been discussed by these genuine hunters of lore.

A deer! No. Joe, the old fellow with the white beard and Budweiser cap said he "bagged" a large one last year.

A bear? No, Henry, a small, squat football coach—-the only one with overalls—already told about the grizzly he skinned in Alaska.

A moose? No, John, the Deacon wearing the waterproof boots, told the story of the dangerous animal he had stalked for three days. He was running out of animals and the group was waiting for his answer.

A light went off—he had it, why no one even mentioned it . . .

"We hunt veal!" Joe shouted with glee as he sat with his chest puffed out.

"You hunt what?" Robert asked, scratching his head like he wasn't sure what he heard.

"Veal," he said again, "you know, veal, . . . the kind you bread and fry!"

The guys looked at one another in confusion.

'Wow,' he thought to himself, 'they don't know what veal is!'

"Hey, you know veal is cow?" Red Cap cut in.

"Uh . . . Yeah! I know . . . I know what veal is." He stuttered as a glowing, warm feeling traveled from his toes to his head. "We hunt cow!"

Joe wasn't pressed for details. Either they did not want to know how an Italian hunted cows on someone's farm or they knew that he was fibbing and accorded him great honor and dignity by glossing over what had obviously been apprehension and desire to be a man among men. Joe would say it was the latter, for over the next three days, he was taught lessons of stealth, tracking, emergency survival, and how to interact with men. He learned that the killing of animals was not for sport alone; that every animal bagged was used. He learned that drinking caused you to become a clown; laughed at by all. He learned that you don't have to boast of accomplishment to belong—shoot . . . when it was discovered he was a greenhorn, the entire group pushed and shoved each other in their haste to show him the ropes. Those men were proud of their knowledge and gained joy in sharing it. Yes, Joe learned much that summer and fall in the redlands of South Georgia—how to laugh, how to see, how to hear, how to feel, but most of all, his first true lesson of being a man.

One of the after-effects of this experience with love and caring was that Joe became confused by his feelings. It was difficult . . . not what he had been used to! Had he found a permanent father figure? He was caught up in a triangle of feelings: self-deception; revenge; love. Robert was like a father. Gail was like a mother. What of Joe-Pep and Jeanette? What of all of those wiseguys he swore revenge on?

"What is love?" he pleaded one night as he gazed at stars blooming in a glorious burst of twinkling.

Then he met Ginny.

Robert got Joe his first "real" job at Fords Dairy. A twisted, modern day Juliet to Joe's Romeo, she was a Protestant, English-American daughter of a well-to-do family, employed by her uncle as a part-time cowgirl herding cattle for their daily milking. Joe was a thirteen-year-old runaway; a Catholic, Italian-American pauper of a deceased gangster; employed cleaning the walls of the milking stalls. They were complete opposites attracted by the same God. Unchecked by the words racism, bigotry or class, they remained entranced with one another for several weeks as they explored through their clear, unfettered eyes, and uncompromising hearts, God's realm of beauty. Their ignorance became their wall of confidence, held firmly in place by a mortar of innocence—though only until rudely breached and demolished by a storm of prejudice.

A few years older than he, Ginny and Joe hit it off immediately. As he told her his sad stories, she listened with understanding. As he shouted with the fury of a lonely, fatherless boy; abused, embarrassed, left to journey the land in search of answers; she talked of faith in God. When he spouted anger at his perceived torment, she returned love to his heart.

He had expected shock and horror at the revelations concerning the degradation of his family and his past . . . instead, he received compassion. His fears of discovery—which caused his own secrecy and denial—were vanquished by truth! Through her compassion he was cleansed of all grievances, he had peace, and his heart became open once more to the possibilities of life.

Soon, he was riding horses with her every day. She became his resource to what was but a trickle of happiness and normalcy thus far in his life. His greatest thoughts were thoughts of the moment. No father had played ball with him. No mother had quelled his despair and raging bitterness. He did not have friends with which to hash out life's differences. These tranquil moments in time became the essence of what he deemed to be but a fragment of true reality waiting to thrust itself upon him. He cherished each romp through the still green pastures, sparkling with dew. Those resplendent, tiny, delicate mirrors that brought each morning's dawn bursting into view, illuminating their days like none other before. Lost for hours in the cool, rich breeze of that fall's beauty, he knew that God was there upon a great, white, magnificent stallion, guiding them through His beauty of nature: serene and quiet, yet loud and imposing—boasting with colors, fragrances and life.

'Was it love of Ginny . . . or was it His nature overflowing with magnificent powers of healing that made him feel this way?' Joe soon concluded that it was God, and God's love, multiplied through Ginny and His nature. Yes, he was learning truth; he was feeling His power every day! He that created this abundance of beauty in nature, held the supreme powers of cure.

After a short three weeks, it seemed "The Curse" took effect—again! Ginny's parents were informed of their innocent relationship; with speed of recoil upon touching a bare hand on a hot stove, Ginny was sent to a boarding school . . . and Joe's job was at an end. He never saw her again . . . and never had the opportunity to thank her for her gift of renewal in Faith and God!

It was not a total disaster, for among the tattered remnants of their journey, sifted through untold ages of uncompromise, fear, and misunderstanding, memories of that brief moment in time, when the joy of innocence and compassion were discovered in the presence of God's peace and love, would remain etched indelibly, forever, into Joe's mind. These seeds would begin to bloom, without interruption—most often during his most trying times when the world convulsed with hate and denial—into fundamental feelings of understanding, love and faith. It was thoughts of Ginny that would bring back feelings of love. He often wondered if Ginny continued to carry her goodness and understanding as a badge of courage or had she secreted it away in a compartment in her heart. He wondered if she would roam the earth in quest of that time when two innocent youths met upon a minute portion of the Lord's magnificent creation of earth, and discovered through Him, the meaning of love. Would she remain satisfied, as he was, that their brief meeting was a planned encounter that became, in essence, their beginnings . . .

Those beginnings were a wealth of future vision into his predicament. His mother loved him, even if he had opposing thoughts running amuck within his subconscious mind—and there was nothing wrong with finding others who would provide cure and care in times of need. Even a relationship—innocent, he would admit—of young love, could sweep him along a journey filled with compassion and joy.

But, the truth of Aggie, waiting patiently for him in New York, soon overcame his emotions. He was prepared to journey once more back to his roots. All thoughts of revenge were vanquished by his new understanding of God. And then—as happens whenever Satan sees the power of God at work and decides to throw a monkey wrench into the cogs of a wheel—an event occured which would temporarily end his vision. Sadly viewing the ending of Joe's joyful relationship, Gail stepped in to offer her sympathy, and the next thing he knew, her sympathy turned to emotion and she seduced him.

One moment she was holding Joe in her arms, comforting him, talking to him, encouraging him to forget Ginny; the next, she had him naked, rolling upon the bed!

Joe was soon drawn into Gail's wild abandon, his mind relinquishing all thoughts of shame or consequences to a cosmos of exotic feelings. Lost between the covers of sexuality, in the center of some strange and bemused world where life existed only for the moment, they acted like teenagers brand new to love. His "mother figure" had turned into his "lover," and this fact crashed his entire thought process; this new information rushed with speed of light to explode into that file marked, "Accident: Personal." Every fact, question, and thought of life, family, love and God; which Joe had thus far utilized to reach a conclusion to his puzzlement; were shredded once more into a new puzzle containing bits and pieces of ragged doubt, betrayal, and confusion. Hopelessly entangled in the depths of this confusion, Joe was now at the mercy of both these new and wholly unfamiliar feelings and the need to understand Gail's actions.

One evening, a terrible fight ensued between Robert and Gail. The next thing Joe knew, Robert was smacking her around. This turn of events brought back memories of the abuse prevalent in Joe's home. The memory of such an episode flashed before his eyes . . .

Joe-Pep arrived home from one of his business trips at five a.m. Young Joe was awakened by a fierce argument that reverberated throughout the house. A slap led to another; then all hell broke loose. He could hear the moaning of his mother and the angry voice of father as he hit her.

"Don't you ever question me or lay a hand on me," he shouted as he smacked her around some more.

The next day, his mother was bruised and in a terrible temper. She asked Joe to throw the garbage out before he went to school. He hesitated for a moment because he wanted to ask her if she was O.K., but before he could speak, she turned around grabbing him and hitting him hard. He was thrust into the window sill head first. Though the blow resulted in a huge, black and blue eye, the emotional pain far exceeded it.

She began to cry out, "Oh my God! . . . What will your father say? You gotta tell him it was an accident."

> Jeanette's fear of Joe-Pep was greater than her fear of the consequences to Joe's feelings, emotions, and pain. He knew she was sorry; but her fear and anxiety of his father's repercussions overruled any other thought. He never understood the violence, and though he'd cringe at the thought, he believed all men did it . . . that it was a part of a relationship.

. . . Joe jumped out of his bed, grabbed the .410 off the wall, rushed into the front room, and pulled the hammer back . . .

"You leave her alone or I'll blow your brains out!" he screamed before he realized what he had done.

There he stood, feet spread apart, sighting down the barrel of the shotgun at Robert.

He didn't know what to do. He just stood there, wondering in his rage, what to do next.

The damage had been done. What excuse could Joe give Robert? Robert had invited Joe to live with him in an act of charity Joe could never repay. He'd repaid him all right; with a transgression on his hospitality. Joe had butted in where he had no business. The burden lay heavy upon his heart.

Clicking the hammer back into its neutral position, Joe showed Robert it was empty all along. Then Joe tried to explain, "You shouldn't be hitting her. She's like my mother!" as he handed the gun to Robert. He tried to apologize but it was no use.

Robert was on his feet in a moment. Snatching the gun from Joe's hands, he smashed the stock against the fireplace.

At least Joe's explanation had achieved its purpose—if only for the moment. But he knew he'd have to leave now.

The following day the air was charged with uncertainty. Gail had called him to the side and informed him that all was well, but he knew that it was time. He believed he'd been the cause of a disaster which had ruined this couple's happiness; that he, in fact, brought the Curse along with him. Several days later, while Robert was at work and Gail was busy shopping, he wrote a note thanking them and left for the bus depot. Joe's adventure began with a demonstration of love, attention, and a few facts of manhood, and ended at the expense of his thoughts of what a new and "real family" would be like, reinforcing his desire to discover truth and somehow end The Curse of Alphonso . . . which had once more revealed itself in its devastating power over Robert and Gail.

With his yearning to return to the city and his family no longer occupying his priority mind-set, he caught a bus to Miami and its lush, tropical wonderland—full of sights, sandy beaches, clear blue skys . . . and a guy named Shorty.

Chapter 29: The Rape of Miami

Mounted on a huge billboard, the Coppertone Girl and her dog announced Miami's welcome in mechanical movement.

Beautiful and variegated, the city gleamed in reflections of smooth, clear, salty-blue skies and kaleidoscopic foliage which seemed to swamp everything in multiple shades of green, red, and yellow. Royal palms, rich with luxurious green crowns mounted upon enormously high, thick stalks of gray; coconut palms, peaked in minty green, split-blades brimming with brown and green coconuts; arica palms, their green and yellow elegant fronds heavy with red, berry-like seed pods blowing in the sea-swept breeze; massive, grand-old oaks, spreading their arms in shaded lanes; tremendously huge ficus trees, with trunks smothered in brown, wax-drip, massive root systems . . . tendrils wrapping trunk and ground alike. Clean-Fresh-Perfect.

"Wow, look at that!" Joe shouted. "See the Live Alligator Wrestling!"

Signs, boasting of prosperity and nature, splashed the roadsides in fervent expectation: "Send Fresh Oranges Home!"—"We Ship Anywhere!"—"Visit Coral Gardens!"—"Monkey Jungle!"—"Coral Castle: The Last Love Story!"

Joe had found his 'Garden of Eden.' His visual excitement peaked as the driver announced, "Last stop! Miami! Fun, Sun and Surf! Last stop!" His voice boomed over the intercom as he swung the large bus into the crowded depot. Joe exited the bus and was immediately met by a wall of humidity, thick enough to swim in.

Busy with tourists and refugees from Cuba, the language, aroma, and visions of the city overwhelmed his senses. Unlike familiar New York, Miami's year round tropical atmosphere spoke full of mysteries and delights waiting to be uncovered; and with fifty dollars and the clothing on his back . . . he was set! Joe began walking among the shops and restaurants exploring with eyes, nose, and thoughts . . . The first Cuban Restaurant he came upon he entered, found a seat at the counter, and ordered a $3.95 feast of Cuban food: yellow rice with fish, breaded Cuban steak, plantains, and cafe' con leche (a strong sweet brew of rich Cuban coffee and milk). When he had completed his meal, he paid the bill and walked out the door; happy, full and ready to explore some more.

As he turned the first corner, they swept down on him like a pack of wild, mad dogs. Before Joe knew what had happened, he was seated on the ground—dazed, bleeding . . . pockets clear, cleaned out; a traffic of richly arrayed tourists moving around, over, and through him . . . none stopped to offer assistance to the vagabond in his misery.

A group of young toughs (who had seen his cash through the window) had relieved him of his only money!

He was lost and alone again, without any means to survive. He walked all night until a car pulled alongside him. An older gentleman inquired if he had a place to sleep. He replied he did not and the man offered him one; said he was a youth worker who assisted newcomers in getting work and lodging. In no position to refuse, he entered the car and it zoomed off into the hot, humid night.

They arrived at an apartment house and parked the car. In minutes they were in his apartment. The sparsely furnished two rooms didn't seem out of the ordinary. But an absence of pictures, momentos, or any other object, made the room seem sterile. He told Joe to sleep in the bed;, he'd give him a ride to a youth center in the morning. Exhausted, Joe was soon fast asleep.

Rough hands pulling off his clothing awoke Joe with a start. His "host" stood totally naked; A beast of determination! Joe soon found himself in a desperate, losing battle as the man beat him—turning him over in his quest of perverted imagination. A rush of fear and embarrassment flooded Joe's very being as his attacker, with one arm around Joe's neck suffocating the breath from his lungs, used his free hand to begin his act of copulation.

"No, God, no," Joe screamed out loud, struggling in a living nightmare.

Grunting like a pig, one arm wrapped around Joe's neck, the beast continued to beat him . . . Joe, struggling and screaming, suddenly realized he could soon be dead—and this thought caused him to will his panic away and remember a street-fighting lesson Sergio taught him!

Joe ceased his struggle and, as the attacker relaxed his grip, Joe pushed upward and toward the left.

The attacker countered by applying pressure toward his left and Joe twisted suddenly and precisely to the right . . .

His attacker fell to the floor.

Joe shot his hand out, grabbing a glass resting on the night stand.

As the man attempted to rise, Joe hit him hard with the glass.

While blood poured from a gash on the attacker's face, Joe jumped up, raced into his clothing, and shot through the door.

Once again Joe was running for his life. His tired and twisted feet that once confined him to a chair, became wings of an eagle; he flew down the stairs and onto Biscayne Boulevard—a musty, surreal landscape of warm, hazy, salty air, huge royal palms, and blinking traffic lights . . . only an occasional car breezing by to break the dead silence of the night.

Joe's mind was beyond confusion: rage, grief, and the pain of humiliation conquered all. But Joe would soon discover that many runaways down on their luck and beguiled by these demonic creatures, would become prostitutes who sold their bodies to men in every city—large and small. He was there, he saw it with his own eyes! Those who grew old on the streets and were cast aside for younger men, would evolve into beasts who preyed on those same men; robbing and beating them for pleasure.

He found it was they, the learned, that must teach the innocent.

Chapter 30: South Florida Outlaw

"Hey, kid, where you from?" The question came in a soft, liquid drawl.

"The city."

"What city?"

"The City, man . . . You know! New York!"

"Wachya doing in Miami?"

"Looking. My folks died and I left."

"So, your family's in the ground?"

"Yeah, in the underground . . . I didn't want to stay in the orphans' home!"

Four weeks of living under a bridge, eating coconuts and thinking of how he arrived here, brought back painful memories; his family was deceased . . . homemade deceased . . . again . . .

The group of kids gathered round a giant palm tree were fascinated by his accounts of adventure. He had become a celebrity, telling tales of New York, Alabama, Georgia and beyond. He was accepted immediately.

"Are you hungry? My mom will probably welcome you to dinner."

Her name was Diane. Her father was a black sanitation worker; her mom a white motel maid. And they, along with Diane's seven brothers and sisters, and her grandmother, lived in five rooms that made up the interior of an apartment in a housing project. Sometimes, during the day when her folks were at work, Joe slept in the livingroom; otherwise it was under the bridge in the woods bordering a canal several blocks west of Biscayne Boulevard. His nights were spent roaming the streets or hanging out at a bowling alley close to the pastel green and pink buildings of the housing projects on 79th Street.

The projects were one-story buildings spread out for approximately twenty blocks square. Within this zone, the buildings were spaced twenty-feet apart. Though inhabited by poor folks of various races and cultures—black, white, and Latin people were of the majority—they seemed to get along together in their shared misery. Bordered by 79th Street to the South, I-95 to the West, 2nd Avenue to the East, and 95th Street to the North, it was close to the bustling glamour of the motels and seasonal fruit and sundries businesses which lined Biscayne Boulevard—yet another world completely!

Poverty ruled the projects: no Ficus, Oaks, or Royal Palm trees filled the landscape . . . just yellow, weedy scrub-grass and diseased black olives. Like their human counterparts, the foliage struggled in competition for the precious natural resources among the dusty, faded, vermin-infested buildings and landscape. Even the air had a unique composition that altered the immediate sky-line; you could walk twenty blocks and feel as if you were entering another country.

Violence, Hunger, Boredom, Lack of Love and Attention; the struggle to survive—altering the norms of this independent society. The rules of life changed once you entered this forbidden zone.

In the projects, words such as Police, Politicians, Law and Order, Society, Right, Wrong, Rules, Regulations, Father, and even Mother carried an alien significance to all but those who abided by the code of poverty. Gravity, Pain, Love, Crime, Consequences, Actions, and Fault, were all words based on reactions versus any definitions in a Webster's Dictionary.

For those embroiled in day to day heated conflict with the emotional and physical poverty of their lives, the outside world was a dream, based on television commercials full of happy children, loving moms and dads, new cars, bountiful meals, pot-hole-free roads, and big houses in the country.

Imitation or limitation at all costs!

Yes, we were promised . . .

LOOK! CAN YOU NOT SEE!

The American dream!

For all . . .

'But why,' they asked, 'did so many wind up with nothing?'

How many truly made it? . . .

At what cost?

So, they tried and failed by the droves and did soon bequest their lives, their feelings, their experiences, their poverty-twisted facts on theirs and those . . .

And Joe? He fit right in.

Within several weeks, Joe had two new items to add to his list of accomplishments: A job landscaping and a professional tattoo.

Diane's grandfather ran a tattoo booth in an arcade and carnival on 79th Street. It remained open the entire tourist season. One night, they walked there and before he knew it, he had her name tattooed on his biceps within a ribbon held in the mouth of a bird.

"Now I can pass for eighteen!" he thought, as he viewed this art.

Joe's life on the roads and streets required him to figure a way to look older than he was. Every time he was stopped by the police and pulled out his fake ID, he'd worry about passing.

"So, 'Mike Clark,' where'd you say you live?"

"Honest officer, I live in the projects with . . . "

"It says here you're eighteen? You don't look . . ."

Flexing his tattooed muscles, standing as tall as his five-foot-two-inch height would allow . . .

"If you don't believe me then take me in and . . ."

"Just get the heck out of here and don't let me catch you out this late again . . ."

"Thank you, sir," snatching his ID and racing to the safety of the projects.

The projects offered all sorts of safety. The police only came by when there was an explicit reason to . . . and even then, they were quick to leave. Kids were always "hangin" all hours of the night. Once in the safety of its borders, he didn't worry. Things were proceeding fine. He was proud earning fifty dollars a week "planting sod." He had moved in with Diane's family, and was happily contributing a portion of his earnings to the household. He was having fun as a man of respect. Until the night of the bikers . . .

Diane and he were on their way to the bowling alley. Diane's heritage, plainly visible in her dark, creamy, brown skin and curly, long, loose hair, had caused three fist fights since he had met her. It seemed there was always someone who would overtly use racism to make her cry . . . out popped the fists!

Though she was fantastic at hiding her feelings Joe could see her pain—especially when covert racism reared its head. He recognized her genuine beauty and innocence—many others did not.

On this night, "they" were the group of hard-nosed bikers who happened to chance by on their way to the 'Tattoo Man': South Florida Outlaws-Mean-Large-Ugly-Loud-Racial-Antagonists.

"VAROOM, CHUG-A-CHUG-A-CHUG-CHUG!", went their bikes, as they approached the brightly lit bowling alley.

"What have we got here? A spic and a nigger!" spouted an ugly, overweight monster as he dismounted.

Joe never could keep his mouth shut! He was with a girl . . . right? They had belittled her . . . right? He couldn't back down. He had to open his trap.

"Yo, who do you think you're talkin to? You call my girl a name again and I'll . . ."

"You'll what!? Kick my butt? Hey, Yo . . ." the beast exclaimed, calling his entire group to the attention of something big that was going to happen . . . something they'd enjoy!

By this time Joe knew he was in the worst trouble he could ever be in. He could not think of what to do.

"So you're a brave guy, huh?"

"Listen, man. I faced worse than you . . . I battled with the mob in New York. I ripped off the Don himself. You don't scare me. You'll have to kill me before you beat me. This young lady has nothing to do with this situation. Why don't you jerks go and terrorize someone your own size . . . or are you just a bunch of faggots?"

The group became totally still, all eyes staring at this profound thirteen-year-old who stood all of five-foot-two and spoke as if he were eight feet tall. Joe was definitely in a bind as he awaited the outcome. Joe's mind churned as he stood on that road in front of the 79th Street Bowling Lanes. He was looking at all avenues of escape, but there were none; not with Diane hanging tearfully upon his arm. Just at the moment the group seemed ready to pounce upon him, a voice, loud and commanding, roared above the approaching storm—Thunder Had Preceded Lightning!

"Yo! Animal. You heard me! Animal!"

Joe discovered the name for the beast . . . and it fit him to a tee!

"Yeah, Boss," Animal answered, his demeanor changing.

"This kid thinks he's bad! I got an idea . . ."

Joe knew something was up; something he'd not necessarily be happy to oblige.

"Let the punk show he's a man by performing a task of endeavor!" The cheers went up as he was grabbed and lofted above the crowd. A task of endeavor seemed the knightly course of action—not that he had any great success with his last knightly duel. But . . . the idea of a joust or a duel! Like the swashbuckler movies of Errol Flynn! 'Yes, this seemed to be what they were talking about!' he thought.

"Listen, the place is busy, see . . ."

In front of The Castaway Hotel, on 163rd Street, Miami Beach—its colorful decor straight out of the Orient—they stood out like a pack of barbarians at the Chinese Wall. The entire group parked bikes rumbling and revving, leather groaning, bandannas flowing like bright war banners in the salty air; and, across the street, a motorcycle rental store, its neon lights announcing: "RENT A YAMAHA 125 TILL TWELVE MIDNIGHT FOR ONLY $15.00." The sidewalk was crowded with tourists.

"You're goin' over there and steal that bike . . . the red one in the front."

It was not a question. It was an order. With Diane safely at home, and he about to be released with only a minor situation blocking his way, Joe decided the best course of action, was to do it.

"How do I get a key?"

"A key?" The response was immediate; everyone began laughing loudly.

"You're the wise guy from New York who defeats godfathers and loudmouth outlaw faggots . . . what do you need a key for? Just flip the switch on the top like this"—showing him the approximate area the ignition would be—"then rip these wires out"—showing him a group of wires—"then connect the green and red, and touch them with the yellow one! You got that?"

"Sure, I got it . . ."

Watching the crowd, figuring out who's an operator and who's a tourist, he reaches over and snaps the ignition, twisting the wires together . . .

"Hey, how about that red one?" a tourist interrupts.

"I like the blue one," another replies.

He's ready to jump aboard when . . . "Can I help you?"

The guy is standing four feet away and Joe knows if he comes any closer he'll see the wires.

"I'm just looking, my parents are staying at the Hotel across the street." He points towards the Castaways . . . not realizing he is pointing directly at the Outlaws!

"Look, he got caught! And he's ratting on us!"

"Let's get out of here!" VAROOM! . . . SCREECH! . . . VAROOM! . . .

The bikes careen down the road.

Joe is so frightened he fails to recognize the racket for what it is and, as the salesman looks over toward the hotel, he jumps aboard, twists the starter wires—and VAROOM!

The rendezvous was to be at Wolfie's Restaurant on Miami Beach. Joe was to park the bike and wait two hours before showing up. Happy to get his "endeavor" over, Joe arrived a little after twelve p.m. at Wolfie's—packed full of bikers—more than had previously been at the Castaways. As he rode into the parking lot, he recognized one of the guys from the original group. Joe un-twisted the wires, popped the kick stand down, and walked toward the front door; a dozen surly bikers greeted him.

"It's a set-up," some one whispered. "He could be wired."

"Wants to pin it on us," another hushed voice joined in.

"What's a kid doing on a rent-a-bike? It's too late for a little punk to be riding on the beach," one of them snarled as he patted him down.

"What the hell are you talking about?" Joe finally asked.

"We don't like kids hanging down here!" another interrupted as if to keep Joe from saying another word.

"Oh man, you guys are stupid," Joe began, having figured out what was going on.

"Who you calling stupid?" someone exclaimed as a hand shot out and slapped his face.

Joe's reaction was immediate, he lunged for the offender and was immediately wrestled to the ground.

That's when some girl, watching the situation, called the boss out.

"So, you managed to do it!" he exclaimed, as he handed a bottle of Jack Daniels to Joe.

Remembering the incident at the hunting camp in Georgia, Joe refused the bottle. But, it's not a good idea to refuse to drink with the leader of the South Florida Outlaws.

Joe woke up in a clubhouse in Hallendale Beach, Florida. He was soused and hung over at the same time. It seemed that after he refused, they grabbed and forced the liquor down. For the next month, he became the gang's mascot. They crowned him with a black French beret, placed him on the "black" 125, and he zoomed all over South Florida alongside those blasting, heavy-throated Harleys. They traveled up and down the highways, terrorized Hollywood Beach every Friday and Saturday night, and scrapped it out on several occasions—just like in the Marlin Brando movie!

Had he found a friend and father figure in The Animal?

By the end of the month, reality looked expensive. Though Joe was having the time of his life, he had grown tired of making excuses for not accepting the drugs, sex, and offers to participate in some sort of larceny at every turn, stop, and go! But when the order came down he was to get his colors (his very own colors!) he put aside those feelings and jumped at the chance.

All bikers who received their colors had rode with, participated in, and were part of, the acts committed by the group for a particular time. They had proved their "colors" by their deeds, often demonstrating they could be trusted through a specific act. Now, for Joe, due to his age, his special act was to assist in the delivery of 'speed' for distribution to the Outlaw's Orlando chapter.

Drug dealing provided the group's main income, and since Joe's youth afforded some protection and camouflage, he was the one selected to carry the dope! Up until this point it had been a game; a game most youth would not even dream of, but a game nonetheless. It had been fun: no one to tell him what to do; freedom to roam and explore; riding a motorcycle all over the place; attention from fifty "father figures." But, this experience had to be leveled with his knowledge of the streets. He was soon recognizing how similar these "father figures" were with "the tough guys" who he'd hung with in New York; the wiseguys his father hung with before his demise; the drug dealers who swarmed 117th Street in Spanish Harlem. When the chips went down, you went down.

His first run went by without a hitch. With the fake ID and registration for the stolen bike Animal had secured, deep in his pocket, and a straight looking couple riding alongside him, he could have been the teenager with his family on vacation: the alibi!

They zoomed off and returned in two days.

Joe was paid one "C" note and an induction ceremony was immediately organized.

The induction for the older guys was intense; Joe had not attended one, but the word was preached to him for the week prior to his trip. In the end, to Joe's pleasure, it was decided he'd go through a less severe ritual.

Twenty-four members wearing leather jackets and holding all sorts of weapons lined up in two rows, twelve to a side. Joe put on two, heavy leather jackets and a helmet that covered his face—some of the special considerations afforded him—took a pint of Black Jack from Animal's outstretched, hairy arm, downed the contents in a straight guzzle (allowing a lot of it to run down his face) and ran the gauntlet. Joe ran through twenty-four men with blows raining upon his person from the many objects they whipped into the three foot corridor. He had been warned not to fall down—the last guy who had fallen wound up in the hospital!—he forced himself to stay as erect as he could as he scurried through, bumping from one side to the other. He was well through the line when a guy who had been given the "honor of the line" (even though he was still on probation and had yet to achieve full membership) stepped up and delivered a blow from a chain so severe, Joe was knocked to his knees—his helmet cracked in two.

Both sides of the line came to sudden halt and Animal, his hulking, beastly figure rushing to assist the mascot with heart, was suddenly held in check by ten members. The rules were the rules: blows were permitted as long as a recruit was within the line, but no one, save "Mr. Probation," continued to lay a single strike.

As "Mr. Probation" continued to shower heavy blows, Joe rose on all fours, to the end of the line. Though "Mr. Probation" was in his rights to continue "the line," the cheering had stopped and all participants were standing one step off the line, giving honor to Joe for completing the line. As the last of Joe's body—his booted right foot—broke the line in the sand, Mr. Probation raised his hand for a final blow.

Eyes bloodshot, all thoughts wrapped up in his own excitement and pleasure, absorbed in the act of delivering submission, Mr. Probation's arm, chain standing as straight as a two-by-four, began its powerful, rapid decent . . .

That's when they released the Animal.

Flying through the thick sand, Animal hit "Mr. Probationer" with such force, he flew like a rag doll fifteen feet and into the surf. Then, for violating the code of the line, the entire group, including those probationers who were not afforded the privilege of the line, surrounded him and, by the time they were through, he stayed in a hospital for three weeks.

Though stunned and sore, the helmet protected Joe. He had survived the line and was rewarded with a three day party: sporting a sleeveless motorcycle jacket with the colors of the Outlaws stitched to its back.

"But how do I escape?" he queried as he sat along the midnight surf; a sliver of moon providing just a glint of light reflecting off the warm surf that gently stroked the sandy beach. "If I leave without delivering the merchandise, I'm liable for retribution."

Three weeks after his induction, Joe learned of the violence that had been done to "Mr. Probation." He also became privy to some of the other ventures and retributions that were being pronounced on various turn-coats: businessmen who owed money, dealers who were slow in paying; favors for mobsters . . . and so on. The message was clear: this is what can happen to you now that you are official!

When he was told he'd be delivering dope two times a week to Orlando and Jacksonville, he realized he was now another tool to be used. Any previous violence or crime he may have perpetrated in the past was thus done for survival, not as a career or way of life! He had tasted the fruits of peace and happiness and had enjoyed it tremendously! These men were no more, no less, than gangsters on motorcycles who were as loyal as their own pleasure and safety allowed; which when threatened, either by innuendo, rumor or paranoia, resulted in death or disfigurement!

The weight of his situation played heavy upon his heart. Events of his life, thus far, were of sudden intervention. Right or wrong, they just evolved from whatever was delivered. His life had become a rush of events; a dash from here to there—never knowing when he'd die! He knew of The Curse; he knew of his father; he knew his responsibility was to get even for his father—yes—he knew how death was, it came and went without any hesitation. Like all of the others in his ancestral line, he led his life thinking his time could be up at any moment. In fact, he'd think of his future birthdays in tens and wonder if he'd be alive that decade.

Joe was lost in thought, when suddenly, with an eerie, silent, bump in the night, someone fell over him and tumbled to the side. In the darkness, he could barely see the person who tripped over him without a sound of foot steps or noise. And he scarcely saw the quick, silent movement of the gun, before its cold and smooth bored blackness was thrust into his face. . . .

Chapter 31: Mother, Mother

When Joe was seven-years-old, a cartoon revealed its secrets to him in black and white. It was entitled "Felix The Cat." Felix was an ordinary cat who possessed a bag of tricks; a physician's case containing an endless supply of wizardry with which all obstacles that chanced upon his way were overcome. Though sometimes a brick would appear to violently hammer an opponent (usually a devilish character) into oblivion, the majority of implements contained in this pouch were designed to conquer in a non-violent way.

"Wow!" Joe would think to himself as he watched in awe, "If only I had that bag!"

One bright sunny day, his mother bought him a gift. She wrapped it and placed it in his room. When he returned from school he saw this cheerful box sitting atop his bed. With excitement he tore the package apart. Through the ripped and tattered rainbow wrapping paper, a black doctor's bag was unveiled! Excitedly grabbing this emblem of his fantasy, he opened it to discover a wealth of plastic instruments. Something red . . . to hear the heart, something blue . . . to tap the knee, something yellow . . . to depress the tongue—but nothing else!

Disappointed, he began to moan. His mother, hearing his grief, appeared at his side.

"Why are you upset? Don't you like the toys I bought for you?" she inquired, as she placed her arms around him.

"I thought this was a bag like Felix The Cat has!" he moaned in despair.

"That is a bag like Felix carries," she replied in all seriousness.

"But where are the tricks?" he challenged.

"You see these tools that you threw on the floor?" she asked, picking up one of the colorful items that he had discarded with haste. "They'll unleash the miraculous powers of God."

"This is a stethoscope; it's used to check the heart," she said, holding the red plastic object to his heart. "Listen to the sound of your heart, and as long as you can hear the rhythm of its beat you can use its power."

"Ah! You're fooling me," he replied with a smirk. "It can't do nothing!"

"Let me show you its magic!" she repeated as she held him in her arms. "You know that I love you," she said, grasping him tighter. "Remember all the times that you hurt yourself and how your crying stopped when I held you like this?"

"Sure, Mom."

"That is God's magic of your heart. You can use its powerful magic any time you please."

She then picked up the blue tool from the floor. "Do you feel me tapping your knee?" she asked as she lightly tapped my knee.

"Yes, I can feel it, but what trick is that!" he asked, sure that this wasn't magic!

"This is God's magic of feelings. As long as you can feel its thump you can use its power. How do you feel when I tell you I love you and hold you tight?" she inquired with a smile.

"It makes me feel good," he replied.

"The magic of feelings can change the world!" she said as she picked up the yellow object.

"This is the most important part of your bag of tricks. With this item all obstacles can be overcome," she continued as she placed the item close to his mouth. "Open wide and say Ah!"

"Ah!" he said, eagerly awaiting the mysterious powers of the yellow tool.

"As long as you have your voice, you can use God's gift of the power of speech. How do you feel when I say I love you?" she asked as she handed the magical trick to him.

"I feel great."

"Remember that this bag holds magical tricks and how you use them will determine how people feel, see, and respect you. The powers of your heart; feeling; and touch; are brimming with God's M.A.G.I.C. They bring warmth and happiness to others, which in turn, become mirrors reflecting that power tenfold. But you must learn, that just to say these words, and not feel them denies the M.A.G.I.C. power that they possess. They become just words of jest."

He picked up the tools and placed them in his black bag of tricks. Then he hurried out of the house to try them out on all his friends!"

* * *

'It's time to get up!' she thought as she rolled over. "Six in the morning and the kids have to be on time." But her body just didn't want to respond; with only twelve hours sleep in the past four days, she was worn out! She forced herself to get up, placed her swollen feet on the worn carpet and, with a painful grunt, lifted herself.

Shuffling to the bathroom, she brushed her teeth and prepared a tub of warm water for Eddy's morning bath. Then trudged to the kitchen and opened a cabinet.

She studied the scarce staples lining the shelves to see what she could fix for breakfast. Another two days and she'd get paid. Then she could re-fill her cabinets. As far as the clothing the boys needed, she could more than likely shop the second-hand store next week—that is—if she could put off the light bill another two weeks.

She shook her head and chose the box of oatmeal she had stolen from the store last night. How she hated living this way. To think that she'd been reduced to shop-lifting. She measured out three cups, poured it into the pot, added water, and turned the stove on.

Turning to the ice box, she opened it and removed her insulin. Jeanette then searched a counter drawer for a needle, filled it, and gave herself her life sustaining morning "fix." And then, like every other morning for the past year, she set the table for four before realizing she had set one too many. After making toast and arranging her children's clothing, she made a cup of instant coffee with saccharin and milk, then sat down with a groan.

"I wonder if he is OK? Oh, how I miss him. Where is he?" she wondered, mesmerized by the ripples her tears were making as they rolled down her cheek and into the steaming cup. "God, can you hear me? I have prayed that you will watch after my little Joey. It was never his fault! You know that? I tried, Oh, have I tried. Why . . . ?"

The sound of Eddy arising snapped her out of her prayer, and she knew she would not sit down again until the following morning—when her daily ritual would begin all over.

Chapter 32: Law and Order

SCREEEEECH! . . . the green and white car slammed to the corner, the doors flew open, and two blue-uniformed predators scrambled in pursuit of the fleeing game.

"Hey! I ain't done nothin!" Donny shouted as Jolly Green Giant slammed him to the ground.

"You wanna stay on the streets? Do you? Well if you do, you'll tell us where Joe and Pauly are! You hear me?" Ball demanded, his face a mass of beet-red anger.

"Man, you guys know—they've been gone a long time! We don't know where, I swear!"—

Wrenching Donny's hands behind his back, Jolly questioned him some more. "Someone knows . . . and you know that someone, don't you?"

"The only one that close is Aggie . . . she might know. His girl friend . . . Aggie . . ."

"Who?"

"Aggie!"

"Aggie who?" Jolly screamed as he twisted Donny's arms with vengeance.

"Aggie, Aggie McDonald! In Woodside, she lives in Woodside."

"Where does she live?"

"I don't know! I don't know! Just go to the projects and ask, I swear, I swear . . ."

After a brutal pummeling of kicks and punches, Jolly let Donny scurry away. Sweating and breathing hard, both men got back into their cruiser.

As they drove off, Jolly told Ball he'd get even. "I'll show that $%%$#@^&! I'll get even for all of the aggravation he and his father caused!"

"Heh, you know Aggie McDonald. It's that little hussy, the red-head with green eyes. The one you're always telling me looks nine-teen! You remember?"

"Oh! That's her name? Yeah, I remember. Let's go and have some fun!"

Chapter 33: Jack . . . The Cat

The phantom was dressed in shoes, pants, shirt, gloves, and ski mask . . . all black!

"Hey, man, get that gun out of my face!" Joe said with indigna-tion.

"What's a young punk doin' on the beach at this time of night?"

"What are you doin' on the beach dressed in black with a gun in my face?"

"You're mighty testy; you earn those Colors?"

"What do you think?"

The next thing he knew, the guy handed him three, one-hundred dollar bills and said, "If you need some real work, come by the Hollywood Dog Track any Saturday afternoon after twelve. Just go by the valet parking and ask the attendant for Jack."

"That's your name?" he asked to the dead-silent emptiness of the night.

But the stranger had vanished as quietly as he had arrived.

The offer of a job, all that cash, the fact "Jack" had the accent of a wiseguy—obviously was from up north—Joe felt strong enough to leave and return to the projects.

After Joe left the outlaws, they discovered an informant had enabled the police to infiltrate the biker's drug operation. The suspected snitch was uncovered and grabbed: Under the Hallendale Beach Pier, as waves gently crested the rocky pilings and sea gulls glided upon the soft, swirling, warm breeze; they tortured and murdered her. The leaders of this operation would be arrested, prosecuted, and finally sent to prison for long terms . . . including the Boss and The Animal!

Twelve in the afternoon and the track was alive and jammin.

"Jack? Jack who?" the attendant asked as he gave Joe this scratch-his-head-who routine.

"Jack! . . . That's who! Listen I just came all the way from New York to see my father's best friend. He died and I'm here cause I was expected to be. I had all the information but I lost it at the airport, now, will you tell Jack the Kid is here? Please?"

"Well, you found the place. Pretty good line you gave Junior. He fell for it. You spend all of the bread I gave you?"

"No. I got two-fifty left."

"I'm impressed, let's go inside. They don't allow kids but . . ."

"Hey, let's get something straight, I'm no kid, O.K.?

"Well, O.K., big guy, let's go."

At the main gate the guards seemed to know Mr. Jack very well. They looked over toward him, winked, and Jack handed one of them a twenty as they entered the frenzy.

"There's the betting windows over there," he said, pointing toward a bank of crowded counters with open windows spaced every three feet. Lines of betters, scowls of urgency written upon each face, jostled with one another in their haste to reach the windows and place their bets—as if each and every one of them had THE BET.

"That's the Club House up there . . . where we're going," he said as they swaggered over toward the stairs that led to a large, enclosed room overlooking the track.

A doorman seated them with a group of men, whom, Joe knew were mobsters.

"Hey, Jacky, whose da kid?"

"My nephew. From New York . . . Joe, meet Shorty."

Staring in semi-shock at the guy Joe was sure to be the same man Bianco spoke of; Joe was at a loss for words. At last, here sat Shorty, a top leader of organized crime, capable of ordering a hit fifteen-hundred miles away; someone who was spoken of, as if he were a God, the man who might have had a hand in the destruction of his family, his father, his mother, his life . . . at last, face to face with the genuine article rather than the sinister and powerful image of a twisted demon he had conjured so many, many times in his deepest thoughts.

Joe found he was astonished by Shorty's appearance. An extremely short, thin, and aging individual; Shorty was outfitted in a loud, wide-collared green and yellow plaid-checked jacket, an alien, black turtleneck shirt, black trousers with yellow belt, and yellow loafers. And this, combined with his deeply tanned, long, thin face, which sported a small, crooked, pointy nose, thin pink lips, and wide-spaced, large, almost black eyes, left Joe feeling he was looking at a sea turtle dressed in yellow and green camouflage attempting to hide in a sea of bobbing humanity.

"Yeah, how ya doin?" Joe said with a mobster inflection, while tossing his computations within his evolving thoughts.

"Where'd you get your tattoos? Sounds like you're from 'The City.'"

"I'm from the Q and Manny Hat. Just visitin'. Got dese in da city."

"You vacationin? Got any people besides old Jacky baby?"

"Some, my father . . ." Joe halted when he realized he almost made a mistake. "I'm jus visitin' Jacky."

"Hey, Yo . . ." Shorty yelled across the table at the bar man. "Bring a burger, a dog, or sumptin for tha kid—an a coke!" Then he patted Joe on the back, pulled a chair out, and offered it to him.

While he consumed a sandwich that appeared almost instantly along with four hamburgers, four hot dogs, four pastrami sandwiches, and several Cokes . . . though no one else ate anything—the guys were busy sending runners to bet on the dogs.

"So, whose ya old man?" the question flashed again.

"Jus' a guy," he said as he stuffed his face. 'I should have said he was dead . . . and mother too!'

"Just what guy?"

"Hey, give the kid a break . . . his father's dead. He just came down from the funeral . . . nobody you know, O.K.?" Jack cut him off.

For the balance of the afternoon, he just acted like he was watching the races while he really paid attention to the conversations that bounced back and forth. It didn't take long until he had figured out Jack's occupation: a thief!

Jack was what was called a "second story man"; a thief whose specialty was robbing homes, hotels, apartment houses, and cracking safes. He began his criminal career "hustling" gold coins—long before it became a popular scam—and wound up learning how to steal them! He'd climb six stories, from the outside, to defeat a doorman. Quite a few jobs were performed while the occupants slept peacefully.

Jack's generosity toward Joe was motivated by business. Jack needed a short, slightly-built juvenile to perform a few tasks. The meet at the track was based on a discussion for the fencing of loot from some big job. Joe's appearance on the beach, combined with his situation, build, and facts of his past, suited Jack just fine.

Now, on his part, the fact Jack dressed well, always had a huge roll of "C" notes, a pretty woman—or two—on his arm, drove a fast, sporty, luxury car, and commanded respect wherever he went, kind of had an impact. Then there was the the link to Shorty.

"OK, just as we discussed: You'll squeeze through the bars of the gate with a bathing suit and lots of sun tan lotion . . . if you get caught, plead you got lost."

'Like who's gonna be sunbathing at two a.m.?'

"Then make your way along the fence line. I'll meet you by the beach wall and hand you your stuff. Then, you'll have to stand on the sea wall, jump on the hood of that there Buick," Jack says, pointing to a wall six feet above a parked black Buick. "As you can see, the parking garage bars you from gaining access to the first balcony . . . but with your bounce off the car, you can grab onto that floor ledge and pull yourself up. You see that telescope on the third balcony up? You'll tie this rope to it"—handing Joe the rope—"lower it down, and then climb down the rope."

Joe had trained for four days at a private spa located above the shopping center on 79th Street and Biscayne Boulevard. This—as Jack called it—was a simple job, it was to be a preview of the real thing! Joe looked up at the fourth floor, knowing he had to climb three balconies—that's if he didn't jump, bounce off the car, and land on his head! Well, he didn't have much of a choice, and after all, Jack was making sure he had plenty of attention, respect, and a place to stay.

"O.K., calm down," Joe said to himself as he stood on the edge of the six foot sea wall. Jump! Dull bang. Pop.

He's flying up . . . Grab it!

"Whoa!"

"Ugh, eeeeeemmmm . . ." He pulls himself up.

Grabbing hold of the cut out designs of the concrete balcony walls, he's soon standing upon the edge of the balcony.

He climbs the corner supports using the open cut design and pushes off on an angle without looking down!

He reaches the next one . . .

"Ooooommm" . . . and grabs the edge.

And so on . . .

Looking over the side of the fourth floor balcony—including the raised parking area under the building—'It's a long way down!' he thinks to himself.

Jack is waiting outside the twelve foot fence on beach-side. The balcony is three feet from the edge of the wall. He ties one end of the rope to the telescope, the other to the balcony concrete railing. Holding six feet of coiled slack in his left hand, he uses his right to lower it down, gently swinging it back and forth until it clears the wall and then lets it go. Jack grabs it, unties the rope and puts it on the ground, then he ties the rope onto the fence and begins to motion for Joe to climb down.

"First, let me check the door out," Joe says to himself as Jack frantically waves to him.

'I'll just check it out! Show him I'm cool. What I've learned. Heck, he's acting like a father figure, right? I'll please him!' Joe uses the nail he carried specifically for this situation. Wedging the head under the door, he pushes down on it while pushing upwards against the glass with his body . . . the door gently slides on its well lubricated track. He enters the pitch-black and drops down.

So far everything goes like Jack taught him. His eyes adjust and he begins to grope his way to the back of the room. He sees that this is one laid-out apartment. He begins to explore. Entering the bedroom. He hears a light rustling. Probably the breeze coming from the open door . . . but . . . what's . . . that . . . over there . . . Is Tha . . .'

The Doberman tore at him . . .

Joe blasts towards the balcony as lights flash on, a gun's cocked.

"BLAM! BLAM!" shots careen off concrete . . .

He's going over the wall as the large dog rips the legging off his pants . . . on the rope . . . sliding down so fast his gloves are hot . . . it seems . . . they're burning . . . crash.

He's up and running as several balconies come to life with lights, noises, and shouts, "There he goes . . . Call the police!"

"What the heck is wrong with you? You're supposed to snatch a five-hundred dollar telescope and come down! Not wake up the entire shoreline. Next time . . . if there is a next time . . . you do what I say. Got that?"

"But you said that . . ."

"Forget what I said! Just do what I tell you!"

For the next several weeks they hit various places along the beach as Joe's education continued—an education leading up to "The Big Job." Jack's territory ran from Miami Beach to Pompano Beach. He had all kinds of tricks and systems to generate the bucks. One of his favorites was renting a group of adjoining suites in a luxury hotel and jamming the doors that separated them. He would then wait several days and inform the desk that his expected associates canceled their trip. Keeping only one suite, with the connecting door jammed to make it seem it was truly locked, he'd wait until someone rented the adjoining suite. In the middle of the night he'd open the door in stealth—while the occupants slept soundly—and remove all the cash from their wallets and pocket books. The strange thing was, he never had a problem. The tourists would wake up and go about their business, only to discover that somehow they had lost their money.

Credit card use was still far away . . . cash was the way.

Another operation—one to be used when the big pre-planned pickings were slim—was to go along the hotels on the beach and pick out wealthy tourists. Once all information such as room number and sleeping habits had been secured, he'd swallow some booze, walk along the breezeway with a stupor-like shuffle until he reached the one he had staked out, and, using a pick kit, he'd open the lock. If any one came out he'd feign drunkenness, say something like, "Oh! Sorry . . . got the wrong room"—and walk off. If no one walked out, he'd place one hand at the top of the door, the other on the knob, and using his foot and top hand to push while pulling on the knob, he'd open the door without a sound. Then, crouching down, so as to protect himself against a possible wary occupant waiting behind the door, he'd enter effortlessly. If someone was in fact waiting behind the door, and they came around, he'd jam the door against them and get away before the person knew what had happened.

The track soon became Joe's home away from home. The wiseguys got used to him hanging and he was in demand as a runner. He'd run numbers for them, make drop-offs of receipts, and get them coffee and things. Though he had not forgotten his predicament—the Shorty deal—he enjoyed the attention and the feeling of belonging so much, he began to see Shorty in a different light; one that made Shorty seem innocent and cool. In fact, the only time he thought about New York was when he went to sleep. It was in his dreams that his guilt raised its head. . . . 'That guy is Shorty . . . your sworn enemy! . . . '

"The big job's tonight," Jack stated as Shorty grinned and slapped him on the back.

"You just make sure the goods get to my place by nine in the morning."

"I'll get 'em there, don't you worry!"

"Who's your climber?" Shorty asked.

"Someone who's an expert!" Jack replied as he winked at Joe, who sat close enough to hear yet far enough not to raise eyebrows.

"You wanna leave the kid at my place? He's more than welcome." Shorty asked winking at Joe. "He can hang in the arcade room."

"Thanks, but he promised he'd stay with his grandmother for the night."

It was a major hit in a major neighborhood.

Golden Beach meant money; lots of it. And the chosen mark was a mansion owned by a very wealthy businessman! A beautiful place with walls, fences, and a state-of-the-art security system. Jack would have to defeat the system and break into a safe; his specialty! Shorty had agreed to pay Jack up front —that is when he received the merchandise—and fence the jewelry and negotiable bonds later in New York. The score was said to be worth two-hundred-and-fifty G's; which meant at least seventy-thousand for Jack in cool, hard, ready cash!

A full moon lit the lawn as two dark shapes zipped the shadows unnoticed. Outer perimeter devices, rigged trip switches, active and silent alarms were defeated, and a primary and a secondary route swept to the mansion—one in front, one in the rear—the units were then switched back on, leaving the majority of detection units operational. In this way, if by a twist of fate, someone approached outside of the narrow corridors of safety, they would trip the alarms notifying the two silent figures working the mansion wall of the violation!

Jack knew it all. He was "In Like Flint, It Takes A Thief, Mission Impossible and OO7," all in one! At the mansion wall, Jack defeated the primary alarm and rerouted the phone lines into an electronic black box that would send a code of impersonating pulses and ohms! Even if they missed a wire, switch, button or sensor for the mansion itself, the alarm would never ring, beep, scream, nor telephone anyone. Though a secondary system with micro-switches randomly placed under Persian carpets was always a tickler, the sophisticated main system was a mute and blind ignoramus. They set out to gain entrance to the main building.

Straight to one of the stained-glass windows which lined the garden, Jack removed three pieces [with a sharp steel knife;] enough to reach in and open the window. Joe slipped in, "walked the wall" to the Persian-covered, marble-floored, double staircase and, walking the edge of the lower marble riser, climbed the carved, mahogany outer railings until he reached the place opposite one of the outer wall windows which dressed both ends of the stair case. Jumping from the rail to the marble ledge, he opened the window, tied a nylon rope to a decorative wrought-iron mold-cap on the interior window's edge, and swung it out and down to the ground, where Jack tied it to a marble statue.

Jack climbed the rope and, from a long, black, nylon backpack, pulled out flat, steel bars, which he placed in a series across the floor to gain entrance to the main study; the bars wedged into the sides of the hallway walls so they could step on top of them and never touch the carpet! Once at the door to the office, he ran a battery-powered device locating two wires running through the walls on both sides of the door. Gently chipping the plaster off the wood underlay of the walls, he used pins to pierce the wires and then connected jumpers across them without cutting them. He opened the main doors to the study. Joe never saw how he managed to traverse the floor of the study nor how he "cracked" the safe. His job was to remain down the hall at the window and keep look out.

Thirty minutes later, Jack emerged with a grin and weighted-down backpack. Going through the whole procedure in reverse, Jack and Joe climbed the rope and disappeared into the tropics of the city called Miami!

One-hundred-and-seventy-five thousand dollars in bonds alone! And the jewels! We're talking diamonds, diamonds, and diamonds! Jack also discovered a host of other items which brought the total to three-hundred-and-forty-thousand! A sure ninety-five thousand hard cash! Joe was assured at least thirty-thousand dollars cash! Jack had promised he'd get a third.

Joe was set to go home and rescue his family!

He'd return, 'The Knight in Shining Armor,' to rescue everyone!

He was so excited! He even decided to go to church and give a thousand-dollars to the priest! He promised to God, thanked God, gave God the credit! "Oh Lord, you have seen fit to end my family's nightmare! Thank you!"

"Listen Joe, you wait here, and I'll be back in a couple of hours. Then we'll take a trip to the Islands for a few weeks; allow the heat to die; and then you can return to New York a man of respect! Now, how many teenagers . . . though I'm not calling you a kid . . . but how many young men get to start their lives with that kind of cash?"

Jack left, and returned several hours later, upset and talking to himself. When Joe asked about the money; Jack cut him short.

"The %$%^& didn't have the damn cash! He ^%^&^% me! Said he'd have it by the end of the week. He's a wiseguy—made and connected—can't steal a damn hotdog without his permission. I had to give the stuff to him and wait! I cannot believe this $%^%!! He said something came up and he had to use a hundred-thousand to bail someone out of a bind . . . I bet that ^%^&%$ has three times that much in his safe!"

On and on he ranted until Joe decided to go down to the pool and chill out, leaving Jack (who he never saw yell once, let alone have a fit) to burn himself out.

Joe had a rough time and awoke within his dreams.

He had journeyed back in time with visions of priests, pastors, and demons awash in his mind—though the gulls cried across the waves and a cool breeze wafted in through the open balcony doors of Jack's luxurious apartment—it was the vision of darkness, pain, and the heat in which he was swimming, that overwhelmed him. That story of life in which Old Man Bianco's voice came back to him; that story of continuation; that story that in fact was not story but reality, rattled inside his mind; "What is my purpose? Why did I have to discover the truth? What am I to do?" It took all of his concentration to finally entomb this dread and retake reality. Was it an omen?

Two weeks had gone by and other than the quick jobs Jack put together they sat simply waiting. Jack seemed to be worried he was not going to see a "red cent" from one of his best heists. Joe soon discovered this was Jack's first deal with Shorty. Though Jack had sent money up to him from his action for seven years, he never did a "job" in partnership with him before. In fact, Shorty didn't even know of the work Jack did; not the actual jobs nor amounts. Shorty collected his "tax" on Jack through Sonny Black, one of Shorty's guys. Sonny ran a car rental business on Biscayne Boulevard. Jack had only met Shorty on Sonny Black's word of the big heist!

After Joe dressed and ate a light breakfast he checked on Jack, who was sleeping—he never awoke before noon. He then went down to the pool and began a conversation with the pool boy. They were deep in conversation when he heard the distinct sounds of a large caliber, semi-automatic weapon: "BANG. BANG. BANG. BANG. BANG!" Its sounds shattered the morning silence. But, as quick and fast as it came, it left. He looked at the pool guy who acted like he hadn't heard the sounds.

"You didn't hear those gun shots?" he asked.

"What gun shots?" he answered as he continued to sweep the water with his net.

Joe looked up toward the area the shots seemed to originate from. Due to the layout, it was difficult to determine its source, yet it seemed to come from the area of Jack's apartment. Feeling strange, he got up and decided to leave and go back to the apartment.

The door was unlocked—Jack was a stickler for locking his door, and Joe knew he had locked it! Entering, he called Jack's name out loud. No voice returned his greetings. Slipping cautiously down the hallway, he reached Jack's door. Warily, he turned the knob and rushed in.

Jack was snoring loudly.

It was time to go . . . he knew, deep inside, that this entire awakening was a message from somewhere, someone! Gathering his clothing—he had purchased an extensive wardrobe—he scooped up the money he had hidden under the carpet, and silently closed the door behind him.

Hailing the first cab he could find, he rode back to the projects and Diane.

Does God work in mysterious ways? No, He works in well thought-out ways: two nights after he left, Jack was found on the beach—suffocated with a plastic bag. The man who began his career hawking gold coins and worked his way into a spot as a preeminent second-story man—who racked in ten large a week—was gone.

Mob respect had claimed another. Joe did not know if he had a family, if he had been married, or if he had a child. Joe realized he had journeyed to a place very rare for a teenager. None of the players were the type who "hung" with kids! Joe concluded that Jack really wanted a son. That had to be it because after Joe began to hang with Jack, Jack would introduce him as his nephew and treat him as if he were his son!

Things he'd missed came crashing to the front of his mind; how everyone reacted when they discovered Jack had an orphaned nephew; how the word swept the underground and he was accepted even though he was a teenager. What irked Joe was the fact that the same guy he was sure murdered Jack, might be the same person who murdered his father.

> A gentle, caressing surf stroked the shore line as the black shadow whisked across the sand dunes . . . to settle against the rustling palm-covered tiki hut. With deft ability, it wavered only for a moment's moratorium and then flashed up and over the pitted railing to land upon a darkened landing. A spiders grasp, and the shadow covered the vertical until arising above the third-floor bal-

> cony. Its outline imposed against the chalk-white exterior wall, it disappeared once again; only a glint of reflection as a patio door slid effortlessly; proof of its reality . . . Silent and determined, it slithered across the smooth, soft, snowy-white carpet until it rested against the lavender, hide-covered sofa. Timing deep bursts of nasal breathing emanating from the target, it shifted its route until contacting the supple down of the black and white checkered comforter. Once there, it reached for the metallic object it carried with reverence and placed it against the comforter. Once connected to an outlet of energy, the shadow proscribed it to pay due homage to its host. Once more, it whisked back to its origins . . . leaving not a trace of its existence!

One week after the death of Jack, before the dawn of a clear and cool morning, an electrical fire broke out in Shorty's condominium. Lucky for him, a sidekick rescued him; he escaped with only minor burns. Though his condominium was a total disaster, he had good insurance—yet "the word on the street" was he had lost a fortune in "undeclared" assets . . . ?

"So, what happened to you?" she asked . . .

For the next two weeks, Joe lived in a motel two blocks from the projects. Partying. Dressing up. Showing off. He spent the seven hundred he had saved, on all of the guys and gals who lived in the overwhelming poverty of the projects. Though he visited the track a couple of times, he knew it was time to go home and deal with his situation. With tearful—on the ladies's part—parting, he gave away all of his goodies and clothing and with fifty dollars, put his thumb out and headed for New York. He began his trek home . . . a seasoned traveler.

Chapter 34: Louisiana Kidnap

He placed his thumb out for a ride,
new memories, visions by his side;
an' hops aboard sleek racing stripes,

or cluttered jalopy—he hardly gripes.
He's hooked: adventure, travel finds
all responsibility left far behind!

"Hey, kid, . . . need a ride?"

Red—bright red—fire engine red—souped up and rumbling with a deep throaty sound, full-blown engine, double, four-barrel carbs, high-rise intake, dual exhaust; the '65, two-door Ford came to a stop. With delightful exuberation, Joe ran toward the car.

The front passenger, a large, heavy, hairy, swarthy-looking man of fifty, dressed in a greasy mechanic's uniform and once white, now mottled brown tee-shirt, his blonde, oily, chop-cut hair receding along the top of his massive skull, a skull which dominated a high-browed, red-flushed face which held a pair of green, narrow-spaced, cat's eyes swimming in an ocean of blood-shot red, steps out of the passenger door and holds the front seat down so Joe can enter the back seat. Joe squeezes himself into the tight interior and makes himself as comfortable as the space between the rear passenger and the window allows. Roar, the engine revs to life, and with a Oooommm. Click! Screech . . . Oooooooommmm . . . Click! Screech . . . Click! Oooooommmmmm . . . they were on their way to cruising altitude in what seemed like three seconds, in a rocket ship with tires and a gear box.

"Welcome aboard, where ya headin'?" the mechanic asked.

"North."

"Oh, Greaser-Wet-Back territory," the front passenger, a thin, straggly bearded individual, who wore torn, filthy over-alls and a ragged straw hat from which poked sprouts of thin, dark brown hair—piped in—leading to a barrage of greaser jokes and back-slapping.

It was not long before Joe realized something was wrong with the picture! Three men, two in their fifties and one twenty-four—but looking sixteen—drinking moonshine straight from a jug; riding hell bent in a bright and shiny race car with Florida tags (in Tennessee) without five bucks between them—and no destination!

Joe soon discovered the driver's name was Davis; from New Mexico. The other two men were from New Orleans. Their names were Papa Joe (the mechanic?) and Pigny (the farmer?)—or was it Pigmy? He really couldn't understand their accents!

Since they bought the car with a check stolen from Papa Joe's ex-boss, the big question in their minds seemed to be "Was the car therefore stolen?"

Joe came to several conclusions, One: these guys were crazy. Two: they were drunk. Three: they were armed. Four: there was no rear door to escape from. Five: why were they so open in their conversation of their misdeeds and circumstances in front of a stranger unless they planned to rob him . . . or worse?

With keen, shark-looking eyes; which jittered back and forth in a nervous environment of white twitching pallor which made up his face; Pigny sharpened the twelve-inch blade of his Bowie knife on a strip of leather with the dexterity of a butcher . . . all in tune to the Louisiana Bayou music twanging from the radio.

'Hanging music . . . yep, that's what it was, hanging music,' Joe thought. He was sure he'd heard this tune in some damned movie where people butchered hogs, drank corn liquor, and groped bare foot women deep in the swamps of Louisiana—or was it Georgia?—as they prepared a New Yorker for the hangin' party! One thing was for sure: Joe would never set foot in a swamp!

Joe shifted uncomfortably when Papa Joe, who sat in the back with Joe, began passing gas in time with the sounds of a banjo that suddenly appeared in his hands.

The racket of Papa Joe's twanging and 'dwanging' mixed with the roar of the engine and the loud, quick tempo of Davis's hands tapping the dashboard as he steered the car with his knees in wide, sweeping, screeching motions across a thin, crumbling, black-top road.

Pigny yelled, "Hey, Mike . . . he be doin the tune? Eh?"

"Yeah, man. Cool!" was all Joe could say; his knuckles turning shades of purple and white as he grabbed the seat with both hands. "I like that music, but listen, hey, Pimgny, I was going north . . . not west. You can let me out at the next crossroad. O.K.?"

"His name's Pigny, got that? Why don't you drink some of this?" Papa Joe said, handing a jug to Joe. "You'll git where your goin soon enough."

Joe took the jug, pretended to take a long swallow, then wiped his mouth in the fashion of the trio. With a forced burp, he handed the jug to Pigny and thought his best chance of escape was to get them drunker . . . unless Davis crashed first!

"Hey, we're almost out of gas."

"You got some money to chip in?" Pigny asked.

"I ain't got a nickel." Joe replied as his stomach began to twist.

"You gotta pay your way somehow." Papa Joe said, belching to make room for another swig of the corn.

"I got an idea . . . ," Pigny interjected, " we can do the thing using the kid!"

"Yeah! Good idea!"

Joe began to worry. What was this great idea they'd agreed on?

As the car roared on a journey through the outer-limits with Pigny and Papa Joe dozing off, Joe set his eyes on the rear of Davis's head and began to think of a plan.

Unless Davis was spitting gobs of slushy chewing 'tobaky;' leaving dripping streaks as wide as the tires of the car across his face, which he promptly wiped away with the sleeve of his stained denim jacket; the eagle-eyed, pimple-faced guy, whose cheekbones were the most prominent feature of his otherwise flat, broad-lipped and dark countenance, seemed out of place in this environment of toxic waste. Educated and well spoken, he lacked the communication skills of Pigny and Papa Joe—his words didn't creep and crawl through a minefield of broken teeth and slurred thought.

Joe knew, if he was to escape this cargo of dramatic destiny, Davis was the key to his release. He began to encourage conversation and soon discovered that Davis had been picked-up by Pigny and Papa Joe several months before. He was from New Mexico. Said he was a half breed, Navaho and Irish. It'd been four years since he started his hike to Michigan and fortune—he had yet to make it! He kept getting blown off course—sounded familiar!

This, his most recent detour, was the worst; the guys from New Orleans were using Davis in con games; they drove the entire breadth of the Southeast, drinking, driving, and stopping frequently at large, expensive homes to beg for money . . . using a teenage-looking Davis to plead for "a few bucks to help me an' my son!" Or, pulling up to a major shopping center and, after bruising Davis about his body, pretending that "My son just fell and hurt himself."

Papa Joe drifted out of his stupor and cuffed Davis across his right ear as he shouted an order for him to "Pull the hell off the highway and head towards the lights of that damn house on the hill."

Davis was intimidated by Papa Joe, therefore, whenever Papa Joe spoke at him, he'd start to stammer. The stuttering excited Papa Joe in some perverse way. Joe had seen that look before: in Miami—on the predator's face!

"Pull over here . . . STOP! You, Mike, get out of the car with me".

Once outside of the car, Papa Joe continued, "You just keep your mouth shut." BAM! Papa Joe smacked Joe so hard his face reddened and his eyes watered. "That's it, you look perfect, let's go . . ."

"Can I help you?" a wary, middle-aged woman asked.

"S'cuse me, ma'am, but we; my son and I; have had some misfortune," Papa Joe began as he shuffeled his feet and anxiously played with the brim of a dusty, old and weary hat. We seem to have gotten lost an used all of our gas tryin' to git back to the main road. We haven't eaten since mornin.' I was hopin' you nice Christian folks could see your way inta loaning us a few dollars . . . I could send it back to ya when we git home?"

Though intimidated by Papa Joe, the woman did not blink; her compassion for the young boy whose face looked so sad was apparent. "Wait here," she said as she closed the door.

Several minutes later she appeared with a large sack of food and twenty-five dollars. "You take care of that child . . ."

Joe sat in the rear of the car not paying attention to anything but the sandwich he was wolfing down. They had stopped for gas, and as Davis filled the gas tank at a cost of six dollars, Papa Joe sauntered into the package store/gas station to buy a fifth of 'Bonded Bourbon.' For several weeks they'd traveled the country, stopping whenever the money for booze and gas ran out, to ask for charity. Though lately, through the good fortune of a real teenager, Papa Joe began to get greedy—stopping all of the time!

The previous night was the worst demonstration of his new pattern: Papa Joe lost his temper when an old woman's son came to the door of the house he chose, and demanded that Papa Joe take his kid and get the hell off his property or he'd call the cops!

Papa Joe wanted to go back and "Do him right."

If, in fact, Pigny had not voiced his opinion that they had two-hundred-dollars in the kitty, Joe was sure Papa Joe would have carried through his threat. Instead, Papa Joe ordered Davis to stop at the next truck stop and demanded he follow him to the restroom.

When they returned—Papa Joe with a large back-slapping, grinning attitude, and Davis with tears and a halting walk—it became apparent that he had taken his anger and pleasure upon Davis.

"What a team. We ain't did this good for seven months. Mike there, seems to make them want to give . . . Eh, Pigny?"

"Yeah, let's head to Nashville; the Christians are strong there!"

Pigny and Papa Joe sat in the front of the car, guzzling bourbon and singing loudly out-of-key; occasionally, they would peek into the darkness of the rear compartment to wink at Davis and Joe with twin, perverted twists of their thick, tobacco-stained lips . . .

Joe's mind was going twice as fast as the car. He knew he was running out of time. The Orleans duo were talking of upping the ante. They wanted to "do sumthin' bigger;" what that 'sumthin' was Joe didn't want to know! Eventually, the booze and the singin wore them out. Pigny stopped to let Davis drive, crawled into the back seat, and soon, the car's gentle throaty sound and light rhythmic bumping along the tar-streaked highway had Papa Joe and Pigny in a deep, snoring sleep.

Joe tapped Davis on his head and, with a hasty motion of his finger to his mouth, warned of silence. He then slid next to Davis's left ear and began to whisper.

The sun arose to welcome the late, fall morning: crisp, clean, cool air, falling leaves—turning colors of the rainbow—squirrels running along the ground of the rest stop—gathering legions of nuts in preparation of the coming winter. A scene reminiscent of Georgia, brought yearnings of freedom to Joe. One month had passed and Papa Joe had grown tired of his cat and mouse game with Davis. He began to show more attention to Joe than Joe wanted. In the past two weeks, Joe had spoke with Davis about escape, he'd convinced him that it was more than possible and Davis had begun to trade in his fear for friendship. Joe told him that whenever the opportunity presented itself Davis had to be prepared. With Papa Joe leaning towards his new ideas, Joe was sure that he'd have to prompt that opportunity.

As everyone stretched their legs to limber out the cramps of sleeping in the confines of hard, plastic-wrapped, bucket seats, Joe noticed a sign identifying a large truckstop off the next exit 100 yards down I-80. "Hey, why don't we stop at that truckstop, wash up, and eat . . ." Joe blurted to Papa Joe. "Wouldn't you like to stop and use a restroom?" Joe continued, teasing Papa Joe.

Papa Joe's eyes glimmered and his smile twisted in a familiar crooked grin. "Yeah, that sounds perfect."

The truckstop, crowded with huge rigs parked in neat orderly rows, swarmed with a multitude of truckers.

Papa Joe, sensing that this many people might not be ideal to retaining his captives, decided to continue down the road; he ordered Davis not to stop . . . but Joe was not going to give up.

"Hey, I gotta go! Come on, let's use the restroom," he said as he jumped over the seat and forced Davis to make an abrupt, tire-screaming turn into the overflowing parking lot.

Sensing the futility of causing a scene, Papa Joe's anger was overtaken by this temptation of opportunity. He ordered Pigny to pull behind the restaurant with its collage of humanity and park by the outside restroom. When Pigny stopped, Papa Joe wet his lips and opened the door. Motioning Joe to get out, he held the door and told Davis and Pigny to wait. When his feet hit the pavement, Joe turned and began to rapidly walk around the building. Papa Joe rushed to overtake Joe as he entered the restaurant and plopped down in the first booth he saw. Papa Joe, an arms-length behind, cautiously sat down. "I thought you wanted to use the restroom?"

"Later. Let's eat some real food for a change. Hey, waitress," Joe yelled—loud enough for every patron to stop what they were doing and turn their heads—"Papa Joe, get the guys."

Papa Joe was steaming mad but he could do nothing. As he contemplated his next move, Davis appeared with the car in front of the window that the booth faced, and parked. A wide, ear-to-ear grin swept his face as he exited the car with Pigny in tow.

Forks clattered, plates clanked, and a hum of rapid murmur, occasionally interrupted by loud barking orders of waitresses and cooks, filled the large dining room. "What a place," thought Joe, viewing the concoction of color, language, and custom, with awe. He was always amazed at the diversity of a truckstop. There was not another place in the entire United States in which such a contrary group of individuals mixed with more harmony: Tall, bearded Texans, in western boots and plaid shirts, sitting with short, balding, Italian truckers from New York; men dressed in brown khaki pants and black, high top industrial boots, wolfing their food in heaps, while New Englanders cut theirs into small, precise shapes—with the deftness of plastic surgeons; conversations of laughter exploded ethnic and racial barriers, conveying one word in a multitude of accents: Friendship!

You could hear a meeting of minds pushing aside the everyday prejudice and disharmony blanketing the towns, cities, and countryside's these road warriors came from. In the high sounding, boisterous laughter of truckers, from a rapidly expanding West Coast as it broke in sharp, rag-tag tempo, through the long, slow, drawling molasses like texture of the Southern truckers—whose soothing sounds softened the hard edges of the serious laughter from those who represented the crowded East Coast cities, caused Joe to sit back in bewilderment: "How come men did not behave like this all of the time?"

A grunt from Papa Joe; signaling he was still engaged in the process of stuffing his snout, brought Joe back to reality. Though the world moved upon its continuing journey into the future, he was stuck in the present with no change in sight! He looked at Pigny who was also gorging himself. Reminiscing the diner episode with Carmine when his journey began, Joe began to wait for Pigny to vomit! As they dug into their platters, Joe signaled Davis to slip him the keys to the car—a pre-planned idea they'd agreed to do at the first opportunity—and made an announcement. "I have to go to the bathroom."

"Pigny, go with him!" Papa Joe blurted.

"Hey, I don't need a chaperone, besides, the bathroom is over there," he said, pointing to a door with a sign that said "MEN'S ROOM" not ten feet from the booth.

"Well, make it quick!" Pigny said.

Joe entered the bathroom confident he'd find the customary window he could make his escape from—but he was stunned to see there was no such window!

"#$%#!" he said out loud, "What the $#%$ am I gonna do now?" He went to the door and peeked through; the trio was still eating. He knew if he attempted to leave through the front door he'd be committing suicide. He contemplated notifying someone of his and Davis's predicament, but he was unsure if Papa Joe would not come up with some con about Joe and Davis being rebellious kids or something; this would prove fatal also, for then the police would be called in and Joe was sure that he'd be returned to a juvenile home or even worse—possibly to New York and the wiseguys!

Finally the answer popped into his mind. With great purpose, he began stuffing the five commodes with toilet paper and paper towels. Moving from stall to stall, in rapid succession, he began to flush them. The water began to rise, and soon it flowed across the bathroom, then under and out the bathroom door. Within seconds, like a stirred-up nest of ants, a rush of employees, mops, buckets, and towels in hand, invaded the bathroom. In the confusion, Joe slipped past Papa Joe's table and out the front door. He ducked down and made his way to the car.

Keeping his head down, he opened the passenger door and crawled across the front seat. Placing the ignition key into the slot, he turned it until he heard the click and the dashboard lit up like a Christmas tree. He was ready, except for one other item: he'd never driven a vehicle with a stick shift!

Though it seemed an eternity had elapsed since Joe had entered the restroom, it had been only fifteen minutes. Papa Joe sat wondering what had happened to him, and in the commotion of the restaurant staff, he stood to investigate.

Joe peeked out over the dashboard as he squeezed into the driver's seat. Papa Joe was rising from the booth, looking in the direction of the confusion that blocked the bathroom door. Pigny had already begun to walk toward the mess, and Davis was edging his way to the door. Joe shifted the driver's seat forward and began concentrating on the shifter. He'd watched Davis and Pigny for more than a month and he was sure he could do it. Placing one foot on the clutch and the other on the gas, he put his hand on the key and cringed as he gave it a twist, "VAROOM!" The roar of the engine crashed through the parking lot and into the restaurant.

As the familiar sound of the super-charged engine of his beloved Ford broke through his conscious mind, Papa Joe instinctively turned to face the window. A look of shocked horror ripped across his face as his eyes met Joe's, and the action began . . .

Joe revs the engine, pushes the clutch in, and moves the shifter.

Davis hits the door . . .

Pigny grabs Davis by his jacket.

Joe jams the gear shift into reverse, jumps his foot off the clutch and jams the gas.

Papa Joe opens the door and heads towards the car . . .

The engine roars but the car doesn't move!

Davis breaks free by shifting out of his jacket.

A horrendous sound of gears clashing together rips through the parking lot.

Papa Joe grabs the car door handle . . .

Davis opens the restaurant door and comes tearing out . . . with Pigny in hot pursuit . . . just as Joe jams the shifter and lurches off in hopping movements.

The car jerks forward.

Papa Joe is thrown from his feet.

Davis is almost to the door when his leg is grabbed by his leg by Pigny.

Joe pulls the shifter out of first.

Papa Joe reaches up and grabs Davis . . . Davis grabs the door handle . . . Joe grinds the gear shift into reverse and slams down the gas pedal.

Davis falls on his face.

Joe, his feet attempting to work the gas, brake, and clutch, all at the same time, causes the car to move in hard, jerking movements down the drive . . . in reverse . . . Davis is almost at the door.

Joe slams the brake!

Papa Joe, and Pigny are tearing behind . . .

They're almost caught up . . .

Joe slams the shifter and rips down the gas . . . just as Davis slips his hand in the door handle . . .

. . . just as Pigny grabs Davis's leg . . . again . . .

. . . dragging Davis and Pigny . . .

. . . they all fall . . .

. . . Joe looks in his rear view mirror . . .

. . . just as Davis rises and races toward the moving car . . .

. . . Davis is in the lead . . .

. . . catching the car . . .

. . . Papa Joe catches up . . .

. . . Causes Joe to start and stop, in crazy, up and down motions all the way to the road.
. . . until Papa Joe falls, tripping Pigny . . .
. . . and Davis reaches the car . . .
. . . Joe slams on the brakes . . .
. . . Davis snatches the door open . . .
. . . Papa Joe is up and at the rear window of the car . . .
. . . he jumps on the rear deck . . .
. . . Joe slams the gas peddle down . . .
. . . leaps the highway . . .
. . . with Davis holding on for dear life . . .
. . . half in and half out of the car . . .
. . . Papa Joe slides off . . .
. . . Davis climbs in . . .
. . . Joe gets the hang of the clutch . . .
. . . they hit the open road to freedom . . .
. . . leaving Papa Joe and Pigny gesturing and carrying on like a pair of comics in a 1920's silent film.

Chapter 35: Warrior Nihanio on Dream Catchers

Joe and Davis cruised down the interstate. They were one hundred and fifty-five miles from Albuquerque, New Mexico—just twenty more and they would be at the Navaho, Indian Reservation where Davis had grown up.

Davis decided to sell the car to a group of Mexicans who would drive it over the border. He figured they should be compensated for their adventure. Joe agreed.

Though Joe felt physically great, the tribulation of the last two months had taken a toll on his mind and he could not remove the nagging thoughts that cropped up once more. Had the last experiences become just another group of stories . . . reduced to just memories? What were the actual results? Did it contain a hidden meaning? Had it become just a thought? What of God . . . and Ginny, Aggie, and Diane crossed his mind—they sometime did whenever God came into the picture . . . relieving the pain!

Davis, who was driving with a case of absent-mindedness, habit, or a combination of both; said something which caused Joe, absent-mindedly himself, to look over at him: a figure, mouth moving in slow motion, relief plastered to its face like a Greek actor's serene mask of play, rambling on about this or that . . .

Bang! Like an exploding bomb it hit him: to Davis, who had experienced more than the mental anguish—a word he was thoroughly familiar with—of the experience, the entire episode had become more than real! Joe was sure his entire life had been changed by the treatment he had received . . . after all, he could hardly recall as many events as Joe could. Joe knew from his own trials and tribulations that an accumulation of events brought on a sort of dulling of the senses—an ability to "numb out!" Had Davis attained that level? He doubted it.

"Hey, Davis, where you goin' to go when you get paid?" Joe asked in his haste to end his thoughts.

"Michigan!"

"What's in Michigan?"

"My mother. She left the reservation ten years ago. After I stop and see my father, I'm gonna find her. You see . . ."

Joe sat stiffly in his seat as Davis rambled away about Tribal Elders or something. Once again, Joe was not listening. In fact, Joe's mind was on his own family. He missed his mother, Angela, Carmine, and even his little brother Eddy—who he hardly new! And the sharp pain of his father, dead; yet alive in the deep recesses of Joe's memory, in that file marked "Accident:Personal" in that abyss, with no future, no present, no hope; cried for release.

He refused to open the door—he did not want to recall those vivid pictures and begin a new cycle all over again. The Shorty episode had put that life to rest . . . or had it? No, it was only these "situations" that masked his thoughts. He decided he'd telephone his mother when they arrived at the reservation. She'll be surprised at how well I've handled myself. She'll be proud!'

No signs announced the reservation; just a simple sandy road revealing a group of shacks. Built of a variety of materials, were massed together and naturally landscaped with sage brush, twiggy looking bushes, and a heap of dust.

Joe became excited as Davis drove down the road toward the buildings. Real Indians; he was going to visit with real live Indians! Memories of his first trip and the stories that wafted across the table of that truckstop with so much pomp and circumstance, cried out, "Andrew Jackson! Naked Ladies! Long standing bridges without columns! Alligators! And now, Indians!"

Joe was surprised when they didn't come riding out on painted ponies with bows and arrows to confront and challenge their red chariot. For a kid from New York, who only saw Indians in John Wayne movies and history books, it was a letdown to see that Indians were nothing more than a memory of motion pictures.

Joe was confused when a group of ordinary looking people, dressed in hand-me-downs and cast-offs, began murmuring and pointing excitably as they surrounded the car.

"What happened to your people? These are Mexicans, aren't they?" he asked Davis.

"No, Navaho."

Embarrassed, Joe began to say something in apology, "I was jus . . ."

But before he could finish his statement, the group (who seemed to recognize Davis) drew closer and formed a curious half-circle around the driver's side of the car. It was then that Joe began to distinguish their prominent features: high cheekbones, black hair, some with long braids, reddish-brown skin, dark, piercing eyes—which seemed to contain an immense store of both sorrow and intrigue.

Joe was suddenly face to face with his vision, but something was missing? It lacked "color" . . . Yes, that's what it was: a once colorful vision whose definition had become a black and white barrage of texture and thought due to its poverty of life. Once more, in black and white, in have and have not, Joe was reminded of a fact of life which he had been continually exposed to thus far: Poor had no color; Poor had no qualification for race, religion, nor creed! Its lethal injection into society was epidemic; its causes wide and varied. But then, from the center of the half-moon, a short man, who looked ninety years old, with long, gray streaked, jet black braids—which were tied with bands of red cloth and silver objects—stepped forward and began to paint in the color between the lines.

With a short backward wave of his left hand, he silenced the group. And then, as if viewing a magnificent canvas with a keen eye, he motioned to the land with both arms in a gentle, sweeping manner and began, in a sing-song, melodic voice, to speak in his native tongue. His vocals, rising and falling like a rhythmic, flowing and ebbing of a peaceful shore line, reverberated in sweet, smooth, harmony.

He began to walk forward, his voice rising with each deliberate step, until he reached the car. He halted and bellowed a crisp, sharp cry, while grasping Davis's arm with his right hand and signing with the other. As if on cue, the group, melting into one, warm-hearted mass of happiness and friendship, converged on the car welcoming Davis "Lost Cloud" home.

Tribal Elder Nihanio, one-hundred-and-two-years old, was the oldest surviving member of "the old way."

Born in 1865, in the face of a high, full moon, he was gifted the name, Night Warrior.

Night Warrior Nihanio, man of a thousand truths and the oldest living repository of the history of his once great and powerful people, sat upon a threadbare sofa in a plywood faced shack, surrounded by fifteen young tribal members. His face was flat, high-cheeked, with piercing, eagle-like eyes, thick, broad lips, and strong, white teeth. Joe was amazed at his mental energy and his vibrant, physical demeanor. The first thought that ran through Joe's mind was the fact that the guy talked "normal"!

"The Great Spirit has honored our people for our care of Mother Earth; for welcoming all who seek peace and consoling; for behaving in the Right Way—with goodness and beauty . . . therefore, with much joy and honor, we welcome Lost Cloud and his friend Mike to our home. We thank The Great Spirit for watching over him and showing him the way back to his roots."

For the next several hours, Nihanio entertained an eager Joe with stories of the Navaho's past.

"Before I was born unto this earth, the Navaho were called the Diné. "The Diné" translates in English into "the People" or "the Folks." The Diné began as a small group of people related to the Apache. After settling in this very land, we began conducting raids to capture people—who we allowed to join our tribe—and wealth. Up until the coming of the Spaniard, with his horse, steel sword, hot musket, and tendency to scalp his conquered, the Diné were a group of peaceful people who loved the heat of the occasional fray like all of the other tribes who made the desert's mesas and cliffs home.

After the coming of the Spaniard, with his sly intrigue, wealth and power, the Diné began a specific routine of warring to satisfy their need for people and wealth with which to combat the Spaniard. Eventually, through this continuing war-like atmosphere, the Diné were able to become the most numerous and prosperous peoples of the painted land.

Reaching more than 10,000 by my birth, my people were very industrious: Our women wove the finest blankets; we worked the Spanish metal of water into great works of art; we raised thousands of peach trees and great patches of corn. Our hogans, what you call houses, provided the necessary shelter we needed. Our flocks of sheep were as great as our desire to hear the Singers sing the Songs of Talking God. We cherished philosophy, poetry, and art. We were a happy and healthy people. But, due to many confrontations with our brothers the Apache, who were being pressed by the Spaniards and their descendants, the Mexicans—who enslaved vast numbers of people for their personal and economic pleasure—we eventually became fierce warriors and raiders.

After the Americans defeated the Mexicans, Americans began appearing in great numbers. We began to experience much outrage. After many retaliatory raids and skirmishes, a fort was established in the very heart of our country. The presence of the Fort brought peace until our people attacked and the struggle began.

Our stronghold was overrun and all our stocks stolen or destroyed. They cut down our peach trees, trampled our corn, and butchered our flocks. Our people were starved into submission, and moved to a reservation. That is where I was born! By my third birthday, we were allowed to return to our lands—which were greatly reduced—and begin our lives again. And then . . ."

Thus, for seven hours, Night Warrior told tales of bravery and legend; of laughter and desperate struggle; of love and death.

By four a.m., the old warrior had used his last remaining drop of energy and finally conceded to sleep.

In the end, Joe felt proud and special, he knew the old warrior was treating him to the most fantastic oral history lesson that he'd ever be privy to!

As Joe lay upon a heap of blankets, along with seven others who slept in the single, small room of the shack, he thought of Nihanio and his history.

The old man had been delighted to tell his stories to Joe. He reminded Joe of Old Man Bianco! What a father figure Night Warrior was: proud yet humble; old and weak yet strong in his youthful memory! Nihanio had committed himself to more than storytelling; he had delivered a strong message to the young boy who had seen so much yet knew so little: "The past was so important to the future; Without memory one has no dreams; Without dreams one does not move forword; Without knowledge of the beginnings, one cannot determine the endings; Without truth, one is prone to repeating fallacies."

Nihanio also told Joe of Dream Catchers: "Dream Catchers were once more than the intricate works of feathers, twisted saplings, beads, and animal fur of the plains' tribes.

Dream Catchers came in human form: men who had the ability to perceive and interpret dreams; men who once roamed the lands, coming and going in their eternal quest to discover man in his many modes. Dream Catchers were medicine men, great healers of the mind, spirit, and body; religous men, philosophers, scientists, and astronomers all packed into one. Dream Catchers were usually excepted in any tribe or peoples they came upon on their often long journeys."

Nihanio said that a dream was nothing more than the mind gathering, digesting, inquiring, and formatting all thoughts, ideas, and happenings that men pushed aside into their subconscious minds.

The mind sorted them just like Mr. Bianco sorted the rumors and facts of the neighborhood before analyzing them and willing the benefits!

He said that the mind was powered by the Great Spirit, but that man, limited by his consciousness, could not understand their dreams.

"Only in the subconscious can they truly gather the entire power of their mind to assimulate their buried thoughts!"

"The Dream Catcher, with his vast experience, was the only one who could decipher the information!"

It was then that Joe knew Mr. Bianco was a natural Dream Catcher!

When Joe asked who of the tribe was the Dream Catcher, Nihanio's face went sad before he began, once again, to educate Joe.

"When the tribes were allowed to return to a small portion of their original and vast ancestral lands, every portion of their way of life returned except two: The Warrior Spirit and Raiding; they ceased. The "Navaho" became a peaceful people and why is this fact so important? The Navaho were not communal; a long history of success and wealth had delivered a system of stability. No great chief ruled, instead, individual families or clans controled the economy. The only way a warrior could break into this circle was by marrying into a wealthy family. But in order to marry into a wealthy family, one would have to secure a dowry . . . and in order to secure a dowry, one would have to raid! Thus peace brought poverty to many; the poor remained poor, while the wealthy got wealthier . . . and the Warrior Way ceased . . . and with this cessation . . . the Way of the Dream Catcher also ceased. "

As Joe lay thinking of dreams and Dream Catchers, he was suddenly awakened to the thought that he himself had so much buried in that file deep in his mind. That must be the reason for all his weird daydreams! His mind was trying to analyze all those thoughts and questions! If only a Dream Catcher was here: alive! I could get the answers I have struggled with for six years.

And then, another wave of sorrow, another thought to be filed into that file marked "Accident:Personal," hovered in his mind: the thought of the look on Nihanio's face when Joe asked who was the Dream Catcher of the Tribe.

Two weeks had passed since Night Warrior first spoke those seven hours of greatness. Joe felt he had been treated with so much respect and honor he decided to level with Lost Cloud, Night Warrior, and the entire clan. He soon told them his stories and his truths. He informed them of his quest and his dreams. In fact, as Joe delivered his own historical heritage, the old warrior sat as amazed and entranced as Joe had, listening to him. The Curse of Alphonso had mesmerized the entire clan. At one point, when Joe got to the part where he had decided to avenge his father, everyone sitting crossed-legged upon the floor, including Nihanio, bent toward Joe so far, he thought they were going to topple over in their determination to hear and memorize every word of this youthful Warrior; a Warrior who had so much Respect for his ancestors, he decided to wage war.

Joe felt pride in Nihanio's respect. 'Yes, what a father figure Nihanio was! He stood straight and lived his life for his people.'

After Joe honored the clan with His-story, he was treated to four weeks of experiences in Diné tradition. He hand worked silver and stone into earrings and other pieces of traditional jewelry; he learned traditional ways to prepare and cook foods of the Diné; he rode a horse bareback into the desert and camped for five days with several, specially chosen, modern day Warriors—in the way of the old!

He felt the pride of the young "Warriors" as they demonstrated and taught him the keys to many of the mysteries of life and survival in the place of the Painted Lands. Later, he took the time to play with excited children; who ran around just as half-naked as the Puerto Ricans of New York—except in the place of the fire hydrant, a muddy hole of several feet wide and two feet deep became their oasis.

Joe had had one of the most memorable experiences of his entire life. And then, Joe went to Old Nihanio:

"Great Father Nihanio, Night Warrior of the Painted Lands, I feel as though I have known you all my life. I, in fact, wish that I had known you all my life . . . but then, I wonder if I would have truly appreciated all of the welcome I have received by your truth. I have never spoken like this before, Nihanio, so you can be assured that you have become a part of my mind. Therefore, I make the promise of the Earth, Sky, and Waters, I shall remember you and your peoples; I shall hold as a part of me, like you have taught me, all your words of thought so that I may tell them to others long after you have joined your ancestors in the land of the Great Spirit of the Sky."

And then, with much regret, he informed his adopted people that he'd have to leave.

"Your words are truth, spoken like a true Diné." Night Warrior replied, "I shall call you Warrior Who Travels. Yes, Who Travels, you are welcome as long as the Great Spirit warms the Earth and the Moon rises to cast the Shadow of the Warrior"

Lost Cloud and Joe sat talking on a bluff overlooking the encampment under a sky splashed in blush and golden clarity.

Lost Cloud had sold the car for two thousand dollars. Neither of the two felt any regret nor crime—they had endured much. When Lost Cloud (as Joe preferred to call Davis) handed Joe one thousand dollars in cash, Joe refused all but one hundred dollars. He informed Lost Cloud to give the rest to Night Warrior and his people after he left as a gift. Then they talked of their plans.

When Lost Cloud said he was going to resume his journey, Joe spoke with much determination. Joe had met Lost Cloud's father; an influential member of the council who was hoping that Lost Cloud would stay. Joe had seen such a change in Lost Cloud since his return he knew he belonged with his people. He began to tell him of his own needs; of his own dreams and wishes. He told him he had such a gift in his father—and his peoples—he would be foolish to leave and chance another Papa Joe and Pigny.

Joe was not sure if Lost Cloud would heed his advice, but he could tell a great impact had been etched upon his mind by his story; he hoped it would remain so.

Joe had already told everyone he was leaving and one of Lost Cloud's friends was waiting to drive Joe to the main highway. Joe felt he'd have a better chance of catching a ride at night when most of the truckers would be "hauling butt" down the roads. So, with much regret, Lost Cloud walked with Joe to the car.

As they hugged in Diné tradition, a hawk, screeching loudly, flew in circles high above as if to say, "I also am leaving in the night. I sing my song for all those who sacrificed their dreams so we might have ours. Have no fear, for our strength is in our friendship, bonded through memories to be passed down as leaves falling to a ground of eternity."

Joe sat in the car as it made its way back down the road. Before entering the highway, Joe asked the driver to stop a moment and rolled down the window to view the village one last time.

Turning in his seat, he was struck with a vision he had been unaware of when he first saw what he viewed as a group of dusty, run down shacks, he now could see the real beauty of the village: bathed in the brilliant, receding light of the clean desert air, the village was transformed into cubicles of gold, crimson, and rich amber, a place of elegance in nature—populated by a great people whose legacy swept the very breadth of history. Neither of the great ancients Homer, Virgil, Horace, nor even the venerable Shakespeare, could have put to words the feelings that pounded in the heart of Joe as he rode his memory down that long, long, lonely highway on his return to his great quest.

Chapter 36: The Swamp Man

"Ask and you shall receive!"

"Oh, Mr. God, I need a han', lik ta raise family by some fertile lan'. Black an rich, deep loam place, Oh, Mr. God, I'm ina race: Short of coin, none a dime, this I pray: be so kin'."

"There, Mr. Farmer, short of race, rests a narrow, farmers place. Crystal waters, briny marsh, cool the summers, never harsh.

"Oh, Mr. God, will you listen to me? Worsen piece of lan' ever did see! Plain simple clay of the red'n kind, won't grow a thing for me an mine.

"Listen, Mr. Farmer," said Almighty God, "got the best recipe for this type of sod, for clumps an clods near a Carolina Lake, prescribes a shovel, a hoe and a rake. Best the swamp, the bog an' pine, states the recipe, must drain the brine! Begin with a season, add a portion of toil, toss an' turn in a mixture of soil. A splash of rainfall, a pinch ye take, of summer's sunshine and then ye bake. Follow to the letter and thy will see, why man keeps his faith in me!"

Mr. Farmer began by the Carolina lake; had a shovel, borrowed a hoe and rake. Cleared the swamp, the bog an' pine. Followed the recipe to the very line. Began with a season, added a portion of toil, tossed and turned in a mixture of soil . A splash of rainfall, a pinch he took, of summer's sunshine and then he cooked.

Blowed the squall that broke an' breaked the land, tumble the crops, swept clean the pockets of farmer man .

"Oh! Mr. God, what have thy done! I'll have not with which to giv' my son!. No grain, no corn, no staples: Where? Oh! Mr. God can you hear?"

"Well, Mr. Farmer, do have faith, give thy measure before thy take! Bundle thy patience I gifted thee, an walk rut-furrows and thy will see, adequate grain and corn in husk, enough for a winter's chilled dark dusk. When spring arrives upon the beak, squawked the jay for seeds it seeks, you'll plant and plant and sow you will, and birth my soil upon thy till.

Soon prospered he, and on the land there grew, huge bumper crops; some old, some new.

Now he sits the rocker his golden years, watching them grow, them apples an pears; as drafts of air, cooled circulation, of century planted oaks and evaporation, swirl 'round mint juleps, tall the glasses iced, that quench his longing and the flies entice. And the tingling, tangling, occasional dong, copper clad wind chimes sing their Creators song; their boastful caress soothes musty ears, as he looks to the land he humbled dear.

Across expansive wide the verandah sweeps, the stately home so tall an' deep; on the edge of the lake of granite stone, beamed an' braced, notched an' honed, an' creatures smother a brackish glade, lush the sanctuary—hand-dug made: leather the gators frozen still, as June bugs in November's steady chill, an' soak the sun, bellies deep, lumped with catfish swiftly reaped, when dived the lake fresh they caught, rest an' wonder without a thought, an' view the graceful gaggled geese, soft upon the water as new shorn fleece, an' flowers wild, the butterflies swarm, prancing, dancing, flutter in storm, of color, energy, beauty keen, mirrored the waters glistening sheen. An' cows blare calves an' farm dogs yap, gleeful merriment as the roosters nap, an' crisp vast fields teem shades of green, corn an' fodder an' snap pole beans, an' the red of barnyard tractors race, to do-dads, homemade, halyard braced, smoke sheds, pig pokes, wooded stalls, an' windmills twisting, winds up tall.

"Oh, Mr. God of me and mine! I followed your recipe to the very line! Though ole' the knees so hard they bend, sore the muscles I shant pretend, though callused the hands wrought with pain, joy my heart I won't refrain, My love, My faith, My dignity, For thy who banished my poverty.."

Joe traveled to Georgia to deliver a shipment of fertilizer, then headed to North Carolina where he helped hand-load a couple tons of tobacco and a short run of the leaf to a large processing house in Virginia—Princess Ann County to be exact. After unloading, they were to pick up a load of processed and packaged tobacco products and make the final run to New York! And home!

The temperature was hot, steaming with humidity that draped all in blankets of sweat. After hand loading the semi with tobacco leaf—

from curing flue to barn, from barn to packing crates, where the tobacco was compressed in a farm built do-dad, from do-dad and barn to semi and all over again—all in one day, he was beat!

When Fred, the driver that hired/picked him up, began to roll a homemade with straight tobacco, the once sweet smell of tobacco soured his thoughts—smelling the stuff made him want to regurgitate the roast beef and smoked cheese sandwich he had just eaten.

The sandwich was complements of Carolina Farms, where they grew and processed most of their own staples, roast beef and cheese included. What a magnificent house! Resting smack in the middle of an ancient grove of oak by a beautiful lake: White massive colonnades; huge verandah; crisp white fountains with statues spewing cool water in streams of musical tones upon Lilly pads and burping frogs. The owner told him it had been built after the civil war, around 1870. The renovations had been extensive and many—so had the photographs: historians, tourists, the curious, and magazines.

When he said "magazine," Joe's first thought was a story Mr. Bianco recited of his Great-Grandfather, Antonio. He immediately became depressed with the thought of all the men of his family who believed in This Thing of Ours—until it included them in a way they never recovered from. They never worked the land, rather they would work the people to get what they desired. By planting the symbols of success rather than the seeds, they assumed they had received the legacy which went with those symbols—minus the hardships. But, working the fields, barns, flues, and tractors convinced him the owners of Carolina Farms deserved what they and their predecessors had worked for.

At seven p.m. Fred and Joe pulled into the depot, unloaded the tobacco, and readied the truck with its new cargo. By the time they were through, it was nine p.m. Fred asked if he'd mind waiting until morning to get back on the road. Joe didn't care; in fact, he thought it was a great idea. He could walk the city and see the sights, then, after a night in a comfortable motel, begin anew, refreshed and on the way home!

Sitting on a rock jutting the waters, daydreaming of Pirates and Ships of gold; viewing lights reflecting off the rolling surf, feeling the warm, salty breeze that puffed the air in tides of its own when . . . "Excuse me, sonny, you live around here?"

Experience had delivered the message long before he looked up; he knew who was asking the question.

"But, officer, that's me . . . I'm Mike, just riding through with my uncle who is staying at the Bayside Motel . . ."

"What's his name?"

"Freddy."

"Freddy what?"

"Well, he's not really my uncle. I'm just helping him deliv . . "

"Look, if you don't produce some ID, I'm gonna have to take you to the youth detention center until they can find out who you are."

When the police officer said "youth detention," Joe's stomach turned over.

At the detention center, Joe saw just how far he was from Queens. The place was located next to a swamp. It was clean, the youth were well disciplined, and both male and female children mixed in the day and were segregated at night. The center had individual cells housing one detainee each. Though smoking was permitted, there were no card nor pool tables—nor any other form of gambling. Capable, educated people ran the center with energy. The food was pretty good. A "dorm mother and father"—a couple who ran things during the day—were in charge and were pretty nice folks. During the first five days Joe got to know some of the guys. They were totally amazed at his travels. As Joe told his stories, the authorities were making unproductive attempts at identifying him. He thought they would have to let him go sooner or later, but they had other ideas.

During his sixth day he was called out and taken to a courthouse downtown.

"The Commonwealth of Virginia cannot allow a minor to roam the countryside. You must understand that neither can we hold you here in the youth center. So, even though we would rather send you home, we must send you to the boy's home upstate until such time as you notify us of your true identity. You'll be transferred in four days."

Back at the center, the guys gathered round to find out what happened. After he described his hearing they began telling him stories of the terrible place that was the boy's home. After the experiences he'd endured, Joe wanted no more of such a place. He began to formulate a plan.

Joe had few choices and fewer cards to play. Either he told them his true name and was returned to New York (and most likely a return to Spotford) or he found a way out of Virginia.

Among the fifty or so kids who were detained, five seemed to be leaders. Gathering them around him, he set out to devise, plan, and execute their escape to the North Carolina state line. From there, they would be free! Ultimately, six detainees huddled together and prepared to make their break in two days, on a Friday night.

Two a.m. and, except for the sound of large keys jangling on the waistband of the night watchman—who was making his required bed check—the center was dead quiet.

Samuel Stromberg, the only black inmate, arose from his bed and looked through the small wire-reinforced window mounted in his door. Judging the distance carefully, Samuel waited, and just as the watchman approached his room, he let out a cry and fell against the door. The night watchman was startled by a shout for help and a subsequent loud thump against the door. Grabbing his keys—while asking if Samuel was alright: "Sonny, Hey! You O.K. . . . Hey! Are you alright in there? Talk to me. Oh, no!" He jammed the key into the lock, turned it and, without removing the key, opened the door.

Jimmy, one of the six conspirators, had noticed that only the weekend watchman was in the habit of allowing detainees to be released from their cells to use the bathroom. As the watchman entered the cell and bent over the prostrate boy, Samuel jumped up, pushed the watchman to the side and rushed out the door locking it behind him. But, instead of just quietly slipping out, they had violated their plan and made a critical error. They had assumed the watchman's large key ring contained his car keys and therefore they would be able to slip out without anyone being the wiser. They would "borrow" his car and drive the few miles to the border. Instead, Pandemonium, reminiscent of The Beast, ruled the floor: everyone was released! In the chaos a window was shattered setting off an alarm! In their haste to leave, they left the keys inside.

Among the kids who stood out in intelligence and maturity was a guy nick-named "Swamp Man." He was fourteen-years-old and had grown up next to a Georgia swamp. He told fascinating stories of weekends spent hunting and exploring with his father among cypress and musty waters.

"And I learned to travel the swamp without detection and survive off the edible plants that grow all year long!"

Swamp Man had an idea: "We could avoid detection by slipping into the swamp! Once inside we could travel several hours and come out right on the North Carolina state line!"

As a New York City boy whose only experience with the wilderness thus far, was hunting in a forest in Georgia and the desert of New Mexico, Joe was not so sure.

"A swamp! You want us to go into a swamp! Are you kidding or what? After all your stories of alligators, snakes, and people getting lost . . . and what about those people who live in the swamp?" He imagined a tribe of Pignys' running around looking for the kid who 'stole' their stolen car.

"Hey, Mike, we can do it . . . It's the best choice."

The sulfurous smell of rotting vegetation permeated everything. No snakes or gators came their way, but other pests made them wish to be eaten to end their misery. Mosquitoes and huge horseflys bit into their flesh; irritating their eyes, noses, and mouths.

Joe had almost removed himself from the waist-deep muck and slime by dragging himself onto what looked like a patch of dry land . . . when the patch submerged . . . and once more he plopped into the yuck. The dirt patch was a turtle.

"Swamp Man . . . seems like we've been going 'round in circles for hours. Ain't that the lights of the compound waaayyyy over there?" Joe pointed to a hazy patch of light in the sky about a mile away.

"No, that's gotta be somethin' else."

"Man, it's cold out here in nothing but tee shirts."

They were sitting on what truly was, the only piece of dry mud in the entire doggone swamp; they were sure of this because they felt they had traversed the entire swamp!

Large enough for all of them, (as long as they bunched close together) the defeated group sat upon the only "dry mud in the entire doggone swamp;" a miserable lot of turtles, cut and bleeding from sawgrass, looking as if they had all contracted a case of giant measles, thigh deep in mud with arms tucked into their short-sleeved shirts—more like a bunch of Mr. Potato Heads in sacks with holes cut so they could pop their heads inside, warm their chests with their breath, then pop them out again—as a platoon of airboats and helicopters criss-crossed the swamp and the dawn's awakening signalled the end of their breakout.

"You know what we should call Swamp Man—The Lost Man! What happened to all your talk?" a shivering Joe asked.

"It's not like the Georgia swamp. "

They made it to the road, sat down, and waited for the police to come by. When they did, the boys meekly surrendered and sat down for the dry ride back. Not to the center, but to the county jail where a cell was emptied of occupants and reserved for the "Juvies."

A jail, a zoo keeper, and a hose: he's swamping them with water to remove the swamp mud they picked up from the swamp—for some reason, the word swamp became muck to them.

Joe was locked up in a jail cell again. After a week, three of the break-out crew, including Swamp Man, were allowed to return to the youth center. Samuel and Joe wished him the best and hoped the alligators in Georgia would think the same . . . "The best tasting swampman they ever-did eat!"

Joe and Samuel remained in jail; one the perceived ring-leader of the break and the other a black guy who assaulted a watchman. Threats of lock-down were used to increase the pressure on "Mike" to reveal his true identity. He answered the call by throwing food at the guards and calling them names. He began a protest that spread throughout the entire wing. He tattooed Samuel and himself. When they burned their sheets and mattresses the authorities had had enough!

Joe is naked and in the "Ice Chest" again.The only differences between the ice-cell in Spotford and the one in Princess Ann County, was the latter was colder, the food was worse, and where you could use the shower and bathroom twice a day in the Spot, here you used a pail.

The chiggers were horrendous; living in the cracks in the concrete, visiting only at night. Joe itched all night, but when the sun rose, peaking a beam into the cell through the crack at the top of the door, the chiggers would retire and the itching would stop.

After five days of this torture, they came for him and brought him back to the cell and his buddy Samuel who was going home! A hearing was set on Joe's case; he would see the judge who could set him free. . . .

If Joe was to see a judge, did he not need the proper attire and look if he was to get out? So, he got ready . . . like any other young man! . . .

He cut the sleeves and collar off his jail house shirt and tore them into strips. Then, after cutting along the side seams of his shirt and pants, he cut small holes the lengths of both and used the strips to criss-cross them back together; leaving small pieces to form a fringe the entire length of the pants and shirt sides. Then he sat down for his hair cut!

"OH MY GOD! WHAT HAVE YOU DONE!": the jailer when he came to get him for this very important day.

Docket number 347654B: Commonwealth of Virginia, In the County of Princess Ann . . . calls the defendant, "Mike Doe," Juvenile, tothe Dock."

"OH, MY GOD! WHO ARE YOU!": the bailiff when he walked into the court!

"OH, MY GOD! GET THIS IDIOT OUT OF MY COURT! NOW! REMOVE HIM FROM MY PRESENCE!: the judge when he threw Joe out of his court room!

Exactly one week later they came for him . . . "MIKE, OR WHATEVER YOUR NAME IS, GET YOUR STUFF! LETS GO! GET YOUR STUFF! FRONT AND CENTER!"

Two state troopers in two cars and a city policeman drove him to the bus stand.

"We're getting a ticket to Miami for you." (Joe had told the authorities he lived in Miami so they would not check with New York.)

"MMM, Miami, just where I wanna go." Joe replied.

"One ticket, ONE WAY, to Miami please. The first available bus!"

"Mike you hungry?"

"MMM. Yea."

"Chump, Chomp, Crunch, Munch. That was great . . ."

"Would you like anything else?"

"MMM. Well . . . No Thank you."

"ALL ABOARD! LAST BUS TO Miami!"

"Here is one hundred dollars . . . and don't come back! EVER!"

"Oh, thank you. No, I won't come back!"

"OH MY GOD!": the bus driver when Joe boarded the bus!

"He's harmless . . . and he's got a ticket!": State Trooper to the driver . . .

All the way to the State line, one forward, one behind, the tandem

Troopers made sure he never left that bus!

Now, for your curiosity, . . . a Mohawk haircut and deep, red lines across his face—made by rubbing a tooth brush handle over and over on his face—combined with his self-tailored outfit, had assured the judge that the Commonwealth of Virginia had no cause to detain him any longer . . .

Chapter 37: Barbie and Clyde

Joe wound up back in Miami in the projects . . . living once again in the woods by the canal that ran along the eastern reaches of its borders; a grove of cypress, pine, and palm trees. Bordered on one side by a canal that ran by a boat shop—later to be taken over by the Ted Vernon Car Collection—it was accessible only by a small coral and limestone bridge. Joe had a fortified position.

While his first priority was to shave his Mohawk, the second was to clear a twenty by ten foot area where he built his own "house"—a cardboard refrigerator box and a plastic tarp. Along with several other runaways who became his associates, Joe spent most of his days hangin on the bridge; shimmying up coconut palms for the hard-covered coconuts; playing poker, hearts; and spades with a worn out deck of "naked lady" cards; making out with rich girls who shopped at the shopping center located on the corner of 79th and Biscayne Boulevard—the neighborhood where he had trained with Jack the 2nd story man. The only time they left this secure spot was at night, when they visited the projects or made occasional forays into the outside world to heist food. In short order, Joe's reputation spread: the Virginia, Indian, Tennessee, Georgia stories. King of the Pack.

Joe was back with Diane and she clung to his arm as if she were a permanent part of his physical being. The other guys, noticeably displaying their jealousy at the attention their girls were giving Joe, didn't dare interfere with his storytelling—even though he was telling the same stories over and over.

"And then . . . you know what I did?"

"Ooh! No! What?" cried the girls in chorus as they fluttered their eyelids.

"I jammed the gear in first, popped the clutch, and, as I zoomed off, I fired twenty rounds from my .45 automatic at Pigny and that faggot, Papa Joe!"

"Wow! Did you kill em?" Johnny squawked—much to the dismay of the other guys.

"Whaddaya think!"

Joe reveled in his status.

This exaggerated masculinity would soon become the cause of a unbelievable chapter in his journey.

Seventeen years old and six feet tall, Pete was built like one of those huge, Southern truck drivers. He had a reputation for real violence and had become the sole powerhouse of the projects long before Joe had stepped back into the picture. Pete's main hobby—when he was not beating up one of the guys on the block—was "ragging queers"—robbing homosexual men. He also liked to be "sniffing the rag", a form of getting high from a transmission fluid additive called "Trans-Go".

Pete first got in trouble when he was fourteen. He'd been picked up one night, beaten black and blue, and raped by two older men. After several repeat performances, Pete joined the street life "hustling" the corner of 81st Street and Biscayne Boulevard—an intersection men frequented for the procurement of teen-aged boys.

When his hormones kicked in, Pete lost his youthful appearance and was subsequently discarded for new blood. His deep-seated shame, combined with his anger at being tossed aside and his Trans-Go warped brain, caused him to react in a manner he believed demonstrated his revulsion for those "friggin queers." Pete began hanging out in the back of the mall where the young male prostitutes congregated waiting for "tricks," and when a "John" drove up, he'd frighten the young male prostitutes into refusing to go . . . the John would have no choice but to offer the opportunity to Pete. Pete would hop in, drive to a location in the industrial area, perform his "trick," then mug the John.

When Joe began talking to some of the guys about the evils of selling themselves, Pete took personal offense and waited for the right opportunity to remove Joe from what he viewed as his place.

For several days Pete watched Joe tell his stories. Joe could tell (between Pete's huffs of his rag immersed in the oily red, strong smelling solution) that Pete was envious. Joe was intimidated by Pete, but he never showed it. He knew the situation would come to a head but it happened sooner than Joe desired.

"You idiots believe the $$## this fool is tellin' you?" Pete screamed out, while sitting in an abandoned car alongside the canal.

"I bet this jerk could not kick his way out of a wet paper bag, let alone rob Mafia guys! You know the Mafia woulda buried him a long time ago! He ain't no Italian. He's a spic whose goin' out with a 'nigger'!"

Joe, who was sitting with Diane on the corner of the bridge ten feet from Pete, was struck by the last portion of Pete's comment as if with a sledge hammer. Pete's words were more than a gauntlet thrown at the feet of Joe; more than a challenge to a duel of honor; it was an afront to his lady! Joe immediately recognized the response of the twenty or so others who were hangin: forty eyes turned toward him, each reflecting a lone solitary figure. A deadly silence descended on the grove, the kind of silence that patiently awaits for the first motion or movement to break out into a babble of conjecture about who would be the victor and who, the conquered.

Joe's first reaction to the situation was a total shutdown of all conscious thought other than this confrontation. For several days the bantering between Pete and Joe had gone on, though Pete's attacks had been aimed above the waist and Joe had been able to feint his way through the abuse with keen savvy. But by insulting Diane, Pete had issued the ultimate challenge of domination. The crowd was tasting blood; most of them had spent many a thought on someone kicking Pete's butt, but the odds were not in Joe's favor, and so the majority of the crowd began to hedge their bets.

Joe's thoughts must have slipped past his facade, for the crowd's reaction was swift and to the point . . .

"Yo! Mike . . . you don't wanna mess with Pete."

"Forgeddaboudit!"

"Hey, Mike. Pete's crazy . . ."

Joe could see the envy and jealousy of the guys converting into a savage need for someone's blood . . . Joe's blood . . .

The girls also became excited by the guys's response; an excitement much stronger than the men . . . which excited the guys further!

Joe had hyped his past adventures and experience so much that he had built up an image which would crumble in an instant unless he acted immediately.

"You know, Pete, you should shut your mouth, you're in no condition to fight!" Joe said, though he was sure that this face-saving statement—one he had used on several other occasions when an aggressor really did not want to do battle—would not work. Pete was usually at his best when he was stoned and feeling no pain.

Joe knew it would take a moment for his statement to seep into Pete's warped brain, and so, he launched his attack . . . he tore at the car the instant Pete's face disappeared back into the red rag.

As Joe grabbed the top metal edge of the car door to yank it open, Pete, who had been feinting while waiting for Joe's attack by keeping his right hand on the inside arm rest/door handle, allowed the door to open several inches before he slammed it back closed.

BAM!

The only thing that kept the door from closing entirely were eight fingers of Joe's hands. Pain coursed through Joe's hands like lightning bolts; his fingers swelled into stumps as Pete casually got out of the car with a large grin that conveyed his confidence and Joe's imminent disaster.

Joe could see the crowd changing directions, though no one had yet vocally cheered Pete on—which would have been the right thing to do for a group of street urchins who played the power game—the mood was definitely thumbs down for the short gladiator with the stumpy hands!

Joe backed away in an effort to compose himself and buy a little time to figure out a plan. His mind was spinning.

Pete, savoring his victory, was so sure of his position he began to taunt Joe; to verbally abuse Joe and Diane. Relishing the sadistic pleasure screaming from his lungs, Pete concentrated his energy into whipping the crowd into a pack of sharp-fanged wolves closing on the kill.

Joe stood straight, stiffening his hands into the karate-chop-way of Kato, the Green Something or Other that he'd read in a comic book when he was back in the Poconos.

Pete turned, took a whiff of his rag, and began to walk slowly toward Joe . . . ready to strike the final blows.

Joe crouched in a bent knee judo position he had seen in some book on Japanese—or was it Korean?—martial arts . . .

Pete was still several feet away when he stopped, spread his arms like a barbarian brain cruncher, and . . .

Was that hesitation? Did Joe sense Pete's confusion at the odd sight of Joe, in crouched, karate-type position, with evil intentions blazing from his eyes?

It was all the encouragement Joe needed. With a horrifying battle cry, one he used with success at Spotford, Joe—as surprised as Pete was—advanced in one, swift lunge, and, twisting 180 degrees, slap-chopped with the edge of his right hand into Pete's exposed larynx. In one swift moment, Pete's Adam's apple hit the back of his neck then popped back out as Pete hit the ground gurgling and desperately gasping for air!

The crowd switched sides in the instant victory of the unbelievable kid from New York who not only traveled the country on his own . . . not only rode with bikers and lived with real Indians . . . not only worked with the Cat Man and fought "godfathers" . . . but who had defeated the ogre, Pete. With one blow! . . .

With both hands swollen as a waterlogged side of beef!

Joe had always thought his true Knightly duels always seemed to end in his defeat. Sure, he'd won a few fist-fights but the real 'Knightly' kind of battles had always seemed to go to the Shortys and the Joe-Pags of the world.

But this time things were different. Joe had actually won his first battle of honor, in front of a crowd of fervent worshipers, in front of Diane—his Miami Princess. He won against all of the odds! The good guy beat the bad guy. It was possible!

Long after this fight with Pete, long after the cheers and legends of the "Fourteen-year-old Man of Respect from New York" melted into a quagmire of memories and chipped thoughts by those who witnessed this extraordinary battle, long after they had been replaced by new memories of growing up, of moving on, of responsibility and social duty—Joe could recall this confrontation with the full clarity of his senses. Right down to the sweet, sticky odor of Pete's Trans-Go. Every moment of his first real victory remained crystal clear forever!

But, sometimes a victory can also be a defeat.

From that day forward Joe was at the top of his world. He could move freely about Miami, into the hardest, meanest streets of the bleakest, most terrifying areas without worry or fear. But Joe's world was an underworld. And it was a good name for it.

The word traveled fast. Emissaries came in droves from as far west as Liberty City, as far north as Opa Locka and Hallendale—just to hang with Joe and his guys.

With all of this "hero worship" pouring upon a lost soul who desired to be like Joe-Pep, Joe kept thinking of returning to New York and exacting his revenge. This whole affair had instilled in him some sort of super hero syndrome. Yet, it was this very feeling and situation that kept Joe from leaving . . . at least for now!

One warm and sunny day, at the greatest height of his street success, when thirty or so kids were hanging with Joe, bringing him tribute, making him feel like a king, an excited voice tore through the pines and palms of "Mike's Castle Grove." . . . "They're here! They're in the projects! Bonnie and Clyde . . . They're here."

The messenger ran into the clearing, panting, his brow beaded with perspiration. Bent over double gasping for air, he told the gang a fantastic story about the two famous criminals, Bonnie and Clyde.

"Bonnie and Clyde? Don't you know that Bonnie and Clyde died in the thirties . . . I know, I read about 'em a long time ago. They're dead!" Joe said as he shook his head at such an absurd statement.

"But I saw em . . . and their guns! Even their bodyguard. I saw their body guard!" Tommy repeated as he made every attempt to prove that Bonnie and Clyde were alive and staying in the projects while they nursed injuries they had received in a shoot out with the cops!

It was not long before the traffic to the grove began to diminish. Once again, an entire episode of life played heavy on Joe's mind: Joe had been assured prominence and respect; he had become a central figure in the world of the streets—a world he carved out of its poverty, violence, and uncertainty; a world where love came in the form of the deference he received as "King of the Pack."

Joe had friends, a Princess, tons of tribute . . . His cardboard house had been traded in for a small, two-person, pop-up camper—the type that's pulled behind a car—given as payment by some guys from the Liberty City Housing Projects for a brief excursion where

Joe recruited twenty of his guys to back them up in a rumble on their turf. He thought he was set! And now someone was trying to steal his position.

As Joe sat in his camper, the rain, which tore in sheets from huge and heavy black clouds, poured through the thick canopy of the grove. Cold, wet, and miserable, he had not had more than several of the guys visit in the last week. And, when they did visit, all he heard was stories of the travels of the "Bonnie and Clyde Gang."

He was losing the loyalty of the projects. He knew that loyalty on the streets had to be enforced through domination—he had to have someone to dominate! It seemed that whoever was masquerading as Bonnie and Clyde were receiving the honors and the tribute that was critical to Joe's survival! No way!

A crowd surrounded the doorway into the apartment . . . voices, murmuring respect and awe, sweeping through the air toward Joe, spoke the truth of what he'd known all along. It was a fact that a rival leader was holed up in the projects. He only doubted that leader's identity: Bonnie and Clyde were dead.

"Hey, Mike . . . Mike!

Joe saw it was Tommy who was motioning Joe to come inside.

He made his way through the throng and into the apartment.

As Tommy led him into a back room Joe was shocked by the sight that greeted his eyes. A huge guy with blood-soaked bandages wrapped tightly around his chest and abdomen sat wheezing in an armchair. Joe didn't have to guess at the future of this man. He needed to be in a hospital. Dark, red blood dripped from the corners of his mouth indicating his chest wounds were severe. His breath, coming in shallow spurts, told of his declining situation. Joe gasped out loud before he could catch himself.

"So, is this Mike from New York? The one who's traveled the country and worked with Jack?" came a voice, sweet and alluring.

Joe looked toward the source, and for the second time he gasped aloud. She stood about five-foot eight. Long, flowing, golden hair. Sharp blue eyes which twinkled with a perpetual misting appearance. Full, bright, red lips, moistened frequently with sexy, provocative movements of her tongue. Golden, even-textured skin, peeking through a snowy white terry-cloth robe with every slinky movement of her body—demonstrating she was completely naked under the robe and had no reservations at exposing her long, sexy legs.

Joe felt a wave of embarrassment in addition to a wave of passion course through his body; one ending in the bright redness of his face—the other centering in his pubic area. Standing like a thermometer with an erection, his first reaction was to move his hands in a downward, sweeping action to shield his obvious arousal and embarrassment—which only directed her sharp eyes.

"Ummmm . . . What are you hiding?" she purred.

Joe was thrown for a loop. Here was this totally sexy broad, flirting and stroking her captive youth, as a man struggled for his life! As Joe struggled with his composure—which he was sure had left the premises entirely—another voice, this one deep and masculine, barked an order, "Tommy, get the car . . . we gotta move Mark!"

The man who gave the order was the male twin of the lady from Venus. He was six foot, muscular, with blonde hair and strong, masculine features.

Joe was now sure who these people were. They were not "Bonnie and Clyde," but they were something else: damned Barbie and Ken dolls come to life! They had a beauty of body in shape, color, and texture, but something had gone wrong.

The dolls were known as Harry and Deborah; gangster 'wannabes' well known in the underworld for small-time jewelry heists, armed robberies of dry cleaning establishments, liquor stores, and a host of violent, yet petty, crimes. The key difference between the genuine Bonnie and Clyde and these "dolls" was the fact that they did everything with spontaneity and a rash, brash attitude that left no room for maneuvering. Hardly anything was ever planned. If they were short of cash they simply pulled into a liquor store and robbed it. In fact, that's how their accomplice, Mark, got shot.

Deborah drove into the parking lot of a large liquor store in Hallandale; Harry and Mark "took it down." A concussion spewed fragmented glass, and shooting erupted into the parking lot not two minutes after the duo entered the store. There were four armed employees in the store and Mark was hit three times. He'd have been left there to die if the Barbie duo thought he wouldn't spill the beans. They figured that if they took him with them he'd eventually die and solve their problem.

Joe was impressed more with the sexiness of Deborah than what she stood for. As for Harry, who was strong and determined with everyone except Deborah, he felt no respect nor hero worship . . . just a deep jealousy and envy at his stature and limited passport to Deborah!

Whenever Harry appeared she launched into this super sexy "do me" attitude with whoever-whatever-no-matter-what male within twenty feet of her! Though Deborah never shared herself with anyone other than Harry, she kept his leash short and tied to her ankle by controlling him with her body and mind. In fact, all men seemed to be controlled in one way or another by her uncanny perception of their weaknesses—which she used to her own advantage. They dumped Mark in a canal, so Deborah needed another flunky to drive, steal, and tease. What Joe could not know at the time was that they were broke and in desperate need for some dough. The police were keenly aware of a duo of Barbie look-a-likes running amuck in the fair city of Miami; shooting at the first sign of perceived danger. They were forced to remain in hiding as they contemplated which of these "Project Warriors" they could use . . . or abuse!

Joe sat on the sofa watching TV. He could hear moaning and groaning and hard, rusty, spring movement coming from the bedroom's open door. Tommy, who was nineteen and slightly handicapped, seemed more in tune with the Howdy Doody Show than the excitement of the ravishing that had been continuing for nearly two hours! Joe tried to concentrate on his thoughts: He knew the Miami thing was finished; dead in the waters of that rain last week. It was time again to hit the road . . . but why was he just sitting here doting on the "dumb" smart blonde?

He didn't realize he was her prey; that he had been marked and was being indoctrinated into her nightmarish thoughts by this very act of lovemaking.

She had pre-planned this episode to fortify all of her previous actions—such as running naked to the bathroom many times in the last three days; flashing Joe on every occasion she could; brushing her hard, tight body against his whenever she could. His personal thoughts were rapidly being extinguished . . . and she and Harry knew it! Her perverted pleasure required another player: her orgasm only approached if she had a captive, unsuspecting, third party. And, in this circumstance, a fourteen-year-old would do.

"So Mike, how long did you work with Jack The Cat?"

"Oh, a long time. We did some great work. The Diplomat. The Four Seasons. The Castaways—we hit that place fifty times at least! Oh! And a big job on Golden Beach . . . all without a gun."

The last remark caused Deborah's eye to twitch. "Are you telling me Jack never carried a gun?"

"No, I'm not saying that, only that I know how to get the bucks!" Joe felt a sense of pride that they were actually conversing with him on a subject concerning their work.

"You seem to know what you want . . . Want me?" she said coyly as she muffed a pose that sent desire flowing through Joe's veins.

"Uh, well . . . um . . . well I just know I would, um . . . I would like to be a part, a part of, of, your gang . . . You know . . . I know the road and stuff . . . I have friends all over the whole, entire, place. The country. Everywhere! I can do anything and I just wanna . . ." Joe's stuttering spread to his mind, his thoughts you know; his brain stuttered in silence—he could not summon the courage to say what he wanted to . . . "Hey Lady, Yea! I Wanna . . ."

For the next week the program proceeded as planned with Deborah alternating compliments and questions, and Harry telling stories of wealth and success; how the Bonnie and Clyde gang stretched from Florida to California; how most were in hiding until the heat died down; how, if Joe could prove that he belonged . . . they might let him join!

Joe began to envision his return to New York as a wealthy member of a real gang—along with many stories of his journey and fame—to rescue his family. He began to move once more like a Bantam Rooster . . . squawking and prancing around—like that time when his father had told him on the phone that he was the man of the house, except in this instance, Deborah and Harry were the ones allowing Joe to develop until he was ready.

"Hey, Joe. We been talking. Deborah and me. About you. You know . . . about joining up. We think maybe you're not ready yet . . . We have to move on and we just think you might have been just kinda swept into the thing . . . "

"You kiddin or what?"

"Well, I have been thinking . . . maybe our way is not like yours. Maybe you're too young. Maybe we ought to just forget it . . . no hard feelings . . . O.K.?"

Joe had been talking it up. He had been daydreaming. He had been sure that he'd zoom away to their next job; one that would deliver thousands and thousands of dollars. His stature with the people of the street had reached the highest acclaim anyone could imagine and now—a flash of memory and the bikers.

"Hey, I can prove it. I can prove I can do it! Just name the place. Go on. Name the place and I'll take it down!"

The plan for his "proving" would come the next evening: Deborah and Harry drove him to a hotel at the corner of 38th Street and Biscayne Boulevard. Once there, they showed him the place where he'd flag the cab from, then, where he'd direct the driver, and then, where they'd be waiting for him. They briefly went over the etiquette of the cab robber: how to tell him he was being robbed; what to tell him to do and how to do it; and most of all, where the cabby usually kept his money and how to shoot the .38 they gave him!

Joe's "proof" was to be a cab robbery on busy Biscayne Boulevard in front of a packed hotel—in the early evening of rush hour traffic.

Chapter 38: One of the Gang

Joe, all of five-foot-two, with a gun that weighed ten pounds secured under his windbreaker in the waistband of his pants, stood on the side of the road waiting for a cab . . . Once alone, he began to think, Man, what am I doing? Is this the right thing to do? But the power of his dream of returning to New York in splendor cast those empty thoughts into the traffic.

Standing there, like a fish out of water, with all of those eyes zeroing on him as they passed, made Joe paranoid. He felt that each and every one of them could see he was about to rob a taxi driver! Joe began to get that familiar feeling of fear tearing at his insides. Several empty cabs had already passed him by yet he did not—or rather could not—raise his arm. And then, just as he was going to forget it, a cab squealed to a stop in front of him.

Joe got in and told the driver to head to 125th and Biscayne. The cabbie flipped the lever and squealed into the fast-moving traffic.

The plan called for Joe to "get the drop" on the driver right after they passed the first traffic light, force him to make the next right, then go four blocks to the bay where he'd rob him, take the keys, and scoot two blocks to where Barbie and Clyde would be waiting.

The driver zoomed off with Joe sitting tensely on the edge of the rear seat. After he flicked the lever, he began to speak to Joe, "So, you from New York?"

"Ahh . . . Yeah." Joe was not in the mood to talk, he had his hand on the gun and his mind was in the process of putting all of the pieces together. The light was approaching rapidly and his hand started to shake.

The cabbie, glancing in the mirror to make eye contact, said softly, "Kid, don't do it."

Joe was so nervous he could hear his blood pumping in his ears. He did a mental double-take on the cabbie's advice, and that's what it was: advice. Not pleading, advising. Experience talking. Joe was so confounded by the unexpected statement from the cabbie he couldn't think.

"Don't do what?"

"You know what I'm sayin', kid. I seen it a hundred times. Whatever's goin on with you, don't do this thing. There's no turnin' back from this. You're young, you got your whole life ahead of ya and you're gonna screw it all up in the next five minutes. Don't do it."

Joe sat in the back seat absorbing all of this. His mind raced. What's going on. He's not supposed to talk to me like this. What's up! Joe's gun hand was clammy and wet, he was shaking so bad he couldn't control it. He was trying to make it stop when he realized they had passed the point he was supposed to have turned right several blocks back! Now he was lost!

"Sonny . . . don't . . ."

"Put your hands up!" Joe screamed—holding the shaking gun between the opening of the plastic divider with two hands . . .

The driver, seeing the huge gun pointed at the back of his head through the rear view mirror, began stammering. "S–S–S–Son . . . sonny . . . I can't, I can't pu–, pu–, put my hands up! I . . . I . . . I'm d–d–d . . . drivin . . . "

"Oh, yeah. Well, uh . . . if you don't do what I say . . . I'll blow your head off! Look, I'm scared, too. The gun's shaking. It could go off! Make the next right!"

"I can't turn right!"

Joe didn't realize they were in the "Left Turn Only Lane" of the three north-bound lanes in heavy traffic.

"Make the friggin right . . . now!" Joe screamed, pulling the hammer of the revolver back with a loud click. The taxi slashed across two lanes of traffic and jumped the curb leaving fender benders and angry commuters strewn in its wake.

The cabbie regained some of his composure and asked, in a resigned voice, "Where you want me to go, kid? Just don't pull that trigger. I gotta wife and two kids."

Sensing the danger in the situation, Joe released the gun's hammer.

"O.K., pull over there and park by the curb."

After the driver pulled over, Joe began to direct him . . .

"I want you to be cool, you hear me? No funny stuff or I'll have to shoot you! I want you to put your right hand on the wheel and pass the money with your left over your right shoulder!" (This was Joe's idea to keep a cabbie from pulling a gun.)

The driver, attempting to do as Joe said, was caught up like a pretzel in a box. No matter the contortion, he couldn't put the right on the wheel, reach under the seat to get the cigar box with the money and pass it over his right shoulder with his left hand!

"Sonny, I can't do it. It won't work!"

"Oh yeah? I betcha you just screwin' with my head!"

"Kid, I been through this before. I got experience. You don' gotta make it so complicated."

Joe, not used to this violent stuff, did not think before his pride got the best of him!

"Get the heck out of the car . . . and don't try nothin'! I know you gotta gun someplace! Trying to trick me, Huh? You know I'm right. You couldda done what I told you but, no, you wanna make it hard. Get out, I'll get it myself!"

The cab driver slowly removed himself from the driver's seat as Joe kept his gun leveled.

Twenty minutes had gone by since the armed robbery began.

Joe could hear wailing sirens coming fast from the north. "Must be for those damn wrecks you caused," Joe said out loud as he lifted himself from the rear seat. "Stand over there with your back to me!"

This, like the pretzel thing, was not part of the program. He was supposed to "get the money and tell the driver to face forward for twenty minutes or he'd . . . "

As Joe reached under the front seat of the cab, the cabbie, glanced at Joe, saw Joe's head was turned to look under the seat, and he just flat out picked up his feet and lit out at a zillion miles an hour!

Joe heard the noise, jumped up, and freaked out.

He knew he would not, could not have fired the gun for any reason but his own safety. So, Joe was left with the cab, the money, and a fleeing cabbie who would reach the scene of the accident and the police in less than five minutes. Time to get lost!

Joe cruised the corner twice where Barbie and Clyde were supposed to be waiting before he got stuck in a mess of bumper to bumper traffic.

Unknown to Joe, the long wait and blaring sirens had frightened the duo away; they had not even checked for Joe . . . Like the cabbie, they just lit out of there at a "zillion miles an hour." And with only four blocks running east of Biscayne Boulevard before hitting the bay, Joe had no option other than to attempt to maneuver through the accident at 49th and Biscayne.

Joe crept in first gear up to the corner one block from the mass of flashing red and blue lights. His only option was to cross here! He hoped the cops would expect him to be long gone. As he pushed the taxi through the dense traffic—several times even "bumpering" a few die-hard "Ain't gonna budge an inch" drivers with his massive, rubber covered wraparounds—he looked once more at the money in the box: twenty-one dollars and forty-five cents!

He couldn't believe the driver only had twenty-one dollars and forty-five cents! He began feeling bad about the robbery and the words of sadness the driver spoke to him. Heck the guy was just doing his job, making twenty-one dollars and forty five cents, when some punk robs him! Just as he thought of leaving the money in the trunk when he got back to the projects—which was less than sixty blocks away—he noticed the police cruiser in his rear view mirror.

His first thought was to finish making his way through the center of the intersection without raising suspicion. There were many cabs in Miami and most of them seemed to be here, right on the boulevard. He looked once more, edged his way, and then turned left onto 48th Street.

The way was clear! He stepped on the gas and . . .

The siren cut on in an instant. Three squad cars were coming for the kill. The police must have called in the cab number. He was trapped.

Barbie and Clyde had reached the projects . . . they had to assume that Mike had been caught. Their attitude, which was technically correct, was that Mike got busted because he didn't follow the plan.

Deborah and Harry had already decided to hit a liquor store and blast out of Florida. They figured if Mike was in fact "busted," he'd inform on their hide-away. As she scurried around the apartment gathering the things she needed for the road, Deborah was placing the blame on Harry.

"It was your idea to use that punk!" she screamed as she packed her clothing.

"That's bull and you know it!" Harry blared back.

Joe waited until the squad cars stopped in position and the drivers got out to order him out of the car before he placed the cab in reverse and jammed the pedal to the floor.

BANG! The police car behind him ricocheted into the dense traffic. Bang! Boom . . . BOOM . . . BOOM! Several cars careened into the cruiser and themselves.

The first cop instinctively turned to see if assistance was needed as Joe took the opportunity to throw the shifter into drive and jam the pedal down.

As he tore through the street toward the squad car in front, the one on the side street entered behind him . . . he twisted the wheel as he hit the brakes and jammed the pedal . . . the car spun a "180," and he zipped by, turning into the now clear side street.

Joe raced the streets—turning-dodging-fleeing this way and that—until at 79th and 2nd Avenue, he bounced over the railroad tracks and flew five-feet through the air to come sparking down to freedom.

Joe arrived in the heart of the projects to a screaming, maddening crowd!

"Yo, man, we thought you got busted!"

"Yeah, wow, we checked it out! Saw you tearing through the tracks on 2nd Avenue . . . check it out!"

"Hey, Mike, . . . Lemme drive!"

Joe's subjects were drooling all over the place in their excitement when Deborah and Harry appeared, their faces in great big grins.

"I told you, Harry . . . " Deborah began as she sulked her way over to the car with plenty of swing in her rear. " . . . he could do it . . . ," she purred.

And to Joe, it sounded like, "He could do it to me!"

Just as Joe was deciding to himself where to "bury" the car, several police cruisers entered the projects!

Joe yelled he'd be back and burned up the grass and bushes of several yards as he tore out of the projects.

Joe started to feel invincible. He felt he was in power. He was learning to enjoy the adrenaline which coursed through his body; he enjoyed the fear and anxiety which crept his veins. He felt if he got caught he'd spend some time locked up, but, what of it! He had nothing better to do!

He made it back to the corner of Biscayne and 79th Street with ten cars behind him. It was getting dark out and the traffic was as slow as molasses running up-hill on a cold winters day. The intersection was jammed tight. When he saw the cars behind him moving over to allow the cops (who were inching their way through to him, sirens blaring, flashing more lights than Times Square and Rockefeller Center at Christmas time) he knew he had to bail out! Thinking of a trick Pauly Wheat had taught him in New York, he stepped hard on the brake and jammed his foot all of the way down on the accelerator, causing the rear tires to spin. Within seconds, a huge, dense and smelly cloud of burning rubber completely obliterated all vision with in the entire intersection . . . then he made his move.

Jumping out of the car, he headed on the course he had planned before causing the vision "white out." Running cautiously through the trapped cars, he made it to the rear of the X-rated Pussy Cat Theatre; a landmark that sat on Biscayne next to a steel bridge which ran over a canal several blocks south of 79th Street.

Chattering radios, reminiscent of the transit cops in that New York bust, seemed to be coming from all corners of the bridge embankment. Joe crouched high above the water, in the actual rafters of the bridge, as the police, with dogs, began canvassing the area. As they got closer to the concrete piers, he could actually hear the orders of each cop as they keenly tossed and turned any movable object. Holding still, with both legs and arms wrapped tightly around a steel strut, Joe held his breath.

"Hey, he ain't here. I checked it," one of the brown-uniformed, Dade County, police officers yelled.

Joe's face itched with sweat running down it's surface, and he desperately wanted to move . . . but he held still. It was dark with no moon. He was figuring to himself how they would leave soon, never knowing he was right above them, when his arm slipped and bang, he fell off the strut and into the water.

"There he is. "

The shouts and flashlights soon reached him as he swam under the bridge towards the Playboy Club on the opposite side of the theater. Reaching the boat dock of the club before the cops could figure a way in, Joe climbed out and ran toward the bay.

Joe was hiding on the roof of a large metal shed, face pointed down, a large branch of oak shading his features. His heart was pumping and he was praying they would not discover him.

The police officer, with a large German shepherd on a long leash, approached the shed. Joe could clearly see his features, as well as the dog's face! They were not more than twenty-feet away!

As the officer approached the building, coaching the dog with promise of reward, the dog barked and fidgeted. Joe was terrified of the dog! It seemed he had zeroed in on Joe. Holding his breath, he watched as the cop flashed his light across the rooftop. Joe was sure the cop had made him. Heck, he just closed his eyes tightly and waited for the order to turn himself in.

But the cop was in too big a hurry, he just turned away . . . as he gave his dog verbal coaching of rewards.

Joe lay upon that roof until late that morning. Then, gently climbing down the tree, he leapt the club fence and made his way the ten blocks to the projects and freedom.

Joe had been traveling for six weeks with Barbie and Clyde in a rental car that should have been turned in three months ago.

It was mid-January; cold, windy, rainy, cold and cold. They were cruising the highways of the Southeast, stopping here and there so Joe could use his "Jack the Cat training" at hotels and motels. Joe was tired of the situation. It seemed they would let him do a hotel room and then they would take the money.

He ate, he slept—in the car while they slept in hotels—he traveled, but he got nothing in return, just more of Deborah's teasing.

Away from Miami and friends, feeling like he was caught in a vicious circle, he began to think more and more of Aggie. This led him to think of his family. One day, while the duo slept, Joe slipped to a phone.

He dialed the number and deposited the coins the operator requested . . .

"Yeah?

"Who's this?" Joe asked, the voice vaguely familiar.

"Who da hell iz dis!" the strange voice repeated.

Oh, lord. Joe thought when he realized who had picked the phone up! "Mr. Pagarelli, is my mother there?"

"Oh, it's you! Don' ya know whoze speekin'? I tol you, youz betta treat ya mudder right. She don' wanna talk to you. And, if ya know wads up, ya woodin' come home!" Click.

Joe was speechless, angry, and on fire! He scrounged his last coins and dialed again.

The phone picked up . . . but, before the party could utter a word, Joe let loose, "Lemme tell you somthin', who da hell you dink you are! I learned howda deal with assholes like you . . . when I get back I'm gonna . . ."

"Is that you, Joey?" the voice of his mother cut him short.

"Oh, I'm sorry, Mom I . . ."

"I think it's better if you don't call again . . . You haven't changed. I'm tired of worrying about you. Besides . . ."

Joe hung up.

Harry had gone to take care of some business, so she invited Joe in.

She sat naked on a tiny chair facing the door as she put her silk hose on her legs. Running her hands up and down.

"Listen, we're running low on money . . ."

She's now toying with her breasts as she attaches her bra . . .

"and I was thinking . . . "

She's placing lipstick seductively on her lips, running her tongue around to tamp it down and hypnotize Joe . . .

"We should head for Knoxville where the pickings' ought to be good and I can visit my aunt . . ."

She's bending over to pick up the expensive dress she had just bought with most of the cash she took out of the last "job" Joe had nearly got killed for . . .

It was a dark night. No moon. No lights . . . other than the three bare light bulbs which glared in the night over a sign that read: "TV-Heated Rooms-See the Live Alligators!"

Joe was not amused. Heck, what did "Real Heated Rooms-See the Live Alligators" mean? What if you chose a non-heated room? Would they feed you to the gators? It didn't look good, but Mrs. Barbie Doll kept on about "Needing the money . . . Honey" in her normal duff duff look! Joe wanted to tell her to shove it . . .but he was starving!

"O.K., but this is the last job . . . do ya hear me? I wanna get enough money to catch a bus to New York . . . "

"You got it," she said just like all of the other times before, yet here he was, at a run-down motel in the backwoods of the swamp without a ticket, ready to rob the place. "O.K., Harry, you go with Mike this time!"

"Hey, that's not my thing, I . . ."

"I don't care about you going, I don't need you!" Joe spat at Harry.

"Heh" . . . Harry began as he toyed with a large caliber gun. "Don't you ever talk to me that way, I'll feed you to the gators!"

"Oh . . . Come on, poopy doopy . . . let's just get the bread . . ." "Goldylocks" cut in, silencing Harry.

"O.K. I'll back him up!"

They approached the room, which had a station wagon packed to the roof, parked in front.

The door was four feet off the ground—Joe guessed against possible flooding by the abundant swamps which surrounded the place—it had its own metal staircase. Joe climbed the stairs and carefully picked the lock. Then he moved away and waited several minutes. When no one came to open the door, he swigged a mouthful of Jack Daniels—kept for this purpose—and returned to the door. When no one challenged him, he placed one hand on the upper portion of the door, his right foot against the bottom, and pulled on the knob as he pushed with hand and foot. He opened the door a crack without a sound and blew his alcohol breath around. Then he opened it further. When no one appeared, he walked toward where Harry was waiting.

"O.K., remember, you're the muscle . . . but don't shoot anyone. Just follow me in and if something goes wrong, I'll jump to the side and you'll trip the person, then tear out of there. I'll be right behind you."

Joe crouched down and entered the dark room. Spying a pair of pants lying over a chair, he headed for them knowing a wallet would be in the back pocket.

A noise caused him to halt!

Harry had bumped into something and the large person sleeping in the bed turned over and loudly said something in his sleep.

Looking over his shoulder, Joe motioned Harry to stay where he was and went for the wallet. He was removing it when Harry, who saw a ring on the night stand and went for it, bumped into the bed. The guy awoke and, with the swiftness of a rabbit, jumped up, turned, and grabbed a shotgun laying by the bed.

Though feeling like he was about to be fed to the gators, Joe was sure Harry would remember what to do! All he had to do (because the guy still had night blindness and could not focus) was trip the guy and run. He'd still get the wallet!

The guy was rubbing his eyes when he saw Harry run like a rabbit himself! This left Joe in dire circumstances; caught between the far back wall and the bed with an angry fat man with a shotgun! He knew even if he made it out the door, he'd never make it to the road before the man blasted him! The guy began to yell as he aimed the gun out the door. Joe jumped up and surprised him . . . he had not a clue another person was in the room! As the guy turned toward him, Joe was already rolling toward his legs. He bowled him over and the gun tumbled in a racket to the floor. Joe was up and through the door when he realized he was gonna get it . . .

Grabbing the stairs, he swung down and under them as the guy reached the door and came tearing down, raising the gun.

He could have touched him that's how close he was. As the man ran, firing his shot gun at a long-lost shape, Joe got up, went inside, and seized the wallet!

He made it. He had gone through the swamp and forest area for a mile before he found the duo . . . at least they had waited.

Joe spent the entire trip to Knoxville in the back seat—acting as it he were deep asleep, worried at a turn of events: normally Joe did most of the driving, but on this trip, Harry decided to drive and at one point he awoke to hear the duo discussing him.

"Let's just dump him!"

"What, like Mark?"

"Whatever, but after Knoxville . . . "

Joe knew his time was up and began to plan . . .

"Hey, is that a hotel up there?" Barbie asked Harry. "Let's go there!"

The hotel was right on I-40, which ran through the center of Knoxville. Brightly lit and huge, it was a genuine hotel! 'Boy' Joe thought, 'They must have been stashing away money if they could afford to stay here. It was gonna be great. Maybe they'd let him have a good night's sleep in a real bed. At least he'd be safe until he figured out what to do. They pulled under the glaring lights of the parking lot and parked. From where they were, Joe could see for a mile in all directions. It was beautiful because the entire road was lit like a Christmas tree. A large truck stop was perched on a bluff right across the street. Joe could see the diesel trucks, parked side by side, blowing exhaust through their stacks and multitudes of people coming and going.

Joe knew what he was going to do! He would sleep, shower, and eat; in the morning, he'd cross that highway and get a lift . . . somewhere north and home!

Joe's excitement was temporarily dashed when Deborah's voice crashed his thoughts.

"Mike, go with Harry."

"O.K.," he said as he removed himself from the car, his mind returning to reality.

They entered the brightly lit lobby and approached the desk. Seeing a giant of a man arise from a couch behind it, Joe left Harry to pay him for the room and walked over to a set of stands which held colorful brochures. Realizing they were free, he grabbed a handfull on places in other states bordering Tennessee. Turning back toward the counter, he began to walk as he read the dashing lines that promised much when . . .

"Put your hands up! Don't friggin' move or I'll blow your head off."

"No," Joe screamed in his head, they were robbing the place. Joe couldn't believe it. Here they were, in the center of town, bright lights everywhere, a packed truckstop across the highway, cars cruising along the main highway—which could be plainly seen from the lobby!

"Hey, Mike, grab the dough! Now!"

And Harry had used his name! Though it was not his true name, it was his road name—one which could be traced! Joe wanted to run, but where to? He hurried to the counter and grabbed the huge wad of large bills. He could see the terror in the eyes of the clerk. He could see the death in the eyes of Harry. He wanted to be out of there and in his bed!

"Come out from behind the counter . . . easy now . . . slowly!"

The clerk moved in extra slow motion until he had cleared the desk and Harry, eyes darting back and forth between the clerk and a group of doors—looking like he was going to find somewhere to shoot the guy—grabbed him and opened the first door he laid his hand on.

"Yo!" Joe yelled. "Don't hurt the guy . . ."

Harry just gave Joe a look of "Shut your mouth!" and pushed the guy into what was a back office . . . and followed him in.

Joe almost ran out the door. He really wanted to just take the money and run to the truckstop, jump into a truck, and leave all of them to rot . . . but he could not forget the cabby's look of shock when he first saw the gun.

Joe dashed into the back thinking of ways to halt what he believed was going to be the ending of the clerk's life, when, with a sudden halt of his progression, he was greeted to a sight of Harry tying the clerk up right next to a safe—which was open and had enough money to fill the large gym bag Harry had placed on the floor.

Deborah was ready when they jumped into the car.

She stomped the pedal and they zoomed across the road . . . and right into the truck stop!

Joe, seated in a back seat, with no doors or windows that opened, felt completely trapped. Deborah and Harry were acting like a pair of tourists out for a night ride . . . no cares . . . no worries—not even about the sirens looming in the night.

"Fill it up." She said to the pump boy with a wrinkling of her nose in a soft and cuddly way. "How much we get?"

"Fifteen thou' or so."

"Oooh! Party time!" she cried grabbing Harry by the crotch.

While all of this celebrating was going on up front, in the back seat, Joe sat staring out the rear window while he applied a ton of Harry's Brillcream Hair tonic in an effort to change his look—like slicking his hair back was going to alter the facts.

"Hey, don't you guys think we should be getting the heck out of here?"

"Don't worry. Just sit there and we will be out of here. "

"Well, I'm just saying that . . ."

"Sonny . . ." Deborah called to the kid filling the car, "Get me a pack of Marlboros."

He took the twenty she had in her extended hand and, as he began to walk towards the restaurant for her change, she jammed the pedal down!

With red and blue lights in the distant rear, gas shooting from a gas pump that failed to shut down when the hose was torn in two, and what looked like fifty-thousand large ants swarming a mound, Deborah hit I-40 West at a hundred and ten.

This is it, if I get out of this mess I will light twenty candles, Joe thought to himself as he desperately prayed no sudden arrival of massed cop cars and swarming helicopters, swooping down from a pitch-black sky, would appear.

After averaging ninety miles an hour for more then twenty-four hours, the Barbie and Clyde gang pulled off the road in Flagstaff, Arizona. Deborah was ecstatic: An old member of their group was hiding out in Flagstaff, they were going to meet him at a hotel there—and she was already planning on what to spend the money on. Joe, on the other hand, just wanted out. He made the comment he wanted to go east . . . but they never acknowledged him. Deborah just pulled into a hotel restaurant, parked the car, and told Harry to rent a room. When Harry came back, an ugly, scar-faced man, looking deadly and mean, accompanied him to the car.

Harry introduced him as "Monkey Face" and said he'd "be riding with us."

Monkey Face grabbed Harry and pulled him to the side. After a brief conversation, where they kept looking over at Joe, Harry came over, threw the keys for both the car and the room to Joe and said, "Listen, we're gonna get something to eat. We got some unfinished business to discuss, I want you to unload the stuff in the trunk and we'll bring something back for you."

As they strolled off whispering to one another, Joe decided this was the time to leave—he just had this premonition he might not be around later.

As soon as they entered the restaurant, Joe jumped into the

driver's seat and drove around to the room number listed on the key. After emptying the trunk, he ransacked all of the baggage in search of cash. No luck. He decided to look in the trunk again.

Behind the spare tire he discovered a large packet of papers and photographs. While rifling through them, he hit pay dirt! Two-thousand dollars in small bills! 'Why would they rob a hotel when they had this money stashed?' he wondered. Well, he didn't care, he was on his way home! He decided to find a bus depot and promptly catch a bus to New York.

After dumping everything into the room, he grabbed the package, went into the bushes, and then lit out of the parking lot.

It was not to difficult to find the bus depot. Once there, he carefully drove by to check it out. Then he turned the car and drove several blocks to hide it. Passing a probable location, Joe whipped the car in a U-turn and zoomed to a stop. As he was getting out of the car, a patrol car pulled up and two officers got out.

"What are you doing making U-turns like that?" the driver asked. Then noticing Joe's age, he continued, "How old are you?"

Joe knew if they called in the car, he'd be dead. His mind began to race and then . . . "Officer, don't tell, please don't tell. My uncle don't know I'm driving the car. He's with my aunt at the Holiday Inn. In the restaurant . . . I . . . I . . . I was supposed to be watching TV in the room . . . I just wanted to drive the car . . . Oh, please I . . ."

Joe sat in the back of the squad car laughing and carrying on with the two highway patrolmen like he had known them for years. He was telling them stories as they drove to the Holiday Inn while they reprimanded him for borrowing the car and driving without a license. Even as he cracked a laugh, flashed a smile, and generally acted like a happy-go-lucky kid, he dreaded the outcome when the officers met Harry and Deborah and the killer-looking guy!

The squad car pulled up to the restaurant—right in front of the window in which the gang was sitting at.

With radios chattering and Joe held between them, the officiers entered the restaurant and approached the booth.

Joe's mind was clicking away as they got closer to Barbie, Clyde, and Monkey Face: when they looked up and saw the cops dragging me in, would they begin shooting?

So, with much apprehension, Joe struggled to come up with something . . .

Ten feet away, Harry looked up and his face went white . . . I mean snowy-dead-person-bloodless-icy-cold-white. Joe could see him going through the motions of thought and reaction. His foot kicked under the table and the dude and Deborah turned and did a double-take.

All their faces went ashen white.

And, just as Joe was sure they were going for their guns, he began his show.

"Uncle Freddy, I didn't mean to . . . honest . . . I just took the car for a drive . . . Oh! Please . . . I'm sorry . . . Uncle Freddy."

"Yes, sir. Seems your nephew decided to borrow your car while you folks were eating . . ." one of the officers stated.

Harry stood up and grabbed Joe. "You know you're not supposed to drive unless you're on the ranch! You're going to be punished. You hear me? Officer, where did you find my nephew?"

"He was near the bus depot. A lot of runaways stop there on their way to California. Listen, go easy on the kid. He was wrong, but you know how it is. Your car is several blocks east of the depot. I didn't have it towed in. If I catch this kid driving again I will impound your car. You folks have a good vacation."

With that, they left Joe in the care of his relatives.

"What the hell were you doing at the bus depot! Running out on us? Nobody runs out on us . . . SMACK!"

Joe's head was spinning from the beating. His nose was bleeding and one eye felt hot and sticky. He tried to explain that he was just going to take a bus home, but they had made up their minds—they had other plans.

"Listen, I just wanna go! I don't want anything else!"

"Oh! You're gonna go all right!" Deborah shouted. "Tie him up and let's go get the car . . ."

Deborah was really into acts of violence—she got off more to the endings than the beginnings.

The TV picture had been blacked-out with the volume turned completely up. Some stupid picture about a Japanese monster running amuck in a city, Rhodan or something like that. Boy, talking about running amuck! He had not taken the time to evaluate the things he had done nor his direction.

It seemed so long ago he had a family. Even the Georgia trip was lost in an avalanche of happenings. A jumble of messages crossed against the grain of his thought, spilling in vast tracks of blabber: Is this the way Father felt before his blood drenched the ground? Boy, that cop was cool . . . no matter what the wiseguys said of cops; I bet he was a great father figure! Yes father figure . . . just what was a father figure . . . for him . . . for Joe . . . was it possible? Jeanette had hung up . . . or had he? . . . or they both had—in mind at the very least! Yes mind . . . think. Think. Think! What will, are, can you do. Imagine . . . to die . . . here . . . in a damn city miles above the earth—so much for cities so high and stuff! To die in New York sounded reasonable: But here? What the heck happened to that guy in the sky? Was he so angry he'd forsake one of His children? Who was that Saint who protected the traveler?'

Racking his brain for the answer only increased the headache that came with the twenty blows he received without showing pain or tears. Tears. Just what you'd expect from some damn kid. Yes, but—he was a wiseguy; a descendant of many past soldiers of the hand! PAST? . . . DID HE THINK PAST? Who were these jerks who thought they could be the ones who bowed his knees!'

And then, for some unknown reason, a thought of a ride he had received when he first hiked through the desert after leaving the reservation crossed his mind. It was one of the strangest experiences of his life. At first he thought it to be an experience left over from the Great Spirit of Nihanio . . .

There he was, thirty miles from the reservation, sitting beside a road on a highway in the middle of a dry, hot desert. Not a single sound of a creature wailed its message of existence. No cars or trucks zoomed by that lonely spot of earth without a speck of shade or cover from the sun's brutal punishment. He was alone and silent.

"Hey, God, I need a ride. I've been here twelve hours!" no reply.

"Hey, God . . . You listening? It's me! You know . . .the guy that's always asking you for stuff and making promises I don't keep. If you help me now, I promise to stop in church . . . whenever I see one! I swear!" No ride, no answer.

"Hey, God, listen, just get me something to drink and I'll . . ."

Suddenly, it seemed, from out of nowhere, pitch-black billowing clouds formed high above his head and a thunderous roar—evoking sounds of two freight trains colliding at a hundred miles an hour—pierced the still, quiet air. Startled, he looked up into the sky just as the rain came pouring down, crashing in torrents to quench his thirst. Soon he was pleading again—this time for Him to turn the doggone water off! The rain stopped as quick as it had begun. "Wow!" he thought to himself, "A miracle!"

We've all asked for something in our lives. "Please God, can you?" must be the most asked question since the age of Moses.

"Oh, God, I promise if you . . ."

Usually our prayers are answered—but not with such immediate speed. So Joe viewed this happening with a slice of skepticism.

"Hey, God, if you can make it storm in the desert, then please get me a ride . . . and somethin' to eat!" But no ride appeared.

He sat by the road for another hour until he heard the distinct and obvious sounds of an automobile whizzing toward him. Jumping to his feet in a split second, he rushed into the middle of the highway—frantically performing like a clown.

An old-beat-up, used-to-be green vehicle pulled off the road and a cheerful driver in overalls quipped, "Sonny, need a ride?"

"Yes, sir. I've been waiting for a ride for thirteen hours!" he said with relief as he opened a creaking, rusty door and sat on the torn and weathered front seat. Closing the door, he started talking and soon established a rapport.

"I'll tell you . . . a miracle it was! The rain just came all of a sudden like. Then, when I was soaked from head to toe, I asked God to turn the water off . . . and he did!"

"You do know it usually rains like that here in the desert, this time of year. Yep. Could have been a normal occurrence, that rain storm."

He felt like his bubble burst and the second true miracle—for him—was not what he thought it was, but a normal occurrence.

He sat in the seat watching as the car devoured the pavement. They had gone fifty miles and were approaching a small town—really a village—at the state border when they resumed their conversation. Joe asked the driver why he was traveling through the desert. "Do you normally drive this way?" he asked in curiosity.

"Well, I'm pastor of a church that's about twenty miles back from the spot I picked you up," he said matter-of-fact, "and I got a call about an hour ago. Seems that Mrs. Somnerset needed the Lord's shepherd for an emergency—-never know when ya gotta tend to the flock. Why don't you stop with me and, after I take care of the emergency, we'll grab somethin' to eat at Old Joe's place. You can get a ride from there."

"That sounds great," he said, his stomach growling like a caged tiger.

They pulled into the driveway of an old, sun-weathered, wood frame house and approached the front door.

"Pastor Johnson! What brings you here so late in the day?"

"Didn't you call me?" a surprised Pastor Johnson inquired.

"No . . . but I'm glad you're here!"

"Well, someone called to tell me I was needed immediately. To come this way," he said, scratching his head.

"Well, I don't know, but since you're here, if you and that young fella are hungry for some hot food then come on in."

. . . Joe smiled at the memory.

Then, a light went off in his head. Why the documents and photographs? They must be important! Why were they hidden?

Joe had hid them in the bushes because he didn't want to leave them in the car in case it was towed after he left—a lesson he learned from his father about never ratting nor causing the arrest of anyone. "not even your enemy." Nor did he want to let them know he'd found them by leaving them in the room. They were pictures of people bandaged up—including Mark—and of "Bonnie and Clyde" posing with weapons . . . just like in the movie! He had glanced at them but not given them much thought! They had not recovered the money because it was hidden under the seat of the car. They had no idea he had found it nor the documents and photos.

Someone kicked him awake.

"Come on! Wake up! You're goin' for a ride!"

It was Monkey Face. He held a black revolver in his hand and a killer look on his face. Joe rolled over and tried to rise but kept falling; his legs were bound. Monkey Face untied them and, as Harry looked through the curtains, pushed Joe toward the door.

"Hey, Harry. You know those pictures?" Joe blurted.

"What pict . . . !"

His face suddenly red with rage, Harry came at Joe. Just as he was within striking distance, Joe blurted out, "And . . . those cops will have them in an hour."

Harry stopped cold in his tracks. Monkey Face, who was set to deliver a blow to shut Joe up, looked stunned. Mrs. Barbie collapsed.

"We could beat it out of you! Where are they?"

"I could have gave them to the cops . . . but I didn't. At least not yet. You don't know what I did with them. And, if you do torture me, how do you know they might not wind up in the cops hands anyway?"

Frozen, like they had seen medusa herself, the trio—including Mrs. Barbie—were at a loss for words. Joe took the initiative, "Untie me. Now!"

Two in the morning and icy cold . . .

Joe, without a dime in his pocket, wearing a flimsy wind breaker—one designed for the heat of Miami—stood, once more, praying for a ride. The gang had agreed to allow Joe to leave if he returned their stuff, but Joe had to maneuver to get away. They finally agreed to let him go to the bus station with Monkey Face, where he'd buy a ticket for New York and Joe would inform Monkey Face where he had hidden the stuff.

When they arrived at the depot, Joe looked around until he saw one of the police officers he had driven to the restaurant with. This coincidence cost the trio their stuff . . . and their planned retribution.

"Officer Mack!" Joe shouted across the busy terminal.

The officer looked over with a funny look until he recognized Joe. "Hey, Mike. What are you doing here? What happened to your face?"

"Oh, I fell off a horse. You know us kids think we can do anything! I'm just pricing a ticket home. My pass from school is about to run out. My uncle will stay here but I have to return. "This is—Joe turned to introduce Monkey Face—but he was no where to be seen. He had lit out! ". . . a busy place!"

"Yeah, it is. Well, I have to make some rounds. You have a good trip. And watch those broncos!"

"Yes, sir. Oh. Thank you again."

With that, Officer Mack and Joe went their separate ways. Monkey Face was gone and Joe was free to act!

He still had two problems: first, he was broke; second, it was late and he knew Barbie and Clyde would soon be looking for him. He knew he had to hide out at least for the night.

As he walked along with his thumb out, he passed a motel. Most of the rooms were empty and the doors faced an empty parking lot on the side of the building. The office was in the front and its lights were out. Joe decided to "borrow" one of the rooms until the morning. He slipped into the woods behind the lot and with stealthy movement, advanced to the furthest room.

After jimmying the lock, he entered, turned the wall heater on, undressed, and jumped into the most comfortable bed he had ever laid on. Soon he was snoring.

Cartoon characters—weird faces—zooming in and out—like reflections coming from a group of carny horror house mirrors—haunting Joe's mind . . .

Joe, lying on the bed in his underwear, sweating with unbearable heat, slowly opens one eye to make sure it is a dream . . .

"AAAAAAAUUUUGH!" Joe screams!

"AAAAAAAUUUUGH!" they scream!

Six people, all looking down and yelling at one time, greet Joe's eyeballs! They looked like his dream, complete with big, round, open mouths! Joe leaps from the bed, grabs his clothes, and hits the door at ninety miles an hour. He's running down I-40 in the snow in his BVDs, trying to slip on his pants, while a half dozen Keystone Cops are chasing him, screaming,

"Whatwereyoudoinginmyhotel!!!"

It seems the morning clean-up woman noticed the heater running from the outside while making her rounds. When she checked her list she realized the room was not rented. She went and got the manager . . . the rest you know.

Freezing cold, he slips one leg in his pants and falls on his face.

The group is gaining . . .

He is up and running again . . .

Cars, zooming by, pointing fingers and shouting laughter as they roll their windows down to gawk.

Joe stops, throws his shoes down and tries to slip his pants on again.

Sensing imminent capture, the 'Keystones' pick up their pace.

Joe is off and running again . . . with his pants still off! He keeps a thumb out as he hops up and down in his losing attempt to get his pants on.

A car passes . . . it slows down.

A beautiful Thunderbird, with a black guy in a uniform, driving it. . .

Is that a grin and a "Come on . . . hop in?"

The group is ten yards away, Joe gets his pants half-way up before hopping toward the car . . . which briefly stops . . .

"Come on . . . hop in!"

Joe runs into the roadway and dives through the window of the car. The soldier, laughing up a storm, drives off with Joe, pants half on; half in, half out of the car . . .

Chapter 39: Escape to Oz

Joe sat in the comfort of Henry's sleek, 1968 hard-top Ford Thunderbird, captivated by the meticulousness with which its designers had thought out each minute detail.

Joe couldn't believe that each of the switches dressing the dashboard, console, and armrests (like one of those computers he had seen at the World's Fair in '64) controlled a different and unique gadget! And, like that computer, the car's many gadgets were amazing: electric windows, seats, locks, antennae, and even seat warmers, automatic-floating-stereo-radio, tilt, turn, telescopic steering wheel, stock, super performance engine, electric sun roof, electric defrosters; air-conditioning, rolled, tucked, and pleated wrap-around leather seats—trimmed in shiny chrome with metal embossed Thunderbirds to remind you of the bird who inspired the artist to create this sleek chariot.

Joe could not keep his hands from touching, pushing, pulling, and generally bugging the heck out of Henry. Though Henry, like a father showing a stranger his first-born son, seemed honored by Joe's amazement; occasionally encouraging Joe by demonstrating some of the extraordinary features of his pride and joy.

Henry, Joe's savior of Flagstaff, in green fatigues and baseball cap, huffing away on a Kool menthol cigarette, sat back like he was the "King of the Road;" with gentle taps of his foot on the accelerator, he zipped around cars with the ease of a full blooded Arabian Stallion racing a pack of mules.

"So . . . what were you falling from?" he asked in pun after Joe finally calmed down.

Joe explained the motel episode—leaving out the Barbie duo—and soon they were friends. An African-American, Air Force Sergeant from "Philly," Henry was on the beginning of a sixty day leave. He was headed to a funeral over the mountains. Afterward, he planned to stop in San Francisco and visit friends before reporting to his new duty station—Beale Air Force Base, above Sacramento, California. He invited Joe to come along for the trip and Joe happily and excitably agreed.

Throughout the journey over the mountains which separated them from their ultimate goal, Joe and Henry talked, with Henry pointing out items of interest to an astounded Joe, who had never seen this portion of nature before.

"See that mountain over there?" Henry pointed to a distant, snow-capped peak hidden by a group of clouds. "That's where this road is going to take us. Sometimes, when I make this trip, I think of all the hardship my family went through to raise me. The Air Force has given me the training, education, pride, and resourses to overcome a mountain which was ten times that size . . . without any roads!"

Conversation continued like that for four weeks while they stopped at Henry's relation's and friend's homes scattered along the way. Finally, they began their cruise to San Francisco, with Henry still doing the majority of the talking while Joe listened to his words of wisdom.

When they topped the last peak, and were well into the valley, Joe finally got his message. For, after the grueling, snow and ice-capped climb, after snow chains and slippery, sharp drops, after freezing stops and short hops, they had burst upon a sight that turned Joe's head like nothing in his entire life—-it was beautiful.

From the mountains to a vast ocean—which was like a deep blue canvas, rippling in brush strokes of a multitude of shaded reds and oranges—they drove across the valley floor stretching in greens, golds, and brownish patches that glinted in a glorious, receding, orange and yellow, boiling sun. With snowy, white-capped mountains of purple and black, boarded by huge, white, billowing clouds contrasting the golden yellow, streak-swept sky, Joe felt he was riding on a road where the canvas was painted by God himself! And, for the absolute first time of his life, through the combination of Henry's new lessons and the splendor and majesty of his first Pacific Ocean sunset, Joe truly knew life had much meaning and purpose . . . he only had yet to discover his!

They hit San Francisco late that night.

Henry, wanting to join some of his buddies, "loaned" Joe twenty dollars before dropping him off at Haight and Ashbury in the center of the city. Joe waved as the car drifted into the traffic and became just another memory to be filed away.

Joe was alone once more. To get his bearings, he began to scout his surroundings. As if he had been dropped into the land of Oz, the streets teemed with a multitude of young street people who were dressed in the most outlandish costumes he had ever seen: Purple, yellow, orange, and red seemed to be the colors of choice—all put together! Baggy pants. Pants which had legs ballooning out at the bottom. Pants which had a multitude of patches. Pants which looked like PJs. Pants made of two different kinds of pants sewn together! Oh, and the shirts . . . it seemed that the tee shirt, streaked with one's favorite colors of the sunset, were the rage.

Another item that did not fail to astound our traveler were the hats . . . not the Fedora kind, but other types of hats—hats that made a statement: do-dads, crumpled, high top, low top, put together, torn apart, flipped to the side, top, back, and even low over the face, black berets, green berets, tie-died berets, red berets, military, complimentary, hereditary, contrary, mother goose, red and loose, hillbilly, I'm a filly, cowboy, sailor, bailer . . . Joe's mind was out of breath!

Then, the most telling item Joe recognized as proof of his theories was the baggage. That's right! The baggage: duffel bag, gym bag, paper bag, leather bag, round ones, rectangle ones, rich ones, poor ones, back packs, shoulder packs, dragging packs, carrying packs. Everyone who walked, talked, or rested upon the trash-strewn sidewalks had some sort of "pack"!

What finally caused Joe to take a deep breath and scurry to place his back to a wall to gather his thoughts, were the faces! Dressed in those pants, under those hats, in those shirts, under "them" packs, were the most diversified group of individuals ever assembled in the entire history of mankind! Every color, race, religion, persuasion, background, nationality, and social hierarchy was represented in the crowd. Though most people were between the ages of sixteen and twenty-five, a large group of young teenagers mixed and mingled with the crowd. Joe had never even dreamed—or had nightmares—of a scenario such as the one he was now actually standing in. The first thought Joe had after evaluating his senses—after he kind of self-slapped himself—was that on this side of the Great Rockies, life had in some way evolved into a freak show!

His shock and confusion were the sort which made him wonder if he had landed in a strange place, where at night the people took on the colors of the sunset . . . and the sky was never blue; always setting as in the picture he had seen upon the mountain on his way down.

Joe began to believe that when the sun rose the next day, either the place would begin "normal" with everyone changing with the rising sun, or, that it was in the setting mode—24 hours a day! It was as if he had landed in the Twilight Zone!

When Joe finally gathered his senses and thoughts, he began to notice the physical images of his surroundings, the conversation, the antics of the people.

The inhabitants of the beautiful, hilly terrain of San Francisco, packed with old buildings, old street lamps, and other assorted historical structures, reminded Joe of The Fall of Rome—with a few changes: an old and stately city, sitting upon a hill, is invaded by a group of "barbarians" who, though peace loving and artistic at heart, are unfamiliar and uncaring of its culture, society, history or indigenous peoples, and therefore, change everything but the physical architecture. Soon, a continuing orgy of festivals develops and its streets are strewn with paper wrappers, cans, cigarette butts, and an assortment of food wrappers. Its buildings begin to display the new verbiage of the conqueror: Peace, Love, Stop the War, Head Shop, Meditation. Its art takes a turn and spills onto the streets with: The Beatles, Arlo Guthrie, The Stones, Jimmy Hendricks, John Sebastion, Canned Heat, Richie Havens, Country Joe McDonald, Joan Baez, Crosby, Stills, Nash and Young, The Who, Joe Cocker, Santana, Led Zeppelin . . . names and sounds as alien as the outfits preferred by the barbarians! But, in the reality of the Barbarians, they were like a great resurrection and congregation of every minstrel, court jester, and philosopher, ever to walk the planet earth and beyond.

With musical instruments and voice in song, carrying more tunes than words in a dictionary, their new thoughts resounded off the newly painted, loud, bright-colored store fronts which faced the tangled streets. From harmonicas, wailing everything from Blues and Southern Foot Stomping Jam, to peaceful renditions of acoustic guitars and flutes, their musical statements were offered as testimonials of the manifold backgrounds which were merged into a phenomena of peace, love and joy.

Yes, though the barbarians called hippies had come and begun a revolution, San Francisco flowed and ebbed on the tides of past and future great souls . . .

"Yo, you got a place to crash?"

The voice startled Joe. Looking to his right, he was astonished to see . . . no, it could not be! No way! Is that you?

His hair was now long and tied in a pony tail; it draped his shoulder—loudly contrasting with the purple and orange tie-dyed tee shirt he was wearing.

"Wow, ain't Frisco cool?" Pauly said as he lit a hand-tailored, odorous cigarette—which gave off an unfamiliar, sweet and sticky cloud causing several barbarians to rush over to take huge, long intakes, turn red, and cough in small successive bursts.

Though shocked, and wanting to jump up and down and hug his friend, Joe acted like a man of respect would—with reservation. "I just got here," he said, feeling a wave of relief replace his shock at the sight of his buddy from New York; someone he was familiar with, even if he had been infected with the barbarian's strange disease. Joe wanted to ask him how he was, how the Southwest was, and if he was "clean."

"So you ain't got a pad to crash in, do you?" Pauly interrupted his thoughts.

Joe was stumped to answer Pauly. Pad? Crash? Not only were the clothing, mannerisms, cigarettes, and music completely alien, but the language contained words which were twisted out of context!

"To tell you the truth, I don't know what you're talking about."

"Oh man, cool dude, like I can check your vibes out. You're still like square, man."

"Pauly, hey, I don't care how you speak, only give me more than a clue to your meaning or don't talk to me."

"Hey man, like don't blow your stacks. Check it out, you just dribble your karma all over the street . . . like that's not cool to lose your cool. "

"Pauly, how long have you been here?" Joe asked in an attempt to calm the situation down and find the word on the street back in The City.

"I split the roost six months ago. Your goomba, Big Franky, who was steeming hot, caught the scoop from some guy you were with, a "Jack the Cat" . . . then I got it through the vine you were crashing in some digs in Miami. I hiked the thumb out of there to see ya . . . SEE YA! I sez to those capitalists. But like, you know, it was not cool. Miami was square. The pigs just rut the streets . . . you know? And, at the projects— some psycho called Clyde something or other went berserk when I asked about you. Kept running his motor about his lady friend running off with a Monkey Face . . . weird man . . . really weird! . . . so I hopped the thumb with some cool dudes from LA . . . and now here I be one week!"

Joe was stunned by Pauly's comments. Obviously, Uncle Frank

had known where he was. The connected guys at the track must have lea . . . or was it Shorty himself? What about the score and Jack! Did this mean more questions? But, the fact of how quick "Clyde" wound up back in the projects—by himself—made Joe grin inside at the news of Bonnie's "discovering" a new running mate . . . did she take the money too? Boy, the street news traveled long distances!

"Hey, Pauly, where's LA?"

"Like LA is the place man! THE REAL CITY! Movie stars, Grumman's Theater, Party, PARTY, PARTY TIME!! Hey man, we gotta hike the thumb there, ya know what I mean . . ."

Pauly and Joe wound up "crashing" the night in an open house on the "hill." It was an expensive house, sat upon a hill overlooking LA. Some wealthy adults and teenagers held non-stop parties in its trash-strewn-glittering-chrome-full-shag-covered-interior.

In fact, the home was swarming with people off the street; people who would walk the corner of Haight and Ashbury, the surrounding streets, alleys, hallways, and even rooftops, until they were ready to drop, then take a hit of speed or acid, and eventually wind up "on the hill".

The way it worked was, you just kept asking "Got a place to crash?" . . . or "Got something for the head", nine out of ten times you would be offered a joint, hit of speed, acid, and/or directed to a hippie crash-pad; a place, in one way or another, communally used. It might be an abandoned house, office or store front; it might be a theater, house, apartment or someone's mansion; it might mean a party, a simple crashing (sleeping) place, a group of voyeurs or exhibitionists who would engage in sex in front of the crashers or even a home opened up by the male owners in the hopes of making contacts with young male and female runaways. Whatever the crash pad, there was always story behind it!

The morning came and Joe jumped up eager to see for himself if it had been a dream or nightmare—his thoughts you know—but before he could look outside, bodies, piled haphazardly every where, indicated it was reality.

Stepping over several sleeping figures, Joe found Pauly and shook him awake, "Come on Pauly . . . get up, it's time to go."

Pauly just rolled over and grumbled before pulling a tie-dyed sheet over his head. Joe was a pro at this sort of thing. From Carmine in

'64, to the guys in the grove, Joe knew how to energize sleeping people into action. Walking over the snoring bodies that were in all forms of dress, Joe found the kitchen. Ripping pizza boxes and all types of refuse from the counter, Joe found what he was looking for.

"Hey, Pauly! Wake up!" Joe dumped a gallon of ice-cold water on top of Pauly's head!

"What da $%#@%% do you dink you're $^%^$#$%% doin'! I'll cap your ass!" Pauly screamed as he jumped up (as the Pauly Joe knew) . . . ready to wallop the jerk who had the audacity to dump a gallon of water on his head!

"Come on, let's go. I got some bread, I'll buy you breakfast!"

Joe entered the crowded intersection and was not surprised to find that a legion of street sweepers with brooms and catchers had eventually swept down the corner and carried off most of the debris; there was now space enough for additional "castoff's" who surely would follow when the vampires awakened that night!

With the corner partially cleaned up, it was once more a place of day-time activity: business men traversed the busy intersection; hippies, who had taken up residence in the various, strategic locations of traffic flow, stood with their hands out in begging fashion.

The revolution did have a few pre-planned agendas: while the majority of revolutionaries slept the day away, a few individuals got up early enough to grub (beg) bread (money). Each individual was expected to perform their share of "pan handling" (a new word for begging); the proceeds of which were always shared with the group. Oh, there was always the occasional six shooter-loner-type-person who did everything for themselves, but in order to have a steady supply of grub and drug, one learned mighty fast of the power of team work. After all, even barbarians had brains.

"Hey Pauly, I'm glad to hear you talking New York-speak. For a while I thought you had burned your brains out on drugs or something."

Pauly, who was still steaming after the bath routine, just sort of grumbled and began asking the occasional passersby for some "loose change" (was not all change, loose?).

Joe had never asked anyone for money; even if he was starving—he could not "lower" himself to such a demeaning position . . . he'd starve first.

Grabbing Pauly by the shoulder, he pulled him into a recess of a doorway. "Hey, Pauly, what happened to you . . .begging for money? I cannot believe you would stoop to such a low thing as begging!"

"I'm not begging, I'm panhandling . . . there's a difference!"

"Difference or not, we are not gonna beg for money. By the way, I got twenty, let's go eat . . ."

"I need a joint first."

Joe, the quick study, had overheard some of the revolutionaries requesting "joints" on the "Hill"; he quickly figured what the "joint" was. "Pauly, I thought a joint was a place? Do you mean one of those nasty cigarettes you were puffing on last night?"

"Yeah, man. It's grass, and it's better for you than liquor!"

"How much you need to buy one?" Joe said as he removed his meager resources from his pocket.

"An ounce sells for twenty-five, but I can buy a "nickel" bag."

Joe handed Pauly a five and told him he'd wait where he was until he came back.

Drugs in California were available 24 hours a day, rain or shine.

Everyone seemed to supplement their "habit" with the sale of drugs: maybe Sam would come into a good score of Hashish Oil and sell it—smoke it—sell it—smoke it—until it was gone—and any money that could have been made.

In other words, they would buy, to sell, to use. One week Sam had it and Linda bought it, the next week Linda had it and Sam bought it.

Pauly returned in no time flat. Pauly said the stuff he bought was treated with opium; he called it "Thai Stick"; said folks in Thailand would wrap thin bamboo sticks with potent marijuana and age it in opium—it produced a rare and potent high! A strong, pungent odor drifted into the street when he opened the yellow envelope that contained the minute portion of his "Thai stick."

"You gonna try some?" Pauly asked Joe.

"Yeah, I wanna see how it feels."

Pauly rolled a small joint with what looked like pure talent. He lit it up, took a heavy drag, and began to turn red as he attempted to keep the harsh smoke in his lungs. Then, he exhaled with a loud swish of smoke, and seemed to relax into a dazed stupor, with specks of spittle creeping from the corners of his lips.

The "high" looked like a weakened heroin high. Joe decided he did not desire to become that person he was so long ago and initially refused the joint Pauly held in his extended hand.

"Come on. It won't bite!" Pauly said, holding the smoldering object before Joe's mouth. Joe had heard that line before, but he knew he was strong enough to try it, besides, he'd have to understand its effects if he was to deal with people who smoked it . . . and a lot of people did!

Grabbing the joint, he took a hard drag and began to choke until his head felt like it was ready to explode. Soon, a warm rush flowed through his veins and he felt this serene sensation shroud his body. Not like the strength of hard drugs, but strong enough. And then, Joe had the weirdest sensation he had ever experienced in his life: "Paranoia" and the "Munchies." Joe was suddenly sure that 'Paranoia and the Munchies' would make a great title to a movie . . . so he told Pauly! Soon, both of them were rolling on the ground, right on the street, laughing so hard they could not catch their breath! Anytime one would begin to calm down, the other would say "Paranoia and the Munchies" and the laughing would begin again. An hour later, after the effects had subsided, Joe thought they should take the stuff and force the Presidents and the Joint Chiefs of Staff of Russia and the United States to smoke some: the revolution would surely soon be over—either they would be so stoned and laughing that peace and love would take the place of war, or paranoia would ensue with a launching of the atom bomb—which would end all of this freaking, stupid, madness!

When Pauly lit and handed the remains of the first joint to Joe, Joe just smacked it away. Joe was sure he'd never smoke the stuff again. He felt too worried and not in control; anything that made Joe lose control he stayed away from. Meanwhile, his hunger was so strong he stopped with Pauly at the first restaurant they passed and together ate twelve dollars worth of greasy, terrible, fast food . . . in ten minutes!

Chapter 40: A Funny Thing Happened

It was Joe's turn to stand and hold the sign that said "LA" in black magic marker. He took the sign from Pauly, who immediately sat by himself along a fence that bordered the on-ramp of the freeway; he wasn't alone very long—he lit up a joint!

Joe was amazed at all of the new words he was adding to his vocabulary like freeway. Now, that was a word. Did that mean no one paid for a freeway? How did it get built if it was free? Only in California did words not mean what they were intended to! Well, he'd mull that one over later, right now the situation called for action—the standing kind!

Joe was the thirteenth person in a line of people who held signs informing passing cars of their destinations.'Democracy in action!' Joe thought; but there was one problem—they were all headed to LA!

Twelve assorted hippies all heading in the same direction was a definitive headache. Let's say, the next one up looked like a mass murderer? What could you do? The cars won't stop! No way . . .

Say you're the fourth in line . . . fourth behind this freaky looking guy who in reality is not a mass murderer but a wandering monk! What do you do? Do you rip the sign out of his hands, scribble out "LA" and write "I LOOK LIKE A MASS MURDERER BUT I'M NOT! I AM A MONK! GOT THAT?"

I don't think so; even revolutionary-barbarian-hippies can get awfully mean! Like the story one of the hitchhikers told Joe and Pauly earlier: A group of docile hippies were standing at the entrance to a freeway conducting themselves in the prescribed manner—each one waiting their turn. The next one up was a young girl of perhaps fourteen, hiking with a temporary partner of thirty-five (temporary partners were individuals who would mutually agree to join together for a limited trip, say Frisco to LA, and part afterwards).

A new Mercedes Benz pulled over and its driver informed the male temp partner that she didn't pick up men, but would offer the girl a ride. When the man refused, she offered the next individual a ride—who was a woman of perhaps twenty. The male, who thought he had been rebuffed by this helpful person, went bonkers and attacked her car!

After hours of Joe and Pauly taking turns standing, and still being seventh in line; Joe knew this form of hiking would never work for him. The situation called for Democracy's partner . . . Capitalism! Good capitalists always had a plan; they developed new or better ways to accomplish an objective better than the other guy. Hippies didn't like capitalists; to them capitalists were really cannibals . . . hippies believed that capitalists just consumed one another. Though Joe regarded the true hippie with great understanding and compassion, he was unsure their great ideals for "the wealth of the community to be shared by all" would go well with the capitalists he knew of; some, who at times, used law-breaking as their main technique.

Joe called Pauly aside and told him they were going to hike in the old way: as capitalists. Snatching Pauly's duffel, Joe and he tromped up onto the freeway and headed south.

"Hey, man. You can't do that. It's against the law!"

Joe, who learned a few capitalist ways in his travels, continued walking in the capitalist way . . .

After dropping them outside a small town fifty miles south of 'Frisco, the trucker roared off with a loud toot of his air horn . . .

It was pretty late and the traffic had died down. Joe was upset he hadn't left 'Frisco earlier. He shouldn't have stood in that line! He could have been in LA by now. He was tired, hungry, and knew Pauly would be twice so . . . 'cause he'd smoked all that dope!

"Pauly, there's a barn down there . . ." he said pointing to a building in a field. " . . . we can get some rest in there and start out again in the morning."

"I'm starving, Joe."

"Hey, get used to using "Mike"! If we get stopped I have to use my fake ID! Listen, get used to your hunger also . . . it comes with the job. Let's get some sleep and I'll figure out the food thing later."

"Sorry, man."

Joe acknowledged the reply with a nod of his head and they began the trek down the sloping embankment towards an abandoned, rusty-looking, tin-capped barn.

Climbing through broken windows in the rear of the building, Joe was greeted by a sight that gave all indications the abandoned barn had become a favorite "road house" for hitchhiking wanderers: old farm implements hung in disarray upon walls with gaping holes that allowed the weather to penetrate. Worn and mildewed, tie-dyed sheets and blankets were strewn across the floor; empty cans, some rusted out, some looking recently abandoned, were tossed into tangled heaps.

After kicking aside some of the refuse to make room for a place to crash, Joe noticed a loft above his head piled high with old straw; it could be reached by a rickety ladder.

Joe began climbing to do an inspection when a sudden and immense fluttering of pigeons, dashing to escape their intruder, caused Joe to leap and land right on top of Pauly—who was scavenging the cans . . . Bang!

"You all right? Hey . . . Pauly . . . Pauly, you O.K.?"

Pauly, lying on his back, the wind knocked out of him, struggled to catch his breath.

"Hey, Pauly, you O.K.?"

Pauly slowly sat up. His face was red but he was breathing and seemed to be just fine. "You came down real fast. I didn't even have time to move. Look, I landed on this . . . "

Joe followed Pauly's hand towards the stack of cans he had landed on when he saw what Pauly pointed to: in the center of the pile, partially wrapped in oil paper, a glint of silver poked in contrast to the rust color of the degrading cans; Joe reached down and picked up the .22 caliber revolver.

"It's loaded!"

"Check it out, a $%$#&^%$ iron!" Pauly said, as he began to look and act more like the Pauly Joe knew. "What's a thing like that doing in a joint like this?"

"I don't know, but it's a find. We can sell it."

"Sell it? What? Are you crazy? We should keep it . . . might come in handy . . . lemme see it."

Joe handed the revolver to Pauly with a warning not to fire it and went back to his original objective of scouting the loft.

The following dawn, Joe and Pauly awoke to a flock of pigeons roosting alongside of them in the deep pile of straw they had used as bedding; at their first movement, the birds flew off in a storm of feathers and dust.

Coughing and sneezing, Joe and Pauly rapidly climbed down the ladder, shaking and pounding their hands all over themselves to remove the rancid-smelling contamination.

Stumbling through the opening and into a crisp, cool dawn, the two wanderers looked—and smelled—like they had been living in a pigeon coop.

"You oughta see yourself!" Joe cried at the sight of Pauly standing deep in a pocket of fog, with feathers sticking in all directions. "You know, if a hunter came by here right now, without a doubt, he'd shoot you! You look like a damn ostrich."

"Look who's talking!" Pauly shouted with mirth. "You look like a W.O.P. pigeon-eater!"

"I bet we smell as bad as we look. We need to find some place to take a bath!" Joe said as he turned on his heels and began the trek up the hill towards the road with Pauly following.

Reaching the road, they walked south, occasionally turning and sticking their thumbs out whenever they heard a car approaching from the rear. After walking for several hours—with not one of the hundreds of cars which passed them offering a ride—they decided to find the nearest creek to dive into, and remove the excess, unwanted crud which clung to them with so much tenacity . . .

"Cold! That damn water is cold!" Pauly shouted as he squished up the bank of the pond Joe and he had discovered several hundred feet from the freeway entrance. "Now you're gonna have to sit like a duck in a pond while we wait for some hick to pick us up!"

"Boy, you complain too much. At least we'll get a ride now," Joe replied as he wrung out his pants and shirt.

Unlike Pauly, who, because he had extra clothing in his duffel, had just dove into the water clothing and all, Joe had stripped entirely before he took the plunge into the green-tinged water of what looked like an irrigation pond.

As Joe hand-washed the stains out of his shirt and pants and hung them on a tree limb that jutted over the pond, he viewed a brilliant, rising sun beginning its morning chore of clearing the lands of the protecting and nourishing fog that blanketed everything within a cool, moist, low-hanging cloud; energizing life into action. It would soon rise above the distant peaks of snow-capped mountains which formed an impressive wall between Joe's old and newly discovered worlds. In shorts, socks, and his old, worn windbreaker, he sat on a decaying stump, soaking up the sun's warming rays. Though it was the end of November, the sun burned bright and hot. Only in the shade was one reminded of the fact that a slight chill had invaded the valley and its complacent inhabitants. So, there Joe sat, silent as a mushroom on a stump, viewing the developing picture, storing energy for thought . . . his thoughts began their favorite pastime—nagging Joe whenever he stopped or slowed down .

Whenever Joe discovered he was growing lonely, frightened, or hungry (physical or mental hunger), he'd become entranced within his mind, rolling over and over past and present events and circumstances that led to his predicament.

Thus, thought only led to further loneliness, fear or hunger. So Joe began to experiment with views and sounds around him as "food for thought"—as stimulants: A harsh, cold, landscape, devoid of active life, could produce thoughts of a warm, soft bed, or the death of his father.

A lush, tropical forest, chattering with delightful, rainbowed creatures, could produce a vibrant thought of Ginny and Georgia, or Miami and the pervert.

The factors which determined which thought would rule in this symbiotic relationship between his mind and eyes, was his own determination to block out the loneliness, fear, or hunger.

He would mull his thoughts over and transform them into what he desired by concentrating on the good experiences rather than the bad—utilizing the picture of life before him.

When facts and realities caused his emotions to play the strongest tune, intensifying his circumstances, he dropped them into a void and used his gift to alter his mind: "I'm starving": see the restaurants and their signs? . . . think "That all you can eat buffet, bread, pancakes . . . food" . . .

Now he could remain in thought, overcoming his hunger for incredible amounts of time.

"I'm so tired": See the winding twisting road? See "The gentle hum of that super-charged engine . . . breezing the road . . . comfortable . . . I'll just snooze on the way."

He could walk incredible distances regardless of his condition.

Though this "newly discovered program" was a way to withdraw from the agonies of his life, enable him to temporarily forget his loneliness, fear, hunger; he lacked the knowledge to physically change the situation, thus his created thoughts ruled his actions.

The problem was this fantastic power of concentration, without proper education, became his weakness too—he'd continue dropping into unbelievable situations because he had yet to come face to face with cause and reaction.

When his mind asked, 'Why had this thing occurred?,' he'd place blame on his family, bury it away, and then produce a good and favorite memory in its place!

He would just eliminate the pain, misery or suffering by ignoring it and therefore, he became immune to reality.

Like a child who continues to initiate fights with neighborhood children and then rushes to his parents for relief, Joe's mind became his parent; it supplied the relief, and yet, it was Joe who ultimately controlled the very parent!

He would refuse to slow down, rushing from one situation to the next, all the time driving his memories deeper and deeper into that file labeled— "Accident: Personal." One day, it could blow up in his face, but, until that happened, he'd journey on a road to experimentation and event without cause or worry.

"Hey, Joe . . . I mean, 'Mike', how long you gonna sit on that damned log? I'm starving and cold!"

Joe's thoughts were suddenly interrupted by a shouting Pauly. He was just about to sit down to a great Italian feast: ravioli, the cheese, meat, and olive-stuffed kind . . . his favorite!; veal cutlets, lightly breaded and fried in olive oil; a side dish of tomatoes, smothered in olive oil, oregano, garlic, with a touch of red wine vinegar; Italian bread—dipped in garlic flavored olive oil.

He had implemented the thought when, through the evaporating fog, laid out in neat, orderly fashion on the slopes of the rolling hills, an olive grove appeared . . . but it all began with his mind telling him he should return home . . . but home brought those memories of wiseguys or sitting at the dining room table with Aunt Connie!

He got up and dressed in his damp clothing and then informed Pauly he'd figure out their breakfast arrangements shortly.

Up and running once more, Joe and Pauly walked to the on ramp of the freeway. Climbing the embankment to a bridge overlooking the entire area, Joe began to scout. From his vantage point, he could plainly see they were two hundred yards from the edge of a village that contained thirty or so structures.

No signs identified the name of the town, nor did it look busy. Joe scanned unsuccessfully for a truck stop and, as far as he could tell, none were within walking distance. He knew better than to venture directly into the town. His experience thus far forewarned of small towns and eager cops; not a good combination for two runaway pupils of the revolution!

But to his right, not thirty yards from where they were, stood a restaurant: The Steak and Egg. Joe could see cooking smoke coming from a huge chimney in the roof. 'They must be preparing breakfast!' His mind immediately began to think of a way to join in.

They approached the restaurant like two Green Berets on a great and secret mission in a jungle, deep behind enemy lines . . . Using hand signals and grunts they made their way to the rear and discovered, much to their joy, a wide open door. It was a storage area separated from the kitchen by double swinging doors with one small window. And, not ten feet inside, was a huge walk-in freezer with its door unlocked.

Moving into position to view the kitchen interior, Joe entered the room and looked through the window; from his vantage point, he could only see a small portion of the actual kitchen, and no employees were within view. He decided to check the freezer; it was fully stocked!

'What a find!' thought Joe as he went back to the outer door, signaling for Pauly to come in and watch through the glass in the swinging doors.

Joe, his stomach turning, and nerves on edge, sprinted to the freezer. After slowly opening the door, he turned and grabbed two huge, commercial type, potato bags—which were heaped in a corner—and returned to the freezer door. Looking once at Pauly to let him know he was "going in", he scurried into the cold and packed room. Huge amounts of lunch meat, pies, bread, and other items of interest were piled in every nook and cranny. Joe, his hunger made more prominent by his "find", began stuffing huge amounts of supplies into his bags: Large blocks of cheese, ham, pies . . . and PEPPERONI! Whatever he could lay his hands on he dumped into the rapidly filling sacks. When he had both of the containers full, he made his way out. Up the hill they went, a couple of heavily burdened pack-rats, scurrying to find refuge from discovery, and feast on their captured prey!

When Pauly saw the first plastic-wrapped hunk of pepperoni come out of the bag, with "Not For Re-Sale/Restaurant Use Only" stamped in prominent series all along its length, he just snatched it up and took a huge bite . . .through wrapper and all!

On the grass that bordered the on-ramp, upon a large "ROCK-AWAY BEACH, New York" towel, the feast was displayed: cheese, meat, pie, bread.

By the time Joe and Pauly had finished devouring—even some frozen apple pie—they were bloated. Pauly wanted to nap before they did anything else, but Joe, who realized the chefs might notice the theft and call the cops—which would lead them to the culprits hiking only ninety feet away—urged Pauly to dump whatever he did not absolutely need from his large duffel bag so they could stash their horde. At first, Pauly objected, but after Joe turned the thing over, spilling its contents all over the on-ramp, Pauly agreed.

The contents of the duffel bag were as diversified as the substance of a teenager's room . . . and that's just what was in the duffel: comic books, electric shaver, two model airplanes—still in the box, fifty letters, ten pairs of jeans (of which only three fit Pauly?), and . . .

When Joe actually viewed all of the stuff, he felt kind of sad for Pauly. Pauly was a rough and tumble guy, ready for anything, yet this exposure demonstrated the unique difference between him and Pauly: Pauly had a great family; a mother who worked for the power plant, Con-Edison, and made a decent living; a father who was a successfull contracter who did business with racketeers . . .

Pauly had all of the things that Joe wanted—down to the airplanes and comic books! "How could someone leave all of that?" he wanted to ask. "Why are you here, three-thousand-five hundred miles from your warm and caring family, with your memories dumped into a muddy green, duffel bag? I would trade lives with you in a heartbeat.

"Can we trade lives?" he wanted to ask.

But Joe's sorrow—and his hidden compassion—overruled such absurd questions. Heck, what would Pauly think of Joe after a conversation like that? He had become weak!

Instead, he decided to attempt to limit the damage he'd caused by dumping his one and only friend's life all over the dusty, debris-scattered, on-ramp.

"How did you fit all of this in this small bag?" Joe casually asked.

Pauly did not answer. With a weird, lost look on his face, one at a time, he began picking each object off of the pavement, giving it an intent stare, then replacing it in the bag!

It was then Joe realized they were going to have to carry the supplies in potato sacks emblazoned with the restaurant's name all over them! They had enough grub for a week—most of it able to remain edible—and there was no way Joe was going to dump it! So, Joe began looking for a place to stash the bags—somewhere they could retrieve them the moment they were offered a ride.

'Over the fence in the bushes!' he thought, viewing the heavy foliage over the four foot, chain-link fence separating the freeway from the ramp! Joe grabbed the sacks—and what remained in them—and hopped the fence and bushes which blocked the ramp from view. As he was pushing them into the bushes, he heard a car come up and a familiar squawking and chattering.

The Highway Patrol Officer who exited the black and white patrol car was six-two and dressed as sharp and neat as a Marine Drill Sergeant. With long, slow, deliberate steps, he sauntered over to Pauly—who was freaking out, most of his stuff still dumped all over the ramp . . . along with the towel and remnants of "breakfast" strewn all over it!

"What have we here? Does this road look like a breakfast table or what?" he yelled as he kicked food down the ramp.

"You know what's worse then a tie-dyed, communist-freak, hitchhiking, California hippie?" he asked a wavering Pauly.

"I . . . I . . . I dddon't know . . ."

"A tie-dyed, communist-freak, hitchhiking, New York hippie who dirties my damn freeway! Who the hell gave you a right to have a picnic on my road?" And then, just as Pauly was about to light out of there, the trooper grabbed him, cuffed him, and had him on his face in the car.

"Who was here with you?" he asked Pauly.

"No one . . ."

'Don't give me that, I can tell there was more than one of you! There always is! Where is your partner?"

"Oh, Go ^%$% yourself!"

The old Pauly had broken through, the one who had no fear but plenty of loyalty. For Joe, those items tumbled upon the road would always testify to Pauly's true strength: his ability to hide his fear in a muddy-green duffel bag.

The trooper reached in, pulled Pauly from the car, and smacked him around. He then began to walk toward the bushes. Joe, who was shaking in the bushes, was both angry and terrified he'd walk over and discover him but the cop stopped suddenly, he didn't budge, he'd seen something . . . the gun was lying in plain view!

The ramp was soon the scene of a policeman's convention. Five cars of various law enforcement agencies sat chattering away as the officers who drove them drilled Pauly as to where, when, how, and who.

"Take him out of the car," a plainclothes officer demanded of the trooper.

Standing in the middle of the group, Pauly, though nearly six-foot tall himself, looked small. He kept covertly glancing at Joe's position as if to say: "Don't worry."

"Well, this gun was stolen in an armed robbery three miles up the road. It happened two days ago. We had this town shut up as tight as a squirrel's ass. How did it come into your possession?"

"Hey, I just got here. Been here since last night. I can prove I was in 'Frisco yesterday! Hell, would I be eating breakfast on your road if I just robbed someplace? And have the gun sitting in plain view? Hey, I found it, I swear, man."

"Listen, you can swear all you want. The fact is, one robber was tall like you and the other shorter. We had reports of two guys swimming in Johnson's irrigation pond? Ring any bells?"

"Hey, Junior. Check these food wrappers out! They're from the Steak and Egg down the hill!"

"Where did you get these? Huh? From 'Frisco? Or does your family always send you food which is wrapped in plastic with the name of our one and only restaurant painted all over it? I think you're gonna escape—how do you feel, Phil?" he asked one of the local cops who stood behind Pauly.

"Yeah, I think he ran . . . "

Three officers then moved off and huddled in a group and began to talk. Joe could see Pauly's eyes as clear as day; he might run but they would surely shoot him. But what if he did not run, what then? What are they talking about?

As Joe contemplated what the result of the officers conversation would be, they began talking and pointing toward the restaurant, the stuff lying on the ground—and Pauly. Soon they were arguing so loudly that Joe, eyes intent on the situation, failed to see a sixth cop who had made his way behind Joe.

'Put your $%%$$##$% hands on your head and don't move."

Joe did as he was ordered and soon he was cuffed and literally thrown over the fence.

"So, who's this?" Junior asked Pauly. "And why does he have these bags full of stuff from the same restaurant!"

"I think we just blew our case wide open. Both fit the description. Damned hippies!" Fred said with his voice reeking jubilation at busting both of the subjects.

"Hey, you can call him a hippie," Joe yelled as he pointed to Pauly. "But I'm no damned hippie. Do I look like a hippie . . . dress like one? What he said is true. We just came down from Frisco. Slept in a barn. Found the gun. Swam in the pond. And that's it!"

"Then explain these sacks? You can't! Anyway . . ."

Joe knew he had to think of an explanation fast. He knew it had to be the best line yet. So he cut Fred off, "Hey, I found the food on the ground behind the restaurant. It was dumped in a pile there. I took it. I thought they were throwing it out! You ought to check it out yourselves! We're only guilty of being hungry, not robbing people with guns!"

When he had finished telling the "truth", Joe realized just how stupid his gross lies were: he had stolen more than he needed, in fact, he got greedy and stupid, what a combination! He knew his prayers—the ones he was reciting in his head—would fall on deaf ears!

And then, four of the officers, leaving two to guard both Pauly and Joe, huddled once again in a circle. After talking, often pointing toward them, the food, and the restaurant, they adjourned and informed the original officer they were going to checkout the restaurant to see if all was O.K.

"Hey, Fred, you and Sam keep an eye on them, we'll be right back."

They scurried down the hill. And, with swat-like movement, they converged on The Steak and Egg.

A funny thing happened on the way to . . . LA!

Joe could see two of the officers, guns drawn and ready, move to the rear of the restaurant as the other two approached the entrance. He was already forming his thoughts on the situation that lie ahead: since both he and Pauly were runaway "juvees" they would more than likely be returned to New York . . . at least they wouldn't be charged with an armed robbery they didn't commit! And then, as he began to think of Aggie . . .

"BAM! BAM! BAM!"

Both of the officers guarding Joe and Pauly split in a dash down the hill, leaving them cuffed and wondering what was going on.

Not for long. The gunshots stopped, and three guys came barreling out a side window of the restaurant. But, with six cops drawing dead shot beads on them, they had no choice but to give up!

"No thanks, this will be fine." Joe told Fred, who had just finished packing ten pounds of food into a brand-new, small, gray gym bag—and had asked if he wanted more! Joe watched as Pauly accepted twenty dollars, an apology—and then . . . shaking hands with nine police officers and the owners of The Steak and Egg Restaurant!

With stomachs once more bulging, this time with two orders of steaks and fries—each—the crime busting duo from the "Great State of New York"—at least that's the way Fred had phrased it when he awarded the duo with the proceeds of the collection—got into the cruiser and rode, first class, with sirens blaring, the twenty miles to the county line . . .

"If luck had a name, Pauly, it would be called The Steak and Egg!" Joe said between hand slaps, back slaps, and a whole bunch of leg slaps.

"Can you believe that the restaurant was being robbed while we were stealing food? I mean what are the chances?" Pauly yelled back.

"And, can you believe we found the gun, the one linking those guys to the other robbery? I mean, it sends chills down my body when I think about it. It was almost heaven sent!"

"Joe, we got forty damn dollars each, new clothing and gear, ten pounds of food, and a ride in a cop car with sirens blaring—and no cuffs!"

"Or arrest!" Joe interjected.

"Well, let's put our backs to the north, and our thumbs to the south, and catch us a ride to PARTY TOWN, LA!"

Chapter 41: A Mother's Pain

Jeanette sat at the dining room table talking to herself, "Why'd I throw Joe-Pag out? I was so foolish! I should've put up with him for the kids!"

As rough and mobbed-up as Joe-Pag was, he had treated the kids like his own. But as long as he was around, the mob was around. Memories are hard to bury. And the beatings were as frequent as his use of the pay phone on the corner. But the extra money he'd been giving them made up for a lot of things.

"Bills, nothing but bills! I can't keep up with these bills. The kids need so much . . . Eddy, my little Eddy, he needs shoes and a warm coat. And Angela . . . she needs some nice things. I can tell she feels bad going to school wearing the same clothes as last year. Carmine needs dental work and sneakers for school . . . that's if he continues going school! He's missed two weeks already playing hookey! He's following in Joe's footsteps . . . I can tell. Yes, just like Joe. Oh my little Joey . . . where are you?"

Tears swept down her face and her body shook with tremors of deep emotion. "Why . . . Oh, Lord! Why?"

The word on the street was that Joe had been sighted in Miami riding with some bikers who ran drugs in connection with a southern arm of the Genovese family. Then word was he was sighted with a known mob associate—a well-known cat burglar. Then he'd been seen traveling with a couple of whacko take-down artists who were wanted by the FBI. When she asked Joe-Pag about what she'd been hearing, as always, whenever questions involved his own destiny, he kept his cards close to his chest and ignored the question—which meant there was more to the story.

Joe-Pag's predicament could be made worse by Joe's actions. She knew the truth. She knew Joe-Pag could be as responsible as any of the others in her late husband's demise and her misery.

Did Joe know something? He was coming of age; the age where he was a definite threat. No longer "untouchable!"

Joe's recent history made both his, and their, future plans undeniable: Joe would fight them and they would try to swat him like a fly into the hereafter!

They knew—they always did—who was a threat and who was not. Threats to the Family got whacked. Those that were a directed threat, that is, a threat of action which could be used by the Family against others, were accepted.

Joe had proven from an early age the hate, anger, and blame he felt toward the Family. Like the time Biagi's son—whose father was a heavyweight Greek associate of the Bonanno Family—broke Carmine's nose . . .

> Carmine, only four-foot-nine and overweight, minding his own business, was walking through a walkway which ran under the buildings—from one street to the next—with both hands full of grocery bags. Jimmy Biagi, a big, strong, bully who beat up regularly on the small neighborhood kids, decided he wanted to have some fun. He walked up to little Carmine and just bopped him in the nose. Carmine had not only suffered a broken nose, but his mother's entire weekly budget of food was stolen.
>
> When Joe (who was living on the streets) heard about it, he swore to get even. The word hit the streets that Joe was looking for Jimmy B. Franky heard about it and picked Joe up. After telling Joe that he "could absolutely *not* touch Jimmy because that was the word of the big guy," Joe, like his father before him, went ahead and did it anyway.
>
> It was a late summer afternoon. Every neighborhood kid within fifty blocks was 'hangin' in Astoria Park, among them Jimmy B.—with a large group of wiseguy's sons. As sudden as a summer rainshower, Joe and his guys—including Pauly—appeared next to Jimmy . . . they'd crept into the midst of this so-called dangerous group unnoticed!
>
> "Hey, How ya doin', Jimmy?" Joe says in "MOBKIN" as he wraps his left arm around Jimmy's tall shoulder. "Isn't it a great day!" he says as he begins to lead Jimmy for a walk. "Listen, I waz dinkin, maybe weez gotta forget everythin' and all ya gotta do iz 'pologize."
>
> Jimmy was going to tell him to shove it when . . . "BAM" Joe's

> "right" shot out and flattened Jimmy B's nose. And before any of his buddies could react, Joe beat the living hell out of the bigger, stronger boy. Joe then challenged anyone of the others to "Go ahead, any one of youz wanna piece of dis action," before dragging Jimmy—by his hair—twelve blocks to Jeanette's apartment. Once there, he made Jimmy apologize, on his knees, with blood dripping all over the floor, to both his mother and his brother! Later, Jimmy's father sent his oldest son, Saul, to "break his head."
>
> Joe heard the word on the street and hid out for three weeks.
>
> On a beautiful sunny day he appeared behind Bernies' Candy Store—where Saul was hanging—and slipped around the building. Inching his way along the wall, around the corner from the group of wannabes, he waited patiently until Saul began walking toward the corner. When Saul had passed him by, Joe yelled his name, "Hey, Saul!"
>
> Saul stopped, and before he could gather his thoughts, Joe leaped to the ground and, rolling fast into Saul's legs, tripped him flat on his face. Joe jumped up and kicked down on Saul's face.
>
> After making sure that Saul would never, ever, attack Joe again, he and his guys—their reputation stronger than ever—walked triumphantly away!

. . . That incident, plus Joe taking down the wiseguys' places and cars, was enough to warn of larger things. With all the street experience he was getting—that is, if he could stay alive—he was more than a threat: he was a fact. And Jeanette knew, from all her experience with the men of her family and the mob, that the odds would never favor Joe. She desperately wanted to warn him. She jumped whenever the phone rang, hoping it was him!

She felt bad that day not long ago when she spoke harshly with him. She wanted to ask him to come home. She wanted to tell him she loved him, forgave him! She wanted to tell him so much . . . but with Joe-Pag standing over her shoulder, and his message to her that, "Idda be betta he didn' come home, da gize don' wan' him . . . ," she knew he could never come home as long as Joe-Pag was around.

So, with great regret, she started a fight—a bad one—which led Joe-Pag to storm out the door. She threw all of his gifts out the window: the children's clothing he bought, the electric guitar he bought for Eddy, the dresses. Oh! how her heart skipped a beat as she flung those four beautiful dresses out the window—they were the best she had ever owned!

She might as well have thrown Joe-Pag out the window . . . now the bills and the sorrow—and poor Angela's late night tears . . .

Angela got along great with Joe-Pag; in fact, she was attached to him. She was hurt when Jeanette threw him out. Angela was also upset at losing the things he bought for her—the only nice things she'd ever owned . . . though she tried to keep her pain hidden.

Jeanette never told her why she booted Joe-Pag; Jeanette knew if she did, it would come down to telling her why her father, grandfather, great-grandfather, and great, great, grandfather had died. And then, the question would come, "What about Joey?"

She gave a temporary sigh of relief as her emotional valve shut down and the tears ceased to flow. A curse had been placed upon her family . . . of this she was sure. There could be no other reason for five generations of sorrow! How in Jesus' name could her family suffer so? How could it continue after all of the constant praying; after all the constant abuse she suffered in penitence, after the deaths of so many, after all the pain and agony of the "little ones"! But, to her credit, after years of wondering "How could it continue?" she started to reason, "How could they end it . . . "

Chapter 42: A Cult of Father Figures

Rah Lum Nah's usual question chalked upon the black board asked, "If art reflects its master, then who is its slave?" Thus the lecture began in precise repetition with the first counter questions,

Question: "But does not art reflect society? Its statements coinciding with reality . . . no matter the style? Cannot one look at all artists and their styles, put them together, and discover the path of an era?"

Rah Lum Nah: "Art not only reflects society's history at the time of its inception, but also drives society. For instance, an artist sees, hears or witnesses an act of violence, he then produces a motion picture displaying that violence; the largest percentage of its content now reflects the very violence which inspired the artist. The viewer of this motion picture sees the violence as everyday reality and soon becomes an artist in life, painting a canvas of the streets in his actions. Another artist sees this magnified "new painting of reality" in those actions and soon paints another picture, writes another book, films another motion picture. On and on the cycle grows! In this way, both the artist and his patron become enslaved to art and its companion . . . a degrading society!"

Question: "But, is it not true, that to keep art as man's slave, one must paint the good side of society or write and produce stories which end with successful and positive results. Cannot art become man's slave . . . with society its master?"

Rah Lum Nah: "Yes, in a matter of speaking, if art is allowed to progress without check and balance to its content, in the end, it will always deliver its subject society into slavery of itself. As art grows through TV, radio, and motion pictures, it has the power to change, corrupt, demoralize, and in general, bring society to its knees!"

Question: "But, Rah Lum Nah, is this not a form of censorship? Is this not preaching an end to free speech?"

Rah Lum Nah: "My son, one does not desire the conclusion of free speech. Free speech is the cornerstone of art in its purest form! Yet, one must judge if free speech means uninhibited art; art that demeans, art that subjugates, art that breeds hate, art that plays upon the emotions of a minority people in a way that delivers hurt and pain, art that produces greed, hate, and violence into our children! Yes, free speech is of utmost importance . . . and, utilizing free speech, we must educate, teach, show, and demonstrate to those who will become our future visionaries how to paint visions which are strong, free, educated, helping, and loving! Yes! Good visions! We must teach that art can enslave through its enticement to profit from man's weaknesses."

Joe looked around as he listened to the mass of forty-year-old priestly men assembled in the small room of The Los Angeles Free Press. He realized, that once more, he and one other teenager were the only ones under thirty! New "chosen ones" were allowed to attend only one of the Rah's personal teachings, on the other hand he had attended them all! He had been attending the political/social debates for several weeks, ever since he and Pauly received the ride into LA.

* * *

They were walking along, content with the cash in their pockets and food enough for several days, when an old, beat up station wagon pulled over.

"Heh, come with us. We're going to LA." A friendly voice in "ragtag" face cried as he removed himself from the front seat..

Joe and Pauly ran over to the car amazed at the dress and mannerisms of its occupants: Each of the four men—who looked in their late thirties—had long hair and beards, flowing robe-type dress, beads and charms hanging from their necks and wrapped 'round their wrists, and their feet were sandaled.

When Joe saw those sandaled feet under their flowing robes and heard the gentle, philosophical way in which they communicated, he was struck by the thought of the book his mother had given him: The Lord's Prayer.

"So, are you brothers journeying from the great city of San Francisco to Los Angeles?" the man asked .

"Yes, we are, but we're not brothers . . . just good friends." Joe replied.

"Are not all of Him, the sons and daughters of He, and therefore brothers and sisters?"

"Well I never thought of it like that."

"Well my brothers, please seat yourselves in the rear and we shall ensure your safe delivery to Los Angeles."

Joe and Pauly soon were on their way . . . They couldn't believe they were riding all the way to LA . . . No walking! No waiting! No more nights on the side of the road! A straight shot deal!

After they settled into the old but roomy and comfortable back seat, they offered five dollars toward the gas—which was more than happily received—and food from their reserves. As Pauly snoozed off, Joe listened with both ears to the soft and mellow conversation unfolding in the two front seats

"So, Rah Lum Nah is going to be there himself?" the driver asked the front seat passenger—who seemed to be the one in charge.

"Yes! For six weeks! And, he is opening the lectures to personal friends of The Order!"

"Does that mean we can bring who we want!"

"Well, brother Shaom, I do believe that each one of us can offer admittance to one person each . . . but, I do believe this is a great occurrence!"

"Oh, yes, brother. Mighty is the word of He that sees all!"

"I look forward to His wisdom and power. He shall be speaking of life and its meaning. We shall hear from his glorious lips the writings he has penned with much truth and compassion. Rejoice brothers, for we shall hear directly the way to discover our purpose in life . . . we shall see and hear from our Father himself, the one and only Figure on earth who can offer the gift of life and love."

Life, love, father, figure, truth, purpose.

These were words Joe wanted to know. Hadn't these gentle, robe-draped men offered a ride to Joe and Pauly with gladness and enthusiasm? Joe couldn't believe his ears. Was it for real? He would have to discover a way to attend this great and mystical gathering of brothers and sisters and learn for himself his future.

Joe had figured a way to attend. With his remarkable communication skills and his trial and error street education—which did not limit the use of "small lies and grand boast"—he was able to relate his trips as planned events "in the discovery of purpose and truth."

From the Navaho Reservation to the Georgia woods, Joe built such an interest in his journeys that soon he was invited —"You shall be our guest to an awe-inspiring event which will be greatly appreciated by a young man of such worldly travel."—by Shaom and Troupah, themselves. They were going to attend the Rah Lum Nah visit!

"So, what does our young brother, who has journeyed much for such a young pupil of the way, have to say about that?"

Joe was suddenly brought back to his place by the loud question which boomed across the room to land upon his lap. He had been lost in his mind thinking of his first chance meeting with Shaom and never heard all of the question . . . and every eye in the place was intently focused on him.

Joe could not detect if it was jealousy or respect that glinted in all of those keen eyes at the honor of the directed question by The Rah Lum Nah. He figured his best option was to give his answer to the original question . . .

"I have learned . . . that one can subjugate art for the better of mankind. I have learned . . . one must use and utilize all forms of art to deliver their message; by doing so, one masters more than art—one masters the people. And, if one masters the people, one has no fear of the loss nor gain of free speech! One controls free speech through art. Therefore, whomever controls the vast majority of art—and its messenger—controls humanity. Let the good control art and it makes no difference that it enslaves its viewers, for their very enslavement can, and will, produce a strong and powerful society who work for its good!"

It was as if everyone in the room had been stricken by a heart attack, en-masse, the silence and looks of astonishment conveyed shock! Even the Rah Lum Nah, who was now standing upon his portable dais, had his eyes intently upon Joe's face. Joe was beginning to think he had said something wrong when suddenly the Rah Lum Nah did something which had not been done since Joe began to attend the meetings: He invited Joe to come upon to the dais and sit with him . . . he had received the lessons well!

Joe soon found himself handing out tracks, *panhandling,* recruiting, looking up to Rah Lum Nah as a father figure; arguing with Pauly about his "infatuation with a religous/political movement which was brainwashing people with its art and words of false truth!

"Sir, your copy of the Rah track . . . donation please . . . Sir, your copy of the Rah track . . . donation please . . . Sir, your . . ."

Joe was collecting nearly one-hundred-fifty dollars on the weekends pushing tracks and collecting donations. On the week days, he handed out the two page Los Angeles Free Press and averaged sixty dollars. "Sir your copy of . . . "

"You still on this corner?" Pauly ribbed him with a feint of his fist to Joe's jaw.

"Hey, it's a living . . . Sir, your copy of the Rah tract . . . Donation please?"

He collected seventy-five cents and placed it in a leather bag he wore around his waist. "What did you do today?"

"Hell, I partied . . . and I'm gonna party tonight!" Pauly said sarcastically.

"Hey, here's five bucks, put it away," Joe said, removing five one dollar bills from his pocket.

"Ain't they gonna say something about you giving me all this money?"

"As long as you don't tell them they won't know! Any way, the Rah said that we should love and share. That's what I'm doing . . . sharing with you—I damn sure don't love your ugly ass!" Joe said as he playfully punched Pauly in the chest. "Anyway, I don't take a dime. I eat rice and vegetables cooked by the sisters twice a day. They gave me my own futon and a place in the old gym the brothers refurbished. And, I am learning a lot! That's the best part. I'm learning history and political science!"

"Yeah, right. The only thing they want to teach you is how to collect money for them! I bet they live like kings . . . with steaks and lobster—while you eat damn "gook" food! You've been doing this garbage twenty hours a day for four weeks! GIVE IT UP FOR CHRIS-SAKE!" Pauly grumbled, a serious look splashed across his face.

"Look, every time you stop by you gotta say something! I'm just checking it out. You know? Like you checked that stupid language out! Hell, you sounded like a #$%$#$ dorf! And, O.K., I gave you hell . . . but I got to see if this thing, is it!" Joe replied to Pauly's sarcastic but well-meaning statement.

"Well, I gotta go. This girl I just met is gonna meet me at the crash-pad tonight!"

"Tomorrow is Friday—my best day—stop by . . . I'll give you twenty!" Joe offered.

"Well, I'll see you . . ."

"O.K. , Hey . . ." Joe yelled as Pauly walked across the street, "You keep your stuff together . . ."

On the way to the gym and his next "lesson," Joe stopped by the beach. The beach was Joe's new place of power. He would sit upon an outcrop of rocks and meditate like the Rah taught him every evening for twenty minutes. He would balance his Karma and complete his Wah. The Yin and Yang would then balance out and he'd be one with nature once more. Then he'd return to the gym and his study and chores.

As Joe sat upon his favorite rock; one that looked as if it had been warn smooth by twenty generations of Karma seekers; Joe looked upon the setting sun. Powerful and soothing, the sun was the balance of this wonderful galaxy; it not only supplied the energy for life to exist, but it also was source of the Rah's power!

That is what Rah taught. The Rah said God did not exist. He said that God was in each one of us. He said we in fact determined our destiny. Joe remembered asking Rah, "If God existed in each one of us, if we determined our own destiny, then how did other self determining individuals effect us?"

Rah said: "When you reach the level of Rah the answers will come as the rays of the sun . . . Rah said, "You should share and give of yourself for the better of others."

Joe had asked Rah, "If we should share and give, then why did we not open a food kitchen or a place for the multitudes of wanderers to sleep in?"

Rah said, "When you reach the level of Rah you will learn the answers to many of life's confusing questions . . . but we must first look after ourselves."

Rah knew. Rah cared. Rah loved. Rah was reborn twenty thousand years . . . Joe only a handful, what did Joe know? When he got to the gym, he'd ask . . .

The pounding of the surf awoke Joe . . .

'It's high tide!' he thought as he glanced at the stars. Rah had shown Joe how to gauge the universe by its lights and it didn't look too good . . . 'Heck, it must be past midnight!' He had fallen asleep! 'Man' . . . he thought, . . .'I've been working and studying too much.'

In the last week, Joe had worked the corner for over sixty-five hours. When you added the amount of time for study and prayer, he was lucky to sleep for more than four hours a night! He got up and ran toward the gym.

The gym was an old building the Rah had converted into his headquarters. The main area was nearly three hundred feet across by two hundred feet wide. One half of the gym was for communal use, the balance storage and off-limit areas. The communal sleeping space measured fifty, by fifty feet, the same amount of space was used for the kitchen/dining area. The balance of the communal space was divided into sections for training, offices, and meditation. Finally, a space, seventy-five by seventy-five feet, was used as the living quarters for the Rah and his assistants; it had been specially refurbished at Rah's own commands. Joe had never seen it. It was off limits to all except Rah and his High Disciples.

Joe was at first surprised by the fact that Rah lived in the city. Joe recalled the conversation with Shaom and Troupah in the car; they said the Rah was going to be in LA for a short time to give a special session or something. It turned out the Rah lived in LA, and that all converts were taken to a meeting just like Joe was, where the same question was written on the board! When Joe questioned this discrepancy, he was informed that only the chosen were invited . . . and what would the chosen say if they were informed they were the chosen without actually knowing the Rah? What would Joe have said? Would he have come? Shaom himself told Joe that by using the principles of "Art and the Way," disciples of Rah were able to recruit by deception—deception being the right way if it ended in the chosen discovering themselves! Yes, Joe had gone along with this explanation; remember his speech in the chosen meeting . . . Control the Art, Control free speech, For the better of man, For the better of society, For the good of society, Society needed the Rah . . . the society for Rah!

Joe entered the building to a loud chanting that reverberated off the high ceiling. Classes, taught by The High Disciples of Rah, were going strong. Joe knew how the new chosen felt . . . it was their first time! He could remember the excitement on the faces of the twelve chosen who began with him. One at a time, for three days, they brought them to a Chosen meeting, until they had twelve—then Wham! The power of the Rah!

The funny thing was, out of twelve young disciples, only four were left after two weeks! But, Rah had informed Rouii—which was Joe's conversion name—that he could look forward to rapid advancement due to the fact that even the chosen sometimes did not "make it do" to their "still yet shallow minds." Rah had said that sometimes it takes three, four, even seven times—which was his very own sacred number—to feel the force of Rah!

Joe had discovered the force in two days! Since, he had collected three times as much anyone else; had recruited 18 people—of which 11 excepted their Wah and were earning funds for the community; had implemented several ideas which had produced revenues twice what they were before! Yes, Joe was feeling great. Any day he'd be taken off the streets to train . . . that's what the Rah said!

As Joe walked over to the collections table—where all proceeds of the daily outside activities were deposited—Troupah suddenly appeared. "Rouii, come, we have been waiting your return."

Joe walked over to the huge, oak and stained-glass doors that led to the section he'd never seen. As he walked, his heart pounded, 'Would he be chosen to move to the next level! Was this the day he'd be given a better place to sleep and the right to teach?'

Joe stumbled across the room in his haste to discover his reward.

The floor was covered in highly glossed maple strips, and a large, carved dais of red cherry shaped in the form of a lotus bloom; large and plumply stuffed pillows in black silk and satin billowing over its petals, seemed to grow from the floor in the back of the room. Rah, dressed in a red and gold silken robe, sat cross-legged and serene on top of the pillows. The lighting was soft and indirect and incense burned with the fragrance of a Catholic Church on Christmas Day. Joe was impressed by the visual aspects of the large room.

Rah and four of his High Disciples—who sat on the floor facing Joe—had their eyes sharply focused on Joe's face, watching his every reaction. After Joe gathered the visual image into a total picture and filed it away in one of his many files, the Rah spoke,"So, my son, how goes your ministering?"

"Father Rah, it goes well."

"Why was our son so late for his duties?"

"Oh, I went to meditate by the sea and fell asleep."

"Does Rouii not enjoy the family of Rah?"

"Oh, no Father Rah. In fact my collections are up twenty percent since last week!"

"Then why does Ruii still talk with the outsider? Why does Ruii give the offerings of Rah to this lost soul?"

Joe was dumb founded. Had they been spying on him? Why were they upset that he had fallen asleep?

"Rah, Pauly is my friend. I've known him a long time. Besides, I work for those collections and don't take anything for myself."

"Yourself? Did you say 'YOURSELF'? There is no 'self' in the world of Rah! Only Rah! All that is, is Rah! You are but one of the whole, and the whole must decide on the part!"

"What about the 'Way'? What about sharing? What about truth?" Joe asked as his world spun into the vortex of letdown and sadness.

"SHAOM!"

"Yes, Rah?"

"Bring to Rouii the elixir of dreams."

The chanting of thirty people, dressed in bright-colored, silken robes, dancing to the sounds of various instruments held in their hands, continued to circle Joe in an alternating, fast and slow fashion. Behind Joe, who sat crossed-legged on a silk covered pillow, two High disciples whispered in his ears.

"You of Rah . . . Rah of you . . . No friend other than Rah . . . No life without Rah."

Joe's mind was swimming in an ocean of color and fast moving, blurred vision. As if his mind had become a time-lapse motion picture camera—every time he turned his head—the objects in his vision followed in a bright and blurry stream. Sounds, sudden and sharp. Then crashing . . . then ebbing to a low rhythm of heartbeats . . . then crashing in a crescendo of sound . . . over and over . . . reverberating . . . in his ears . . . whispers . . . those damn whispers . . . got to stop the whispers . . . . people . . . colorful people . . . dancing . . . cymbals, tambourines, drumbeats . . . movement . . . Where am I? What's that fragrance? Feeling sick . . . trying to catch my breath . . . stop the noise, please stop the noise . . . heartbeats . . . where are they coming from? Is that my heart? Why is it beating so loud?

"The Rah . . . The Rah . . . only The Rah . . . "

Screaming . . . who's screaming?

Joe awoke feeling he had been wrung through an old-fashioned rolling-dryer. He was completely exhausted with a soft hum running freely inside his head. After gathering his thoughts and memory, he had this awful feeling he had been drugged and hypnotized. He slowly sat up and unconsciously began to feel the roof of his mouth with a swollen and dry tongue; deathly dry; dry-paper-dry.

What's that next to his Futon? A small, wooden tray, delicate bamboo legs, a cup of herbal tea! The tea, swirling mists of vapor and fragrance, enticing him with thoughts of refreshing, sweet, warm, quenching fervor . . . reaching over, lifting the cup . . . use both hands. Sipping its contents in even, short drafts, warm liquid . . . so thirsty. Sounds ebbing . . . Blurred vision . . . Intense colors running rapidly Blurring into one another . . . lights . . . chanting . . . sounds . . . Sounds! Voices!

After three days of a non-stop acid trip, Joe desperately wanted to come down; to end the motion, the sounds, the visions, the whispers tearing into his mental file marked "Accident:Personal." Someone, something, demanding answers, questions, questions. No! You! Can not! Ask that question! . . . I am . . . I am . . . a man of respect! Father? . . . Dead! . . . on the ground! . . . blood running . . . an ocean of bloody red agony! Brother's name is . . . you cannot have me! Think of Ginny . . . What? Who is wrong? Ginny? Oh! No don't think.

Something was pulling at him; grabbing his arms and legs.

"FIGHT!"

No sound uttering from his lips. Ears don't hear.

"SCREAM!"

"Something is eating me!"

"HELP! HELP! SOMEONE HELP!" No sound in his ears.

Joe screams again . . . he hears in his mind BUT NO SOUND COMES TO HIS EARS!

"I AM DEAD . . . I AM DEAD . . . NOOOOOOOO!"

Chapter 43: Someone's Eating Me

Pauly skittered to the ground behind the "gym," rolled over, and looked to see if any of the security disciples had heard his tumble down the slope.

Confident, he'd entered the grounds to the rear of the building without notice, he scooted to the stained-glass windows which filled the rear wall like a multitude of scavenged church windows; windows which had been placed at odd angles into whatever space they would fit—a massive jig-saw puzzle of rich color and angles; heads under feet, arms over legs, abstract symbols mixed with written words. He scurried from one window to the next, looking for a clear opening . . . and then he saw one, a small sliver of clear glass! Peering through the crease of clear glass, Pauly was greeted to the sight of an orgy of sound and movement: A multitude of colorfully dressed zombies, dancing round and round a person lying on a group of pillows . . . the windows reverberating with blows of cymbals and drums . . . and then, the figure moved . . . it was Joe!

Sharp sounds, occasionally breaking the stillness of the night and filtering to his position, had Pauly constantly looking over his shoulder in paranoia. "Must be cats!" he murmured to himself.

It was nearly dawn and the ceremony had ended, with Pauly going over his plan to rescue Joe for the hundredth time.

After being tipped off to Joe's predicament by one of the many converts who had left the Order of Rah—"Joe is in some sort of bind over his friendship with Pauly. The Rah doesn't want Joe continuing any personal relationships. He wants to wholly show him the way. Joe is too valuable to lose!"—Pauly had scouted the area. A door to the kitchen was always open. The problem was the kitchen was running full steam 24 hours a day! At first he decided to create a diversion of some kind, but after thinking of alternatives, he came to the conclusion that to do so would threaten Joe's life. He finally decided on using a robe from one of the defectors.

As Paul made his way to the kitchen, he grasped the white cotton robe tightly around his body. Grabbing an empty garbage can, he hoisted it onto his shoulder and walked into the busy kitchen. Once inside, he was unsure how to find the room Joe was in. Placing the can next to several others, he walked through the first door he saw and found himself in a large training area.

Disciples crowded around a table as a guy motivated them to collect, collect, collect every dime they could, "In Rah we go and build our world!"

Pauly ignored them and, as if he were a disciple himself, he just walked through a large set of stained glass and oaken doors that led to the area he had seen through the window.

In his delirium Joe fought Pauly . . . He was struggling and screaming!

"Joe . . . Joe!" Smack! "Joe!"

Pauly was worried if Joe continued to scream, someone would discover them. "Joe, it's me, Pauly!"

Joe looked directly into Pauly's eyes and, suddenly, without warning jumped up and ran through the door screaming, "Someone is eating me!" Pauly chased after him. He would not, or could not, get a hand on his own mind; kept fighting and screaming—even as Pauly carried him right through the group, who was shouting, "HEY! YOU! WHO ARE YOU? YOU'RE NOT SUPPOSED TO . . . HEY! . . . THAT'S ROUII! WHERE YOU TAKING ROUII?"

"GO $%$# YOURSELVES! I'M TAKING HIM!

Pauly sat on a large bean-bag feeding Joe (who was tied down in a bed) some soup, that had been mixed with a sedative the doctor had given him. They were in a house run by a group of people who spent hours assisting those who left the various cults, drug houses, and communes to recover from drugs and "bad trips." Until his girlfriend told him of this group, Pauly had no idea what to do with Joe. He seemed to have enough LSD in his system to drug ten people.

Three weeks passed by and Joe was his old self once more. Occasionally, he'd have bad dreams, but otherwise, the incident was left behind in LA.

'You know, you kept saying someone was eating you!" Pauly said as he gave Joe this I-told-you-so look. "You know if it wasn't for me, you'd be a frigging loony-toon . . ."

"You make it seem like I was nuts! Hell, I agree I was on some damn trip into the Outer Limits, but at least I checked it out!"

"Yeah, you almost checked out!"

"O.K., O.K., I agree you rescued me! Now, let's see if we can get ourselves to New Orleans . . . and then New York! Home! Home! Home!"

"Yeah, that's a great idea! But, what about you getting even?"

"OH! Heck man, I'll figure something out . . . after this trip, I just want to forget fights, jails, arguments, and hate! Just want to see my mother! And Angie!"

"What about Aggie?"

"Paul, whaddaya think? I've met other girls, but Aggie's my love!"

"YOUR LOVEY DUVEY! HA! HA! Check you out! IIIIN LL-LOOOOOOVVVVE!"

"That's the very reason I didn't mention her! I knew your sorry ass would start that bull, 'cause you ain't ever had a girl!"

"Ah! Man . . . that's bull! What about . . ."

After a series of experiences, from Laguna Beach—where Joe and Paul hung out partying up a storm in a motel that war protesters had taken over (and wound up sentenced along with the protesters to painting the City Jail!) to San Diego, where Paul and Joe worked on a fishing trawler, Joe and Pauly finally found themselves in Indigo, California!

"Who in the hell named this place Indigo? It sounds so cool but hell, it must be two-hundred degrees in the shade!" Pauly yelled to Joe—who was ten feet ahead and advancing. "Hey, Joe! Slow the hell up! I don't know how you do it, but I can't keep pace!"

Joe slowed and then stopped and sat on the road waiting for Pauly to catch up.

"You know Pauly, we've been in this damn desert walking and waiting for a ride for twenty-seven hours."

"You don't have to remind me! Why don't we catch a ride at that train depot back down the road. Must be one train that's going east," Pauly said as he plopped on the ground like a sack of potatoes.

"You're right. Let's go back!"

Laid out on the desert floor, the trainyard loomed large; with tracks running east, west, north and south, it was a spaghetti-bowl of steel and train.

Pauly and Joe had scouted the place but were at odds as to which one to hop and how to do it. Joe came up with an idea to check the town for a hobo; one would surely be there.

"Hey, You! I'm heading to New York by way of New Orleans with my buddy here," Joe informed a group, of what seemed like, seasoned hoboes.

"Listen, we were wondering, what's the best way to hop a freight? I figured a group of educated road warriors, such as you guys, would teach two apprentices such as us?"

The shabby group of bums seemed to lift themselves up at the compliment Joe had just bestowed upon them. With pride in their eyes, they looked at one another until one of the group took it on his own to be the main spokesperson, "Sonny, first may I ask where you got that "Laguna Beach City Jail" tee shirt you're wearing?"

"Hey man, me and my sidekick have been living on the road for months . . . had to get some grub and a nice bed to sleep in, we checked into what we thought was a hotel . . . It's part of the wardrobe, if you know what I mean!"

"Well, if you'll part with that there tee shirt, I might be able to assist you young grasshoppers on your journey."

"No problem!"

"Well, the most important thing is water . . ."

Joe and Pauly entered the railway yard. They had a jug of water and were concentrating on a train moving east just as the old geezer said.

"Paul, let's go . . ."

Pauly and Joe began to jog in pace with the boxcar they had chosen. The train picks up speed . . . Joe and Pauly pick-up speed.

Running along the boxcar . . . its' door wide-open, beckoning them to throw their bags in.

Joe heaves his gym bag . . .

The train continues to pick up speed . . .

Pauly heaves his duffel in . . .

Joe grabs ahold of the door and pulls himself up.

Pauly is right behind Joe . . .

He's almost up . . .

His feet are dragging . . .

The train picks up more steam and begins to lurch on the tracks.

Joe pulls Pauly in . . .

"Hey man! We're on our way!"

"Yeah!"

"RIDE, BABY, RIDE!" Joe yelled as he walked over to the open steel door. "Hey, Pauly, look, it's those old bums we talked to."

Pauly got up to walk toward the door just as Joe was putting his head through the door to wave to the old guys who were frantically waving and jumping up and down when: BANG!

Joe was lifted up into the air just as the steel door slid with a bang, crashing closed, barely missing his nose by a hair's width . . . ZOOM! He flew—in sitting position—legs straight out . . . two feet off the ground . . . WHAM! . . . like a cartoon creature into the back, side wall . . . BOOM! Joe trying to gather his senses and lift himself up and BAM! . . . in the opposite direction . . . WHHEEEE . . . in rhythm to the train's motion as it reverses direction . . . BOOM! . . . into the opposite wall on his belly . . . BOOM! Joe grabs ahold of the steel door opposite from the one originally open: JUMP! PAULY! JUMP! . . . they jump off the train and land on their faces in the hard gravel of the track side . . . on the opposite side they had originally entered.

Picking themselves up off the ground, Pauly and Joe walk, bent over from the wallops they received in their "train ride" to nowhere, away from the yard and its confused trains.

"Hey man! What the %^%$ happened!?" Pauly asked.

"I don't know, but I almost had my head guillotined right off by a damn boxcar door!

"Lookit!" Pauly shouts.

Joe and Pauly watch as the train moves back and forth as it connects empty cars with loud, crashing, booms!

Sitting, or rather, lying in semi-agony on their packs, Joe and Pauly swore they would never, ever, attempt to ride another train.

"Hey, Pauly. We did just like they said! We got an old Clorox bottle and filled it up with water; then we watched for a train that was moving in an easterly direction; then we paced ourselves and jumped in . . ."

"Yeah, but they didn't tell us about that first movement—the part where they connect the damn train cars!"

"So whatta we do now?" Joe asked Pauly as he stretched his bruised and sore body in effort to assure his mind nothing was broken.

"That's your job, man! I only know how to steal cars!"

"Hey, I got an idea! You still got that tape recorder? The one I saw when your stuff was . . . uh . . . You know, the one that don't work?"

"Yeah, I still got it. But no one's gonna buy it! The only people we saw alive and kicking in this forsaken place were the train engineers and them hobo-bums who stood on the road and watched us make asses out of ourselves!"

"Give it to me. Come on! If I can get us a ride out of here . . . ' Cool Water! Food! Hamburgers and fries! Shakes! A ride out of this damn desert! "GIVE THE THING TO ME!"

Darkness crept the land and a crescent of light in a sea of crystal black cast a gentle glow upon the road. The temperature had dropped drastically and Joe was deep in thought of his friend Nihanio and the painted lands; a beautiful place when people like the Dinè added warmth and civilization to the landscape.

"Hey, Pauly . . . Pauly . . . wake up! Is that a car I hear? Can't see no headlights . . . just the sound . . . you hear it? PAULY?"

"I don' hear nothin', man! Must be that Navaho training or something. I'm going back to sleep!"

"Pauly, wake up . . . get your stuff. You gotta be ready . . . a car's comin down the road . . . real fast! Pauly . . . PAULY!"

"Listen, ain't no . . ."

"Pauly, if a car comes around that bend . . ." Joe said, pointing to the wide sweeping turn in the highway, "and you ain't ready— with all your damn stuff in your duffel and closed up tighter than that damn squirrel's ass that cop told you about—I'm gonna leave your dumb ass!"

The high-set lights cast their beams two hundred feet in front of the car as it barreled down the silent, ghostly road.

"Get ready Pauly. I'll stop him and, as soon as I begin to talk to him . . . Do you hear me? As soon as I begin to talk to him through the driver's window, you . . . You listening Pauly? . . . you open the back door and jump in! Remember, you gotta jump in while I'm talking! And, don't let him see you coming up or it'll blow the whole thing! Got that?"

"Yeah man, but I think you're nuts! Here! You want to do that here! In a damn $%^&^%$$# desert? Dressed like we are! Being easily recognized for who we are? YOUR %$%^%$# CRAZY! That's all I got to say . . . CRAZY . . ."

"Hey, Pauly, repeat the plan!"

Pauly repeated the plan just as Joe had laid it out . . .

Chapter 44: By the Force of Two

A bullet with two flaming beams rumbled down the road, four miles, two miles, one mile—ZAP!

Joe was in the middle of the road jumping frantically up and down, the object barreling directly toward him . . .

SCREEEEEECCCCHHHHH!

By the breath of a prayer, a sleek, black Oldsmobile skidded to a halt, no more than two feet from Joe. He immediately rounded the car to the driver's window! "Hey, how you doin'! My name is Mike Clark, Jr., and I'm reporting for the Los Angeles Free Press!" he cried through the closed window at the driver who seemed to be in shock. "Open the window, I'm doing an exposé on hitchhiking from LA to the Mardi Gra! See! Look, this is my press credentials. Who are you and where are you headin'?" Joe screamed as he displayed his Free Press ID in one hand and the broken tape recorder in the other. "I wanna ask you a few questions."

Pauly had come upon the rear passenger door just as Joe began his "idiotic" plan and was surprised to find both the door and his courage open; he'd had enough of sitting in a desert for thirty-five hours! He opened the back door and sat down before the stunned driver had time to catch his breath!

"Well, you young men really gave my heart a run for the money!" The salesman stated as he cruised down the road. "Aren't you fellows kind of young to be working for a newspaper? What did you say the name was?"

"LA Free Press. And we're just doing this for our school project. We have a special pass for one month and our article is going to appear in the Los Angeles Free Press! In fact, you are the fifth person who will be featured on the east trip! With you going all the way into New Orleans, we—my partner and I—will feature not only your views on the revolution and the art of hitchhiking, but also your company and its products! To start your interview, what is your name, address and age?" Joe said as he held the dead recorder's microphone directly into Jose's mouth.

All the way to New Orleans Joe interviewed "Jose," patiently "recording" every word. Even when the guy began to talk non-stop, Joe held that mike regardless of Pauly's snoring and his own fatigue.

In between his encouragement and "Wow! you're cool," Joe slipped in that they, his older cousin—who was really watching over him for his mother—and he, had agreed to take the assignment only if they could travel with no money nor supplies: "Just like the real hikers, depending on the Christian goodwill of those who assisted them! And, upon arriving in the center of New Orleans, Joe thanked Jose for "adding his strong and educated common sense to the problems of youth, the anti-war movement, and the ridiculous hippie movement," then asked him again for his address so he could send him several dozen copies to give to his girlfriend and others.

Jose promptly reached into his pocket and gave Joe two crisp and welcome twenty dollar bills!

After Joe handed Pauly one of the twenties and the tape recorder, they both smiled widely and congratulated one another in the middle of the street.

"Damn, Joe! You're a natural! That's what you are . . . a NATUU-UURAAAL! No one's gonna believe me! No one else coulda ever thought of it, let alone did it—and pulled it off!"

"Pauly, I was . . . we were desperate, and desperate people do desperate things! That's what that Air Force Sergeant told me. He said that when pressed by circumstance, the mind can accomplish anything . . . but he also said that "anything" is only limited by the tools at your disposal! Our tools were the tape recorder, the ID card, and the salesman in his bigotry, hate, and greed! What we did was not right by the Sarge's standards, but what alternative did we have? He said all people are basically good! Well, that's something I don't wholly agree on, but maybe . . . that's why I have second thoughts of that revenge stuff! I just wanna go home and get a job."

"A job! You! You gotta be kidding. Didn't you just see the magic you created? I bet we can make some real bucks!"

"Pauly, I don't want to! I can be a man of respect using my brains rather then a gun!"

"That's what I'm talking about! You and me in business! We can run a legitimate racket and still be cool! Our own brand of wiseguy. You know what I mean? All business men gotta have a sidekick that sort of keeps things right! I can be your Under Boss . . . except we're gonna be a legit concern! Don't Gambino own a whole bunch of legit companies?"

"Pauly, I accept your offer. And speaking as the President of our new partnership, we gotta come up with a business plan! You are now my one and only Vice Prez! Now, let's go and eat, check out the city, and then get our butts back to the REAL CITY!"

Thus, Pauly and Joe sealed their bargain of dreams to join society as young businessmen. They would soon discover just how well they worked together through a very lucrative business opportunity that would drop into their hands!

Chapter 45: A Taste of Legit

On the tail end of the Mardi Gras, Joe and Pauly were treated to the time of their lives.

"Check her out," Joe said, placing a dollar bill in the woman's garter. "Isn't she hot!"

"Can you believe we're in a strip club?" Pauly added over the wild and drunken cheering bouncing off mirrors draping the walls in reflections of exploitation; both on the part of the men—who juggled for position to place cash in the garters of the numerous women—and the women—who juggled for position to encourage them.

"You better not say that too loud, someone's liable to hear you!"

"Well, you just about saw all you wanted to see . . . Indians; the Golden Gate Bridge; alligators . . . did you get to see the alligators?" Pauly asked, cutting short his rundown of Joe's tales.

"No, but I was in several swamps!"

"Well, we gotta go and see some 'gators!"

"Yeah, on the way back!"

"Yeah! Back to the city!"

New Orleans was a party-party-party town this time of year: hawkers, standing outside the numerous night spots dotting the French Quarter like bumps on a log, literally snatched Joe and Pauly—along with several older gentlemen—off the street and jammed them into a crowd that swept them like coconuts on an ocean of sound to the stage—on which ten woman gyrated on top of glossy walkways not two feet away!

Joe and Pauly soon forgot their discomforts and pains of the road; sitting in the crowded strip bar as they groped and slipped dollar bills into garters. Soon, both were down to five bucks each—which wasn't lost on the massive bouncers who kept a sharp eye on the patrons.

"I'm sorry, but you gentlemen will have to leave! We do not allow minors . . . "

Joe and Pauly began to complain.

"You find yourselves some more bread an I'll see what I can do," the bouncer said as he hustled them to the door with a "Don't come back!"

Joe and Pauly were not stupid, they knew the score!

"Ain't that a bunch of bull? Come back when . . . yet we don't," Pauly exclaimed.

"Yeah, they just wanted our money. Well, I think I had enough of that place anyway! Let's check out some of that gumbo stuff we heard about. I'm starving."

"But, we only got a ten between us."

"Don't worry, I'll figure something out."

Joe and Pauly soon found themselves in a restaurant where the menu consisted of dishes more alien than the menu Joe ordered from in Mississippi!

"Crawfish!" Joe exclaimed. "Do you suppose that crawfish are those creatures that zip along in the dirty water of Central Park?"

"They look the same . . . look over there! What the hell?" shouted Pauly; loud enough to catch the attention of a demure waiter who made a point of appearing at their table as if he had floated upon a swift current.

"Gentlemeen, dos yorn appiteets desire ourn crawdaddy platter?" he asked as he pointed to the heaping, steaming platter which Pauly had alluded to: bright red creatures—their legs and feelers still attached!

"What did he say?" Pauly asked Joe, his face all squinched up as he intensely watched the folks—using their hands!—dig into the platter with relish . . . and a squishing, cracking, slurping sound.

"He asked if we wanted some of those little lobster-looking things."

"THEY LOOK LIKE LARGE, PAINTED, COCKROACHES!" Pauly exclaimed—once more in a loud voice.

"Sirs, dis restauroont serves only da finist Cajun in dese Quaters. an' has doon so for geenerations! Mabee you shood try anata place dat servs HAMBURGOR!"

"Listen, give us . . ." Joe began . . .

"WHAT THE HELL IS THAT GUY EATING?" Pauly exclaimed as he jumped up from the table! Every—and I mean every—head turned and was stuck in frozen, time warped amazement at Pauly's rudeness.

"Sirs, I am goona have . . ."

"Excuse me gentlemen, you seem to have a northern accent . . . New York?"

The table was soon heaped with platters: Oysters, Clams, Musssels —raw, fried and baked; Crawfish—steamed, baked, fried, cold, hot, and HOT!; Lobster—steamed, boiled, sautéed, cold, hot; Chicken—grilled, baked, fried, cold, hot, HOT!; Gumbo HOT! . . . a list of edible creatures astonishing Joe—he began "sampling" each one!

"So, how long has it been since you gentleman began your journey?" asked Mr. DuPlaintis, a cultivated, distinguished gentleman who turned out to own the restaurant, and had appeared at Joe and Pauly's table, in the nick-of-time, to rescue and invite them to a feast.

"On and off for three years for me and one for Pauly," Joe answered as he reached for another serving of raw oysters with the best manners he could muster.

"Well, I have seen many vistitors enjoy our cuisine, but none with more relish . . . I do hope our meager fair will satisfy such a hearty appetite!"

"I never tasted stuff like this! It's great! I really like the hot stuff," Joe said as he stuffed another serving of the Grilled Blackened Cajun Red Fish onto an already overflowing plate.

"So, are you to remain long in New Orleans?"

"Mike is gonna start a business and I'm gonna be his Und . . . his partner!" Pauly answered, correcting his slip as he toyed with his plate.

"A business? What type of concern are you interested in creating?"

"Well, I don't know, but I can do anything! Just gotta figure what's available. Heck, I have worked the trucker routes, fishing vessels, dairy business—where I actually herded the cattle! And many other things. I got plenty of experience! I began my journey when . . ."

Mr. DuPlantis, who had sat all night with an amused, attentive look upon his clean-shaven face, took on a serious look and began to rub his prominent chin as he listened to Joe describe his thoughts.

" . . . and then we thought we could begin here and return to New York later to show everyone . . . and bring them back! You see . . ."

With a delicate hand that bore a large signet ring in twenty-four carat gold, DuPlantis continued to rub his chin and listen until, suddenly, like a light bulb going off in a pitch black room, his face lit up in an enlightened way. "Hold on, hold on! Perhaps I have the perfect opportunity you young fellows would be interested in!"

Pauly and Joe lifted the carpet out onto the balcony . . .

"Hey, Pauly, this is our twelfth today!"

"Yeah, that's . . . um, four hundred dollars so far this week!"

"But you're not adding the extra ten dollars we're getting for each one from the Pelican Hotel!"

"Yeah, that's . . ." Pauly began adding the carpets they had yet to remove. "Um. Wow! Another hundred-and-fifty!"

Mr. DuPlantis had secured a contract between Joe and Pauly and a large commercial carpet installer. Joe and Pauly would remove old carpet from contracted sights such as hotels, motels, and other multi-roomed facilities and get an average of five dollars per room. The duo was also responsible for hauling the old carpet off . . . but they were already reaping the reward of Joe's ingenuity. He convinced another fellow he met, Jack Johnson (a black guy with a large truck) to join the team and then came up with the idea to clean and market the old carpet to other businesses for $20-50 dollars installed! It had been four weeks and Joe, for the first time of his life, was happy and saving money to return home. Together, Joe and Pauly had fourteen hundred dollars in a bank account Mr. DuPlantis had set up for them. Joe had been talking non-stop about going home and convincing his family to move to New Orleans!

Joe and Pauly continued to expand their business. In fact, Joe and Pauly made so much money, they met with DuPlantis and offered to donate two hundred dollars to a orphan charity he was involved in as a way of demonstrating their thanks! Joe began to build his self-respect and forget his animosity toward the old way. He stopped thinking of being "a man of respect"—because he had in fact, became one! He now could return home and rescue his family.

Part Five: The Beast Celebrates

IN THE YEAR OF THE BEAST, NINETEEN HUNDRED AND SIXTY-NINE . . .

ROARRRRRR! Initiating a thunderous detonation of suffering, the Beast's horrifying exhalation launched a gaseous sheet of red, crippling pain across the mounted, ghoulish skulls writhing in torment upon the walls, ceilings and daunting throne . . . "Captain

Jobuly, your miserable servant has come home and delivered a most scrumptious morsel for thy master's palate . . . but is it satisfying?"

At the Beast's question, hanging precariously above Captain Jobuly's head in the foul-breath air of the crimson cavern of living death, multitudes of distorted, chalk-white faces, grimacing, contorted; in perpetual grief and inconceivable agony; momentarily halted all signs of their suffering. With their only means of temporary absence from agony a compulsion for inclusion, an intensifying, rhythmic rumble swept the cavern until the cries multiplied:

Take! Take! Take! Take his skull!! TAKE HIS SKULL!!!

"Well, Captain, does it?"

Pause in the cavern as Captain Jobuly shivered in the wake of deathly silence; all but the multitudes of warriors—who jostled for position to be the next chosen one at the Captain's inclusion upon the throne—frozen in anticipation.

"Duh . . ." the Captain began.

"DUH? . . . NO!" The Beast roared . . . and the howling, deafening, clattering sound of millions of macabre skulls, gnashing their teeth, greeted the Captain's indecision—

"You have merely whetted my appetite for Joe's soul! Yes! AN APPETITE WHICH DESIRES SATURATION; DRENCHING AND DRIPPING WITH THE PUTREFIED FLESH OF THE FIFTH GENERATION OF THE CONTRACT!"

"But Sire, I had yet to complete my endeavor before you hastily summoned my wretched and undesirable apparition. At long last, you shall have your hunger satiated . . . this I swear by the blackest, foulest, most degrading oath of your Realm of Evil!'

The Beast writhed in pleasure of the unsanctified oath of the Captain's loyal respect . . . "GO AT ONCE, BUT TRAVEL THIS TIME AS YOUR EARTHLY SELF! GO BACK, BACK, BACK TO BATTLEFIELD EARTH . . . ENGAGE THE POWER OF GOOD! BRING TO ME HIS SOUL. BLACK, WRETCHED, FULL OF EVIL AND WRONG! YOU HEAR ME ?

Foul with obnoxious defilement, the Beast's breath tore through the cavern fanning the winds of eternal damnation!

Chapter 46: The Man of the House Returns

The bus pulled across the state line. All during the ride Joe had great thoughts of arriving home as the man of the house; as a man of respect.

He'd done it! He'd accomplished the impossible! It had taken four years from that first trip at eleven; it had taken blood, sweat, and so much fear and agony; it had cost him his childhood and most of his teenage years; it had denied him school, friends, and memories he'd have had of proms, Boy Scouts, his first football and baseball games, rides with girlfriends to the beach and movie theaters. It had denied him family and joy and all of those precious moments we hold so dear to our hearts: "Memories of love and happiness with family." But when the bus pulled across the New York state line, Joe was the happiest young man in the world!

He couldn't wait to see their eyes light up in recognition. He was the first to journey to the places he'd been and couldn't wait to tell everyone. With three thousand dollars in cash in his pockets, he had plenty enough to pay for his family to go back with him! Pauly, who snored loudly next to him, even made the decision to return with Joe and help him move his family. They'd left the business in Jack's loyal hands—their hard-working partner who was running a crew of ten people! Joe was on top of his world; he'd leveraged two dollars more per room and had expanded his realm to include four other carpet installation companies—including a mill which actually produced and installed commercial carpet!

Joe and Pauly had become the youngest businessmen to eat regularly at their mentor's restaurant! And now, with the train coming up on Ditmars Boulevard—the last stop on the route—he would soon be home and happy! He would have to go to Bensonhurst, Brooklyn; Ravenswood, Queens; Long Island City, and, of course, Astoria, to visit with relatives! It was a high priority to demonstrate that he had in fact accomplished more than all of his cousins put together! Then, to Manny-Hat, to see good Old Mr. Bianco! Oh! Yes! He was on the top of his world as the train rounded the bend. When it stopped Joe flew down the stairs . . .

"Hey Pauly, take this five-hundred and add five of yours and buy us a car! I'll call your house in a few days."

"My father might still have that '57 Chevy for sale! You got my number . . . right?"

"Yeah, I do. Hey," Joe added as Pauly took off to dash to his house, "Stay in touch with Jack!"

Joe began the walk to his mother's house. All the way, he thought of his mom's face when she saw her "rich" son return . . .

Combing his hair he knocks loudly on the door.

"Who's there?"

"Me!"

"Me, who?"

"It's me! Open the door!"

"Who's, 'me'?"

"It's Joe! Is my mother home?"

"Who you lookin' for?"

"My mother."

"Your mother don't live here."

"Look, I don't know who you are, but if you don't open this door, I'm gonna break it down!"

"And I'm gonna call the cops if you don't leave."

He'd planned a grand entrance. He'd figured the best way to receive the splash of joy he desperately needed was to dramatically appear at his mother's door—the prodigal son—home at last, and in one piece.

"I had it planned! Don't you understand? I had it planned!" . . .

"Mom! I'm home!"

"Oh, My Joey! My Joe!"

"Oh, Mom, stop . . . lemme tell you about . . ."

After the initial shock of his arrival had worn away, they'd have a grand feast with his favorite dishes on the old dining room table. Tomatoes with garlic, onion, and oregano in a pond of vinegar and olive oil; day-old Italian bread, smothered in olive oil and garlic; lightly-breaded eggplant, fried and simmered in a red sauce smothered in mozzarella cheese; yellow apples for dessert (all the kids disliked apples, and for this reason—along with Mr. Bianco's "Apple Attention"—they became Joe's favorite). When his father was alive, once a month his mother would go shopping. When she returned she'd take out a dozen ripe, rich and yellow apples and say, "These are for Joe, no one touch them!"

SOMETHING-ATTENTION-THAT WAS HIS-ALL HIS!

Joe's mind was swimming in pictures so vivid they seemed real . . . the family would gather round the table and hastily devour everything in sight in a rush to get to the storytelling episode.

Accounts of his journey would leap from the depths of his memory, hurdling all opposition with vivid color, exotic oration and multifarious movement! He would hold the entire audience spellbound.

It really wasn't a question of rescuing his family as much as it was of the honor and love of his family: a love he felt he never received.

. . . "I'm calling the %$@ing cops!"

Of course he knew who would appear . . . so he did what anyone in his position would do.

After quizzing the neighbors and friends of his family, he discovered where they had moved.

Another quick comb of his hair and another knock on another strange door.

"Who's there?"

"It's me."

"Who is it?"

Not again, Joe thought to himself as he tried to figure out what was going on.

"It's me! Is my mother home?"

'Click,' the lock is turned. 'Scrape,' a chain is removed. 'Creak.' The door opens and a tall, thin stranger, with neatly trimmed black hair combed into a pompadour, and a large, thin, pointed nose overshadowing tightly creased lips, suddenly appears.

"Hello, you must be Joe?" he says casually as if he knew Joe all his life and was expecting him.

'The funny-looking guy speaks!' . . . "Yeah, can I come in?"

"Oh, sure. I'm sorry, I didn't mean to leave you standing in the hallway."

'I bet you didn't,' he thought to himself as he entered the unfamiliar apartment.

"Your mother's out shopping and the kids are in school." He had a German accent and wore a Jewish symbol on a thin chain around his neck.

"Would you care for a beer?"

"No . . . thanks, but I'll take one of those smokes."

They chatted until his mother came home and then ate a dinner of cabbage and knockwurst.

What a change. Not only was his family living in new digs, but his mother had quit dating Joe and found this guy, Loui Fleugal! Joe had a new stepfather.

Later that evening, before he could tell everyone why he had returned, he grilled his brothers and sister on who, what, and where. In the front room an argument raged between Jeanette and Lou.

"He's my son!"

"Well, I heard all about him. If thinks he can just show up at our door unannounced he's a fool . . ."

Jeanette dated Loui with the hope that a non-Italian, hard-working truck driver would provide the family with a father figure of sorts and some prosperity. But to Joe, it seemed that Jeanette was telling him he was no longer the "man of the house." A mental position of respect that had become his only motivation. On top of this, his reception was not what he had envisioned. He tried to tell his mother about the business and why he had come home, but his mother just looked at him disbelieving.

"How can a kid have a business like that? I think you're just making it up because I'm with Loui! Listen, Joey, I love you, but you don't really expect me to pack the family and move to New Orleans, do you? A few years ago I'd have taken you back in a heartbeat, but Joey, you gotta understand . . . with Loui and stuff? I can't just say, "O.K., come home! You understand, don't you? Take the money you have and find a place until I have time to talk this out with Loui . . . O.K.?"

"But I got a business to run in New Orleans . . . I can't stay in New York for more than a few days!"

"Well, that's what you're going to have to do! We can see what Loui has to say about this . . ."

"Mom, I'll call you. Give me your number."

How confusing that conversation was; he had to get permission to rejoin his family? . . . after all he'd done! Jeanette would ask Loui if Joe could move in? Joe didn't want to move in! But he felt it was his family and he'd already decided life could be just like the picture he had painted in his mind. Joe couldn't comprehend the changes. He returned to Queens expecting everything to be the way he left it, as it was in his mind. If it wasn't that way, he'd turn the clock back! The only clock to be turned back was the Curse of Alphonso. The Curse would ring "twelve midnight and all's not well . . . "

That entire first night, Joe walked the streets meeting up with all of his old buddies and telling them stories of he and Pauly.

He could tell whenever he told the stories of Bonnie and Clyde—even the Reservation and Nihanio—the guys couldn't believe him!

Was it their small worlds? Joe asked himself. They'd never seen America outside the city. Joe decided to called Pauly. He'd not informed Pauly of the situation at his home, he couldn't . . . Imagine, after all of the times and plans, his family refusing him; disbelieving! He would surely look the fool! Might cause him to drop a notch or two! Oh! No! Joe could not tell Pauly.

"Hey, Pauly. Listen up. I'm gonna take a few days to visit my relatives. I'll call you in about four days . . . did you get a car?"

"Yeah! It's a beauty! It's in mint condition! Your Mom ready to go?"

"Yeah, but we'll give her and my brothers and sister a few days to get ready. You keep cool . . . and don't wreck the car!"

Joe combs his hair, jacks his collar up, and . . . KNOCK, KNOCK, KNOCK. The door slowly creaks open and Aggie's face lights up in recognition! "Joe! Joe! Joe!"

Joe bursts through the doorway grabbing her up in his arms, his face full of happiness at seeing Aggie once more. "Wait til I tell you what all's happened, where I've been, what I've seen . . ."

Suddenly he notices something is wrong with Aggie. He was so drawn into the circumstances of a happy reunion that he simply had not noticed at first. He'd wanted to see Aggie after he visited his mother, wanted to invite her to come along on his journey! He had just barged in the moment Aggie opened the door and hadn't noticed at first . . .

"Are you pregnant?" a dumbfounded Joe asked as he stared at her belly . . . a belly that was four times too large!

"I was hoping to tell you on the phone before you came over . . . I waited but . . . "

"Who's da father?" Joe cut her off.

"I was raped . . . "

"You were–wha–what? –by . . . by wh–who did it?"

"You remember Jolly Green Giant, the cop? . . . he . . . he was looking for you . . . and he kept . . . he kept coming by here! One night he forced his way in and raped me . . . Oh, God! He raped me . . .I couldn't stop him, Joe, I couldn't . . . I begged him . . . he wouldn't . . . he . . . "

Aggie couldn't stop the tears.

Joe's head was spinning so fast the ground seemed to be moving with it! He couldn't believe it! He simply couldn't comprehend the world he had been born into! Could it be true? Could it be?

Then he took his arms—arms that longed to hold someone forever—and wrapped them around Aggie. Holding his own tears and anger inside of him, he comforted her with all of his powers until her sobbing ceased, her emotions washed-out by her revelation; one she had fought to hold deep inside . . . deeper than any Joe had ever had before . . . all he could think of, was his anger, and the blame the "Family" deserved.

Sure, Joe-Pep had chosen his own course in life, but had he not been delivered into the "Family", encouraged by the "Family", died in the "Family?"

Joe-Pep was the proverbial racketeer; he liked to play in the fast lane until the "auto accident" . . . the one where the traffic caught up to him in the form of seventeen copper-clad, lead slugs. But Joe, on the other hand, knew from his travels that crime did not pay, he knew that jails, detention centers, and confinement in general, were terrible. The loss of your freedom tore at the very heart of "This Thing of Ours." Death. Confinement. Pain. Sorrow. Fear. Hate. Selfishness. Greed. These were the vocabulary of the Mob. But there was one more word in that dangerous vocabulary; one word that would override all of the others, for Joe, until he was satisfied: REVENGE.

Joe stalked out of Aggie's door like a cruel zombie. His mind was flooded with images of revenge against all of those who had wronged him, his family, his friends, and Aggie. Joe walked aimlessly until a car came out of nowhere and snatched him into its belly.

Chapter 47: Vengeance Is Mine

"WELL, WELL, WELL! Look who's come home ta roost! Da wandering $%$#$%^ monk!" Tony Black exclaimed as he walked into the room and sat down in his chair, cigar poking from the corner of his mouth, polishing his diamond ring on his suit jacket.

He slapped at Joe and made his ears ring once more. The room was spinning and blood ran from a gash across his brow—put there by the ring Tony wore.

He had been snatched off the street, knocked in the head, blind folded, and dumped into the trunk of a big, black, Lincoln Town Car. Joe awoke in some place cluttered with chairs and tables—card tables—he thought. Chips and cash? The noise of a cardroom coming through the background of the pounding in his ears. Pictures on the walls. Peeling wallpaper. Some run-down social club?

"So, you got Franky's nephew?" A voice—a new voice—asked.

"Yea boss, weeze got da punk dat ran out on ya!"

Joe struggled with his brain, trying to get it mobilized to deal with this new threat! What should he do? Think! Think! It can't end now! Think!

"Waddaya wan' me ta do?"

"How ya doon, Joe? Oooh! Look at that mug! Someone's been dumping some mighty heavy whacks on your noggin!"

Hey, wake up! Come on brain, do your thing! But Joe's mouth didn't want to work!

"Been having fun running with the Cat? Oh! I can see that twitch. What, you dint think I knew what and where?"

"Listen, . . . I knew I had to get your dough . . . I got it, I got it! That's the reason I came back!" Joe's mouth spit out.

"You got six grand?"

"Yeah, I got it!"

"Untie him! Now!"

Joe counted out two-thousand, eight-hundred and fifty dollars and placed it on the table.

While the Don counted it, Joe made his call.

"Hey, Pauly. I need the cash."

"What?"

"Listen, don't say nothin'. Just get the cash . . . meet Tony Black and give it to him!"

"But . . ."

"Pauly . . . Tony Black . . . Just give it to Tony Black . . . like I told you we was gonna do! He's drivin' a black Lincoln. Listen, on the corner at Bernies' in . . ." Joe stopped and asked Tony how long it would take until he arrived.

"In about an hour. O.K.?"

"OK! But . . . somethin's wrong."

"Hey, I'll call you later."

"Ya knowz whad iz gonna hapin ta yose gyz if ya leave . . . Right?"

"Yeah, I do."

"Remeba, da Boss got gize in Orleans . . . friends!"

Joe's fate was assured. He couldn't return to New Orleans without having the wrath of the Don follow. He'd made the mistake of informing the Don he had "started a business which was making money hand-over-fist"; how no one had realized the cash that could be made ripping out carpet and reselling it.

The Don began asking the particulars and Joe, in his pride, told him EVERYTHING! Only after the Don made a few calls to New Orleans, did Joe realize his mistake!

The mob was into any and all cash situations including Church bingo games,used furniture and second-hand stores—where sometimes they moved their swag—moving and storage businesses, pizza parlors, tee-shirt businesses, scrap metal businesses, junk yards, and now . . . the "cash cow" carpet removal business in New Orleans!

The Don liked Joe's ability: He was "gonna" keep him around to "groom" him for the family! But Joe soon discovered the Don had not known where he'd been; that he really never cared.

Only Tony Black, the rat who was spoken of by Bianco . . . the guy so low, he once stole money from a blind bookmaker (before running off to Florida!) was aware of Joe's travels.

"Why?"

Chapter 48: A Plan of Action

All Joe could do was think of his anger and place blame on "The Family" . . .

It was after dark when they arrived at Joe's Bar and Grill. A place where Joe-Pep used to hang out. The same place Great-Grandfather Antonio had visited on the eve of the contract on Jimmy, back in the '30s.

An odor of stale beer saturated the atmosphere that greeted them as they entered the morbid, dark establishment. Packed with an amalgamation of lost souls and creatures of The Hand, it brought visions of a nocturnal watering hole on The Plains of Serengetti—complete with vicious hyenas and docile zebras . . . whose stripes identified them as prey.

Leaving Pauly and Sergio at the bar, Joe strolled to a door in the back of the bar and knocked in code upon it before entering without waiting for a reply. Entering the room, Joe halted to inspect the crowded gaming table in the center; he was looking for a particular face . . . but Feranzi was absent. As he turned to leave, someone called out, "Yo! Joe! You looking for Feranzi?"

Joe turned and recognized Nicky D, who he knew from the old days as Feranzi's driver. "Yeah, you know when he'll be in?"

"Dat's gonna be difficult, da old man passed away last year. Listen if deres a ding youse gyze need, den come back lata . . . afta weeze close, say two or tree. O.K.?"

"Yeah, I'll be back." With that, Joe turned and, jacking the collar of his shirt with an exaggerated shoulder movement and a shake of his head, he sauntered to the door in a display of supreme dominion as if these assorted wiseguys and wannabes were his personal fan club.

* * *

Hanging from an antiquated frazzled cord, a single light bulb's harsh glow competed with huge pale clouds of cigar smoke drifting above the table.

Huddled in the dimness of this hazy setting, three intent figures, dressed in black fatigues and combat boots, contemplating an illustrated, penciled in, hand-drawn map. Displaying the interior of an apartment house, the map's most prominent detail were the names of Tony Black, Ball Buster, and Jolly Green Giant. Boldly traced over and over, each name seemed to be the primary interest of these resolute warriors: they would all be there.

"Let's go over the details one more time," he said for the fifth and final time. "The layout of the interior is the most important. The bottom floor is empty, the top has been converted into three sections of which only one portion is utilized. Though only one door allows access, we gain our own entrance by moving through one of the southside windows—which opens into a room with a door leading to the private office; a designed escape route which I will utilize in reverse!"

"The office, as you can see", he said as he pointed to the penciled drawing, "is to the right, behind Tony's main table. I will enter from it and force them to open the door allowing you access, otherwise, we can't catch them in a cross-fire. Remember, the abutting counter where the old cash register and phone are placed, is here . . ." he continued, pointing to the map, "it will block your immediate movement, but, it will also offer protection! You'll have to come around it to enter the main gambling room."

"The kitchen, right here"—turning the map around in his determination that each soldier know each detail perfectly, he stabbed at a circled section—"is off to the left of the main room; set up to serve sandwiches and snacks—make sure you neutralize it by taking full notice!"

Everyone shook their heads in agreement as he stood up. "Heh, you're the driver, you're also our security and our eyes on the street. Anything, and I mean anything, you deem to be suspicious, you react! I don't want no shooting other than what's planned unless it's absolutely necessary! You're the only one with a fully loaded and operational gun! You need to have it because your responsibility is the most important. We were only able to get three guns. Mine is a .38 revolver but we got no ammo for it. His gun is a .25 automatic but it jams. You have the .45 with the full clip! The two of us can take the place down, get their guns, and take care of business, but, our weakest point is our escape route. You are the most important! Got that?"

"Yeah, I got it. Hell, I want those #$%%$# just as bad as you!"

"At my signal, you are to go directly behind Tony Black and put your gun to his head. Remember, he won't allow any shots to be fired. He cannot afford to have a blood bath on his hands. Everyone will obey! They'll think they can get us later! SO DO NOT WORRY! I'll play the hand and control the situation. Just everyone do what you're supposed to do and we'll be set! We'll take care of our business and be on the road to Georgia before they have time to get over the shock!

Chapter 49: The Score

The old brownstone apartment building sat like a huge and silent, expressionless, solitary beast; its glassy eyes coated with cataracts. There were no guards at its entrance—only a single, unattended door blocked their way. Climbing out of the car, a pair of black leopards on the prowl—hungry—each movement attentive to sound or movement, stalking the ten feet into the darkness of the entrance.

Sliding up beside the door, blending perfectly with the black soot shrouding the once rich, brown brick, they cautiously remained in position until satisfied they were unnoticed. Then, one stealthy shape placed its right foot on the bottom of the door, its left hand on the top, and with his right hand wrapped tightly around the tarnished brass door knob, pushed with its foot and left hand as it pulled with its right: the door opened without a sound.

A set of tired stairs loomed up and into a darkened landing where there was a single steel door. With hand signals, one configuration informed the other to take the stairs while the first swept back through the door and zipped around to the side of the building.

A shadow, slick as oil on water, shimmied a fire escape, three tall buildings down from the old brownstone, and rapidly skimmed the rooftops until landing above the target . . . as sleek as a stalking black cat, it glanced once over the steep side of the building and leapt the clay capping to land silently upon the black iron rails of its fire escape.

With the only occupied section of the otherwise dormant building on the opposite end, the figure placed a "Rockaway Beach, New York" towel over a smudged window and, with a quick, effortless rapof his gloved hand, broke a small pane of glass right above the lock. The only sound: the faint music of falling glass on the interior floor; he entered the black interior; the shadow became one with its conquered subject.

Though times had changed, events remained the same: seated at five, felt-covered tables, on brown and weathered bent-cane chairs, was a variety of men—from known gangsters to local wannabes—playing cards. Behind the tables, on stained and peeling papered walls, were pictures of the old country, each a demonstration of fealty, respect, heritage, family, and politics. The room buzzed with the racket of a gambler's den.

"Eh, Charley. I'll give you five, for six-an'-a-half."

"Go @#$# yourself, Cheech! That's why they call you Cheech the Fleece . . . Sal already offered five for six."

"Yeah, but where is he?"

Schooled against the walls viewing the action, predatory loan-sharks waited patiently for a potential kill that would line their pockets, 'Who would go bust and need cash!'

At the head of a large, cash-cluttered poker table—by a door with a sign that read "Office-Keep Out,"—sat a man dressed in a "guinea tee" and slacks, dealing cards to an assortment of men who were drinking and placing bets—among them . . .

"Hey, you up or what?" Ball asked Gregory as he raised the bet by throwing another twenty into the huge pot resting on the table.

"The %^%$ is bluffing, he ain't got a $%^%$%& pair of %^%$&* deuces!" Jolly spat.

"Hey! Com'on, ds bet's on de table . . ."

"CRASH!"

"Everyone up off the tables! You! Yeah, you! You stay right where you are . . . and put your $&%*&^$# hands where I can see em—on the table! The rest of you hug that $%$^&^% wall . . . Now! Yeah, you too . . . you $%^&&%^$# jerks! What are you lookin at? Huh? Whaddaya tink now? Huh! A couple a %^&^$# plastic pigs! Face the %^&^%$$ wall! . . . You, open the %^&^$%^ door . . . now!"

Waving the gun around so as to keep the fact of its impotency secret, Joe noticed that Sergio had not budged! Joe was demanding the attention of over thirty Mafia figures and their subjects! The room contained over thirty guns—in the hands of experienced wiseguys who made a living killing! Yet Sergio had not moved an inch from the counter.

"Yo, cover Tony! Now!"

Sergio got hold of his senses and scampered around the counter. Soon he had his .25 placed at the back of Tony Black's head.

Suddenly, the torrid anger boiling for years beneath Joe's world frothed to the surface, keeping his impotent revolver pointed upwards, he began stripping everyone of their guns and cash as he hurled bitter abuse upon their persons: "What you looking at? Get your #@%$ against the wall . . . yeah you, I'm talking to you! You punk! How long have you—Tony—ripped off the dreams of so many? Gimme that watch . . . and the $%^%$#$ rings!"

"Listen, take whatever you want, but I think you're making . . ."

"Did I ask you to speak?" screamed Joe, as he whacked Tony Black across the mouth with a loaded .38 he had taken from one of the shylarks. It was not difficult for him to terrorize them, for each man could see the absolute anger drilling from Joe's eyes; even Ball and Jolly remained quiet and subservient. They were sure it wouldn't take much for this raging bull to blow one of them away! Just like those mobster movies he'd seen, Joe became the person in the role he was playing. Scooping all the cash from the tables, Joe ordered his subjects to empty their pockets inside out, and strip. Then he ordered Tony, Ball, and Jolly to get to their knees. The trio did as they were told and Joe, who had picked up another gun, this one an automatic, stood behind them . . . with both guns cocked!

"You guys knew my father, you're responsible . . . a part of the problem. I'm gonna blow your %$%^$%#$ brains out! What you gonna say to that? Huh? You %$%%$#$%^!"

"Heh, hold it, wait . . ." Ball Buster began.

"Shut up! I don't want you to say nothin' . . . you just think before you die!"

The room had now become so quiet the sounds of tense breathing became a roar. Trembling with hate, Joe stood staring at the back of their heads, ready to blow the three into the utter darkness of death.

"Please, please . . ." Jolly Green Giant began begging. A dark stain spread down his legs.

"Jolly, shut ya moud . . . ya make me sick!" Tony had cut him off.

BANG!

Joe shot off his automatic by the side of Tony's head . . . just like the story Bianco had told him.

Everyone's ears were ringing, acrid smoke wafted through the air. Tony clamped his bleeding ear and asked of no one, and everyone, in the loud voice of the near-deaf, "Iz my ear still dere? . . . my %$%$#%^ ear . . . did he shoot my ear off?"

Ball and Jolly began crying. Joe took a step back. These were wiseguys? Mobsters? Men of respect? Men of the Black Hand? Soldiers of This Thing of Ours? These dribbling, whimpering pitiful men . . . Joe's thoughts began exploding in contrast with his anger. Children . . . did they have children . . . remember! . . . no, shoot! Shoot! They're responsible. Are you sure? . . . just take the dough . . . they'll come for you . . . so, shoot 'em!

"Ah, $%#@ you, you're not worth it . . . Joe spat at the three heads and backed off. Calling Sergio from behind the main poker table—where he had remained, entranced by a performance he could not believe—they backed their way toward the door.

Spying the register out of the corner of his eye, Joe hit the sale button and removed all of the bills; he then took the change tray and, like an actor in a scripted James Cagney movie, threw the change on the floor with the statement.

"Save it for the sweeper."

Opening the door, the duo flew out and down the stairs, jumped into the waiting car, and zoomed away.

YEAH!

YEAH!

YEAH!

We did it! Joe thought to himself as they celebrated by throwing money all around the car. Thirty thousand dollars in cash and egg on "Dem Gyze" faces!

He didn't think about the consequences, nor the implications of his act.

He had avenged his father . . .

He had avenged his mother . . .

He had avenged his uncle . . .

He had avenged his ancestors . . .

He had avenged himself!

Chapter 50: Calling In the Loan

Arriving back in Queens with his share of the loot, Joe went to his mother's house to give her some cash under the pretext of winning it at the track . . . He would tell her that in the hopes she would take it—though he knew in his mind the truth would not be far in finding her—then he could leave with Pauly, Sergio, and Aggie. In spite of Loui, and acting once more the man of the house, he gave her five thousand dollars.

"Where did you say you got the money from?" Jeanette inquired as he laid the money on the table, beaming with pride.

"I won it at the track off the money I brought with me . . . it's yours! Really, I got lots more!" he repeated, boldly showing another several thousand dollars.

"What track and what race?" she asked with a doubtful look.

" Won it, that's all. Listen take the money, you know you need it! I'm gonna head for Miami," he lied.

"I don't care where you say you got it. I know it had to come from dishonest means. God will punish you, do you understand what I'm saying?" she admonished as she swept the money off the table.

He was devastated. He was blown away. "This is not right! There is something wrong here! Why are you doin' this to me?" Joe screamed as he began picking up the money. "God does not exist—if he did, then why did we end up like we did? Huh! Here you sit, acting like I'm wrong and your friends have taken my life; my freedom; caused me to suffer . . . Hell, you didn't even care what happened to me . . . did you? Who the hell do you think stole my business in New Orleans? . . . huh? Here I am, returning to help you! Do you hear me? You! And who was it told me I couldn't come home, huh? Who?"

"I . . . I . . . I wanted you to . . . to . . . to come home . . . I did. I swear, it was . . ."

"See, I told you!"

"Listen, I've done the best I could. I'm still . . ."

Snatching the remaining cash off the floor . . . "Let me tell you something! I robbed the damn card game! Tony's game! That's what I did! And I don't care if Franky, Tony, Shorty—or those cops . . . or anyone else cares! I got even . . . Oh, I'd like to blow all of their heads off . . . but I got mine back!" With that, Joe stormed out of the house.

He could hear Jeanette weeping as he flew down the stairs and ran toward the waiting car and Pauly.

"Oh, God, why my family?" he yelled—so loud, that passers-by, mostly couples lovingly holding hands and smooching as they strolled the block on their way home, froze on the spot—their eyes warily following the madman.

"What the #$@# are you looking at?" he screamed at them. Their heads turned away instantly as he jumped in the car and roared off.

The car lurched from the curb with a screech of tires against hard pitted blacktop and zoomed into the filth and grime-coated city he awoke to in November of '61 . . .

With Pauly as quiet as a tree on a windless day, Joe roared down the road . . . deep in thought.

She refused the money which would have helped her tremendously. 'Why? Father, I wish you were here. I know that it was wrong, but I just did it—it had to be done! I know deep in her heart she loves me . . . or does she? If she did then . . . '

Joe was in the worst turmoil of his entire life. Demons screamed in his head. The void holding that tremendous file of facts and thought—the one marked Accident: Personal—heaved its compilation of emotions, feelings, anger and questions into the forefront of his mind. Even a Dream Catcher would have stumbled in his attempt to gather all of the pictures and visions and facts and feelings that rushed in painted opinions, 'Who should he pray to? Was father in hell? Was there a hell? Was there a God? Was he right? Should he have just let the thing go? Was it wrong for the Don to take what had taken Joe four years to get? Was his family right? Was there a curse on his family? Is there really such a thing as a curse? What of hell . . . was there a hell or was he there already?'

The thoughts of his experience in the semblance of hell sent shivers coursing through his bones.

"Joe, your Uncle Frank came by. He was very angry and excited! I don't know how he found out where I live or how I knew you, but he did. He said it is very important that you meet with him . . . tonight! Something about a problem in Brooklyn last night. What does he mean?" she exclaimed as soon as the door opened and he scrambled in.

"I don know, honest!" he lied, all the time concentrating on his departure and freedom from a place he was sure he would never return to. "Where did Franky say to meet him?"

Joe agreed to meet with Frank. He had to. He had to know how and what to do . . . Leaving both the car and Pauly waiting ten blocks away, he scurried in the shadows of the night to his rendezvous.

""What the hell were you thinking? Did you think you'd get away with it?" Uncle Frank demanded of Joe as they drove the neighborhood. "Where's Sergio and the money!"

"Uncle Frank, they owed me! They deserved it! They raped Aggie! You gotta help me get . . ."

"I ain't gotta do nothing! You just give the money back . . . or you're in big trouble. In fact you're in a bind anyway! Your father would have . . ."

"Why does everyone bring up my father, huh? How'd he die, huh? Mr. Bianco told me! It was his own friends and relatives who stood by. They had to, the word was on the streets for weeks! Why didn't anyone lift a finger to help? Or did his own friends set him up! What do you know? You have the . . ."

SMACK!

The blow caught him on the cheek as a torrent spewed from Franks lips. "You little $%$#@#%$, who do you think you're talkin to. I want you . . ."

Joe's hands instinctivly flailed. A right-cross to the bridge of Frank's nose and Joe turned and hit the door. Frank never had the chance to stop him, nor to catch him. Up and over the first fire-escape he came to, over rooftops, down alleys; he disappeared.

Chapter 51: Reality Sets In

Heart pumping, head spinning, gasping and wheezing—as if approaching a heavily defended home plate with two pit bulls chasing him—he rounded the corner in one motion, dropped to the ground, and slid down and under to the presumed safety of a silent, rusting, red Ford.

Finding himself wedged between the cold wet pavement and the hulking remnants of a once proud symbol of the American way of life, Joe felt scared, defeated, and worn out. He was fighting to control his breathing, which was producing clouds of steam in the cool, pre-dawn—sending an SOS that would surely catch the attention of the rapidly advancing beam of light that pierced the darkened street. His vision, impaired by the narrow crease of space between the road and the rocker panel, afforded him a view of the four blue legs with black feet moving not ten feet from his hideout; a surreal, giant pit bull, determined to capture its elusive prey, Ball and Jolly approached, leash of light in hand, barking and baying, "We're gonna get you! Com'on out! We know you're hiding . . . come on you little rat!" Holding his breath, heart pounding so hard he swore it could be heard a block away .

Ball and that rat Jolly had had the entire area surrounded, Joe lay there thinking just how close Jolly was to him; if he only had a gun, he'd get him . . .

Joe remained where he was for four hours until the duo disappeared. Then he slowly made his way to the train station.

The train moaned and groaned to a stop on Ditmars Boulevard. Joe exited the car and apprehensively, in stealth, moved along the stairwell. What was he to do? Where was he going to go? He couldn't go to Pauly's house, his father was connected and Joe was sure the word was on the street! Everyone would be looking for Joe and Sergio! They had no idea Pauly was there . . . but, what of Nicky D? Would he include himself by informing he had sold the guns to Joe? No! But where to go? He needed a safe place to plan, to wait, to find Pauly and the car—to escape. The only place he could think of was home! He could get Carmine to somehow notify Pauly. Get him to meet somewhere! But, he couldn't let his mother know . . . Wow, just like the old days . . . he could hide under the bed for several days without her knowing!

Taking all of the back alleys and byways he wound up at his mothers apartment house. The front door was swarming with police officers; he had both the law and the criminals out to get him. Waiting in the dark until all but one strategically placed car remained, he climbed a fire escape several apartment houses down the block and silently made his way along the buildings until he came to his mother's building.

Climbing over the wall and down to the upper landing of the fire escape that opened into Carmine's new bedroom, he tapped on the window. Carmine's face appeared in the window. With relief, Joe asked him to open the window.

"Carmine, open up."

Carmine just stood there.

"Carmine, the cops are down there, open up!"

Nothing

"Carmine, will you please open the window?"

"I can't, I'll get in trouble."

"No you won't—just open the window!"

"I'm telling!"

"Listen, if you open the window I'll give you some money!"

"I don't want nothing."

"Open the darn window!" he shouted so loud the cops heard him and began flashing their lights up at him!

Over the roof he went—with the sound of their feet climbing the fire escape right behind him. He leapt two stories down to the ground and ran as hard as he could. As he turned a corner several blocks away, he tore down into the subway, jumped the turnstile, ran across several live rails, and like a cowboy in a western movie, jumped aboard a fast moving train headed back towards Queensborough Plaza.

As soon as he arrived at Queensborough Plaza, he exited the train and wracked his brain for Pauly's number.

Rolling numbers over and over, he began dialing them until, like a safe cracker on his tenth turn of the dial, he cracked the combination and Pauly's voice came crackling over the line!

"Pauly, baby! Pauly! Man am I glad to hear your ugly voice! Listen, grab the car and get your butt over to the Plaza! Don't tell no one and watch your back . . . you know what I mean!"

"Right! I'll be there on the short and quick! Man, this town is buzzing. I was waiting to get the heck out of here!"

"I'll be where the street ladies hang—in the back!"

As he waited for Pauly, Joe checked the large pockets of his leather jacket for the wads of cash that made them bulge. One part of him wished he had never stolen the money; wished his nightmare would end . . . the one consuming the little life he had: no peace, no happiness, no family! Worse than that was the fact that "mother" had become a word of so much conflict and emotion. Confusion was the order of the day . . . though he once relished the thought of leaving New York forever with the knowledge of the defeat of his enemies, he now knew they could never be defeated! Yet the thought of Aggie, his princess, and he, her 'Knight In Shining Armor,' demanded sacrifice . . . but whose? The right thing would be to leave and let the whole thing die down, then come back and take care of business . . . that he was sure of.

Pauly's arrival halted his thoughts, at least until they drove to a hotel where they would sleep the night away.

The following day, after they ate breakfast, Pauly and Joe drove to get Sergio: he was not at his place—only a dark gray sedan with four guys out front . . . so they kept going.

After driving to all of the places he might be, Pauly made a last call and lucked out when he discovered where Sergio was hiding out: The Italian Feast of St. Gennarro!

When Joe heard that he was, of all places, at the feast, he went crazy. "What, you think we can just go tromping into the Feast and not be noticed? What, is he crazy or what? The Italian Feast? It's the worst place to go! The wiseguy's own it!"

"But Sergio's friend said it was the perfect place to meet," Pauly replied with a shrug of his shoulders. "They'd never think we'd go there . . . in fact it'll be so crowded we'll be lost in the crowd. Let's just go there, get him; then jump in the car and leave for Georgia."

"Well, they never saw you. It's my butt not yours . . ."

"Look, we'll be in and out before any wiseguy is the wiser!" Pauly laughed at his unintended pun—he was right.

The area was blocked off and it seemed the entire Italian community was all crunched into the ten blocks or so that made up the progression route for the celebration of The Feast of St. Gennarro. The festive carnival atmosphere took control of his thoughts and visions. All he could see were colorfully dressed participants jostling for room as they crowded the food concessions that poked out into the streets like so many brightly lit cubes of color and aromas; sausage, fried with tomatoes, onions, garlic and peppers; connoli's—freshly made as you waited. His stomach growled as he grabbed Pauly and they sauntered with heads downcast to a small stand that sold meatball sandwiches. He purchased one and devoured it.

And then, above the music filling the air with vibrant sounds of emotion, and the loud pops of firecrackers filling the streets, he heard someone calling his name . . .

"Hey! Joe! Over here!" Sergio shouted.

As he looked up, Joe saw Sergio walking toward him. He was in the process of making rapid motions to tell Sergio to "hurry let's go," when he noticed three vaguely familiar faces on top of huge muscular bodies, roughly shoving people out of their way, in a beeline to Sergio. One of them looked over toward him and excitedly grabbed the guy next to him in recognition. At that very moment the scene of Tony's gaming house came to the forefront of Joe's mind . . . they were among the wiseguys at the job!

Desperately, Joe snatched Pauly around and pointed as he began yelling and jumping around to notify Sergio of the situation, but Sergio acted like he thought Joe was goofing off . . . Joe and Pauly started running toward him. Sergio stood there joking around while the trio gained several yards in their determination of evil intent.

"Sergio, watch out, turn around, they're almost behind you! Run! Run! Run!" Joe shouted at him as he picked up speed—but Sergio, making funny faces, remained where he was awaiting Joe's arrival.

Joe reached him just as the soldiers of the Hand were pulling black automatics from concealed leather holsters under their jackets.

BLAM! A shot rang out. Then another . . .

Sergio was hit before he realized the reapers were upon him.

Grabbing hold of Sergio's arm, Joe tripped the guy closest to them and pulled him along.

BLAM! BLAM! BLAM!

More shots rang out as Pauly and he ran, jerking side to side in effort to limit themselves as targets.

Through the crowd they pushed and shoved their way, until a pitch-black patch between the red bricks of the houses lining the street, offered escape.

Turning into the alleyway's darkness, they were rewarded with a false sense of vision-less safety. His feelings magnified through his fright of death, Joe squinted his eyes in tight cracks in order to keep a rage of threatening tears from bursting the dam; releasing pent-up waters in a flood of a long lost boyhood. With his breath on fire, he turned his attention to Sergio, who was steadily weakening in his arms as his life's blood poured with blackness upon a black ground in a black alleyway from his blackened heart. Right at that moment, Joe was faced with another reality: Sergio's blackened soul was doomed to a worse fate than that place he had once visited before.

Finally, pushing him to the ground, he groped for Pauly, whispering his name. No one answered him. As he crawled in the dark he stumbled across a limp figure!

Pauly was not moving.

Those tears that welled in his eyes, daring to burst forth and drench his soul, were diverted to anger once again! Desperately fighting a need to cry, he plunged forth from that alley of shame and death.

The crowd, seemingly unaware of the seven or eight shots which had been fired, nor of the situation of life and death underlying the Streets of Saints, was a maze of color and movement. With his back to the alley-way, stood one of the men who had fired the first shots. As he fought through the mass of bodies, Joe hit him in the back with a chair he wrenched from a vendor. He dropped instantly—due more to the shock of the unexpected blow than to injury—and his gun went careening down the street. Joe jumped upon the gun, picked it up, and aimed it at the prostrate man.

Chapter 52: Rescued by God

He caught a train and made it to Ditmars Boulevard, and from that most familiar place, a place full of memories of he and Pauly having a blast; of talking of what they would become; of friendship, and of boast, he trudged to his mothers house with his head down, as if in a dream.

It was near midnight, he knew his "friends" were home and, having had dinner with their folks, were now happily sleeping in their beds of comfort and dreams . . . while Pauly and Sergio lay upon the ground, in a filthy alley-way, stone-icy-cold; no comfort, no dreams, no pulse of the heart informing you that you yet are alive; with people walking their dogs, stepping all over them!

Sobbing internally, fear and dread viciously snapping at the remnants of his attitude of invincibility, he suddenly realized he had been more than simply lost . . . he had never been found!

"So, Oh Lord! Who was that child so long ago who prayed to you upon bended knees? Who asked and received? Who was it that looked upon that liquid encased battle between life and death, the one who had lived the lives of so many dreams . . . and nightmares. Yes! A series of lives . . . some which required sleeping in hallways and abandoned cars while the world slept in beds with blankets. Where did he belong? With his family? With the children of the street? In California and hippie land? With Nihanio and Lost Cloud? Barbie and Clyde? Pigny and Papa Joe? On a trawler, a dairy, pulling dirty old and rundown carpet off floors, painting city jails, lost in a swamp, in a reform school, a mental hospital . . . "or, Oh Lord, in my room . . . forever . . . condemned to pull that old suit of armor down—over and over!"

With an awful shout that reverberated off the ghostly buildings, Joe reached for the gun he had snatched off the ground at the feast and placed it at his head!

"Should I die on these filthy streets? My body to lie so people may walk their dogs over me like my father before me . . . and his . . . and his . . . and Serg's and Pauly's? I didn't shoot that man who killed my friends! Twice I couldn't take from another what was taken from me! What must I do? Where is the vision I desperately asked for so many times? Are you real? Do you live like Aggie said? Tell me, Father in heaven!"

Suddenly, looming in the shadow of his dreaded thoughts, a picture of sanctity, of cleansing powers, of hope and love . . . the strongest he had known in his life . . . a love of forgiveness swept clean his profane thoughts and he looked up to see the place that offered refuge so many times before: The Immaculate Conception Church. He knew he had to stop, that he must stop, even if only to say a prayer for those in the other place . . . a place one never returned from!

Though it was past midnight, the doors were wide open . . . beckoning. He mounted the warm and white stone steps and looked hesitantly into the sanctuary with hope; wishing the old priest who scolded them back when he robbed the poor boxes would appear and offer comfort to his tired mind.

As he entered, a soft, gentle breeze brushed the alter—causing candles to flicker in the darkness like the many stars which had lit the night skies in Pennsylvania; twinkling in hypnotic gesture, beckoning him to enter.

The Saints stood perched upon their thrones, silently viewing his every move, patiently waiting for him to defile their sanctuary. He walked into the chapel, made a sign of the cross, and proceeded quietly down the long lane between the ornate benches on either side.

When he reached the black, wrought iron railing that separated the alter—with its huge Christ Crucifixion—from the Cathedral, he knelt upon the red, velvet-lined knee board and felt like crying. He somehow knew that crying would begin the process of cleansing his heart and soul . . . and show his sorrow and penitence, but his attitude—or the evil internally battling for domination—demanded otherwise.

"Blasphemies . . . Blasphemies. Scream blasphemies," it demanded!

Twisting, tearing; his anger welled to his throat, choking him with its intensity: "Why?" he asked out loud. "Why did you take my father? What did they do to you? What! Now look what's happened! Why did you allow my father to be murdered? Why did you take him!"

A voice abruptly startled him . . . the words interrupting all thought . . . loud and clear . . . the chapel reverberating with the Lord's resounding voice, "I am your Father!"

. . . He was dumb-struck.

The words continued . . . "Jesus said that! Yes, my son, those were the words of Jesus. He declared for you. He died for you. He said he was your Father. Father to all His children! So, he did not take your father; for he *is* your Father!"

He turned just as a priest swept down the aisle in his black flowing robes. "What do you know? Huh?" Joe whined at him. "You all say things that aren't true! Where is He now? Why don't He come down and get rid of our problems? Why don't He do something?"

The priest put his arms around Joe's shoulders to comfort him. He told him a story Joe had heard many times before; the story of their Savior's last days on earth. He explained His last words and then he asked Joe if his troubles were as bad as His.

Joe did not answer him. He felt so bad. He had taken His love and help and stepped all over Him. It was then that the priest said, "Sometimes you must put aside your anger and let love into your heart. You have plenty of time to find your place and the reasons to His will. Don't you worry. Take the time to study all those around you, and you will discover many things. If you desire His intervention you must pray and leave your ways . . . leave your ways! Leave this city!"

The priest asked if Joe needed a place of refuge for a few days.

Joe replied he did not and that he was fine. He thanked him and he left . . . his mind twisting within its confusion. The priest had shared his love and patience at just the precise time Joe needed it . . . just like all of the other times . . . yet what about the world outside—the dead and the living, the pain and the sacrifice, the lost and the found. And what of his father? Had he lived, how different would his life truly have been?

A thought flashed through his mind, 'Would he have grown up like Tony Black; like Tommy?'

But the sorrow was something he knew he'd never forget: father and his last day on earth; his experiences thus far; his friends's deaths;

the fact he continued to place blame on his mother . . . when would it end?

Joe sat alone on a hard plastic seat in an empty car of the Queens express . . . one of his hands stained with the blood of Sergio and Pauly, the other holding a sack he had placed the money in—money he had been so determined to reap on the justification of revenge; of honor; of father and mother; of hate; on the pretext that life was going to be different. Death became the reaper of change, yes, death had become the difference in his life once again—only this time, it was his fault!

"Oh Lord . . ." he cried internally. "What have I done . . . I have killed someone's love and caused the death of others!"

Those tears that had welled within his eyes so many times, threatening to flow and release the agony of his heart; were released internally; rage erupted from within. He could not wash away his guilt. Oh! The agony of desperately wanting to cry and wash away his guilt, his sorrow, his impotency, his inadequacy to rectify his situation. His guilt was not of self-pity . . . it was of loss—both his and theirs! He did not know Sergio as a brother or as a long-time friend, but he had known him as a human being with hopes, dreams, and a life as hard as his. And Pauly? Pauly had been his only friend; his only true brother! He continued to hold his tears in check until he could not hold out any longer . . . they were consuming his very being.

As the train rambled down a long dark tunnel, screeching, screaming, laughing, flashing bursts of Lucifer's lightning along the way, Joe screamed to his God in Heaven to take him home!

Thrusting the sack through an open window, he released it and prayed that Jesus would take his guilt along with it. And then, a flash of bright, white light flooded his soul. An heredity of tears burst the dam of his legacy; flooding, washing, battling with the filth and grime that coated his life. In heaving torrents of rains of grief and sorrow, of pain and of agony, of his and all of theirs, they rushed forth draining . . . emptying . . . cleansing.

Part Six: The Spirit of God

IN THE YEAR OF THE BEAST, NINETEEN HUNDRED AND SIXTY-NINE

Built upon twelve layers of stone, each inlaid in succession with a separate type of gem stone—jasper-sapphire-chalcedony-emerald-sardonyx-sardus-chrysolite-beryl-topaz-chrysophrase-jacinth-ame thyst—were the walls of jasper 216 feet across. Within these walls, twelve gates, each formed from individual, massive pearls, stood wide open in invitation to the multitude of worshippers who were entering the Holy City. In the center of The Holy City, The Knight of Good, The Prince of God, He who carries the Scepter of Earth gathered his Angels in a room deep within His Father's Kingdom. With His Warriors assembled, an offensive was devised, "We have heard the prayers and tears this Earth Year of One Thousand, Nine Hundred and Sixty-Nine, A.D., which have electrified The Holy City. It is time to invest the reserves. Before we send our young apprentice on another quest of discovery; before we train, equip, and fortify him for his future battles; we must drop in on the Evil One."

Serus Jebilia, six-foot-eleven, with vocal cords made of steel; the greatest Warrior Orator of them all; stood up and enouraged the Warriors on their way to do Spiritual Battle against The Beast.

"Very few men . . . nor women for that matter, can meet her record of achievement and dedication to the Knight of Good Over Evil! For forty years, she has fought The Beast. For forty years, she warned of his existence. For forty years, people just laughed when ever her voice was raised in protest. Most of those who opposed her views are now in The Beast's Cavern of Eternal Suffering! We must continue our battle for our brothers and sisters who are being swept away like matchsticks in a raging river of blood and destruction! Are we to sit here and allow this insidious monster to continue on his way, oblivious to the rampant destruction of mother's souls standing as sacrifice for their children! Are we to forget those who have kept the faith while many sank into depravity! Are we to balk at the mere mention of quest, of battle, of sacrifice! Shall we allow those of ours on Earth to bicker amongst themselves as even this very moment millions are battling a swift current of suffering and trepidation! What do we care who gets the job accomplished as long as we realize victory! The final battle is close! The end of the War between Good and Evil will end with victory for Good! But will you taste that victory! Will you share that V-I-C-T-O-R-Y! Let us stuff The Beast's Demon Warriors into his belly as victory fodder! Are we not to rise, our shields of faith protecting our souls; our helmets of salvation assuring us ultimate victory . . . even in death! Are we not to raise our banners in the defense of the weak, the maimed, the suffering believers of the Word of God! Are we not the true brotherhood of the Almighty: The Knight of Good over Evil! Have not our ancestors battled The Beast to stalemate for 5000 years! Are we to forget their sacrifice! Are we? Do I hear you! Rise, you sons of God and defend Him that knows all . . . to victory! To victory! Rise up and shout His name!"

Five thousand Warriors were standing, cheering as one, the cries of jubilation resounding off the walls of the mammoth chamber! And then, from one lonely mouth, began the Oath of Allegiance . . . and then, everyone, with all their heart and mind, joined in . . . "

"I am with Him. I, a Warrior of The Order of The Knight of Good over Evil, sit round the table of man, ready to do Battle. Oh, Hear me, Knight of Darkness! I am here! Ready! A protector of the weak! A deliverer of the Mighty Word of God! I shan't turn my cheek to thee! Only the side of my Blade of Wrath shall I give to thee! I shall cast thy demons out and into the fiery pits of hell!"

"Hear me, Men of God, Warriors of The Faith," Serus bellowed once more, "I have done all things with Him in my heart. I have done all things with the knowledge that He sheds a tear in his love and sorrow for so many of His that have been swept into the abyss of living death! He has given all the power of Choice, Dominion, and Reason! He has done so because He loved us. It is time to rise and bring the Battle to The Beast once more! It is time to deliver destruction to The Beast's Demon Warriors! It is time to cast his Demon Brigades off the face of the earth! Even as I speak, our Great and Honorable, Captain Warrior Nihanio, gathers with seventeen of our finest Warriors for an attack that will set the pace of things to come! The Beast shall toss in his Cavern tonight! He will move his rage onto his own! He will snatch the very skulls of many of his leaders of the Red Forward Warriors of The Devil's Brigade! You hear me my brothers! That is the way of The Beast! That is the weakness of The Knight of Darkness and Evil! We can and will defeat him because his ways are not our ways! He revels in death and suffering. His mind sees any defeat and suffering as enjoyment! As reason to take and take and take! He receives pleasure for the suffering of others—especially the suffering of those who think they are immune because they are his own Lieutenants and Captains!! I say, let us give him his true enjoyment!

Epilogue

Chilly, silken rivulets rain
and break the bound
by their chains
those tears of sorrow
loss and shame
began the dawn
and swept the pain . . .

Joe dropped into the city for one day to visit his mother; the entire affair lasted one hour before he decided to leave before Loui got home or someone heard he was back. Jeanette was happy to see him but spent most of the time begging him to be careful when he left.

After he left, he made an attempt to locate Aggie . . . but he did not have enough time; she had moved. And now, two-hundred miles south of the city, tired and hungry, Joe was in deep thought once again: of his family; of his ancestors; of his future.

Joe's quest had changed once more, yet he knew he had a Father in the Heavens, someone who would continue to watch over him during the tribulations of discovery that lay ahead. He realized many journeys, many trials, many experiences, many tests of faith awaited him, on this, his newest quest: one of the ending of The Curse!

Though doubts would arise—for this he knew from experience—he would continue to journey in search of discovery knowing in his heart that God would one day answer him. Yes, experience had taught him what faith could accomplish . . . but, are faith and fate intertwined? Do they exist as opposing forces? Could fate have decided his life long before he was born? Attempting to block these nagging questions, he briefly thought of his last days in New York a year ago . . .

He had called his mother, but she refused to take the call. He wound up riding the train to Aggie's house. Poor Aggie—now entwined within The Curse of Alphonso—was still glad to see him. She had decided to have the baby in a home for un-wed mothers; then give the baby up for adoption. They spoke of the future, but they both knew Joe had to leave again; at least until the heat died down. He and Aggie spent several days exploring Central Park for the final time. During those brief days, as if they were the only people in the world, the park became theirs and only theirs. With Bianco's assistance, a rumor began that Ball and Jolly (with full knowledge of Tony Black) had recovered the thirty thousand bucks and rid the city of all evidence of the culprits! They say, the streets can both deliver truth and remit retribution.

When it was time to go, he called a trucker he had met and secured a ride to New Mexico and new places and adventures beyond. He remembered the bright, sunny day, when the tractor-trailer pulled up: a brief kiss and hug and he was up and in the cab—a forlorn Aggie, brilliant torch-red hair blowing in the breeze as he huffed and puffed down the road.

. . . and now, once again, Joe stood upon some dusty gravel beside a quiet, black-top road concentrating all of his powers against the perpetual silence . . . as if on cue, a soft, distant sound pierced the still air. Louder and louder it grew; closer and closer it came until finally, the sound became a roar and two tons of steel and rubber hurtled around the bend—heading directly towards him!

Prepared for a war of minds, he clenched his fist, extended his right arm perpendicular to his worn and tired body, and willed each finger's energy to that lone, fleshy part of his body: the thumb.

Callused by winds of time; chapped and peeling from continual exposure to the sun's rays; bruised by endless opening and closing of car doors; it remained strong and determined, an emblem of his faith. Joe's only certainty was in his faith. He knew that faith was something that remained forever in a state of living, perpetual growth. As long as you have faith, all of life's roadblocks will soon become insignificant. Words such as hunger, pain, and the sleepless agony of life's desperate journeys would evaporate—replaced by opportunity. Though lately, tired, hungry, and alone, he began once more to question that faith. As he had so many times in his life, he asked for a sign of God's will.

Looking up toward the sky, he shouted a prayer with all of his remaining strength, "Show me once more your power, Oh Lord! Stop this car and deliver to me, a ride and something to eat!"

In battle stance, his thumb pointed toward the south as he faced north toward the sharp bend in the road, he saw the approaching car with a determination matching that of his thumb. It was written upon his face—as if he could will the two-ton hulk of moving steel into disobeying its master by pulling over on its own!

The vehicle rounded the bend and began to slow down as it advanced toward him. Joe summoned his waning resources, "Come on! Stop! . . . STOP!"

The brown and white sedan slowed even further.

His heart jumped with expectation, "Is he going to stop? Where is he going? Who is he? Where would the ride take me?"

The vehicle passed him and began pulling over; he could clearly see three young men waving frantically for him to hurry, "Come on! Come on!" They shouted as they came to a stop one-hundred feet ahead of him. Dragging his old companion and best friend—a muddy-green, army duffle bag, behind him—Joe began to half-run, half-limp toward the waiting car.

They shouted for him to hurry. With his heart pounding so loud he could hear it, Joe reached deep and wrested the energy to continue.

"Only fifty feet left," he urged himself.

The car stood still, engine rumbling, exhaust spewing, brake lights glaring; contorted, shouting faces cheering him on; a jumble of hands and arms mish-mashed in movement, beckoning him further.

"Just a short distance left, you can make it!" he said to himself.

"Only a few feet, come on!" Three pairs of lips mouthed.

Joe reached out . . . touched the rear panel . . . he made it! He made it! And then . . .

"Sucker! Hah! Hah! Suckerrrrr . . ." Strange voices called out in unison as the sedan took off in a cloud of dust, leaving Joe to fall into a lump of rage and exhaustion.

He sat on his duffel bag praying. Six hours had passed, and other than those three teens, not a single car, truck, or bus had zoomed by! He felt like shouting his anger and blame at God . . . but he knew in his heart that it was not His fault. He continued to believe that God would come down to earth, wrest the steering wheel from some unsuspecting driver, and steer him to his feet. Hadn't he before? Or had he? Was it Him or not . . . Was it fate? . . . Or faith! When would his faith conquer his doubts? So much doubt; on so many roads; on so many rides; in so many places.

Joe had become the perpetual wanderer. Coated with dust and perspiration, a hunger of spirit gnawing his perplexed mind; while hunger of the physical kind growled deep in the pit of his stomach. Like many believers, when situations seemed desperate and the answers were not immediate, he'd question his faith. With plenty of time to question, he'd invent all of the answers—which would lead to the very invention of the questions! A confusing predicament at the very least.

"Why'd you leave in the first place?"

"I had no choice!"

"Why'd you have no choice?"

"Because God gave me no choice!"

"But God did give you free will and you chose to look for more choices!"

"That's confusing. If He gave me choice, where are they?"

"He gave you the option of choosing which road to take!"

"But who designs the road? Who determines which road will lead to what place?"

"You decide where the road will lead and you decide which place you will go to!"

"Hold on a minute . . . if I decide which road to take and where it will lead me, then why am I still searching for the right road?"

"Maybe you chose wrong!"

"I did . . . ?"

On and on the questions and answers would begin to revolve within his mind until they would occur without interruption, continual . . . even in his sleep: "Listen, God, I know you are there in Heaven where it's cool and there are no worries . . . or are there? . . . are there worries in heaven? Is that it? No, it can't be! Or could it? Well, anyway, I have faith in you. You rescued me so many times I can't recall them all. I need another favor. 'My body is hot and my mind seeks your kind intervention . . . and friendship!'

The road remained silent. No answers cried out—no intervention. So he resumed his thoughts. 'Why am I here? For what purpose?

When will I discover the meaning of my life?'

"You are here because you chose to be and right now that is your purpose! You will find further purpose when you choose to!"

Joe sighed. His conversation with himself reminded him of Abbot and Costello doing their "Who's on first" routine—would it ever make any sense? Noticing waves of heat rippling off the black pavement, he stretched out his arm, picked up a thin, dead branch, and tested its surface—the asphalt road was soft enough to depress with the stick, so he wrote upon its surface: "God was here—but I was not . . . Joe." He turned and tossed the stick.

Immediately, a cocoon of dry, hot air blanketed his body and his body's defenses began to cloak him in a blanket of sweat. Salty beads of perspiration formed upon his brow until it collected into huge rivulets that tumbled down his face, down his back, down his legs, immersing him, cooling him . . . depleting him.

With a dirt-caked sleeve, he wiped his forehead and felt the rough texture leave imprints in chaffed red upon his face. Thoroughly exhausted, his body signaling in desperation for fluids and rest, Joe collapsed upon his duffel bag in an awkward, lonely, position.

Roaring down the road, the '57 Chevy answered its master's every touch: a gentle movement of hands upon the steering wheel and it negotiated sharp, winding curves with precise, immediate response—zoom it went, roar it barked, passing all in predetermined fashion.

In starched, white cotton shirt, and bell bottom blue jeans, the driver sat comfortably in control within his climate-controlled atmosphere. He had one well-heeled-black-velvet-side-zip boot planted firmly on the floor board, the other pressed upon the accelerator as he tooled along.

As the Chevy raced against a never-ending series of dots, dashes, and double lines painted in faded shades of yellow and white, the driver rounded a turn and spied a crumpled figure lying amid what seemed to be an old, muddy green, duffle bag. His foot came off the accelerator and hit the brake pedal. The Chevy acknowledged the command with a screech as it pulled over to the side of the road.

The driver had stopped instinctively, not because he felt he should, but because he saw what looked like a green duffle bag . . . could it be?

He opened the door to a rush of hot air that swept the breath from his lungs. "Boy, it's hot," he said out loud as he placed his feet upon the hot, soft tar. Arising to his six foot height, he looked down, and read the inscription gouged in the surface of the road.

A sudden feeling came over him as he approached the familiar looking body . . . the excited driver began shaking Joe with both hands in a "come-on-get-up" way.

"Joe, wake up, wake up . . . Come on, wake up!" he said while actually lifting Joe's body up and violently shaking him back and forth.

Joe awoke feeling like he had entered the gates of hell in the midst of an earthquake. His head was spinning within a tornado of heat and pain. His vision reduced to a hazy mist of colors and shadows. Through blunted senses he could hear a voice.

'Whose voice is that?' he thought as he peered intently into the shrouded apparition. 'Is that you, God, . . . or . . . it cannot be . . . the devil?' . . . No, it was a familiar, earthly voice . . .

Hands suddenly reached out, roughly lifted him, and placed him onto a cool, dry, comfortable seat in a vehicle of some kind. It felt so good Joe briefly wondered if a chariot of God would have air conditioning!

"You just sit there, Joe, and I'll drive you to a hospital," a familiar voice commanded as the stranger turned the key in the ignition, causing the car's engine to leap to life. Joe was jammed into the seat cushion by the force of the Chevy as it launched itself like a missile out of a chute.

Over the roar of the engine as it wound out, and the sound of rock and gravel being sprayed by squealing tires across the roadside like bullets from a Thomson machine gun, Joe's focus began to slowly return and he saw an outline of a face, also vaguely familiar—he was sure the stranger who stopped by the road to assist him had blue eyes, a strong, solid chin, and long, rich, golden hair. Like Thor—the comic book hero—driving a souped up Chevy. He attempted to say something like, "I'm alright," but a dry, tasteless feeling had invaded his mouth, choking all attempts at speech; his vocal cords, strung as taunt as violin strings, would not respond . . . even a thanks would have to wait until his body recognized that safety was at hand and began its rejuvenation. In the meantime, he'd thank God for the reprieve.

The Chevy tooled along at a high rate of speed, three-hundred-and-fifty horses of souped up engine humming with glee, radio set to a local top-forty station spitting out verbal messages of societies ills.

Joe drifted off . . . a surreal world of bright lights and coordinated confusion greeted Joe as an assortment of attendants rushed him, strapped tightly to the transport gurney, directly into a private bay where doctors and nurses began their diagnostic process in determination of his condition. Standing over Joe, a concerned doctor gave orders for a liter of glucose to be brought down.

"Start the IV! I need vital signs and ice-packs . . . NOW! he commanded. With a crowd of white, starched, uniformed attendants performing their appointed duties, he turned toward Joe, whose check-up had indicated severe sun-burn, heat exhaustion, and dehydration. He ordered Joe be kept overnight for observation; a room was assigned him.

Joe awoke the following morning. He felt like he had been tackled by the entire Oakland Raiders football team. With private grunts and groans he made it out of the bed and into the lavatory. He was welcomed by a severely swollen and sun-burnt face when he viewed himself in the mirror.

"Thank you God for watching over me," he praised, and then turned, limping back to the bed.

"How are you doing, young man?" a cheerful nurse greeted him as she entered the room with her hands full of gadgets to test, prompt and inform him.

"I'm doing great, just hurt here and there. How did I get here?" he asked.

"The young man that brought you in, is in the lobby. We will let him know you're awake," she replied as she placed a rubber sleeve around his arm. "Your blood pressure is fine, you should be able to leave in a few hours. I want you to eat your breakfast and get dressed. O.K.?"

"Thank you, I will," he answered as thoughts of the stranger began coming back to him.

"Did God save me because I have faith?" he asked himself.

At that moment a knock at the door interrupted Joe's thoughts.

"Well, well, well. Check you out! A $%$#^%$ Indian!"

"Pauly!" Joe exclaimed, is that you, you bum?"

"Who did you think it was . . ."

"Pauly! Pauly! It's so good to see you! I didn't think I'd ever see you again! I thought you died!"

"Cool it, Joe . . ." Pauly said, " . . . we don't want my visit to screw your release up! We gotta go to Georgia yet!"

"But, how did . . ."

"Heck, I just, like, got a shoulder wound and went into shock. My pops got me out of trouble, said I was just going to the feast and had given you guys a ride. I heard you was visiting, it was all over the neighborhood, jumped in the car and scooted south . . . talk about luck . . ."

"Yo! Check it out," Joe replied, "it wasn't luck . . . "

Joe recovered, and for the next two years, up until he went into the armed forces, he traveled the country with Pauly; they journeyed the land together, experiencing many situations of difficulty and faith, but through it all, through thick and thin, they knew God traveled with them.

There Is Life After Death!

Jeanette's story ended last night; seven days after the birth of my second daughter—born a tiny, wriggling, joyful bundle of life—I carried my mother's heart by naming her Jeanette.

You've heard the story, you know I felt I had been the black sheep of my family since I was born with club feet. And even though, Jeanette, had demonstrated her love and care, I blamed her—along with the world—for what I conceived as my personal misfortune. And when, at eight years of age, my father was murdered in gangland style and my family thrust into a world of poverty and inequity, I began to question the meaning of life, love, truth, and family. Finally, embarrassment of my condition and situation begat a lasting fear of discovery.

At eleven years of age, in desperation for answers, I ran away from home on a quest that would take me on a road that covered every nook and cranny of human endeavor and situation—right and wrong! Contact with my family became few and far in between; besides a once yearly call to Angela, they all but vanished! I hid my heredity, my legacy, my family, in that file marked, "Accident:Personal." I changed my name and created a fable. I created a family and placed them on father-figured thrones of marbled thought and dream!

After a series of disasters and broken relationships, I married and the union produced two beautiful children, Danielle and Jeanette. Though the curse continued to affect me, by the time my second daughter was born—seven years after the first—I began to see and understand the true nature and greatness of a mother's labors. I searched that file deep in my mind for stories I'd tell these lovely children of my own mother; one kept coming to the forefront of my mind . . . I had a special Jeanette-story instilled deep in my heart, of the message that the power of my heart, feelings, and touch were brimming with M.A.G.I.C.; bringing warmth and happiness to others—which in turn became mirrors reflecting that power ten-fold.

I recalled it as her greatest lesson: "You must learn that just to speak these words and not feel them in your heart denies the power they possess—they become words of jest . . ." The emotion and power of this story at the very moment of little Jeanette's birth, made me think of my mother, like I never had before . . .

"Hello, Angie? Hey, how's it going? We've been blessed with another daughter! Named her after mom . . ."

"Joe, listen, mom's in the hospital. She's really sick. She has cancer! I think you should forget your feelings and think of hers. You should come down."

. . . A year previous to my call, Jeanette had begun her battle with cervical cancer. For the first six months she underwent chemotherapy and looked and acted as if the cancer would become just another of the mishaps she had overcome with her robust tenacity. After all, was she not a veteran of wounded survival, her heart pumping in perpetual purple?

Yes, she survived much: a lonely, fatherless childhood, where she was shuttled among relatives . . . paying her dues by scrubbing floors and making beds—none of her own; survived her father's death and a mother's abandonment; and then the brutal murder of the only other person who she truly loved: my father, her lover, a man who used fists as talk, a gangster who left her with four children who were little more than tots in shorts.

My mom had survived the worst of poverty and inequity, where "one house dress and 'baloney' survival" ruled her life. She had survived the pain of a son who was born with club feet, and endured five more years of pain as she wondered if that son would ever walk. She survived the worry for her sons, who followed in their father's footsteps, disappearing for months —and eventually for years on end. Though my mom had few lessons in love, through the haze of my childhood memories, I could always recall her devotion, care, and belief in God. In fact, from birth to Communion in the Immaculate Conception, Catholic Church, in Queens, New York, my mom made sure she instilled a path to God in me. Though I vanished for months on end in my battle of wills, it was that most spectacular gift of God that enabled me to survive some of the most horrific situations imaginable.

You see, my mom was the sort of woman who mastered all with an indifference towards hardship. A five-foot battering ram, mom would rumble her heavy frame through all obstacles—real or imagined. She had survived for fifty years based upon her belief in God and an innate ability to hide her sorrow in His robes. "His strength," she would say, "allows me to strive with every last drop of God-given energy."

I was shocked to hear she had cancer and was in a hospital. I believed she would overcome this set-back. I hastily packed my family and traveled to Miami where my family had relocated. We arrived at the hospital ten hours later on a rainy, windswept day . . .

Entering the sliding doors to the hospital, I asked directions to the intensive care wing and then found an elevator that would take us to the third floor and destiny.

Hospitals . . . Oh, how I hated them! When I was a child I spent an enormous amount of time in brightly lit sterile corridors of freezing cold tile and stainless steel. Just entering the close confines of an elevator, with white-uniformed attendants at elbow's end, brought a revival of my memories of isolation and terror—the sort of isolation and terror that induces a perpetual fear of sickness. The sensation of the hospital, the elevator, and those starched, linen troops, reminded me once more of a fact of my life, a fact that led to another of my "fibs," namely; I didn't go to doctors because I was a man. Exiting the elevator, my family and I were greeted by a stern and foreboding sign, notifying us that we had entered the: "INTENSIVE CARE WARD—-SILENCE PLEASE!".

I made my way to the nurse's station and saw Angela, eyes red and misty, looking like that day so long ago when I awoke to find her seated in the rubble of her own dreams.

We talked for more than a half-hour before I asked where our mother's room was, and, before Angela could tell me, without a glance, several quiet, pink-chilled hands raised above the counter and pointed in unison toward a large glassed-in room with several occupied beds. I asked my wife and children to wait with Angela at the station and walked toward the room. As I approached, I saw one group of white-uniformed, squeaky-soled attendants sitting deep in their own thoughts, and another group scurrying about on familiar errands. My mental file, the one marked "Accident:Personal," exploded into a series of rapid, visual, motion picture movements . . .

'Nihanio . . . dressed as a Dream Catcher . . . holding a picture book of lost and forgotten memory . . . whose memory was he holding . . . is that mine? . . . Mother's? . . . did those things occur? Is that mother holding me . . . in the hospital . . . tears flowing down her cheeks . . . begging doctors for help . . . Bianco . . . is that you? Why are you standing within a cloud of moving pictures ? . . . is that mother crying? . . . Family? I see family . . . Ginny . . . Robert . . . Aggie . . . Diane . . .

Gail . . . Pauly . . . Father . . . Sergio . . . what are you . . . family . . . they are family . . . pictures-rapid-in motion!

Three sets of white-uniformed hands raised me from the floor. 'Why off the floor?' Angela, nurses . . . "I'm all right . . . I AM ALL RIGHT!"

I shooed away the concerned mob and walked back to the station and approached her door. Stopping for a moment, I put the remnants of my fragmented thoughts into series, added Angela's information, and pulled a mental switch . . . a vivid picture began to roll . . .

She was born to continuance: alone, lonely, desperate, wanting change, desiring a father, a father figure, a family, embarrassment, journey, forget, deny, change, opportunity.

She rushes for love and family, never completing school; a debonair man named Joe-Pep sweeps her off her feet with three piece suits, brim-feathered fedoras, and diamond pinkie rings. His swaggering, boastful attitude, and flashy bank-rolls speak of unlimited opportunity. He appears as a 'Knight in Shining Armor' whose battle dress consists of a trench coat and .45; ready to rescue a damsel in distress . . . She became that damsel . . . and in short order gives birth to three boys, one girl, and a heap of visions of things she never had.

Her visions of a happy, God-fearing family, with a caring husband and father, and a lively, lovely, bunch of school loving children, who would one day become doctors, lawyers, businessmen and women; are dashed in one terrible instant. Joe-Pep enjoys playing in the fast lane until one night in 1961, in his restaurant on 81st Street in Manhattan. The traffic catches up to him in the form of seventeen, copper-clad slugs. A vicious tornado sweeps her peaceful village on the shores of life in the dead of night. She awakens to a heap of rubble swept by tides of memory; a life of drifting sands blown hither and dither regardless of want or desire.

Left an uneducated mother with four children, all her life was spent cleaning other folk's houses and taking care of other folk's worries; menial positions were struggle, long hours and minimum wage were synonymous. Yet, her ideals and faith in God continued to occupy her every moment's thought and action.

Eventually, she discovers her children have grown up, married, and are well on their way to being successful and self-sufficient; she decides to attend a job career seminar sponsored through a government grant. She graduates a program teaching low income citizens various careers.

She proudly displays a certificate—notifying all—she is a genuine nurses aid. But irony and the curse of continuity rules her world: after living in slum after slum were she struggles alone to raise her children; after finally seeing her children on their way to successful independence; after completing a rigorous six month training program at fifty-six that promises her own independence; she begins her career assigned a position in a prestigious hospital only to be struck down with disease . . . and now is a patient in the very hospital she had recently been employed in.'

. . . Oh, how proud she must have looked, standing in her starched, white uniform, holding her fancy diploma with its colorful calligraphy . . . as if she had attained a doctorate degree . . . and, when I thought about it, I realized she already had a doctorate . . . on ending The Curse of Alphonso!

At that precise moment, I knew she had traveled my road long ago—I was but repeating her journey, and her mother's journey . . . and so on! Yes, the Curse, in full bloom of perennial revival.

Turning into the room, I was greeted by an unfamiliar picture. "Mom?" I asked. Can this be the large, happy woman who was the champion in the ring of life? Her frail bones and loose, wrinkled flesh draped the bed like a hundred-year-old worn quilt; its once supple down peeking in ragged tufts through ruptured seams—only its faded color and design left to prompt recognition. I was stunned! Mom was but a mere, rough sketch of my memory. Her eyes were tightly shut . . . a grim red slash replaced her once plump lips that had planted many a tender kiss upon my cheeks in the hour of my needs . . . they trembled. Was it with hope? Fear? Or were they in rhythm with the memories of her dreams?

Silent and furtive, as if attempting to locate my seat after arriving late to a theater of life, I approached her bed. Oh! How I desperately desired to rescue her . . . to reach out and hug her . . . to lift her back into the real world of life and love with her favorite saying, "it's gonna be alright" . . . but I feared awakening her—for I knew, at that precise moment in time, this parody of life and death would reveal itself as to what it truly was . . . REALITY!

The impact of my sudden awakening to life's frailty jolted those guarded questions; questions clutched deep within the mind, only to be released after life teeters over the brink of death's abyss: 'Had I ever told her I loved her? Had I become what she envisioned? Was she happy in her thoughts with my endeavors? Did she truly know that I placed no blame upon her for my misfortunes of life . . .only joy in my fortunes?'

Questions ruled my thoughts once more. They built upon each other until my mind was a frenzy of unanswered questions which I knew would haunt me to my last breath. And then, as if God was shouting to me: "My son, you are blessed with the miracle of second chance . . . you have the time and opportunity to tell her of your thoughts!" My mind traversed an invisible link in thought with hers and her eyes suddenly opened in recognition, revealing an internal light, energized and dynamic; clear, sharp and undivided by her battle with her pain and hope. A smile broadcast through the interference of her sunken cheeks and tore asunder my emotions . . . My arms instinctively reached out for familiar ground and touched more than the leavings of her physical being; they touched that very sacred portion of her existence: her very soul and spirit.

Electrified, I was immersed in the waters of eternal emotion. A thunderstorm welled the core of my being, threatening to burst forth and release my personal fears of pain, death and sorrow. But, I would not open that dammed up raging flood lest it cause her, in turn, to join my river of tears; I was sure a lop-sided victory would ensue, where the soothing of my emotions would come at the expense of her few remaining precious drops of life's sustaining liquids. I forced myself to batten down the hatches of my trembling emotions and sailed, full-blown, into that rare, incredible port of destiny, where life flowed on the edge of death.

"Mother, I love you—you know I love you—I've always loved you—you have given me so much—I'm so proud of you—I have brought Pat, Danielle, and a new baby—your namesake—we named her Jeanette—after you—she's a spitting image of you—you have to see her." I blurted my stream of thought in an instant of both apprehension and joy.

Her eyes glistened with droplets of twinkling lights as her smile intensified in joyful acknowledgment and recognition that her son, Joe, had returned; and her little boy had become a father himself!

The angry, grim red slash, violently etched upon her face earlier, was temporarily vanquished along with her pain. In that humbling moment, I could feel a transformation and bonding of our souls through our mutual love and understanding. For so long, we had been at odds; each one of us believing that the other did not care . . . and now, with the beginnings of one life and the ending of another, we were drawn together in a mixture of joy and grief.

Forced to withdraw—lest I comment of her impending future—I kissed her and said I was going to get my family. I then turned in my haste at composure and sauntered through the door in a show of false bravado. After telling my wife about my mom's condition, the first thing she asked, was if it was rational for us to allow Danielle, who was seven, to see her in such a state. This sensible question did not require much forethought on my part, for I immediately recalled the morning of my father's funeral.

"Oh, my poor father . . . If only I had the chance to have told him I loved him. "

Informing my wife of my decision, I began explaining to my daughter Danielle that Grandma Jean was sick and to my best ability illustrated what had occurred so she could understand and tell Grandma Jean she loved her. Grasping Danielle's hand, we shuffled our way into the room.

It was clear that my decision had been the correct one. Danielle's delicate voice and genuine love radiated throughout the room. She asked Grandma Jean why she was so sick, and soon, Mom and Danielle were talking and laughing away.

I was so proud of this child of God, who looked beyond the mere physical attributes of this sick woman and into her heart. After ensuring the oldest daughter went first in conversation, I presented Jeanette.

Jeanette summoned her reserves of strength and reached out to hold this newborn child in her arms. As if her bed was bathed in the light of the innocence of a summer's dawn, I could see and feel the warmth and pride that mom felt in knowing her hard work and determination had planted the seeds which bloomed this abundant life—life that bore her very blood . . . cleansed of all continuity of a bygone era! Yes! Even cleansed of the Curse of Great, Great, Grandfather Alphonso! After thirty minutes, I gathered the girls and escorted them from the room and then returned alone.

As I entered the room, it was apparent Mom had been crying; her eyes were moist and red; and she swiftly crumpled a tissue into a ball, concealing it in the closed palm of her hand—I was sure it was not a matter of dignity, as much as her desire not to elicit a tirade of tears, which would impact upon the joy this visit had created. I sat next to her and held her hand. As I summoned the courage to humble myself by informing her of all the feelings I'd held within my heart for so long, she hushed me.

"Listen to me," she began. "I know how you feel. I know what you have gone through. I also know that you have matured and realize the struggles we all went through. You do not have to tell me anything . . . your visit has proven your love and understanding. God has blessed me by allowing us this extra time to share this moment. I just ask of you one favor. "

"Oh, mom you will be . . ." I began, but she interrupted me once more.

"All I ask is that you and your brothers and sister stay together. Do you hear me? Because family is so important . . . and I want you to raise those children in God's sight! I am very happy you named your beautiful child after me. I am proud you have become a young man. I am proud your daughter Danielle is a 'princess.' These things have demonstrated your concern and the fact that my life has not been in vain. I am tired now and must rest. Please, do not worry or pain for me. I have seen my wishes come true. I shall rest tonight like I have never rested before. I shall rest knowing that God has at last answered my eternal prayer. Now, you must go and take care of your family. Go get them something to eat, and some rest. I am sure they are tired."

With that said, I reached out and held her in my arms, kissed her, and thanked her for being my mother. In a few minutes she was in a deep, exhausted sleep.

Later that evening, while my family and I were sleeping at my brother Eddy's home, in Ft. Lauderdale, Florida, mom passed away. Angela had agreed to stay by her side that night. And, it was with an amazing exuberance, that temporarily shrouded her sorrow in a cloak of mystery, that she told me what had happened.

"Mom woke late that night," she began. "She seemed unaware I was by her side. She opened her eyes, smiled, and, as if she were viewing another entity in the room, said in a clear, sharp, voice, "I'm ready to go." Then, she closed her eyes, and left this mortal earth."

Up until Mom's passing away, I'd forgotten how to forgive, I'd forgotten how to love, I had forgotten how to cry. Shedding a tear was like squeezing water from the desert's sands. I had been taught to be "a man of respect . . . and men did not cry."

Many a tear of revelation has since fallen upon the yellowed pages of my life, quenching a thirst as dry as that desert's sands. Seeds of destruction, sown so long ago, once nourished by forgiveness, have blossomed the bouquet of truth I desperately strove to uncover. You've got to look beyond the transparencies of this mortal life if you seek truth—I had.

Through the truth gracing these pages, I've had the pleasure of a heavy burden lifted: no fear, no embarrassment, only happiness for a quest that had taken me three-hundred-and-sixty-degrees . . . back to my roots. A journey which began with death and ended with what seemed like death; but where life became death's bouquet.

Oh! How sweet and fragrant His blossom's ring. They shout their beauty in the colors of His deeds. They spread their roots into the fertile minds of His youth. They spring forth on the most windswept, dark-cast, winters day, to shower my family and I with care, love and hope.

Through God, my mom became the quintessential hybrid mom of moms; providing her remaining green leaf of energy as fodder for our minds, souls, and futures. One small child, born to more than mere name and continuance—my family and I know, for we have crept her vines of endless love, we have quenched our thirsts in her heart of forgiven streams, we have discovered much through this simple woman who, through her ultimate faith in God, delivered her very wishes, visions and dreams.

My life began anew at the revelations coinciding with my mother's death. I was reborn in the eyes of Jesus Christ and began to comprehend my duties and the gifts given me from God through my journeys . . . and the sacrifice and prayer of that 'Knight in Shining Armor' who had touched my heart and soul in secrecy: A Woman of the Curse of Alphonso—a true warrior who battled her war to victory's profound legacy: Many times must we birth our children: First, from the womb, where nourishment means more than the substances of our bellies—vast amounts of love, compassion, and understanding must be portioned with our repast. Second, we must birth our children with forgiveness and education to overcome and persevere. Thirdly, and most importantly, we must birth our children with the gift of God, planting His seeds of hope, protection, and prayer. And finally, we must strive to teach them through our experiences—lest the winds of continuance blow their dreams to shreds . . . for the absence of what may seem but a few words can alter our futures. We must never wait again until life tumbles into death's abyss.

Thus, the frail woman's life ended and another began . . ."

A Woman, A Wife, A Mother, A Grandmother, A Friend

Was the trembling of your lips —so slight
A manifest of earthly, cowered might
When death announced itself that day
With wind and rain and banished ray?
And when you rose unto the gates
Assisted by the wings of faith
Did you fear the golden light
In all its glory . . .
. . . So searing and bright?
Did you worry . . . For within the book
Your name was absent—or mistook
For someone else who never cared
A life thus ended, so unfair?
Were you astonished when trumpets blared
And joyous voices joined in prayer
Welcoming your yearning, tired soul
. . . from a life so often cold
For God knew your heart: like a soft, summers' sun—
Showering all with its radiance; its warmth;
Its glowering remembrance
. . . invigorating.

For God knew your touch: like a cool, gentle,
mountain stream:
Clean; Clear; Providing—
Coursing through the lives of all who passed . . .
. . . Sweeping; . . .Altering; . . .Purifying.
For God knew you: as essential as a newborn's
first breath of air;
As beneficial as springtimes first drop of rain;
As lasting as time itself!
To all who wandered by—Needing, Feeling, Hurting-
You were a well of life.
Your motto:
"If you are thirsty . . .
Drink . . ."
. . . Touching them with your compassion
. . . Understanding
. . . And truth
So put aside your haunting fears . . .
. . . For even God and HIS ANGELS have shed a tear . . .

Appendix

Rocky (Joe)—Though Joe maintained contact and shared his love with his family since the passing of his mother, the Curse was not truly broken until 1993. Currently residing in Atlanta, Georgia, he is now happily married and was blessed with a baby girl (Juliana Ariel was born free of continuation at the time of the completion of this book, 8-19-96). He is President of The Lighthouse Sanctuary for Youth Foundation (a non-profit foundation dedicated to assisting youth) and L.I.G.H.T.S. (Lighthouse International Giving Hope Through Sanctuary), an organization dedicated to ending continuity through the Empowerment of those whom desire change through training and opportunity. [770) 982-0467].

Carmine (brother)—single, Ph.D., writer, speaker, currently living in Atlanta where he operates a private practice engaged in Neuro-Linguistic Programming; helping others overcome their fears.

Angela (sister)—a happily married and accomplished business woman; currently resides in Hollywood, Florida where she is a mortgage broker.

Eddy (brother)—accomplished restauranteur and business man; happily married with two beautiful children—free of the Curse of Continuation—currently residing in Ft. Lauderdale, Florida.

Uncle Eddy—retired and living in upstate New York.

Nana Lou—89, continues to play the piano at retirement clubs and organizations in Hollywood, Florida.

Uncle Franky—91, resides in Virginia,

Joe-Pep—Murdered in New York

Uncle Carmine—Murdered in New York

Grandpa Jimmy—Murdered in Chicago

Great Grandpa Antonio—Murdered by the torture of time and events.

Great, Great Grandpapa Alphonso—Died of a stroke caused by the revelation of facts at a sit-down.

Aunt Connie—Died of a heart attack caused by obesity in the summer of 1982.

Sonny Black—Currently resides in a federal penitentiary.

Tony Black—A gangland murder ended his life.

Fritz (Ball)—Died after a long bout with cancer (The devouring beast of cancer reckoned to stay with him for a few years!)

McDonough (Jolly)—Died of a heart attack in 1976.

Joe-Pag—Died of throat cancer.

Sally—A gangland murder ended his life.

Jack the Cat—Found beaten to death with a plastic bag wrapped aroiund his head in South Florida.

The Animal and the Boss—Currently serving life sentences in a Florida prison.

Shorty—Died peacefully, yet his relatives were left without a dime; they never could find any cash, deeds, stocks, or any other form of wealth—seems he hid it in fear of losing it in a fire or something, and never trusted anyone!

Gina—(Anne you know who you are!) Owns and operates a bar in Queens, NY . . . still gardening.

Aggie—Married, three children, currently resides in Queens in NYC.

Pauly—Married, currently resides and owns a carpet business in NYC.

Pete (NY)—Died from an overdose.

Donny and Danny—Reside in NY, both married with strong families.

Nicky the Greek—Graduated college, married, and became a professional wrestler. Resides in NYC.

Crazy Eddy—Institutionalized.

Bernie and Yetta—Sold their store and retired in 1976 and lived a happy life.

Feranzi—Murdered gangland style.

Pauly Ham—Murdered gangland style.

The Ape—"Disappeared", his body was never found.

Mickey "Two-Shoes"—"Disappeared", his body was never found.

Tommy—Became an informant for the FBI

Nicky-D—I saw him in the summer of 1993 while I was researching my father's death as an "associate" of the Gambino Crime Family in Coconut Grove, Florida. He was retired and living in a condo on Miami Beach.

Don "Boccala"—He sleeps with the fishes.

Don Joe "The Boss" Masseria—Shot to death in Coney Island.

Don Maranzano—Murdered with guns and knives.

Don Charley Lucky—Died of a "heart attack" in Italy.

Don Genovese—Died of natural causes in prison.

Don Gambino—Died peacesfully of a heart attack.

Robert and Gail—Reside in Georgia; raised 5 strong and healthy children.

Diane—Completed high school and married.

Pete (FL)—Died from complications of AIDS in 1987.

D.T. Williams—Became a Judge.

Ginny—I pray our brief meeting and ending was her beginnings . . .

Papa Joe & Pigny—Probably still looking for their "stolen" car.

"Mr. DuPlantis"—Passed away in 1984 and left his wealth to a youth charity.

Lost Cloud—Found his mother and was the spark that joined his family together again.

Night Warrior Nihanio—Passed peacefully into the spirit world in the late 1960s.

Harry and Deborah—Married in prison; at the time this book was published, the street news said they were still incarcerated.